W9-CBT-831

Dagger and Coin

Also by Kathy MacMillan

Sword and Verse

DAGGER AND COIN

KATHY MACMILLAN

HarperTeen is an imprint of HarperCollins Publishers.

Dagger and Coin

www.epicreads.com

Library of Congress Control Number: 2018947992
ISBN 978-0-06-232464-1 (trade bdg.)

Typography by Ellice M. Lee
18 19 20 21 22 PC/LSCH 10 9 8 7 6 5 4 3 2 1
❖
First Edition

For Manuela Bernardi,
my OTE and fairy godmother to
all my characters

The Gods

Sotia, goddess of wisdom and the sole surviving god

Gyotia, king of the gods, Sotia's brother and tormentor, killed by his wife Lanea to prevent him from exacting vengeance upon Sotia

Lanea, goddess of the hearth, Gyotia's first wife, accidentally killed by Sotia in her rage against Gyotia and the other gods

Suna, goddess of memory, sister of Gyotia and Sotia, killed by Sotia

Lila, goddess of war, Gyotia's second wife, killed by Sotia

Qora, son of Gyotia and Lanea, god of the fields, killed by Sotia

Aqil, son of Gyotia and Sotia, god of sacred learning, killed by Sotia

ONE

MY FATHER WOULD have been ashamed that the assassin didn't target me.

But then, it had been my scrimping and planning that had made this Festival of Lanea celebration possible, that was repairing the bridges and cleaning the fountains so city residents wouldn't die of the flux, and no one seemed to appreciate that either. Certainly they'd enjoyed the roast lamb stews and nut puddings that had been served all day in the marketplace; people had streamed in and out since midday bells despite the heat, and if Qilarites and Arnathim mostly avoided each other, no one could be too surprised. It had been less than thirty days, not even a Shining and a Veiling of Gyotia's Lamp in the night sky, since our new Ruling Council's decree outlawing slavery and declaring all Arnathim free and equal citizens of Qilara. Though tensions between Qilarites and Arnathim had occasionally erupted into violence in that time, most people had been too intent on survival and rebuilding to spend much time fighting.

I'd argued that, given all the shortages in the city, it was ridiculous and wasteful to mount this celebration for Lanea, a goddess widely believed to be destroyed.

"But Soraya," Raisa had said, brown eyes wide in her pale, scarred face, "the people need *something* to bring them together." No one dared contradict Raisa ke Comun, High Priestess of Sotia, the only surviving goddess, on matters relating to the gods—not even me, and I happily contradicted her on just about everything else.

Besides, if the celebration was a success, it would send a message to people throughout Qilara that the new Ruling Council knew what we were doing, despite our youth. We would need the support of the viziers and stewards and townmasters to enforce our new laws and taxes. So I'd kept a sharp eye on the supplies all day, determined that nothing go to waste, but that the food wouldn't run out either. Any servers who offered too generous portions heard about it from me, and I'd scolded a group of boys earlier for throwing crumbs at the asotis perched on the abandoned slave pen building bordering the marketplace. I wouldn't have anyone blaming my budget for shortfalls.

When twilight came, I'd had enough.

I edged closer to the bonfire and smoothed my hair so that it fell straight down my back—"a sheet of midnight sky," the flirting boys of the Scholar class used to call it. The familiar gesture helped me suppress the anxious twisting of my stomach that darkness brought on, and I looked around for the other members of the Ruling Council. Mati Villari, former king of Qilara and my former fiancé, was ladling out stew for merchants and peasants at a table near the entrance—something about breaking down barriers between the classes. Jonis ko Rikar, erstwhile leader of the Arnath Resistance, was talking to a group of Arnath men over by the bread ovens, chewing with his mouth open. Raisa was . . .

Gods. She was passing out flowers.

There wasn't an eye roll in the realms of gods or men that could adequately address her naive idealism.

Nonetheless, Raisa was the one I approached. After all, it had been Raisa's invitation—uttered in public, in front of a crowd that adored her—that had gotten me on the Ruling Council of Qilara in the first place. The fact that she was the reason my betrothal had fallen apart was minor compared to that.

"It's past time to head back to the palace," I said when I had pushed my way to her side. Three peasant women had parted respectfully when they saw me coming. Being a Gamo and a member of the elite Scholar class still meant something, even if it wasn't supposed to anymore. "Letting this go on past nightfall is a security risk, and expensive."

I'd kept my tone brusque, so no one would guess how the darkness pressed at my lungs, how the walls of the surrounding buildings seemed ready to close in at any moment.

"Soraya! Here, help me pass these out," Raisa said. "Then we can go." Without seeming to realize how much the world had changed, that an Arnath woman would tell a Qilarite Scholar to do anything, she handed me a bunch of flowers—roses, lilies, lotuses, all taken from the abandoned gardens of Scholar nobles who had either died or fled after the earthquakes and floods (or, depending on who you talked to, the day the goddess Sotia destroyed the gods of Qilara and brought down the monarchy). I sighed and passed them out perfunctorily, gratified when a few of the Qilarites in the crowd shifted toward me instead of Raisa.

Most of them, Arnath and Qilarite alike, gravitated to Raisa as though they couldn't help it. As though receiving a flower from her hand and a few inane words from her mouth would somehow bless them and their children. I watched one young man, fourteen or fifteen at most, move up to the front of the crowd and back several times, as if screwing up his courage to meet the great heroine who had raised the floodwalls and saved the city.

The next time he moved closer, I saw the dagger in his hand.

I didn't stop to think. I launched myself at the assassin, shoving him away from Raisa, who had held out a flower to him, like she thought the blade was some ridiculous Festival of Lanea gift.

I got tangled in my skirts, but grabbed the attacker's wrist—thinner than I had expected—and tried to wrestle the blade from his grip. He tumbled backward, sending the crowd screaming and rushing out of the way. My right ankle twisted violently as I went down with him.

"Guards!" I yelled, but our ragtag force was too far away, spread around the marketplace.

The attacker shoved me aside and rose. With a shout, someone burst out of the crowd and tackled him. I heard a cry and steel clattering on stone, and then a grunt. By the time I knew where to look, the attacker was lying limp on the ground, another man—rugged, dark-haired, Qilarite—kneeling over him.

"Are you hurt, my lady?" the newcomer asked.

"No, I don't think—"

"What's going on? What is *he* doing here?" said a hard voice behind me. I turned to find Mati at Raisa's side, glaring at the man who had emerged from the rapidly thinning crowd to help. Several guards had finally arrived too, but they hovered, unsure who to arrest.

"The boy was coming at her with a knife, you idiot," I said. Ordinarily I tried to maintain the illusion that our Ruling Council was united, in front of other people at least, but the falling darkness pushed me to the end of my patience. As did the way Mati's arm went immediately around Raisa's shoulders.

"Soraya saved my life," Raisa said dazedly.

I looked away. I suppose it had never occurred to her that the entire council had something to lose if an assassin took her out. "This gentleman helped subdue the attacker," I said.

Mati scoffed, so unlike his usual irritating cheer that it made me look more carefully at the unconscious assassin—or rather, at the man still kneeling by him, his bearing rigid and military despite his threadbare clothes. His black hair flopped over the smooth brown skin of his forehead, and stubble coated his jaw.

"Captain Dimmin," I said. He hardly resembled the handsome, clean-shaven guard who had directed my security when I had been the king's betrothed, but there could be no doubt.

"Not captain any longer," he muttered.

No, he had been one of the many guards who had deserted their posts during the disasters that had killed most of the former leaders. From the way Mati glared at him, it wasn't hard to guess why he had stayed away after our new council took over; Dimmin had been the one to wield the whip when Raisa had been punished by the old Scholars Council for disobedience of the writing laws.

Well. If Mati was going to hold everyone's past allegiances against them, our allies would be few indeed. I pushed myself up to tell him so, but crumpled and yelped as pain bolted up my leg.

Dimmin caught me and supported my weight as though it were nothing. "My lady?"

"My ankle," I gasped. "I think it's broken."

"We need a doctor!" cried Raisa.

Mati eyed the crowd behind me. "Jonis! We need to get them out of here!"

I wanted to remind them that I'd said from the beginning that we should shut the celebration down before sunset. If they had listened to me, none of this would have happened. But my mouth wouldn't work except to let out a little keening sound.

And then Dimmin was shoved aside and I was picked up by the last person I wanted touching me. Jonis's curly head bowed as he got to his feet, staggering to support my weight with his skinny frame.

"No, get the attacker and the knife," I panted. "Where's Valdis? He can—"

"What do you think he's doing?" Jonis snapped. "Just shut up and let me concentrate, will you?"

I had no choice in the matter, because once he stumbled across the rapidly emptying marketplace, my ankle flopped with every step he took, with a wrongness that turned my stomach. *Breathe,* I told myself. *You will not throw up in front of Jonis.*

And I didn't throw up. I did something even worse. I passed out completely.

TWO

I CAME TO as Valdis was carrying me up to my room in the palace. He must have wrapped my ankle tightly in something, because the floppy sensation was gone.

"I gave you castromana leaf," he said when he saw that I was awake. "To dull the pain temporarily." Though Valdis was officially my family's taster, he had also been treating my mother's headaches, nausea, and bleeding pains for years, and he knew herbs as well as he knew poisons. He'd been one of my father's most valued men since serving under him in the border war with Emtiria twenty-five years before, and even now refused to cover the Gamo eagle tattoo that stood out against the brown skin of his neck. Valdis had been the one to bring me my father's signet ring after his death, walking right past my mother to do so. After all, Mother was merely a Gamo by marriage, and Father had long ago declared me his heir when it became clear that she would bear no sons. But I wouldn't have put it past her to steal the ring from

Father's corpse, and I suspected that Valdis had gotten to it before she could. In that quiet act, Valdis had declared his loyalty to the Gamo family and to me as its head, and I had rewarded him by immediately announcing that he would stay on with the family in the same role he'd had with my father.

"And the dagger?" I asked.

"I have it," said Jonis's voice behind him, and Valdis's mouth thinned under his mustache. I understood. I didn't like the idea of an Arnath, especially Jonis, creeping behind us with a dagger any more than he did. But I was on the Ruling Council of Qilara now; I had to play their game, even if that meant putting up with Jonis. My family's power, and my access to my own inheritance, depended on it.

When we arrived at my door, I fumbled with the key to my room. The corridor was dark enough to steal my breath.

Inside, the shutters were open, letting in the evening breeze and enough dim light for Valdis to step around my trunk and deposit me on the bed. I scrambled to light the lamp with shaking fingers.

My breathing didn't slow until its yellow glow lit the room. I collapsed against the pillow, my forehead damp, my hair in sticky tendrils against my neck.

Jonis had followed us inside. I considered having Valdis eject him, but I wasn't about to let on how much it unnerved me to have Jonis hovering about while I was incapacitated. So, as usual, I went too far in the other direction in an effort to prove that I wasn't frightened.

"Tend to the attacker," I told Valdis. "We need him alive for questioning. Send the doctor up."

Valdis cast a dark look at Jonis but did as I ordered.

The moment he had left—pointedly leaving the door wide open—Jonis turned on me. He had a scar over his left eyebrow, a souvenir from the day that he and his Resistance fighters attacked the palace, probably given to him by one of my father's men. It stood out now, the shiny dark pink of pig flesh against his pale skin. "Why do you keep your room locked?" he snarled. "What are you hiding?"

I gritted my teeth at being addressed like that by anyone, let alone an Arnath rebel who had kidnapped me and held me in a pitch-black *tomb*, and who was lucky my father hadn't caught him and ripped him limb from limb. I bet it would please him that I hadn't been able to sleep without a lamp lit since I had returned from the tombs, that I grew short of breath whenever I couldn't see the sky. But I wouldn't ever give him the satisfaction of knowing that.

"Of course I lock my room," I snapped. "Only an idiot would leave her room open."

. . . or someone with nothing to steal, I realized. Jonis had probably never even owned anything worth locking up.

"May I remind you," I said icily, "that I just saved Raisa's life?" I held out my hand. "Give me the knife."

"That could have been a setup, to earn our trust."

"Me? I'm not the one with experience in assassination."

That shut him up. My father may have been part of the plot to usurp Mati's throne, but Jonis's Resistance had killed Mati's father.

He finally handed me the weapon. It was slightly larger than the jeweled knife my father had given me three years ago on my sixteenth birthday, the one that was only useful for paring fingernails. But this blade was sturdy and sharp. I held it close to the lamp, but there was nothing to see on the smooth surface of the heavy handle.

"The design's not Qilarite, not Emtirian. It's not anything I recognize," said Jonis.

"And since when are you an expert?"

"My master sold such things in the marketplace. Had to know to wait on the customers, didn't I?" The acid in his tone was a reminder that Jonis had, until recently, been a slave to Horel Stit, one of the cruelest merchants in the City of Kings.

I didn't know what to say to that, so I ignored it. "That boy was hardly a skilled assassin," I said, placing the dagger on my bedside table to hide the way my hands shook. I hadn't realized until now how lucky I had been. For all the preparation I'd had to become queen of Qilara, I'd never learned anything so unladylike as how to defend myself. I'd assumed I'd always have bodyguards for that. I hadn't considered how risky and self-revealing it had been, jumping on the attacker. I hadn't stopped to consider anything in the moment, actually, and that was unlike me—gods, what was being on this council doing to me?

"If you're not behind it," said Jonis, his tone making it clear that he had not given up his suspicions that I was, "then maybe the southern vizier is. I'll be investigating that as soon as we arrive in Lilano."

I let out a groan as the full meaning of the night's events hit me. The council had agreed that Jonis and I would head south to the garrison city of Lilano the day after the festival, to court the support of the southern vizier for our new government. He was the most influential of the remaining viziers, largely because his city was home to the South Company of Qilara's army. I'd insisted on going because I had contacts in the Lilano court, and I hoped to turn Vizier Tren's vague mentions of monetary support into loans that would reduce the amount that my family estate was putting into the rebuilding effort. More importantly, I needed to check on my family's southern investments, especially our huge salt mine. Jonis had whined that an Arnath councilor should go as well, and the others had agreed. As it would clearly require an act of the gods to separate Raisa and Mati, that meant Jonis would accompany me.

But the attack on Raisa tonight, and my injury, had changed that. "I can't go to Lilano with a broken ankle," I said. "And you're not going either."

His green eyes narrowed. "What are you talking about?"

"That assassin targeted Raisa. Whoever sent him might have been happy to kill all of us, but when he had to choose, he went for her." I didn't mention that I'd been standing right there when it had happened, that he easily could have attacked me instead. That it was something of an insult that he hadn't. "They're not going to stop, either. If she dies, every shred of credibility our Ruling Council has goes with her. Getting her out of the city is the only way to keep her alive."

Jonis's face went so pale that I wondered if the time I saw him kissing Raisa in the tombs had been more than just a show for my benefit—or at least if it had meant more than that for Jonis. Maybe it was the Gamo in me, but this realization only made me want to twist the knife a little more.

"If you think Mati is going to let you go with her to Lilano, you're even more deluded than I thought," I added.

His cheeks reddened. "Just because you handle the money, that doesn't mean you make the decisions."

"This has nothing to do with money. I'm telling you what makes sense."

The doctor entered the room then, followed by Raisa, who scurried to the bedside and took my hand, not seeming to notice that I flinched at her touch.

The doctor eased the wrapped cloth off my ankle. It hurt, and I called him something that would have made my mother slap me if she'd been there to hear, but he ignored me and examined the mass of swollen flesh. As he set the bone and rewrapped it, I only managed not to scream by clutching Raisa's hand and repeating "I am a Gamo" over and over in my mind.

Mati finally arrived while the doctor was preparing medicine for me and Raisa was surreptitiously flexing the hand I had nearly crushed.

"Where've you been?" said Jonis. He sat slumped on the turned-around chair of my dressing table.

Mati pushed his shaggy black hair out of his eyes. "I checked on the attacker—still unconscious—and informed Kirol and Adin about the situation. The guards are clearing out the marketplace now. There was some fighting after we left."

"Was anyone hurt?" asked Raisa, anxiously touching the ugly

scar on her left cheek. She'd gotten that scar in the battle at the palace, and Mati's right arm had been burned to uselessness by the High Priest. I was, as Jonis often pointed out with a sneer, the only member of the Ruling Council who didn't carry scars, because I had run away from the fighting.

"Too early to tell." Mati glanced at the doctor, then back at the three of us. "We need to talk."

The doctor nodded. "I'll be but a moment—" He stopped abruptly. I would have bet he had been about to add a "Your Majesty."

From the familiar wet-earth smell that rose from the cup he handed me, I guessed it to be the same sharma tincture that Valdis prepared when the discomfort of my female bleeding became too much to bear. Most doctors would have offered silphium for pain, but this one, having been in the palace during my betrothal, knew that my sisters and I had never been allowed to take it; silphium was also a contraceptive, and having a mother with a history of miscarriages and stillbirths made it too risky.

I hesitated, wondering if I should summon Valdis to taste the medicine, but Mati said softly, "Why would he set your ankle and then poison you?"

I hated how well Mati could read me, when he had rejected me in the worst possible way. But I had spent six years training myself to be what I thought Mati wanted, so his words, against my will, soothed my doubts. Besides, the doctor seemed loyal to Mati at least.

I drained the cup.

"Thank you, Nelnar," said Mati as the doctor packed up his things. He looked meaningfully at me.

"Thank you," I echoed, realizing that I hadn't even known the man's name before Mati said it, though he'd been tending to me for nearly a year. I needed to pay more attention to those things. Mati did, and people loved him for it.

As soon as the door closed behind the doctor, Mati said, "Raisa and I will go to Lilano."

I shot Jonis an I-told-you-so look, which he ignored.

"And you think you can just decide that," said Jonis.

"Soraya can't travel like this," Mati went on, as if he hadn't heard Jonis's snide tone, "and Raisa—"

"—needs to get out of the city before they try to kill her again," I finished for him.

Raisa shook her head. "That doesn't make sense. I'm not that important."

She really didn't see it, the ethereal hold she had on people, the change in her since she had done . . . whatever she had done to keep a tidal wave from destroying the City of Kings. Since she had been found delirious on a lower roof of the palace, babbling about the goddess Sotia. Since the temples had burned or collapsed and their priests had all been killed, leaving her to be proclaimed High Priestess of Sotia and revered or despised—or both—by the survivors.

I tried to tap her, but the medicine was already making my limbs heavy, and I ended up whacking her arm so hard that she winced. "You have to go. Don't be tiresome about it. It will be more dangerous for everyone if you stay." Even now, I wanted to insist that I could manage the trip, and I hated her for making me argue about it.

Raisa's eyes fell on my ankle, and she nodded.

Mati let out a sigh of relief. Raisa could be difficult when she wanted to be. "You'll need to write us letters of introduction to your Lilano contacts," he said to me and Jonis.

Jonis folded his arms with a grim smile. "D'you really think mine can read?"

Mati blinked. Before the upheaval, reading and writing the language of the gods had been reserved for the Qilarite nobility only; that was why the nobles were called the Scholar class. Changing that had been among our foundational First Laws for a New Qilara: access to writing for all, equality for all citizens, a ban on slavery, and property rights for women.

We'd worked hard to spread literacy as quickly as possible; controlling the language of the gods was how the kings and Scholars had held power for hundreds of years, so the people of Qilara would never believe that our Ruling Council meant to change things unless we immediately made writing available to everyone. Anyone who could read and write had been drafted to teach others in the newly named Library of the People, and we'd even made taking writing lessons a prerequisite for receiving food rations or joining the guards.

Of course, none of it was happening fast enough for Jonis, who wanted change *now*, never mind how much it cost or how much work was involved.

"I think you have *some* way to communicate with your people in Lilano," said Mati, raising an eyebrow at Jonis, "considering that you managed to steal from every shipment out of the south in the last three years." Raisa averted her eyes; she'd helped the Resistance with that. Mati's voice hardened as he went on. "Managed to set up an assassination of your own too, as I recall."

Mati's challenge crackled through the air, a reminder of who they were: former king and former rebel. It was odd to see Mati, ordinarily the one working hardest to prove that we could all get along, reminding Jonis of this piece of the past.

Jonis unfolded himself from the chair and stood. "Yes," he said evenly. "When people are desperate they'll go to any length to get what they want, especially if they feel like they don't have anything to lose." His eyes shifted to Raisa. "While you're in Lilano, I'll find out who was behind that assassin, and we will stop them."

Mati relaxed a little, as if Jonis had passed a test. Raisa took a shaky breath and nodded as Jonis described his Resistance contacts in Lilano; she would have to be the one to approach them while Mati worked on the southern vizier and the nobility. I tried to catch Mati's eye to ask him, with my expression, whether he thought she could handle this. But he was only watching Raisa with concern.

Of course he was.

I wouldn't think about that. Instead, I cataloged the facts: Qilara's treasury was only surviving on loans from my family estate. Emtiria, the huge country to the east, was a constant threat. And now someone was trying to assassinate us. "It's not too late to offer the Emtirian emperor a trade deal," I said, cutting across Jonis's explanation of Resistance codes, making them all stop and stare at me.

I'd suggested this at our very first Ruling Council meeting, and they should have listened to me then. The Emtirians, who literally worshiped profit, never hesitated to turn enemies into allies for the sake of trade. But no, making special deals with Emperor Adelrik after he had taken part in my father's coup attempt was "dishonest" and "inviting them to take over from the inside again" and "not the way *our* council does things," and I'd been soundly outvoted.

"If we make an ally of Emtiria, we won't have its army breathing down our necks," I said into the silence. "A simple trade agreement would hardly be selling Qilara away. We don't have the labor force to run the mines any longer, and we need the funds. If we agree to use Emtirian output and give their ships port access—"

"We've been over this. We can't trust Emtiria," said Mati.

I rolled my eyes. "But—"

"You don't understand. I . . . did make a deal with the emperor." Mati's voice was harsh, bitter. "Right after my coronation. And as soon as the harbor gates at Asuniaka opened, Adelrik sent in a fleet and took the city. That's how Emtiria got into Qilara in the first place."

It couldn't have been a very well-negotiated deal, then. I opened my mouth to say so, but Jonis spoke first.

"Why is this the first we're hearing of this?" he demanded.

Mati looked away. "Does it matter *how* I lost Asuniaka?" He'd been king for less than ninety days and had managed to lose a major port and continue his father's depletion of the treasury. No wonder it was a sore subject. Raisa put a hand on his shoulder, and he took a deep breath and turned to me. "We can't trust Emtiria," he repeated slowly, as if to a child. "Promise us, Soraya, that you won't go making any deals with the emperor."

"You don't have to lecture," I snapped. "You already outvoted me."

"Then it shouldn't be a difficult promise to make," said Jonis sharply. He and Mati shared a look. They seemed to have found something to agree on: that I needed watching.

Outraged, I looked to Raisa for support—when had that become something I did? But she just glanced at the other two and said, "It would . . . help if you promise that, Soraya."

"I see," I said, stung. "So, this is where all your talk of forgiveness and second chances ends. Del Gamo was a traitor, so his daughter must be too, is that it?" None of them answered; none of them would look at me either. "Fine. I won't pursue any deals with the emperor. Even if I think it's stupid not to," I couldn't resist adding.

"You think anything that doesn't make you money is stupid," Jonis grumbled.

"You two will have to take care of everything here while we're in Lilano," Raisa said over him. "That means that you have to work together. You can't snipe at each other all the time. You're the . . . example of cooperation between Arnathim and Qilarites."

"Whereas as you two *cooperate* so well you hardly let go of each other," I said, gesturing at her and Mati.

Raisa took Mati's hand—the burned right one—and lifted

her chin. "People notice how we behave, not just the decrees we put out. They won't believe peace is possible unless we show that *we* believe it."

"We'll be nice," said Jonis sarcastically. I'd probably hear about his suspicions of me every single day once Mati and Raisa left.

"We have to show that we believe it," Raisa repeated, letting go of Mati's hand, "which is why our best option is to bring in Gelti Dimmin to investigate the assassin." Mati and Jonis made identical sounds of disgust—apparently they'd found something else to agree on—but Raisa ignored them. "He was in the market tonight because he was patrolling on his own—did you know that? The people of the merchant class don't trust us, but they trust him. They go to him for food and help when they won't come to us. I hear all about it in the public audiences." She looked at Mati. "You would, too, if you didn't look ready to murder someone anytime his name is mentioned."

Mati spoke through gritted teeth. "Kirol could—"

"We're past that," said Raisa quietly. We all knew she was right; Kirol Tarn had only become our guard captain because he had remained loyal to Mati throughout my father's attempted coup—and because, though young and inexperienced, he'd been the sole volunteer. Most of the experienced guards, including Dimmin, had fled once it became clear that the Arnath rebellion had succeeded.

"Dimmin is Kirol's cousin. They could work together," I said, because it was true, and because it obviously annoyed Mati and Jonis that I was supporting the idea of hiring the former guard captain.

"You know what he thinks of Arnathim," said Jonis, staring at Raisa.

She clenched her hands at her sides. "People can't change unless they are given a chance to. We have to show that we believe it." She repeated it like she had to keep reminding herself of it. And maybe she did. I'd always assumed that her sunny optimism came naturally to her, but I saw the iron underneath now, saw how much it had cost her to suggest hiring the man who had whipped her. Perhaps it was a decision she had to make and remake, every single day.

I didn't want to admire her, especially after she had joined the other two in forcing me to make that ridiculous vow not to treat with Emtiria. I decided that the strange sensation must therefore be a result of the medicine in my system. My mind was still going at full speed, but my limbs were dull and slow and my ankle throbbed with an odd pressure. I let out a frustrated groan.

"Oh!" Raisa sprang to my bedside. "We need to get you out of that dirty gown so you can sleep." I managed to raise one hand to shoo the two men out.

Their faces reddened comically as they sped for the door. If it had been Raisa about to disrobe I bet they would have climbed over each other to get a better view.

THREE

ONCE, I WOULD have called for my maid to undress me, but I didn't have one any longer—it was all too easy for ladies' maids to sell information about their mistresses, and I had to save my bribe money for more important things now. So Raisa helped me change, then brought me a glass of water and a cloth to wipe my sweaty face. How it would have pleased me, half a year ago when I was Mati's betrothed and rumors had swirled through the court about their relationship, to have her waiting on me.

And then, as if to punish me for such thoughts, there was a humiliating episode involving a chamber pot.

Once I was settled back on the bed, Raisa traced a symbol over my bandaged foot. No doubt she thought she was calling down Sotia's blessing. I was too exhausted to point out that Sotia probably couldn't care less about my ankle, so I just pulled my too big dressing gown around me and leaned back against the pillows. The dressing gown had been my father's, and if I pressed my nose into the black silk collar, I could make out the sweet scent of his jasmine hair oil. The silk was still in good shape, and the dressing gown might have fetched a decent price but for the lumpy blue embroidery on the front. Back when I was seven and had done the needlework, I'd insisted that the designs were flowers, but even to me they had looked more like misshapen coins. I'd gotten better with a needle in the intervening years, thanks to the endless stitching parties that made up the social life of Scholar women, but my father had never let me redo the design, and had worn that dressing gown every morning.

What on earth would Father think if he could see me now? What would he say if he knew that my family's southern investments, which made up the bulk of our wealth, now depended on Raisa and Mati's ability to convince the people of Lilano that the Ruling Council knew what it was doing?

But I couldn't tell Raisa about those worries. She'd see it as selfishness, never mind that those investments were supporting her pet projects.

So I took a different tack. When she had finished her little ritual, I said, "Don't expect to get away with that in Lilano. People there will think you're deluded and you'll only alienate Qilarites more."

Raisa perched on the edge of the bed and fixed me with a stern look. "I'm more concerned about the Qilarites here in the capital. I am counting on you to hire Dimmin. They trust him. We need him on our side."

Bringing in Dimmin was actually one of her better ideas, but I wasn't about to tell her that. "The council didn't vote on it," I said archly. "Mati won't like that."

"Mati won't be here," she retorted with a faint smile. "He doesn't mean to . . . well. He still feels so guilty about everything."

"Everything" meant the fact that Mati hadn't been able to stop the old Scholars Council from whipping her, and that he'd had to bargain for her life by agreeing to send a ship full of slave raiders to the Nath Tarin, the northern islands that were home to the Arnathim. That had been part of my father's plot to seize the throne, a way to use Qilarite hatred of Arnathim to make Mati look weak.

Personally, I found Mati's self-flagellation over the whole affair tedious; after all, he'd stopped the whipping halfway through, hadn't he? And those raiders hadn't actually gone to the Nath Tarin; it wasn't widely known, but Mati had loaded the ship with inexperienced sailors and given them navigational charts that would send them into an uninhabited wasteland.

Where, no doubt, those sailors now rested at the bottom of the frigid sea. He obviously blamed himself for that, too.

Regardless of what had happened to the raider ship, though, we would eventually have to reach out to the Nath Tarin. Raisa had been bringing this up since the first days of our Ruling Council; she'd been born on one of the northern islands, had been brought to Qilara by slave raiders at age six. But what were we supposed to do? Show up on the islands saying, "Sorry about killing and enslaving your people for hundreds of years, but we'd like to be friends now"?

Mati had obviously been grappling with his guilt about all

this. I'd noted, however, that his treatment of *me* never seemed to cause him much regret.

"He'd better find a way to manage," I said crisply. "It's going to be up to him to convince the southern vizier and the Scholars in Lilano that we aren't destroying the country with the new laws." I closed my eyes against a rush of frustration. I would have been so much better at it than Mati. I had the connections. My uncle was Lilano's Trade Minister, and his daughter was engaged to the War Minister's son. My aunt Ema held great influence over the Lilano Scholar class, as her late husband had been a war hero. Not to mention the many Scholars and merchants of the city who owed allegiance to the Gamo name, thanks to my father's shrewd business dealings and political maneuverings.

But I had more than just my name to rely on. I knew exactly which gown I would wear to entice the southern vizier's son, exactly which bits of sensitive information I would dangle before the southern vizier to talk him into a large loan to the treasury, exactly which gifts I would slip to which courtiers to secure their loyalty. But Mati and Raisa would walk into Lilano with none of that. Mati might be aware of such tactics, but he would never use them. Too honorable? Or too stupid?

And Raisa would probably go around offering writing lessons to anything that could hold a quill, stubbornly refusing to even acknowledge old ways and old laws. She would be a novelty, though, and Scholars did love that. She had a certain artless charm; it could be an effective weapon if she ever bothered to use it as one.

Raisa frowned. "Up to Mati to convince them," she repeated. "You mean that Mati's going to have to go back to acting like he owns the universe, even though that kind of behavior disgusts him."

"Vizier Tren and the Lilano Scholars won't take him seriously otherwise," I said evenly.

"And they won't take me seriously no matter what."

"I didn't say that."

"You didn't have to." Her nostrils flared. "I'm not as stupid as you think I am."

I shook my head. "You're not stupid at all. But Lilano is a garrison city, full of men. How do you think they'll react to you? Let Mati take the lead, but don't let them push you into anything."

Raisa's mouth settled into a determined line. "I won't let him get pulled back into that . . . version of himself, no matter how good an actor he is."

Yes, Mati had been an excellent actor. So excellent that I had been blindsided by his very public rejection of me. "At least don't flaunt your relationship while you're there," I snapped. "That won't help at all."

I expected her to argue, but Raisa rarely took bait like that. It was, if I was honest with myself, one of the most frustrating things about her. She tilted her head thoughtfully. "What you said before, that Mati and I never let go of each other. We're not trying to hurt you."

I stiffened. Much as I'd wanted to be queen, much as Mati was now a familiar if frustrating presence, I'd felt nothing but relief at the idea of not becoming his wife. "Is that what you think? That I'm some lovesick—"

"No. I don't think you ever really loved him, but it can't be easy for you when it's all been so public."

"You two don't seem to mind," I muttered, closing my eyes.

"What do you mean?"

"I mean that you never stop touching each other, no matter where you are, or stealing little kisses when you think no one's watching." I hadn't meant for the conversation to go this way at all, but the words flopped out over my swollen tongue. "Do you think anyone in the city *doesn't* know that you sleep in the same room? We know—you love each other. Do you have to be so . . . blatant about it?"

Raisa's cheeks reddened, but she straightened her shoulders. "We're done hiding. Some things people need time to adjust to, but some things people just need to learn to accept. Mati is my husband now. That's how it is."

This was what she believed, though there had been no marriage ceremony before the priests, no dowry, no bridal tent, and though she wore her hair uncovered. I tried for a sarcastic laugh, but it sounded more like a grunt. "It's just not . . . decent, the way you two carry on. That won't help you with the Scholars in Lilano."

A crease appeared between Raisa's eyebrows. "Do you think it's wrong to—" she said, but the sharp look I threw her made her change tack. "Do you think it's wrong to be in love?"

There had been a time when I'd thought I was in love with Mati—or perhaps I had willed myself to believe that I was in love with him, because that would have made marriage to him easier to bear. The truth was, I found Mati insufferably dull. *You might not think so,* whispered an unpleasant voice in my mind, *if he had ever once looked at you the way he looks at Raisa.*

That wasn't even worth contemplating. No one had ever looked at me the way Mati looked at Raisa, and probably no one ever would.

Did I think it was wrong to be in love? No, but that wasn't what Raisa was really asking. I gritted my teeth, hating how much less I knew about the things that went on between men and women in dark rooms than she did. I was one of the best-educated women in the country; she hadn't even been able to name the Emtirian emperor when we'd first begun this council.

And I had never even been properly kissed. Oh, I'd kissed Mati a few times, following my mother's advice to corner him in empty hallways or temple alcoves. Once I'd even dragged him into the garden maze, where, if he had reciprocated in any way, we could have done more than was appropriate. I would have let him, too, so desperate had I been to prove that I could hold him.

"Love is overrated." I tried to put acid into my tone, but it just came out sounding weary.

Raisa's eyes got what I had come to think of as her Sotia light, the one that showed she had seen into the heart of a situation and found some truth concealed from mortal eyes. She suddenly seemed far older than eighteen. I wanted to smack the little smile off her face, the one that said, "You'll understand someday."

"Remember, we're sending you to Lilano to keep you alive," I said quickly. "Just keep quiet and don't give anyone a reason to hate the council. Is that so hard?"

"Don't worry about us." Raisa stood and patted my arm, and I could see that she'd already dismissed anything else I would say. "The bell is on the table. If you need anything, ring. I'll be right across the hall." She bent to blow out the lamp.

"Leave it lit!"

She must have heard the panic in my voice, because that irritating light of understanding came into her eyes again. She nodded and moved away.

"Don't you dare tell Jonis," I muttered after her.

"I'd never," came her soft reply, just before the door clicked shut behind her.

Raisa came back the next morning, dressed in a rose-colored travel cloak, her auburn hair pinned up under a scarf to make her less recognizable on the road. Rather than boarding the ship to Lilano that waited in the harbor, where she'd be a target, she and Mati would ride out of the city with an already scheduled delivery of food and supplies to the towns along the western road, then cut north to the coast and row out to meet the ship a day into its journey. We hoped to keep news of their departure quiet until their ship had turned south along the coast. If all went well, they would arrive in Lilano in four days.

While I finished letters to my Lilano contacts, Raisa wandered around my room, examining the walls and fingering items on the shelves; she certainly did make herself at home in my life. I'd done what I could to brighten up the blank drabness of this room with water-stained tapestries and chipped figurines—everything that hadn't been damaged in the earthquakes and floods and battle had been sold away to fund repairs. Back home in Pira, the walls would have been painted red or gold or blue, not the endless beige of the capital city.

I signed the last letter, and Raisa brought me the sealing wax.

"May I read it?" she asked, reaching for the letter.

It was an odd moment. Not so long ago, her making that request, or me granting it, would have been a death sentence. I handed her the paper; the corners of her mouth lifted as she read the kind things I had written about her—things I would never utter aloud. I hastily sealed my letter to the southern vizier's son, which was embarrassingly flirtatious. I would have broken my other ankle before letting Raisa read it.

"These won't do much good if you provoke people," I warned her as I handed her the pile of letters to aunts, cousins, old family friends and business associates—anyone who might benefit by supporting us. "You're leaving soon?"

"Within the hour. Mati said to tell you he hopes your ankle is better soon."

Which meant he wasn't coming to say goodbye himself. I wasn't disappointed, exactly, but this showed how far I had fallen in his favor. Raisa, it seemed, was the only friend I had.

I almost laughed aloud at the thought of the word *friends* being applied to the two of us.

Raisa reached into her cloak and held out a bundle of cloth. "I never got a chance to give you your Festival of Lanea gift."

I took it warily. Gifts were traditional at Lanea's festival, but they were usually laden with significance. Given our past, I couldn't imagine what Raisa would have chosen.

Inside the bundle was a small, spiny ball the same shade of green as the cloth below—kirit green, the color that Arnath slaves had once worn. The cloth had probably been cut from one of Raisa's old dresses, as none of the Arnathim wore green anymore if they could help it.

"It's a maschari seed pod," Raisa said. "They grow in the desert, and they're supposed to have beautiful blue flowers. You could grow it in a pot by the window."

I frowned. "I thought maschari was poisonous."

"Only if you eat it."

I raised an eyebrow. "You gave me a prickly seed pod that grows a poisonous flower? Festival of Lanea gifts are supposed to be *subtle*."

Her mouth fell open. "No, I just . . . it's a beautiful flower that grows quickly in a harsh place, and that made me think of you."

I stared at her, not sure what to make of that. "Thank you," I said at last. "But . . . when you get to Lilano, don't give the southern vizier any gifts. And remember, let Mati do the talking."

"Stop worrying. Sotia won't let us fail," said Raisa serenely.

I laughed. "Right. If Sotia wants peace and equality and all that, why doesn't she show up and fight for it? Why didn't she stop that assassin?"

Raisa looked startled. "She does. Through us." She touched my shoulder. "And she did. Through you."

She was serious. She absolutely believed what she was saying. I couldn't even begin to form the arguments that might get through to her, so I just sighed and said, "Try not to get killed."

Raisa smiled, though I hadn't been joking. She kissed my

forehead before I had a chance to cringe away. "Don't murder Jonis. Even if you have a really tempting opportunity."

I laughed, though she didn't. Maybe she hadn't been joking either.

FOUR

AFTER RAISA LEFT, I contemplated the eagle design on my father's signet ring—*my* signet ring, I reminded myself—which I wore over my right thumb. I'd taken a huge risk in joining the Ruling Council, but it had seemed like the best option to obtain the power I'd always wanted and to protect my family's wealth. Now my family's southern investments depended on Raisa and Mati's ability to woo the people of Lilano, whether they knew it or not. Could I trust that?

I couldn't. I had to mitigate the risk. My family's salt mine in the Haran Desert was my biggest concern. Salt was the most coveted resource on the peninsula; that mine had once brought in more than our silver, gold, and iron mines combined. But ever since slavery had been declared illegal in Qilara, the salt mine's profits had declined without enough workers.

Father would have sold the mine, I was sure. My fellow councilors wouldn't like that I was considering what he would do;

to them, Del Gamo was only a usurper. But I knew why he'd taken part in that coup: to save Qilara from Mati's father, who was bankrupting the treasury and unnecessarily antagonizing Emtiria. People thought my father was calculating and cold, and maybe he was, but he'd also distracted me with stories the whole time Mother was in labor with the twins, and insisted on wearing the awful embroidered dressing gown I'd made him, and been scrupulously faithful to Mother even though she was ugly and temperamental and manipulative and couldn't give him a son. I'd watched him die trying to save my sister. It was easy for them to make him the villain in their story, now that he was gone.

The Gamo legacy was in my hands now; if I lost my family's fortune, no doubt men all over Qilara would hold it up as an example of why women shouldn't handle money.

I gritted my teeth. I knew exactly who would make the perfect buyer for the mine: the Emtirian emperor, with his high population and seemingly endless supply of indentured servants. But the others on the council had made me promise that option away. I couldn't even approach anyone in the Emtirian court without arousing their suspicion.

The southern vizier was the next-best option. If I'd been going to Lilano, I could have convinced him in person. I just had to hope that I could be as persuasive in writing.

I wrote one more letter, and then, bracing myself for irritation, I sent for my sister Alshara.

She arrived half an hour later in a cloud of rose perfume and flopped onto my bed, sending my ankle into paroxysms of pain.

I bleated like a wounded eland. She was too far away to slap, so I threw my pillow at her. She shrieked as it mussed the beaded ends of her perfectly straight black hair.

"What was that for?" Alshara yelped.

"My ankle is broken! Get off the bed."

"Oh, stop being melodramatic." Alshara smoothed her hair and rose as slowly as possible. "I can't believe you made me come back before all the excitement last night. Is it true that Captain Dimmin saved you from an assassin?"

"*I* went after the attacker. That's how my ankle got broken." It occurred to me that being known for saving Raisa from an assassin's blade could help my reputation in the city. Why hadn't I thought of that sooner?

But if there was anyone I could count on to remain unimpressed, it was my sixteen-year-old sister. "Clumsy," she sniffed. "So is Captain Dimmin still as handsome as he was?"

I rolled my eyes, which was perhaps unfair, as the topic of Dimmin's looks was one Alshara and I had once dissected from every angle. I didn't like the way Alshara always nudged me back into that shallower version of myself. I had much bigger things to consider now.

"I want you to go see Elisia Brooks before her ship leaves today," I told her. Elisia's father was a prominent Lilano Scholar, and he and his family were heading home to Lilano on the same ship that was to have carried me and Jonis. Elisia and Alshara had always had a connection that seemed to thrive solely on their shared love of courtly fashion.

Alshara frowned. "But I want to go to the market and get a new wrap to go with my blue dress."

"Absolutely not. You have plenty of clothes. Besides, this is more important."

She tugged on her hair beads and pouted. "You used to be fun."

"And you used to be slightly less ridiculous," I retorted, and then stopped myself. The smart one, the sweet one, and the silly one—that's what Father had called the three of us. If Alshara had been less ridiculous it was because she'd had her twin sister, Aliana, to keep her in check. Aliana, whose sweetness hadn't saved her.

I'd been the one to find Aliana's body, on what was supposed to be my wedding day, in the midst of a battle and an earthquake. Her skin had been cold and lifeless; I'd known she was dead even before I saw the red slash across her throat.

I took a deep breath. Alshara had been practically catatonic in the days after her twin's death; as irritating as she could be, I preferred her ridiculous to silent with grief. And it wasn't Alshara's fault that Mother had left her behind when she had taken most of my father's men west to hold Pira, counting on Alshara reporting every move I made. Mother assumed that I'd agreed to be on the Ruling Council to keep the Gamo family near the centers of power, that I would readily abandon the others when necessary. I'd let her think so, because it was easier not to argue, and because I wasn't certain that she was wrong. I believed in keeping my options open.

But Alshara did like to think she was useful. . . .

I glanced at the open door and lowered my tone conspiratorially. "I want you to visit Elisia because I need her to deliver a letter for me to the southern vizier. Something I would rather not go by . . . official channels."

Alshara's eyes immediately lit up; she was probably thinking that she would have something juicy to report to my mother. "Is it . . . some kind of—"

"I'd planned to talk to the southern vizier about it in person, but now . . ." I trailed off and indicated my ankle. "Just ask her to deliver the letter and keep it quiet, all right? We don't need the entire world knowing that our salt mine is up for sale. It's embarrassing." I pinned my most serious look on her. "I'm trusting you with this."

Alshara straightened a bit, and I could see that I had said exactly the right thing. I'd managed to make the request just interesting enough to make her feel like she was in on Gamo intrigues, and just boring enough that she wouldn't care about the details. In fact, it was a rather routine business offer, but I didn't need her blabbing; if other potential buyers thought that I was desperate to sell, it could lower my profits.

"After I see her, I'll come back and tell you how it went," said Alshara. "If you want me to send any other letters, I can—"

"Actually," I said, barely managing to keep from grimacing at the thought of Alshara inserting herself into all my plans, "I have another important job for you. Have you been to the Library today? Everyone who can write is supposed to be teaching, you know."

Alshara's nose wrinkled, and I quickly added, "It would be helpful to have someone keeping an eye on Deshti. She's so close to Jonis, you know. And I'm not sure it's wise, having an Arnath head librarian, especially not one who was so involved in the Resistance. I'd feel better if her assistant were someone I trust, someone who could make sure she wasn't working against Qilarite interests. Do you think you could do that?"

Alshara nodded so hard that her hair beads clacked. It was almost enough to make me feel guilty that I'd only asked her to spy on Deshti to keep her busy and out of my way.

Almost, but not quite.

Later that afternoon I finally got a full report about what had happened after we'd fled the marketplace the night before. Though at least fifty witnesses had seen me jump on the boy, people were attributing Raisa's surviving the assassination attempt to her mystical connection with Sotia. Typical.

No one was sure exactly how the fighting had started. Undoubtedly someone had spoken sharply to someone else, but whether it was Arnath to Qilarite or Qilarite to Arnath, no one could say. A cart was overturned, pinning an Arnath girl under it. When a Qilarite man tried to lift it off her, some in the crowd thought he was attacking her and dragged him away. They lashed him to a post and beat him while the guards fought their way through the brawl that had erupted in their wake.

The Qilarite man was well known in the city as a maker of ale, ready with a smile and joke for anyone who had a coin to spend. He'd been the only alemaker who would agree to supply the festival celebration. When I'd met with him to place the order, his three-year-old daughter had been playing at his feet, and he'd often turned away from our conversation to answer her questions.

The man died of his wounds a few hours after the attack. No one remembered seeing him at the festival that day, not even the men currently crowding the dungeon cells whose bloodied, bruised knuckles had beaten him.

Valdis carried me down to the dining room for the council meeting that night, as I flatly refused to let Jonis into my room again. I gritted my teeth against the pain from my jostled ankle—I would not pass out again, I would *not*—but the sight that greeted me at the bottom of the stairs drove everything else from my mind. Four Arnath guards were escorting about a dozen Qilarite men toward the exit, from the direction of the dungeons. Behind the group strode a burly Arnath guard with a thick red beard, loudly reminding the Qilarite men that they could be brought back in for questioning at any time if the council found their actions suspicious. This was Adin, formerly of the Arnath Resistance and one of Jonis's closest friends, and he seemed to be thoroughly enjoying his position of power over these Qilarites.

"What's going on?" I asked Valdis.

"It's the latest round who were held for questioning about the assassination attempt, my lady."

I frowned. "But they're all Qilarite."

Valdis nodded, and I sensed his relief that he didn't have to point this out to me. Like many other Qilarites, Valdis must have wondered about where my loyalties lay now that I was on the Ruling Council.

The guards led the group through the outer doors, and Adin clapped one of the Qilarites on the shoulder and said something to him in a low voice. From Adin's expression, I guessed it to be a threat. The Qilarite man, who had a strange thick patch of dark hair right in the middle of his head, strode on as if Adin was beneath his notice. I watched Adin's face darken and his fists curl, but he let the man go and headed back toward the dungeon.

Valdis continued down the stairs. "That man he spoke to was Horel Stit," he said, then glanced down at me, probably wondering if he had to explain who that was.

"I see." And I did. Horel Stit was Jonis's former master. No wonder Adin had looked at him with such venom. Valdis's tone made it clear that he thought Stit had only been questioned because of this.

I considered telling Valdis that if he had concerns about Qilarites being treated unfairly in this investigation, he needn't have resorted to the theatrics of making sure I witnessed the men leaving; he could have just told me so. But if he feared my reactions the way he had once feared my father's, that was only to my benefit, and I couldn't have him or any man thinking they needed to explain things to me.

When we reached the dining room, Valdis deposited me into a chair and stepped back.

Jonis didn't even acknowledge me: he was too busy arguing with his mother while she set platters on the table. She had taken on the role of our head of household, but this usually meant directing the servants and ordering supplies, not plating our food. After the attempt on Raisa's life, it seemed she was not going to take any chances. I tried, and failed, to imagine my own mother ever doing such a thing.

"I'll be serving your meals myself from now on," she said somberly. "Don't argue, Jonis." She hovered until Valdis was done tasting everything, then patted Jonis on the shoulder and left. Valdis glanced at Mati and Raisa's empty chairs and hesitated, clearly not wanting to leave me alone with Jonis. But our council meetings had always been for councilors only, and I wasn't about to change that just because I didn't have Mati and Raisa here as a buffer between me and the man who had once kidnapped me. I nodded toward the door, and Valdis reluctantly left. It was some small comfort to know that he was waiting out in the hallway with the guards, though.

My stomach was too queasy for the lamb—from pain, from medicine, from what I had just witnessed in the entrance hall—so I reached for the wine. "What exactly do you think you're doing, only questioning Qilarites?" I demanded. "I'm sure there are plenty of Arnathim who resent Raisa, you know, if not for joining the council, then for marrying a Qilarite."

"The assassin is Qilarite," said Jonis sharply. "And as he is still unconscious and may not survive, we don't have much else to go on, so Adin has been questioning—"

"The assassin *looks* Qilarite," I corrected. He, of all people, should have realized that the boy's looks meant very little; Jonis's own sister, who was only four, had brown skin and dark hair and eyes, unlike her mother and brother's pale coloring. From hints Jonis had dropped, I knew that his mother had been raped by her Qilarite master. "I think you're letting your past affect your decisions, and it's dangerous."

Jonis narrowed his eyes. "What are you talking about?"

"I saw Adin with Horel Stit just now."

Jonis's fingers tightened around his fork. "Stit," he said, "has worked for Emtiria in the past. I thought you would have known that, considering that he ran messages from your father to the Emtirian emperor."

My cheeks went hot. It wasn't as if my father had actually told me the details of his plans. "And what does that have to do with the current situation?"

"I had an up-close view of the things that man was capable of for years," said Jonis. He smiled grimly. "I bet it keeps him up at night, thinking about how I'm the one with the power over *him* now."

The expression on his face twisted something in my stomach. It was the one I had expected to see from him when he had held me captive in the tombs—enjoyment at having me in his power. But back then, he'd only been dispassionate, coldly logical.

"And you're going to use that power to get revenge on him? Have you thought for even a second about how that will be perceived?" I said angrily.

"We couldn't find anything to connect Stit to the assassin. Adin had to let him go," said Jonis, looking almost disappointed about it.

I shook my head. "Obviously, Raisa was right. We need an experienced investigator, and we need someone who won't alienate Qilarites further. That's why I've already contacted Gelti Dimmin."

A lot of tiresome arguing followed this, but, as I'd known

it would, the fact that Raisa wanted to hire Dimmin overruled everything else.

I took another sip of wine, realizing how weak I felt. Best to get this meeting done quickly and get back to bed. I went straight to the next unpleasant topic. "There's still the matter of those rioters arrested last night. A prompt public execution ought to stop any further nonsense. The platform at the market would—"

Jonis's fork clanged onto his plate. "What are you talking about?"

"This council agreed that the punishment for murder was execution." Even Raisa had reluctantly assented, once she had been made to see the reality of our situation; prisons were luxuries for better-funded nations. "Those prisoners attacked a man, and he died." I pressed my fingertips together, remembering the adoring look on the face of the alemaker's daughter as she had asked him why the festival would be held at the market and why birds ate worms, as if she was already used to being taken seriously by her father. I'd sent Valdis to see the alemaker's widow, with condolences and a bag of silver asuns and the promise of an investigation. But it wouldn't be enough. The man's wife and daughter deserved justice.

Jonis gaped at me. "That's not . . . no. They got caught up in the anger and the—"

"If we don't make an example of those men, it will happen again," I said coolly. My father's words echoed in my mind. *One harsh punishment, publicly administered, serves as a warning to the others.* He'd been talking about the slaves in his mines, but it applied here too. "We have to keep order."

Jonis's chair screeched against the stone floor as he leaped up. "And what about what was done to them? The Arnathim are just supposed to swallow everything and not fight back when they're attacked?"

He loomed over me like he had in the tombs. I gripped the edge of the table and forced myself to speak evenly. "Does that justify murder?"

"Maybe!" he practically shouted. "You have your stupid lists and your budgets, but you're just . . . surrounded by a wall of ice, aren't you? You have no idea how people really live." He rubbed at a scar on his wrist. "You want to stage an execution of Arnath prisoners. On the old slavers' platform. Do you have any idea the message that will send? Why not make the Arnath merchants move their carts into the slave pen building while you're at it?"

"At least then it would get some use," I muttered. Though every other building in the City of Kings, in every state of repair, had been taken over by squatters in the wake of the flooding and earthquakes, the completely untouched slave pens at the market remained empty, and the other councilors had steadfastly voted against every use I had suggested for them. "Besides, I thought we were supposed to be looking past all that. We are all equal now, aren't we?"

"You're not that naive," Jonis snarled.

I thought of the alemaker's daughter, waiting for her papa to come home, and her mother, who'd had to tell her that he never would. I pulled in a deep breath. "You want those prisoners exonerated. What message will *that* send?"

He stared at me, his chest heaving, then sat back down with an air of deliberate control. "Conscription was always the backup option. We need more guards."

"If they stay in the city, it'll cause a riot. You want them conscripted, send them to the North Company. They can repair the bridge."

"Fine," he spat.

"Fine," I replied with equal venom.

Look, Raisa, I thought. *We're cooperating.*

FIVE

WITHIN DAYS WORD had gotten out about Mati and Raisa's flight to Lilano. Though anyone with half a brain would realize that they were there to keep Raisa safe, conspiracy theories abounded—that I had driven them out, that Mati had fled in shame at losing the throne, that Jonis and I had done away with them in some sort of lovers' murder pact. This last was enough to make me rail about the utter stupidity of people for five full minutes, until Jonis pointed out that the city residents might like me more if I wasn't so disdainful of them.

Just the day before, the doctor had replaced the splint around my ankle, wrapped it in linen, and slathered on foul-smelling wax that dried into a stiff coating. He'd been surprised at how quickly the swelling had gone down. I could walk again, as long as I leaned on the stick he provided and took frequent rests. I considered it an act of supreme self-control that I got through our council meeting that evening without once beating Jonis with that stick.

Thanks to him and his overzealous questioning of Qilarite suspects, the occasional scuffles that had been breaking out at food distribution points throughout the city had turned into armed brawls, with Qilarites and Arnathim alike protesting that the other group got more. We'd had to divert more guards to cover the food distribution, but it wasn't until Gelti Dimmin organized a group of "protectors" to watch over the food distribution points in the most disputed areas that things calmed down.

"See?" I told Jonis. "They listen to him. We need him on our side."

But I wasn't able to convince Dimmin himself to meet with me until four days after Mati and Raisa left. I'd had to enlist his cousin's help. When Kirol arrived at my study door with Dimmin in tow, I'd been listening to a "report" from my sister on what she had learned about our head librarian, Deshti, while working in the Library of the People. I'd nodded seriously as she'd described every petty annoyance; it was clear that, though Deshti might be young and somewhat caustic, she was a competent keeper of scrolls. Kirol's knock had interrupted me trying to explain to Alshara that Deshti asking her to do things like dry scrolls and create basket tags did not mean that she was actually evil.

I told Alshara to return to the Library; when she saw who entered the study behind Kirol, she shot me a meaningful look and then brushed passed Dimmin with a coquettish smile. He didn't even look at her.

In fact, Dimmin looked downright grim; I had the feeling that he had come only so that Kirol would stop pestering him. Dimmin and Kirol had the same deep-set dark eyes, the same strong chin, but Dimmin was broad-shouldered and confident where Kirol was scrawny and skittish. Dimmin's hair fell into his eyes and his chin sported a few days' beard, while Kirol was clean-shaven, his hair as close-cropped as a new recruit.

The two men stood stiffly, apart from each other; the closeness between them that had spurred Dimmin to get Kirol into the guards in the first place must have become strained since the monarchy fell. It wasn't hard to see why: Kirol had stayed, and Dimmin had deserted.

"Wait outside, Kirol," I said. If Dimmin resented that his cousin now held his former captain post, then Kirol's presence would only be a hindrance.

As his cousin started to protest, Dimmin winced impatiently.

"Wait outside," I repeated. "Please."

Kirol's mouth was tight as he turned and left. I wasn't sure whether to be worried that our guard captain was so transparent about his insecurity in his post, or relieved that he wasn't idiotic enough to think he was doing a good job.

I had chosen to meet with Dimmin in what had once been the king's own study, which I had taken over as my work space. Dimmin had stood on the other side of that great blackwood desk before, seen King Tyno behind it, and King Mati after him. I wanted him to understand that I was just as powerful as they were.

"Please sit," I said. "Thank you for coming. We owe you a great deal for stopping that attacker from escaping. I understand that you were patrolling that night, and that many of the merchant class look to you for help and protection. And your work with protecting the food distribution points has benefited everyone in the city. The members of the Ruling Council are impressed."

"I only came," he said, still standing, "to tell you that Kirol is perfectly capable, my lady."

That brought me up short. I frowned. "We both know that's not true."

A muscle worked in his jaw.

"He's told you what we need," I went on. "An investigator. A *competent* investigator."

"Kirol is competent. He's got good instincts, my la—"

"But not experience," I countered.

"He's only twenty-three."

"And you were only twenty-four when you became captain three years ago, weren't you?" I asked innocently.

Dimmin's eyes narrowed. He didn't like me mentioning that. Of course he didn't, given what he'd done to get there.

"I could train him," Dimmin said stubbornly.

I waved this off. "We don't have time for that. We need to find out who sent that assassin. But perhaps we could discuss you training all the guards later." My mind turned over the possibilities there. That would be a strong, visible role for him to take, and would quell some of the ridiculous rumors in Qilarite quarters that our Ruling Council was a tool of the Arnath Resistance.

He started to protest, but I spoke over him. "We are prepared to offer you two thousand gyots per Shining." I knew how much he'd earned as guard captain; I knew how much more it cost to buy a guard's loyalty. And I knew that he wasn't helping people now strictly out of the goodness of his heart. His protection came at a price, but I doubted many in the City of Kings could pay what it was worth. He couldn't have brought in more than a few hundred gyots in the last Shining acting as a private security guard. He would take a better offer when he got one.

"I'm not interested." He crossed his arms over his chest.

"Two thousand three hundred, then."

"No. Your council is turning this city upside down and I don't want any part of it. You throw good Qilarite citizens into the dungeon, and you wonder why you have riots in the streets."

I'd intended to be charming, persuasive, but this made me stiffen. "The Ruling Council is the only thing standing between order and chaos."

He shook his head. "You don't want me working for you. I'm a deserter. I whipped the king's Arnath lover—"

"Two thousand five hundred. And how would your mother feel about a seaside home in the Watch? It must be hard for her, with your father gone so many years."

With amusement, I watched his dawning realization that he had underestimated me. Of course he had; I was *only* nineteen, *only* a woman. But honestly, did he think I wouldn't have done my research?

"Mother wouldn't want me to take anything from this council," he spat.

I lifted my eyebrows. His current home in the Web, the crowded merchant-class area near the market, would be nothing more than a few rooms; I was disconcerted by the idea that money and a lavish former Scholar's home might not tempt him. Had I read him wrong?

"Your mother would want you to remain a soldier, like your father," I said. "She was so proud when you became guard captain."

He didn't answer, but I saw something flicker in his eyes at the mention of his father. Family pride obviously meant something to him.

I smiled. "Two thousand five hundred gyots a Shining and a new house, for now. And later, when you begin to train the guards—"

"I don't want to—"

"—you will, naturally, receive a raise, which we can discuss later. You'd have to learn to write first, though."

He folded his arms. "No."

"Basic writing skills are a requirement for all the guards now."

"The guards have to learn to—"

"The investigation is the priority, but as soon as—"

His hand came down on the desk, making me jump. "The guards have to learn to write, and people have to sit through lessons to get their food rations. You Scholars think you can just make everyone do whatever you want, and you think you can do it to me, too. Well, you can't. I said *no*."

He glared at me, his chest heaving. I refused to look away or let his little display of temper frighten me.

"Everything all right in there?" came Kirol's muffled voice through the door.

"Yes," I called back. My pulse thrummed in my neck. I hadn't thought it would come to this, but that didn't mean I wasn't prepared. "You expressed some concerns about why we shouldn't hire you. Allow me to address them." I indicated the chair across from me, but he remained standing, so I went on. "You deserted your post. And you whipped Raisa, on the orders of the Scholars Council. I expect you have feared retribution for that. I doubt, for example, that it is a coincidence that you only agreed to this meeting after it became known that Mati and Raisa had left the city." He flinched at their names, but I pretended not to notice.

"In addition," I went on, "you did favors for the High Priest of Aqil for years, helping him and my father with their plot to usurp the throne. You undermined your superiors, put guards sympathetic to their cause in place where needed, and even, on the High Priest's orders, secretly facilitated the meetings of former royal Tutor Tyasha ke Demit with the Arnath Resistance, all so you could catch her in the act of teaching them the language of the gods and ensure her execution. The High Priest got to insist that the king was weak for allowing the Tutor system to continue, and you were promoted to captain the very next day. Am I missing anything?"

He didn't answer, but he finally sank into the chair.

"I imagine," I said, "that a number of people would be shocked to hear about the things you've done. I wonder how your admirers in the Web would react if they learned how deeply you were involved in the High Priest's plans. And Tyasha ke Demit was nothing less than a martyr to the Arnathim. If I even mentioned to Jonis that—"

He raised his head. "You would blackmail me?"

I didn't answer, only met his gaze steadily, my index finger moving over the design of my father's signet ring under the desk.

Unexpectedly, a grin tugged at the corner of his mouth. "I see."

His tone implied that there was something more than business being conducted in this room, and I was rattled by the way my heart thumped, as if it agreed with him. I realized that I could take a different tack, loosen my bodice and giggle and flatter him. I was almost sure it would work, and we'd have our investigator.

But then he'd never see me as anything but Del Gamo's simpering daughter. I needed him to understand that I was more than that.

"The offer is two thousand gyots a Shining—"

"You said two thousand five hundred before."

I arched one eyebrow. "Two thousand gyots a Shining, a house in the Watch, and your past stays in the past. That is the offer." I leaned back in my chair. "It's up to you whether you're smart enough to take it."

He sighed, running a hand through his hair. Something sparked deep in his eyes. "You truly are your father's daughter, my lady."

It had been a long time since someone had said that and meant it as a compliment. "Councilor Gamo," I corrected absently. I looked at him, debating, then added, "But you may call me Soraya."

"Soraya," he repeated slowly.

"And I will call you Gelti."

His answering smile was bemused. "How the world has changed," he muttered.

As soon as I had informed Kirol that his cousin had agreed to work for the council—choosing not to take his look of unflattering disbelief as an insult to my powers of persuasion—I led Gelti down to the infirmary. His first task would be to question the assassin, who was still unconscious. Valdis had a stimulant he thought might break through the boy's haze. It might also kill him, but we didn't have many other options to find out what was going on.

With my walking stick, I was slow on the stairs. My ankle still ached, but I hadn't called for the sharma tincture in days. Gelti hovered nearby, holding out a hand to steady me, which I ignored.

"Kirol will need to approve everything you do, but otherwise you will work independently," I told him once I had reached the bottom and caught my breath.

"And the . . . others on the council?"

"The entire council has agreed to this," I said. *More or less,* I thought. "But I will be your primary contact."

There was that grin again. I wondered if it was deliberate. He had to know the effect it had on women.

I turned and led the way toward the infirmary.

"You need to take better precautions," he said. "At least five armed guards when you go out, and two within arm's reach at all times. That boy shouldn't have been able to get so close."

Traveling with that many guards meant that at least half of them would be Arnath. That still felt more dangerous to me than no guards at all. "You needn't worry about security. You are only responsible for investigating the attack."

"It's hardly worth investigating if you're going to make it easy for them. You can't put yourself in danger."

"You mean none of the council can put ourselves in danger."

He paused. "Of course."

I glanced sideways at him. "I did stop the assassin. I'm not completely useless."

"That was nothing more than luck," he said gruffly. He glanced at me, then pressed his lips closed on whatever he'd been about to say.

But I could guess. I'd been kidnapped by the Arnath Resistance, and I hadn't been able to fight them off. Gelti probably assumed what my father had, what everyone had, about what they had done to me.

Their assumptions might have been right, too, had a different man than Jonis led the Resistance. It rankled to admit that, but I knew it was true.

I'm not afraid of you, I wanted to say to Gelti, but saying so would be its own admission that I was, in fact, afraid. But afraid of what? Of the flutter in my pulse when he smiled at me? Of the way the air seemed to have thickened between us?

I didn't have time for such thoughts. "Just get us some answers," I said, and led him into the infirmary.

SIX

GELTI'S QUESTIONING OF the assassin didn't last long; the stimulant only brought the boy to consciousness for about ten minutes before he sank back into a stupor, and he died later that night. The only real information Gelti got was a mumbled reference to something called the "Swords of Qilara," which he thought might be one of the gangs that had flourished in the Portside area of the city. He seemed to take it for granted that any one of those gangs would want the Ruling Council dead. Gelti also examined the assassin's dagger and immediately recognized it as a simple one favored by soldiers, so common that it told us nothing.

At the council meeting that night, I made sure to tell Jonis how quickly Gelti had identified it—so much for Jonis's own expert knowledge of knives. That didn't help his mood; he was already sourer than usual, because we had received a letter from Raisa, and it had been addressed to me, not him. She and Mati had reached Lilano and met with the southern vizier. I groaned aloud when I read how she had openly told Vizier Tren that the Ruling Council wanted to borrow money from him; she had no sense of how such things were done. She should have waited at least three days to broach the topic. The southern vizier had agreed to discuss the issue further, but he had also given her a message for me.

> *He says to tell you, "One thing at a time." Do you know what that means? He's an odd man, certainly.*

I knew exactly what it meant: Tren had received my letter about the salt mine and wouldn't consider business with the Gamo family as separate from council business, no matter how much I tried to keep it so. And if I wanted him to consider loaning money to the Ruling Council, I couldn't expect him to purchase the mine too.

Jonis, of course, demanded to know what the message meant. Though irritated at his attitude, I had nothing to hide, so I told him.

"We sent Raisa there to keep her safe, and you took it as an opportunity to make some extra money?" Jonis asked, tone full of disgust.

"I sent the letter separately," I informed him icily. "It's family business."

"Wrong," said Jonis. "You're on this council now, and everything you do relates to that."

I tossed my hair. "If I don't find a buyer for that mine, then there won't be any more Gamo money for Qilara's treasury. If you know another source of funding, then I'd love to hear about it."

Unfortunately, with Vizier Tren out as a buyer, I had few other options. I wrote to a handful of old family friends that night, offering the mine for sale, but I knew that they would have little incentive to purchase it. So I wrote to my mother too; she would have gone through all of Father's letters by now, and surely many of them incriminated others. At one point he had commanded the loyalty of over half the court in his conspiracy to topple Mati from the throne. I might not have the luxury of concealing my past allegiances, but others did, and I bet they would pay dearly—perhaps even purchase a salt mine they might not otherwise consider, at a price that was more than fair—to keep them concealed. Most of the surviving Scholars, after all, were still hiding in their country villas, pretending they had never dreamed of working against Mati.

I didn't tell Jonis about the letter to my mother, but that didn't stop him from making snide comments about my obsession with personal profit over the next eight days, every time the budget came up. This didn't stop until another letter arrived from Lilano, this time from Mati and addressed to both of us.

It may have been a mistake to bring Raisa to Lilano. There's so much resentment here. I expected some, of course, over the equality laws, but it's not about that. It's about the new law allowing women to inherit property. The men here like to tell about the War Minister's wife—she took her dowry from the family treasury and ran off with a lover, and they were both found outside the city gates with their throats cut a few days later. At least five different Scholars have told me the story. They seem to enjoying repeating it, especially where Raisa can hear.

Arrest the people who tried to kill her, as soon as you can. We need to come home.

"He's afraid for her," I said.

"Of course he is," said Jonis, an odd, almost wistful expression on his face as he read the letter.

I pursed my lips. I'd warned Raisa to let Mati take the lead precisely because I'd feared something like this. Lilano, being a garrison city, had five men for every woman, and apparently those men were threatened by the law allowing women, married or not, to own and inherit property; it had made women all over Qilara far less dependent on men. That law wasn't going anywhere, as it was what gave me—and by extension, the Ruling Council—access to my family's fortune. It was, as Raisa was fond of saying, a change people would just have to learn to accept.

"I'll tell Gelti to step up the investigation," I said.

Gelti had been reporting to me every morning on his progress. If it rankled him to report to a woman, he hid it well. The next morning, I met him in the garden as usual, so that we could talk privately yet still be in view of the guards at the gate.

When I told him he needed to move more quickly, he frowned. "Using more force will just get people defensive. I've been working my way through the alehouses in Portside. I spent some time at the Bleeding Oyster last night, and I'll do Zentner's tonight. But people won't talk if they know I'm working for you."

I leaned on my walking stick. "You don't think they find it suspicious, you hanging about in places like the Bleeding Oyster?" I could only imagine what such an establishment would look like.

He laughed. "Not at all. The company I keep isn't what it once was. I started where I'm already known."

"Could these 'Swords of Qilara' be connected to the army, do you think?"

Gelti tapped his lip thoughtfully. "It's possible, but—"

Another voice drowned his out. "Soraya!"

I turned to find Jonis racing down the palace steps.

As Jonis skidded to a stop in front of me, Gelti stiffened at my side. "We have to leave, now," said Jonis. "Adin has a carriage waiting." He grabbed my elbow and steered me toward the stables. "Remember the—"

Gelti's hand landed on Jonis's shoulder and spun him around. Gelti was at least three inches taller than Jonis, and broader across the shoulders. "Show the lady some respect," he growled.

Jonis shrugged off Gelti's hand with a cold glare. "The *councilor* is needed elsewhere."

I edged myself between them. "What's going on?"

Jonis's mouth twisted, and he kept his eyes on my face as he spoke, ignoring Gelti completely. "Remember the raider ship that Mati sent out? It's been sighted. It'll be back in port within the hour."

"But . . . the tidal wave," I said. "The earthquakes. How could it have survived?"

Jonis shook his head. "Don't know, but it's here. And we have to go meet it. When those men left, Mati was still on the throne.

We can't let a bunch of disgruntled sailors out into the streets."

My mind was working in slow motion. "But even if they survived . . . they shouldn't be back yet." Jonis shot me a warning look, but I had already bitten back the rest of what I wanted to say. Gelti had been in the room when the Scholars Council had forced Mati to send those raiders, in exchange for Raisa's sentence of execution being lessened to whipping. But he didn't know—very few people knew—that Mati had given them false navigational charts that would lead them into the wastelands. Even if they had found their way, they shouldn't be back for at least another Shining.

"We have to be there when the ship arrives," said Jonis. "Those men might listen to you."

He was right. I said goodbye to Gelti and followed Jonis to the carriage, half wishing that Gelti would come too. I could admit to myself, as Hodder, an Arnath guard, offered his hand to help me up, that this was because Gelti made me feel safe.

Which was ridiculous. My father would have been offended if there weren't five different people plotting his assassination at any given time. Being a Gamo, he'd always said, with a touch of pride, meant that you were never truly safe.

"Has word gotten out about the ship's return already?" I asked, peering out the window as our carriage reached the crowded streets of Portside.

"What do you mean?" said Jonis.

"The way people are grouped together. And that Arnath woman selling fruit—she keeps looking around like she expects an attack."

Jonis shot me a withering look. "That's normal these days."

I watched a group of sailors at the fruit seller's stand. They laughed and talked loudly as they filled their pockets with fruit, one even stuffing a melon down the front of his tunic. Their leader handed the woman some money. She looked at the coins in her hand, then ran her eyes over the men and put the money into her pocket without a word.

"And that," said Jonis, as the carriage moved along and the stand passed from sight, "is a fair depiction of how things are."

"What do you mean? They paid her."

"If they gave her a tenth of what that fruit was worth, she's lucky. She's luckier still that they didn't destroy her stand and do worse to her."

I frowned. "They wouldn't dare. The guards—"

"Can't be everywhere. We don't have enough men." He didn't say that our forces would be better equipped if my mother hadn't taken most of my father's men west with her to hold Pira, but I saw the remark burning in his eyes. He'd lost that particular argument, three to one.

I pursed my lips. "But if the sailors are behaving like that . . . I mean, that will affect trade. Merchants can't pay their taxes if they can't sell their wares."

Jonis glared at me. "Yes, *that's* the problem."

"It's one of them! And maybe it's an argument that would change the minds of people who don't . . . well . . ."

"Don't believe that Arnathim are people?"

I looked away. "Sometimes economics and common sense will sway people when emotional arguments won't. We have to do something about the sailors—could we recruit some of them into the guards?"

"How do you propose we do that? Most of them are dead-set against learning to write. They think it's blasphemy. You won't find a more superstitious lot."

That tallied with what my sister had been telling me about the Library. Even with all her complaints about the menial tasks she had to do, some useful information had slipped though. *You can always tell the guards and sailors and soldiers,* she'd said airily a few days ago. *They're the ones who look like they'd rather be anywhere else.*

I pursed my lips. "Then the sailors on the raider ship will be like that too."

Jonis interlaced his fingers—I had noticed that he often did this when angry, as if to keep his hands from becoming fists. I wondered, for the first time, how he had acquired that habit. "Worse, probably. Only the most ruthless volunteer for the raids."

"But these were drafted. Mati made sure the least-experienced men went on that ship." The scribes, too. Young Luka Shann, a hopelessly incompetent palace scribe, and elderly Tril Hait, who'd been in prison, had been assigned to the ship. Most of the sailors had been plucked from prison too—surely it had seemed like mercy when the king gave them their freedom in exchange for becoming raiders.

Mati had done the job neatly. He'd fooled the Scholars Council into thinking they were getting what they wanted, and he had earned the temporary loyalty of the men's families by freeing them from prison. It had been a backhanded stab at my father, I knew now, as his soldiers had arrested most of those men in the first place, usually for failing to take bribes.

"When those men find out they were given false maps—"

"Sailors use charts, not maps," I corrected him.

Jonis glared at me. "When they find out that Mati purposely sent them into the wastelands, they're going to be furious."

"Why would we tell them so, then?"

I expected another scathing look, but Jonis only tilted his head thoughtfully.

"There are many ways that ship could have ended up with the wrong charts," I said.

"True." Jonis nodded slowly. "Yes, that's true."

"We're going to have to arrest them, though, at least until we know what we're dealing with."

"Yes." Jonis's tone suggested that the phenomenon of us agreeing was as strange to him as it was to me. "The captain is young. His name is Savage. Lives up to it, by all accounts."

My reply flew out of my head at the sight of a banner hanging from a house near the harbor: a sheet painted with several Arnath symbols. "Freedom is ours," I managed to read before we passed. I leaned out the window and saw several fair-haired Arnath children playing in the back garden.

This must have been one of the merchant houses Valdis had told me about, taken over by Arnath squatters. I only hoped that the owners had fled or died in the earthquakes and flooding, and not in some more sinister way.

Kirol was already at the harbor when we arrived. He opened the door of the carriage and said rapidly as we descended, "I've got fifty men here, another twenty-five along the road."

"Not enough," Jonis muttered.

"We never have enough. I wasn't going to leave the palace unguarded."

"There shouldn't be more than forty sailors aboard," I said. The raider ship, easily recognizable by its size and the red flag it flew, was just coming around the curve of land to the north. "We shouldn't use the word *arrest*, if we can help it. They were only following orders."

"Orders to kill and enslave innocent people," said Jonis.

"But they didn't," I reminded him sharply. "They never went to the Nath Tarin."

Kirol strode off to organize his men. Jonis and I walked toward the empty dock the raider ship was heading for, Adin and three other guards falling into step behind us. I smirked; as much as Jonis mocked me for Valdis acting like my bodyguard, his friend Adin hardly left his side.

At least, he hadn't since the assassination attempt on Raisa. I wondered, briefly, what it would be like to have friends so devoted.

Word clearly had gotten out about the returning ship. Behind the tense guards, a crowd was forming. There was no shouting, however; the people were still, quiet. Watching to see how we would handle this.

We couldn't tell them yet that there were no Arnathim on that ship—not if we wanted to keep Mati's false charts a secret. But surely once we announced that the ship had not gone to the Nath Tarin as planned, that would defuse some of the tension. Really, I told myself, it might be the best thing we could ask for at the moment. Surely the Arnathim would celebrate.

Right now, though, the crowd was separated as if by design: dark-haired, olive-skinned Qilarites on the right, fair-skinned Arnathim (and here and there a few with Qilarite blood, like Jonis's sister) on the left. Kirol tersely ordered some of his men into the gap between them.

The ship drew closer. The design painted on the prow—the two furious faces of the king of the gods, one on each side of the ship—reminded me of how gleefully the Scholars Council had chosen this ship for this mission, because it was known as *Gyotia's Wrath*.

Jonis and I might have been alone; the only sounds were the lapping of the waves and the creaking of timbers. Three asotis settled on the pilings nearby and ruffled their gray feathers, watching us with unblinking black eyes. Asotis were quill-feather birds, friends to Sotia in the stories of the gods. A desperate laugh bubbled up at the back of my throat as I thought of the symbolism Raisa would read into the birds' presence. *If you really are out there, Sotia*, I thought, *now would be a nice time to show yourself.*

"Are you armed?" Jonis asked abruptly.

I shook my head. He shoved a sheathed dagger at me, his eyes still on the looming ship.

I swallowed. "Thank you." I hung the sheath on my sash, where it drooped and destroyed the line of my dress.

"Ho, there!" cried a voice. I looked up to see two sailors at the rail. "Can we tie up here? Something going on?"

Jonis took a half step backward, reminding me to step forward. "I am Soraya Gamo, of the council," I called. Let them assume that meant the Scholars Council that had once advised the king. "I must speak with your captain before anyone can leave the ship."

One of the men disappeared and came back with a paunchy middle-aged man.

"You said Savage was young," I muttered to Jonis. I felt, rather than saw, his responding shrug.

"My lady, this is an honor," said the man cheerfully. "Or is it my lady queen now?"

I forced a smile. "You and your crew have been gone for a long time, Captain."

He nodded. "Seventy-four long days, and we spent most of them thinking we'd never see home again."

"We are pleased to welcome you back," I said evenly. "But I need to speak with you about a few things. Please leave your men aboard and come down, Captain."

The man's eyes ran over the walking stick in my hand, my bandaged ankle, the guards behind us, but he bowed. "Certainly, if you ask it, my lady."

I motioned the guards forward to help moor the ship. The gangplank thunked against the dock and the captain walked down to meet us, while a knot of sailors watched anxiously at the rail. They reminded me of Adin, hovering behind Jonis. This captain had the loyalty of his men—not the dynamic I'd expected on a ship of convicts and incompetents.

As the captain approached, I automatically extended my hand, palm down, as I would to a male Scholar. After a moment of hesitation, he took it.

"Many Shinings to you, Captain Savage. Things have changed since—"

The man laughed, his jowls shaking. "I'm not Savage, lady. My name's Coe. Savage is dead."

Well, that was a mercy, at least. This man seemed friendly enough.

He sucked his teeth, then seemed to think better of it. "Savage didn't know what he was doing. He and the scribes got us pointing the wrong way."

"Ah, well, I am sure that Scholar Hait and Scholar Shann can—"

"Both dead," said Coe. "Savage thought he'd give me the worst lot, keep me on oars day and night. But I was the only man on that ship who'd ever been out on the waves. Soon the other lads saw what was what. Didn't take much to convince them they'd be better off following me."

I breathed in sharply. "Mutiny?"

"For a good cause. Savage would have had us lost in the wastelands while the food ran out and men turned on one another. We lost twenty-one men, but still had enough to get back on course and complete our mission. I expect the king'll be pleased."

Jonis made a choked sound behind me.

"Your mission?" I said blankly.

Coe drew himself up proudly. "Yes, indeed. Some died on the journey, but we've still got plenty of cargo. Nearly two hundred slaves, straight from the Nath Tarin."

SEVEN

SOME INSTINCT I didn't know I had propelled me a half step to the right, so that when Jonis lunged forward, he collided with my back instead of with Coe. That knocked me off-balance, and Coe caught me. I stared at Jonis, silently pleading with him to find whatever steely composure kept him from throttling me ten times a day.

His wild expression cleared, and he gave me a nod, his mouth a grim line.

I turned back to Coe. "I will take charge of your . . . cargo, Captain. If you and your men would kindly disembark—"

Coe frowned, scanning Jonis, noticing, I was sure, that his tunic was brown, not green. "Well, now," he said, "that's not the usual way."

I smiled sweetly, my pulse hammering. "Things are not as usual just now, but surely you and your men are exhausted after your long journey." I looked over my left shoulder, ignoring the growing, silent crowd and focusing on one face. "Kirol!" I called. "The Bleeding Oyster is nearby, isn't it?"

"Y-yes," he replied, failing to hide his shock that I would know of such a place. And I hadn't, until an hour ago.

"Tell the owner that we will pay him fifty gyots to make his establishment exclusively available to Captain Coe and his men today." I caught Kirol's arm and added, in an undertone, "Make sure the owner tells them nothing." I turned back to Captain Coe. "After we have inspected the . . . cargo, we—that is, I—will come to the inn and talk more with you. Summon your men, now, please. All of them." I motioned to some of our guards to accompany him back onto the ship.

As soon as Coe had stepped away, Jonis hissed in my ear. "What are you doing?"

"If they're happy in the inn, they're not on the streets. Arresting them in front of this crowd could start a riot. We have to find a way to send the slaves back without—"

"They're *not* slaves," said Jonis through gritted teeth.

"Of course not." I was momentarily speechless at the fury in his eyes. "Of course not," I repeated. "But the crowd—"

Jonis spoke over me. "We have to go talk to them, explain what's happened and, oh gods, apologize . . ." He tugged at his hair.

My stomach rolled, remembering how we had put off sending emissaries to the Nath Tarin, but how, how could we convince anyone that we wanted peace after this?

Shut up, I told the fluttering voice of despair in my mind. *You are a Gamo.*

Not that that was helpful in this situation. "You should be the one to talk to them," I said as I watched the line of sailors leaving the ship.

Jonis closed his eyes briefly—praying, I wondered? Then he replied, his voice leaden, "You have to come too. It has to be both of us."

"But . . . they'll think . . ." I had no idea how to finish that sentence. I wasn't used to considering what slaves—what Arnathim—would think. Everything I knew about the Nath Tarin came from reading Raisa's account of her childhood. They spoke the same language we did, but they lived in scattered villages, with no central cities. There were seven inhabited Arnath islands, weren't there? Or was it eight?

My knees suddenly felt so weak that I clung to my walking stick. The ship, the crowd, the yawning sky—everything just seemed so impossibly huge. How were we supposed to keep control of this?

"Come on." Jonis started for the gangplank as the last sailors cleared it.

"Guards," I hissed, hobbling after him. "We need to take guards."

Jonis looked at me, his eyes unfocused, then he nodded and called out several names. I tried not to cringe as Adin and three other Arnath guards fell in around us.

Jonis told them to wait on the deck. His face was white as he grasped the ring on the door of the hold and hauled it up. I didn't ask how he knew where to go.

He peered down into the darkness. "It's a ladder. Can you

manage it?" *Or will you use it as an excuse?* his suspicious frown seemed to ask.

Much as I wanted to flee back to the dock, escape the odors of fish and salt and sweat and human waste emanating from every part of this ship, I found myself oddly drawn to that hole in the deck. I didn't want to see what lay below, didn't want it to *be*—it was not supposed to be a part of my world.

But my father hadn't made his name by flinching at the ugly parts of life. I'd wanted power, and this was part of it.

"I can manage it," I replied. I meant the ladder. I wasn't sure about what lay beyond that.

Jonis swung himself onto the ladder and climbed down. At the bottom, he squared his shoulders. "You'd better get down here."

A guard appeared at my elbow as I laid my stick on the deck. I flinched, all too aware that I was the only Qilarite aboard this ship, but he only held out a hand to help me climb onto the ladder.

I was almost to the bottom of the ladder when my ankle gave way. Jonis caught me and righted me before I could even yelp. Then he put his hands on my shoulders and turned me around.

In the meager light that came in through the portholes on one side of the ship—the others were blocked by the dock—I saw rows of cages on either side of a narrow aisle. And inside each, figures huddled together, some clutching the bars, some hoisting themselves up toward the small portholes, trying to get a glimpse of the outside. The light was so dim, or they were so grimy, that the Arnath paleness of their skin was not visible. That was what struck me as most odd; they didn't look Arnath or Qilarite or anything at all. They just looked like people.

Whispers and mutters came from the far end of the hold, where the bars disappeared into the darkness, but the people in the closest cages watched us silently, reminding me of the crowd outside. Everyone wondering what we were going to do.

My breath thundered in my own ears. "This must have been a cattle ship before," I muttered, but every word resounded in the silence.

Jonis threw an angry look at me, but my comment seemed to have shaken him out of a trance. He stepped forward. "People of the Nath Tarin," he said loudly. "This has all been a mistake. A horrible mistake. We are . . ." He faltered.

"Sorry," I said, stepping up beside him, determined not to wobble even though my stick was still up on the deck. "For what you have gone through." I caught sight of an older woman in the nearest cage, her face full of breathtaking hatred. Even though the woman was easily three times my age and iron bars stood between us, I touched the dagger at my waist, just to reassure myself that it was there.

Jonis walked along the aisle, explaining what had happened, but I was sure that the people on the other side of the bars weren't taking in a word. Just as I had hardly been able to understand a thing in the tombs—his words had been drowned out by the pounding of my own fear through my blood, and the overwhelming darkness.

Suddenly, I couldn't breathe. I bent over, hands on my knees, gasping.

"Light," I said as Jonis shot me a questioning look. "It's too dark in here. How can they hear anything you're saying?"

Jonis didn't question my ridiculous logic, only went to the firepit near the ladder and struck a flame in it, then set it in the middle of the aisle.

My lungs eased as the faces of the prisoners came into clearer view. Some looked angry, others defeated, others wary. I took a deep breath, so deep that it made me gag at the stench.

Jonis spoke again. "We will send you home. My name is Jonis ko Rikar, and this is Soraya Gamo. We are members of the new Ruling Council of Qilara, along with Mati Villari and Raisa ke Comun."

There was a yelp from one of the cages farther down. A pale hand reached out through the darkness. Jonis carried the firepit toward it. I hobbled after him, ignoring my twinging ankle.

A short woman with matted curls was pressing herself against the bars. Her eyes glittered. "Raisa lives?" Though she spoke our language, there was an unfamiliar lengthening to the middle of the words.

Jonis stepped closer to the woman. "Yes. You know her?"

"My niece. Comun was my sister. But long since, she was taken . . ." The woman sagged against the bars. "Where is Raisa?"

"She's not in the city right now," said Jonis shakily.

The woman slid down the bars, whispering, "She lives."

A young man with reddish curls came forward and crouched beside her, placing a hand on her shoulder.

"How do we know you tell the truth? About her niece, about any of this." He spoke with the same accent as the woman, with drawn-out vowels and rasping consonants.

Before Jonis could answer, a man shouted something foul from the other end of the hold, and several other voices took up the call. I edged closer to Jonis and touched the handle of my knife again.

Jonis's fiery reply drowned out the insults and made it easy to see how he had become the leader of the Resistance. "I am Arnath, like you. I swear to you, we will send you home."

"Arnath?" said the young man in front of us. "'Of the islands.' You call yourselves such?" He looked keenly at Jonis. "Which island are you from?"

I had never seen Jonis quite so nonplussed. "I . . . I was . . . my mother's grandparents came from the islands," he said. "But I don't know—"

"We do not say that—Arnath—on the islands. Those taken by the raiders are the Melarim, the lost. That is what we are." He did not raise his voice, but I heard the steel in it nevertheless.

Jonis's face crumpled. My heart pounded in alarm—he had barely been holding himself together since Coe had first told us of his cargo, and this seemed to have pushed him to his limit.

"No," I said, then repeated it so the rest of them would hear me. "*No.* We will send you home. We're here to help you."

"Then why do we sit in cages?" the young man said pointedly.

"She's one of them," shouted a man's voice from the deeper darkness. "Why listen to her? The other one's probably her slave—"

"I am no one's slave," Jonis growled.

I grabbed his arm, realizing too late that it resembled the action of a slave mistress. So then I bent close to him and whispered, "If we can resupply this ship and get a new crew in here, we can send them back after nightfall. No one in the city even has to know they were here. If that crowd finds out—"

Jonis shook my hand off his arm. "What is wrong with you?" he spat. "We're getting them off this ship as soon as possible. They are not riding home as cargo." He strode over to the ladder and called up to the guards to search for the keys to the cells.

I turned to follow him, my hand clutching the dagger hanging from my sash, but the young man with the copper hair spoke again. "Let us out, please," he said. "There are many wounded and sick among us. They need care."

He was right. Of course he was right. But the thought of what would happen when this got out was almost too much to bear.

I glanced at the hostile stares of the others, then chose to focus on the young man who had spoken; he, at least, was not glaring at me. "What is your name?" I asked him.

"Loris ko Puli." Some of the others hissed, as if they thought him revealing his name was dangerous. I couldn't think why.

"Loris," I said, stepping closer. He seemed to have the respect of the others. Maybe if he listened to us, they would too. "We will send you home, I swear. But a riot is brewing outside. If your people march off this ship in broad daylight, it will be dangerous for everyone, including you." There—logic, cold and clear. Just hearing it out loud helped steady me.

"You are Qilarite," Loris said. "Like the raiders."

"Yes, I . . . yes."

Jonis walked back down the aisle, speaking loudly enough that all those in the cages could hear. "We'll get you out of those cages as soon as possible, and find a place for you to stay until we can get another ship to take you home—a proper ship."

"Where will we put them though?" I muttered when he reached me. "We don't have enough rooms at the palace."

Jonis frowned. "Maybe split them up in the houses in the Watch?"

"No," said Loris sharply. "We stay together. All of us."

Murmurs of agreement came from the other cages.

"There is . . . one place large enough," I said. "At the market." The deserted slave pen building was clean and empty and would house two hundred people easily.

Jonis reared back. "No."

In his eyes, I saw that I was only a Scholar again, that our brief cooperation was gone. "Do you have a better option?" I snapped.

Jonis rubbed his face wearily. He knew I was right, but I doubted he would forgive me for suggesting it. "It won't help things in the city when word gets out."

"We'll have them on a ship by tomorrow or the next day."

A thumping, followed by shouts, came from the direction of the ladder. I started; it sounded as if the voices were coming from the hold, but no one was visible.

"What's behind that wall?" Jonis asked Loris.

"The crew quarters."

I clenched my fists. "Coe left spies behind." He had obviously sensed something was amiss. Why hadn't we thought to have the ship searched?

Jonis swore and raced past me. He was already scrambling up the ladder as I limped down the aisle, my skin blasted by the heat of Arnath gazes. It took me four tries to get onto the ladder. By the time I reached the deck, Adin and another guard were at the rail. Jonis was halfway down the gangplank shouting, "Hodder, stop him!"

My eyes found the sailor dashing along the pilings a split second before Hodder's arrow did.

EIGHT

THE SAILOR LET out a guttural cry as the arrow pierced his back. He toppled into the harbor with a splash.

"Find him," Jonis said to Kirol. "Search the ship and make sure Coe didn't leave any other spies. And get those cells open even if you have to use saws."

The guard who had helped me onto the ladder earlier was missing. "Where's the other man who was here?" I asked the nearest guard.

He eyed me with dislike. "Dead. Went looking for the key and that spy got him."

"I see," I said heavily. I'd been afraid of that.

Then I clutched the railing as I saw the crowd, roiling like the sea. A fight had broken out near the road, and guards were dragging men apart. My stomach dropped. The whole crowd had just witnessed an Arnath councilor order an Arnath guard to shoot a fleeing Qilarite sailor. "Jonis! We have to talk to the crowd."

Adin, who had attached himself to Jonis's side again, said, "She's right."

I retrieved my walking stick and started down to meet them.

"It'd be faster if I carried you," Adin said.

I glared at him. "Don't you dare."

Jonis pointed to the raised front of the terminal building. "We can get their attention from up there."

"And you'll be a target for any arrow or knife that comes your way," said Adin.

"Then it's lucky that we'll have you with us to make sure that doesn't happen," I told him.

But I had to admit, as we headed for the terminal building, that I would far rather have had Valdis beside me, or any of my father's men. Or Gelti.

I reminded myself that my money backed this council—no one who wanted it to succeed would let anything happen to me, even if they hated me personally.

Once we reached the second floor, I had to submit to Adin lifting me out of the window onto the wide ledge at the front of the building, but at least no one was looking our way.

The shouting had grown louder now, the gap between the two groups smaller, but the guards had managed to contain the fighting. So far.

"We can't mention the false navigational charts, remember," I said.

"I know that," said Jonis irritably.

Adin put his fingers in his mouth and let out a whistle that cut through the shouts below and resounded against the houses on the far side of the road.

Jonis prodded me in the back, which I took to mean that I was to start. I had no idea what to say, but that had never stopped me at a thousand Scholar dinner parties. "We thank you all for coming," I said. Maybe if I treated this like a routine gathering instead of a disaster, I could make others see it that way too. "I am Soraya Gamo, of the Ruling Council of Qilara. This is Jonis ko Rikar, also of the council. As you can see, *Gyotia's Wrath* has returned—" Something splatted against the building below us, and I automatically stepped back, my heart pounding. A man on the Arnath side of the crowd yelled something incoherent and lifted a melon before lobbing it at me. Like the first, it met the stone wall of the terminal building below with a wet smashing sound, but several people in the crowd cheered as if it had hit me.

"This ship," said Jonis loudly, ignoring them, "went out before First Shining. We assumed that it could not have survived the earthquakes or the tidal waves, but her crew has turned out to be . . ." He faltered.

"Determined," I filled in. I was aware of Jonis's hands curled into fists next to me, and of Adin behind us, his gaze swiveling over the crowd. "Unfortunately, this means that they have also done what they originally set out to do." I took another small step backward in case more fruit came my way.

Jonis shouted over the murmuring of the crowd, his voice determinedly calm. "This changes nothing. Slavery is illegal in Qilara. These people from the islands will be treated as our guests."

"Traitor!" someone shouted from the Arnath side of the

crowd, and several others repeated it.

"These people will be treated as our guests," Jonis repeated loudly. "We will send them home as soon as possible."

"And the sailors will hang for following orders!" shouted a voice from the Qilarite side of the crowd.

"No," I declared. "The sailors will be quite safe, provided they follow the laws of this city. As will everyone else."

I hadn't meant it to sound threatening, but from the set of Jonis's mouth, I guessed that it had. "We're losing them," he muttered.

We'd tried reason and patience. Clearly it was time for other tactics. "Adin, whistle again," I said.

He did, and that set eyes back in our direction. I took a half step forward, not daring to look down at the drop below. "In token of our commitment to peace, and in acknowledgment of today's upsetting events, port taxes will be waived for the Shining for any ship whose crew is not involved in any violent incidents for the next ten days. Taxes will also be waived for any establishment that immediately ejects belligerent customers for that time. And if the city remains peaceful, each citizen will receive an extra measure of grain."

Murmurs and conversation started up in the crowd below, but the tenor of the talk had shifted; I could tell that even from where I stood high above.

"You're bribing them into peace?" Jonis said.

"I'm a Gamo. It's what we do, isn't it?"

Jonis opened his mouth to address the crowd again, but then he shook his head. They were talking among themselves, many moving off down the roads, and we had lost their attention. "I wouldn't have thought of that," he said.

"Let's go talk to those sailors and get it over with," I said. "We need to get the place at the market ready, and I have a budget to rework tonight."

We didn't make it back to the palace until well after sunset bells that evening. First there was the unpleasant business of addressing Coe's men at the Bleeding Oyster, which turned out to be a large, run-down inn a two-minute walk—or, for me, a ten-minute hobble—from the dock. I was out of patience by that point, so I told the sixteen men who remained of the crew tersely of the changes in Qilara since they had left, and informed them that their captain would be held in the palace dungeon as a result of his decision to leave a spy on the ship. As my budget was shot full of holes anyway, I also promised them a bag of silver asuns each if they remained peacefully in the inn until the Melarim had been sent home. This was for their own protection, I explained, as Jonis stood grimly by my side and a half-Arnath guard force surrounded them.

It was a strange thing, to use my Scholar status to make them listen to me, all the while telling them how that status no longer meant anything.

On our way out, I reiterated to the owner that he was to bill the council for the men's expenses, but that nothing would be paid if a single man was allowed to leave before we authorized it, or if anyone from the outside were allowed in. I promised him a bag of gyots up front, which seemed to allay his doubts, and he spoke to me obsequiously, with many a "my lady," even as he deliberately ignored Jonis in a way that made me simmer with surprising anger.

Jonis went to the market to ready the building, and I went to the storehouses to order food and supplies. By midafternoon, coaches and carts were rolling along the main road to take the Melarim to their temporary home, and I was poring over registries to find a ship to take the Melarim back to the Nath Tarin.

I couldn't concentrate. I'd already changed my gown and scrubbed my arms, even though the rotten fruit that the Arnathim in the crowd had thrown hadn't touched me. I kept smelling it. I cringed whenever I remembered it, whenever I thought of the way the people in the hold of the ship had glared at me. Whenever I remembered the deadly look in Jonis's eyes when he'd learned about the ship's cargo.

I was supposed to be in power now, and that was supposed to protect me from fear. This was what I'd always wanted. So why did I feel so vulnerable?

I'd been thirteen when my father had told me that I would be the future queen of Qilara. Our tutor had died that year, and my horrid aunt Silya had taken over educating me and my sisters. She insisted that we were years behind in learning courtly ways.

"Why can't we have another tutor? Why Aunt Silya?" I asked my father, letting my lower lip quiver.

"Soraya," he said sharply. "You're getting too old for that. Your aunt can teach you how to be a proper Scholar wife." I gaped at him. Aunt Silya's husband had died before I was born, and she often said, out of Father's hearing, that the freedom of widowhood was her reward for enduring the trials of being a wife.

But more than that, I was astonished at the implication that Mother couldn't teach me how to be a proper Scholar wife. Even at that age, I'd heard the whispers wondering why Del Gamo tolerated his ugly, unpleasant wife, but this was the closest Father had ever come to speaking ill of her.

"Your mother will bear no more children," he went on, but the grief in his voice told me what he really meant: no sons. "You will be my heir, Soraya. It is up to you make a good marriage and carry on our family's legacy."

"Will I . . . will I have a highborn husband, Papa?" I asked.

The endearment made him smile. "The highest."

"Prince Mati?" I whispered in astonishment.

He placed a finger on his lips. "Our secret, for now. Mind your aunt and learn all you can." He put his hand on my hair fondly. "You are my smart one, after all." This made me beam even more than learning about the betrothal, and when Father showed me the ledgers for the salt mine the next day, and let me go with him to negotiate the purchase of slaves a few days later, I nearly burst with pride.

The betrothal only made sense, I decided. Who better to match a Gamo than royalty?

Still, when I had pictured my future husband, he'd always been tall and handsome, like my father's portrait in our receiving hall. Prince Mati was . . . gangly and awkward and a year younger than I was, and always running around with his cloddish cousin from the Valley of Qora.

But he would be king one day. When next my family visited

court, I spent hours in the garden waiting to run into him. I was charming, and he was bashful. He picked a peach-colored flower for me, and I pressed it under a wooden box on my dressing table so that I could have the seamstress make me a dress that exact color.

It was during that visit that the tests began. I didn't understand, at first, why Father brought a succession of physicians to see me. One poked my arms with a stick, then stared at the indentations as if reading a scroll; others made me swallow smelly concoctions and then watched me for hours afterward. When I was sixteen, Aunt Silya told me that all this was because my mother was incapable of bearing sons. She warned me that if I didn't comply with every test the king's physicians wanted, I would never be queen.

So I didn't complain when a fat-fingered physician smeared my body with oil and made me lie on the cold stone floor, periodically prodding my stomach. I didn't slap away the probing hands of the midwives who poked garlic into my private parts and then checked my breath the next day to make sure my body was open to bearing a child. If children were the way to secure a highborn husband and a throne and a place on the Scholars Council, then I would do what I had to.

Just before my nineteenth birthday, my betrothal to Mati was officially announced, and I returned to the palace to stay. Mati was so charming in the beginning that it took me nearly half a year to notice that he was never alone with me if he could help it. I tried harder, seeking him out whenever I could, and without my father having to tell me to do so, I endeared myself to the ministers and the high priests.

And then King Tyno died and Mati shut himself off from me. I found out later that he and Raisa, the royal Tutor, spent almost every night together during this time, though they hid it well—at least until Mati burst into the courtyard where most of the court was witnessing Raisa's punishment and threw himself between the whip and Raisa's tattered back.

It was the first time I ever defied my father. He ordered me to stay—this turn of events in no way changed my marriage plans, he insisted. But I bribed four of Father's men and fled in the early morning hours, headed home to Pira.

If my coach hadn't been attacked on the western road, if the Resistance hadn't taken me hostage, then my father might have disowned me. When I returned from the tombs with the news that the Resistance was hiding there, and Raisa was with them, Father made it clear that I would comfort Mati's broken heart in every way that I could, and that I would marry Mati even if I had to share his bed with ten slave girls.

My mother understood my feelings, though she did not approve of my running away. "Impractical and self-revealing," she called it. Later that day, she made me practice the cry that I would give when Mati led me to the tent at the end of the garden after our vows, where we would consummate the marriage. The guests could not begin the celebration until the bride's first cry sounded, so she urged me to make it "full and lusty and loud." No one, she said, wanted to wait around for a frigid bride when there was roast lamb to be eaten.

I, however, had decided that I would let Mati touch me for

precisely as long as it took to put a baby in my belly, and no longer. I only hoped it wouldn't take as long for me as it had for my mother—and of course, that I would bear a son.

I'd done all that, tolerated all of that, for a chance at royal title and a seat on the Scholars Council. And when Raisa had offered me a place on the new Ruling Council, I'd taken it, despite the fact that it meant working with my enemies. I'd always wanted to do something that actually mattered, to prove that being a woman didn't mean I was brainless. But how could I do that if I quaked in fear as I had in the ship's hold, if I let the yawning helplessness I was feeling now direct my actions?

I couldn't. I would be useless to everyone like that.

It was time to learn how to defend myself.

NINE

I SENT FOR Gelti, and let him think it was simply to discuss the situation with the ship as I led him along the overgrown garden path. With the Bleeding Oyster closed, he told me, business at the other alehouses had picked up, and there was still lots of talk against the Ruling Council.

He stopped abruptly in the middle of the path. "You need more guards. You're in more danger than ever."

I kept walking. "We've always needed more guards. How are we supposed to get them?"

"The same way you got that crowd to stand down. Throw money at them."

"I gave them incentive to work with us instead of against us," I returned frostily. That was what Father had always called it.

"One thing I don't understand," said Gelti, his voice so low that I turned to face him. "If you knew that people were desperate enough to keep quiet for an extra measure of grain, why didn't you give them more to begin with?"

I flushed. "Because there isn't more. The treasury is bleeding money as it is. With these new expenses . . . but I'll work it out somehow."

Somehow. I had to.

I started walking again, and he fell into step beside me. "How much would have been made from the sale of the slaves?" he asked.

"That's not even worth thinking about."

"But you've thought about it. How much?"

I sighed. "Five thousand saltbricks, at least." Enough to repair the fountains and feed the people of the City of Kings for a year. Valuing my skin, I hadn't mentioned those numbers to Jonis or anyone else.

Gelti made a noise of consideration, but let the topic drop as I took the path that led through the heart of the garden, where my wedding bower had once stood. The chairs and decorations and the bodies from the subsequent battle had long since been cleared away, but the flowers were choked with weeds, and the grass was still torn up where the worst of the fighting had taken place. At least the flooding and rains had washed away the blood. I led him to the left, avoiding the place where my father had fallen, and into the garden maze, straight to where I had already hidden two wooden training swords.

I tossed my walking stick aside—I was wobbly without it, but I told myself that I didn't really need it anymore—and held one of the swords out to him. I refused to go another day without being able to defend myself. And maybe learning to fight would combat the helplessness that I had felt since we had learned about the raider ship's cargo.

"I want you to teach me to fight," I said.

Several different emotions passed over his face in rapid succession. Shock, I had expected. But I also saw satisfaction, and something that might even have been admiration. "Well," he said. "You have good reason to learn. Will you be able to avoid going among those . . . Arnathim?"

"Melarim," I corrected him. "That's what they call themselves. The lost. But it's not just them." I thought of the Arnathim who'd thrown fruit at me, of the disgust in Jonis's eyes when I had suggested the pens to house the Melarim.

Gelti looked like he was going to protest, so I said airily, "I understand that it may be a challenge, as you don't have experience in this type of training."

His mouth tightened. "That's not an issue."

"So, teach me."

He stared at me for a long moment, and then a slow smile spread over his face. He reached out and took the wooden sword. "You won't be using this yet," he informed me. "You have a lot to learn before you get to hold a weapon."

He tossed the sword aside and held out a hand. I hesitated only slightly before taking it. But then he whirled me around, and before I knew what was happening, his arm was a bar across my chest, his hand tight over my mouth, and he had my left arm twisted up behind me.

Panic clawed at my insides, but Gelti's calm voice spoke in my ear. "You've just been attacked. What do you do?"

It was a lesson. Of course. My pattering heart slowed a little as I considered my options, all the while trying to ignore the fact that, close up, Gelti had a smell of metal and sweat that was surprisingly appealing.

I pulled at his arm, but it was only a show of resistance. I didn't really want to get away just yet.

"If that worked," his voice rumbled in my ear, "it would only be luck."

I fought the urge to say that not every woman would fight back in the first place. But I was supposed to be learning, so I kept quiet.

Also, he still had his hand over my mouth.

"What if he did this?" He wrenched my left arm higher and pinned it between his chest and my back, then grabbed my right wrist.

"I'd scream," I said, trying to twist my arm out of his grip.

I felt his nod behind me. "Hold still," he said.

I did, and then he moved so quickly that I registered cold steel at my throat before I even realized that he'd let go of my wrist. "Would you still scream?" he asked.

My breathing quickened. *Aliana, in the garden, a stranger holding a blade to her neck.*

My free hand automatically tried to push the knife away as I had done to the attacker in the market, but I might as well have been trying to move stone. A finger of fear slid down my spine. "You said no weapons," I managed to say.

"I said *you* had to learn without weapons. Never assume

that your opponent is unarmed."

"That's not fair."

"And it won't be when they send another assassin after you. They'll want you in the most vulnerable position possible. Remember, anything can be a weapon. In my day, recruits weren't allowed to even start sword training until they passed three combat tests using things in their environment. So. What could you use, other than the swords?"

"A branch?" The excitement of his closeness was fading now, with my left arm protesting the unnatural position and his dagger cold against my neck.

"If it's big enough, sure. What else?"

"The bench."

He chuckled. "Made of stone. You can't lift that."

"But if I hit your head against it hard enough, it could crack your skull."

"You *are* a ruthless thing, aren't you?"

His admiring tone made me flush with pleasure, though I wasn't sure that "ruthless" was something I wanted to be.

"All right, the bench can be a weapon," he said. "What else?"

"I could strangle you with my sash."

"If you could get close enough. Anything else?"

Once, I would have been wearing beads or hairpins or earrings that could be repurposed. But Soraya Gamo, Councilor, wore only a simple gown with no jewelry. My walking stick was too far away; I'd never reach it before he overtook me.

But I did have another weapon, didn't I? One I had used before, even if I hadn't thought of it that way.

Arching back against him, I said breathily, "Won't you let me go now?"

He froze, and I took advantage of his surprise to slip under his arm and grab a heavy branch.

He grinned and nodded in approval. "All right. Now what will you do?" He advanced on me, and I held up the branch with both hands. He slashed in slow motion, his eyes following my parries as he spoke. "Most men won't go directly for the kill—they'll try to establish dominance. They won't expect you to fight back. That saved you at the market." His breath was even, though I gasped with every step and my arms shook under the weight of the branch. He moved in faster, his blade shearing a twig from the side of the branch as I fought to keep it aloft.

"Consider your strengths and weakness as well as those of the weapon," he continued conversationally. "That lighter branch over there would suit you better. This one would do more damage if you hit your attacker, but you're not likely to get close enough for that." Deftly he twisted the branch out of my weakened grasp with his left hand and pressed his blade against my throat with his right.

I should have been terrified, but the emotion surging through me was only edged with fear. Slowly he lowered the dagger, but he didn't move away. I was hyperaware of the perspiration rolling down my back, my disheveled hair, my heaving chest. He was so close that I could see the scar on his jaw beneath the beard he must have grown to hide it. His lips parted slightly. I tilted my face up toward him, my heart pounding, and not just from exertion.

I saw in his eyes the moment he decided not to kiss me. Hadn't I spent half a year being rejected by my fiancé? So I backed up first, before he could, and asked a question that came out needlessly belligerent.

"Why wouldn't a man go for the kill?"

He blinked and stepped back, as if he needed to put even more distance between us. I swallowed my disappointment. *Noble Gamo daughter,* I reminded myself.

"Well . . . you're a beautiful woman. Most men would . . ." Gelti examined the cherrywood handle of his dagger—probably another of the spoils of his alliance with the High Priest, I thought, as it likely cost more than a year's worth of guard wages. But he had kept the handle polished, the blade keen; he was a man who valued fine things, and knew how to take care of them.

"I know what most men would do," I said.

Abruptly Gelti sheathed the dagger in his boot and looked up. "You can't let anyone get that close. Next time, choose a weapon you can keep hold of. And running is always an option."

I bristled. "A temporary solution." I'd run once, and, as Father had reminded me often, it had led directly to my kidnapping by the Resistance.

Gelti shrugged. "But it might keep you alive long enough to keep fighting."

"Is that how you justify it to yourself, your desertion?"

I knew why I had said it—I was still smarting over that almost-kiss, and I wanted to wound him. I hadn't anticipated his sickened expression, or the way his hands would drop to his sides.

But perhaps Lanea, goddess of mercy, was truly gone as the

whispers said, for I only wanted to press on, to see if I could deepen this little wound I had opened. "And isn't it a kind of running, too, refusing to learn to write? The world is changed, and you will slip further and further behind."

Gelti lifted his head, and the set of his jaw was something else now, dangerous and dark.

Nonsense, I told myself. Gelti had supported my father. He wouldn't touch me.

Even, it seemed, if I wanted him to.

"That's exactly the attitude," he said grimly, "that makes people want to stab you."

I backed up warily.

He shook his head. "Not me. But plenty of others. You've got your council, and your fancy writing, and not a single merchant or peasant represented. And now you're telling people they'd better behave or they won't get their grain. And you wonder why people hate you."

"Do you have any idea what I'm dealing with?" I spat. "Not enough money, not enough men, everybody asking for more, more, more, all the time, and somehow I'm supposed to magically provide it. If I can't, it must be because I'm selfish or incompetent. If I can, then there's no gratitude at all because I must have a magical supply of money that requires no management whatsoever. If we encourage people to read and write, we're tyrants. If we don't, we must be hoarding the language of the gods for ourselves." I shook my head. "If teaching me to fight is so distasteful to you, I can find someone else to do it."

"No," he said. He blew out a breath. "No. Of course I'll do it."

I coughed. "I expect you'll want a raise."

I could have sworn that it was hurt that flashed across his face before he turned away. "It's all part of my services, Councilor."

Our best option for returning the Melarim to the Nath Tarin was the *Shorebird*, a ship that shuttled passengers between Qilara's coastal cities and was owned, unfortunately, by the southern vizier. Vizier Tren's business agent in the capital, Harcus Gard, had received an injury during the earthquakes that had left him paralyzed, so it was his wife, Marieke, who met with me the next morning.

Marieke Gard wore the long veil of a Scholar wife, but hers was so sheer that I could see her square chin and sharp eyes. My mother would have been horrified. I doubted the southern vizier was aware of how much she had taken over her husband's business, let alone the fact that she did it wearing such a veil.

"And what are the terms?" I asked, once the initial pleasantries were out of the way.

Marieke smiled; I had the feeling that the polite nothings annoyed her as much as they did me, though neither of us had been willing to dispense with them. "Before we get to that, Councilor, I have a personal question. I wish to know the status of my request for reparations."

"No one will be compensated for loss of slave labor," I said, my tone made brisk by the fact that I had suggested this very thing and been soundly outvoted. Jonis hadn't spoken to me for three days after that council meeting, as I had pronounced his own reparations proposal—to provide every Arnath family with a house of their own—a financial impossibility.

Marieke gave a laugh that was probably supposed to be charming. "Yes, that has been made clear. I was referring to the three urns, golden headband, and an Emtirian crystal inkwell that my husband gave to you for your wedding gift."

"Those gifts were dedicated at the altar to the gods before the wedding." Not to mention that all the wedding gifts that hadn't been looted or destroyed had been sold away to fund repairs.

Marieke tossed her head, a practiced move of disdain. "Those wedding gifts were the rightful property of the Gard family and any just council would agree. But I suppose your council's justice is a moving target. Good Qilarite citizens forced to sacrifice their hard-earned wealth for no reason. Don't be surprised if the Scholar class seeks other ways to protect itself."

"What's that supposed to mean?"

"It means that if no one trusts your council to look out for their interests, everyone will look out for their own."

I sighed. If I hadn't joined the Ruling Council, I could imagine my own mother making a similar demand about my lost dowry. Really, it was amazing that we hadn't had other Scholars making such requests about the wedding gifts. . . .

I frowned, resolving to check the scribe records from the public audiences, most of which Mati had handled. He studiously avoided all references to the wedding, so it was quite possible that it had come up often and he just hadn't mentioned it.

"You may submit your request in writing to the chief steward," I said, liking the sound of the words in my mouth even though we had no chief steward anymore. Never mind—we would eventually, and such requests were so ridiculously low in priority that they could wait until that time. It didn't matter, I told myself, that this government was being held together with paste and string, as long as people believed that it was something more. "That is a separate issue from our wish to engage Vizier Tren's ship."

"Is it?" said Marieke with a wide smile.

"There are other passenger ships we could—"

"None that can be ready in fewer than twelve days. I checked. The *Shorebird* can be ready in ten. Eight if we receive reparations for the wedding gifts. And you need to get those tialiks out of the city before your council loses control." She folded her hands in her lap, unapologetic about her foul language.

"And the price?" I said evenly, though my hands clenched under the desk. She was right about the timing for the other ships; I had checked too.

She named an outrageous sum. I laughed. What followed was a tiresome back and forth that ended in me agreeing to a price that was more than I had hoped, but less than I'd feared. When I added in the cost of the wedding gift reparations—which I had to, as we couldn't afford to wait ten days to get the Melarim on their way—my budget was once again in tatters.

And worse than that: using the southern vizier's ship would mean that he wouldn't even consider loaning us any money until the ship had returned from the Nath Tarin and been inspected. I remembered his condescending message, delivered through Raisa: *One thing at a time.*

I was already mentally sorting through my jewelry box to see if there was anything else I could sell. I hadn't heard back from my mother yet about Father's records in Pira and the possibility of using information found there to pressure a buyer for the salt mine. With every day that went by, making a profit from the mine became more necessary and less likely.

"Have you—I mean, has your husband ever considered investing in mining operations?" I asked Marieke.

Marieke's nose wrinkled behind the sheer veil. "Without a cheap labor source? That would be a fool's investment. No doubt anyone with a mine in Qilara is trying to get rid of it as quickly as possible right now."

"Indeed," I said with a tight smile as I showed her out.

Then it was back to my ledgers to try to find some way to account for the cost of securing the southern vizier's ship, feeding the Melarim, the waived docking fees, the extra grain that had been promised to the people of the city, and the sailor's expenses at the Bleeding Oyster. There was nowhere near enough money, not even if I put off the bridge repairs for another season.

My family had many investments, but little portable wealth left. At this point, the deficit was so high that selling the smaller mines would do little good. I simply had to find a buyer for the salt mine, and I couldn't afford to wait for my mother to find the right Scholar to blackmail. The best options—the Emtirian emperor and the southern vizier—were closed off to me, but the former Emtirian ambassador to Qilara, Lord Romit, had once expressed interest in the mine, back when it was so successful that my father wouldn't think of selling it. By all accounts, he had fallen out of favor at the Emtirian court after the collapse of the

Qilarite monarchy, so perhaps he'd be interested in an investment.

I'd written to Raisa and Mati the night before to tell them about the ship's arrival, but even with my description of the dire state of the treasury and the need to send the Melarim home as soon as possible in order to avoid riots in the streets, I doubted they would approve of what I was considering. I knew that Jonis wouldn't.

Nonsense, I told myself. The others had made me vow not to do business with the Emtirian emperor, but private citizens of Qilara doing business with private citizens of Emtiria was another matter. Still, this would have to be done delicately.

My eyes fell on the list of ship registries, still open on my desk. At the top was *The Lady with Flowers*, Horel Stit's ship. I'd seen that ship as we had left the docks yesterday, with its unexpectedly sweet figurehead of a small woman, eyes on the bouquet in her hands. It was hard to believe that a man who put such an image on his ship was as cruel as Jonis described him.

Jonis himself had said that Stit used to run messages to Emtiria. If he already had connections there, then he might be my quickest option to offer a deal to Lord Romit.

I summoned Valdis and had him memorize a message, then sighed and handed him my ruby brooch to give to Stit as payment for delivering the offer to Lord Romit.

It was a sticky business, but, I reminded myself, it was still just business.

TEN

STIT AGREED TO carry my message about the salt mine to Lord Romit, and Valdis was back in time to accompany me down to the market that afternoon. Jonis had been spending every free moment among the Melarim since they had been installed in the former slave pen building, but I hadn't wanted to visit until I could tell them about the arrangements for sending them home.

I had never been inside the slave pens before, though I had been escorted with my father into the small, elegantly appointed rooms for wealthy customers above. Those rooms had been converted to an infirmary for the sick and wounded among the Melarim. The others were living in the larger spaces on the first floor.

Kirol had assigned only Arnath guards to the Melarim, which made me glad I had brought Garvin, one of my regular Qilarite guards, as well as Valdis.

Garvin led the way down the narrow entrance hallway, which

soon opened into a wide room lined with benches. Iron rings were set into the walls, but the chains were gone now, and some kind of writing covered the wall in between the rings. I couldn't get close enough to read it, because there were people everywhere, lying on mats and blankets, sitting on the benches, propped up against the wall. They all fell silent as I passed.

A woman's voice, loud and rasping, rose up behind us. "Most Honored Sotia, shield us from the ignorant beasts of this world with the light of your knowledge." Muttering broke out in the room.

Ignorant beasts of this world. That meant me and Valdis and Garvin, I realized, my heart leaping into my throat.

"Let's go," said Valdis, stepping into my path as I turned back toward the voice. Over his shoulder, I saw an old woman writing a symbol in the air with her index finger, as if warding off an attack.

I took a deep breath and followed Garvin deeper into the building. At last the passage opened into a room lit with torches and lined with large cells, the design so similar to the hold of the ship that it could only have been deliberate. Aside from the writing on every wall—which I could now see had been done with charcoal on the stone, and seemed to be prayers to Sotia written in the Arnath script—the cells were impeccably clean; I'd had the building mucked out last Shining, back when I'd assumed that our council would do something sensible with it instead of pretending it didn't exist.

The cell doors had all been tied open with lengths of rope, and people moved in and out of them freely—not nearly as many people, though, as I had seen jammed into the smaller front room, and many of them were lounging in the hallways instead of inside the cells.

Of course. After what they had been through on the ship, they must hate the bars.

No one spoke to me, though I saw their eyes dart to me and then away. All except for one little girl, nine or ten years old, with light-brown hair in two braids over her shoulders, who stared at me openmouthed. A man who might have been her father—at least, he had the same flyaway brown hair—crossed to where she perched on a bench a little apart from the others and hissed something in her ear, and she hung her head.

Jonis sat on the floor inside a cell with the woman who'd called to him on the ship, Raisa's aunt. The woman was much cleaner now, though her hair could still use a comb. Jonis's open expression as he spoke with her took me aback. He'd never looked like that in our council meetings, even before Raisa left.

I swallowed a lump of fear. For all his nodding along at Mati and Raisa's talk of Qilarites and Arnathim working together, it would be easy for him to turn on me. We hadn't done a proper census yet, but it was likely Arnathim now outnumbered Qilarites in the City of Kings, and the Melarim swelled their numbers even more.

I was glad that Valdis was behind me, and that I still had the dagger Jonis had given me the day before, strapped to my thigh. Even if I didn't really know how to use it yet, knowing it was close by was a comfort.

Adin was playing cards with a group of men and teenage

boys, his laughter booming out periodically over the other conversations. He sat across the room from Jonis, which must mean that he sensed no danger here.

A hand on my arm made me jump. I felt for the dagger, but when I turned, I found a stocky young man with coppery hair that fell into his eyes, eyes that were light brown and serious despite his smile. I didn't recognize him at first, now that he was wearing a clean tunic and out of the dim hold of the ship where he had been the only one of the Melarim willing to talk to us.

"I wondered when you would come," said Loris ko Puli.

If *you would come,* I read in his tone, and bristled. He frowned, removing his hand from my arm. In my peripheral vision, I saw that Valdis had stepped forward protectively, and I suppressed a flash of gratitude.

"Of course I came," I said. "We are aware that these . . . accommodations are not ideal, but—"

"No, they are not," he agreed. "But it is better than the ship."

I flushed. "Your return journey will be quite different. I've booked a luxury ship for you."

"We don't need luxury. We just need a place to grieve for our dead. The fate of many on the islands is . . . uncertain."

His heavy tone made me wonder if he had left a sweetheart behind. He seemed about my age, maybe a few years older, and might even be married. It felt rude to ask, though, so I only said, "Our temples were destroyed in the earthquakes, so we don't have a proper place for mourning rites. There are some makeshift altars throughout the city, mostly to . . . Sotia." I hesitated. "Do you know what happened here?"

"Yes, our Learned Ones saw Sotia's destruction of the other gods. That was why we were unprepared for the raid." He met my eyes. "We did not account for the continued hatred of man, once the gods were gone."

I flushed again, not liking how often he made me do that. "That raid was set in motion before any of the rest of it. And now, we're . . . doing our best." I took a breath. "I really need to speak to Jonis."

He led me toward the open cell where Jonis sat with Raisa's aunt. I gestured for Valdis to stay outside, and Garvin took up a position across the room. Jonis, I noted, hadn't bothered to bring any guards back here with him; Adin, in his card game across the room, hardly counted.

Jonis didn't stand as a Scholar would when a lady entered, but I had long since grown used to this. "Loris and Tira have been chosen by the others to speak for them," he told me.

The woman, Tira, shook her head. "Loris is a Learned One. He leads. I help only as he asks me to."

I looked at Loris with interest. Raisa had told me about the Learned Ones on the islands—they were a council of four, the inspiration for our own Ruling Council. They weren't just leaders, but teachers, responsible for passing on the language of the gods. Because of this, the raiders usually killed them and their families rather than enslaving them. Raisa's father had been a Learned One, and she had only survived by taking on a neighbor's family name.

Loris frowned. "I'm just an apprentice. I'm not old enough to—"

"Not an apprentice any longer," said Tira, touching his arm.

Loris pressed his lips together and didn't answer.

Tira patted the bench—the gesture so reminiscent of Raisa that I had an unexpected pang of missing her—and I sat beside her. Loris sat on the floor beside Jonis, and I explained the delay in preparing the ship.

"Eight days?" Jonis's tone implied that I had fabricated this timeline.

Loris shrugged. "We long since had given up hope of returning home at all. Eight days is nothing. But we will need ervadesha so that the children can resume their lessons."

"Erva . . . what?" I asked. Jonis shrugged, equally baffled.

"Ervadesha. With wax? For writing practice." Loris held one hand flat and mimed writing on it with the other, then wiping it and writing again. I had trouble picturing what he was describing—how could one write without ink?—but it seemed to be a device that could be reused, and that would save money. Writing supplies had tripled in price with the increased demand as more people learned to write.

When Jonis and I continued to look at him blankly, Loris dropped his hands. "We can make our own ervadesha if you tell me where to get wood and wax."

"We'll get them for you," I said quickly. "It's best if you don't go around the city."

Loris frowned. "Are we prisoners here?"

"No!" Jonis replied at once.

"Things are tense right now," I explained. "We don't have enough guards."

Loris turned those serious brown eyes, the color of cream tea, on me. "If we can't leave, then we are prisoners."

Jonis sighed. "Of course you can go out. But . . . you should be armed if you do. We'll make sure to provide—"

"May I speak to you privately, Jonis?" I said through clenched teeth.

"So you can tell me what a bad idea it is to make sure they can defend themselves?" he said darkly.

"No, so I can remind you that some people will see that as creating an army."

Jonis stood, his hands balled into fists. "Those people are exactly the ones who will put them in danger. If we can't provide more guards, then we have to provide weapons. It's our responsibility to keep them safe."

"Which would be easier," I retorted, "if they stayed here." I resisted the urge to stand as well; one member of this council, at least, had to behave with dignity if we expected to keep this situation under control.

Loris frowned. "I will not ask our people to stay penned up for so long."

I sighed. "Suppose they could move freely about the marketplace? We have enough guards for that." I did not bother to look to Jonis for his agreement; I knew our resources best, and he had not bothered to ask me about arming the Melarim.

"Limited freedom is better than none," said Tira in a measured tone, looking at Loris. Though more than twice his age, she would clearly defer to him.

"Is it?" said Loris lightly.

"Letting you go out to the marketplace is the best we can offer," I told him. "We can't keep you safe if you seek out danger."

Loris pursed his lips, then nodded. "I will explain the situation to our people. But I won't order them."

"Understood," said Jonis. "And I will provide you with basic weapons"—he held up a hand to ward off my protest—"easily concealed, and not purchased with council funds." He shot me a nasty look. "Don't worry about your precious budget."

I bit back a heated reply. I would not let Jonis drag me into an undignified argument.

Loris looked past me, and his expression went blank. I turned to see the little girl who'd been staring earlier, the one with the braids, standing hesitantly by the open cell door with two tin plates. "For our guests," she whispered.

Loris hesitated, then motioned the girl forward. She cast a nervous look at Valdis as he followed her inside. On each plate lay a bun, one larger than the other, and a handful of slightly shriveled grapes. I hadn't been able to arrange the best food at short notice, but at least the bread was fresh, as the Melarim had been given the use of the four ovens in the courtyard at the back of the building.

"Thank you," said Jonis, reaching for one of the buns, but I stopped him with a look. He scowled as Valdis picked up a bunch of grapes, sniffed it, then popped one into his mouth. He chewed meticulously as I explained to Loris and Tira that our council had to take precautions. I didn't mention the assassination attempt at the Festival of Lanea; I wasn't sure how Tira would react to finding out that her niece had been the target.

The girl watched Valdis curiously as he moved on to tasting the buns, smelling each and then pulling off a small piece to sample. He paused over the morsel from the larger bun, opening and closing his mouth in an odd, fishlike gesture that animated his mustache, then he lifted it to his nose and sniffed again.

"Pinkbane," he announced thickly, staring at the girl. "Garvin, hold her."

By the time I had processed what he'd said and sprung to my feet, holding the wall for support, Garvin was in the cell and gripping the girl's arm. The plates crashed to the stone floor, and within moments, the other Melarim were up and staring, crowding closer to the cell.

Loris looked stunned. "Erinel," he said to the girl. "Why would you do this?"

She had gone white as chalk. "I—I only—Papa said to take the food to the lady. . . ."

"Find her father," Loris said to one of the men hovering on the other side of the bars, just as Adin shoved his way through the crowd and planted himself behind Jonis, who was looking back and forth between the girl and Loris.

I met Valdis's eyes. "What does pinkbane do?"

My heart skipped a beat at the way he opened and closed his mouth a few times, as if reacquainting himself with his lips. Valdis knew his business, I reminded myself, and he had developed a tolerance for many poisons. He would be fine.

With one hand, Valdis loosened the strings of the bag at his belt and withdrew a small dried leaf, which he quickly swallowed. "Causes paralysis, my lady," he said at last. "Perhaps death, depending on the dose. He probably got it from the medical supplies. The doctors use small amounts to numb the skin for surgery."

"I see," I said, looking at the bun he still held. "And only one was poisoned?"

He nodded. I glanced at the Melarim grouped on the other side of the bars. Without a doubt, that poisoned bun had been meant for me. The girl would have offered me the larger bun in a show of politeness, or maybe they just assumed that the greedy Qilarite would take the larger portion.

I forced myself to breathe slowly in and out, to ignore the bars and the wall of people pressed against them, the windowless stone walls behind me, and focus on the open cell door, the path out of the building, the torches in the hallway outside. This wasn't the tomb, and I wasn't a prisoner.

"It's a misunderstanding," said Jonis. "Or an accident. She's just a child!" He glowered at Valdis. "Or he's lying."

"How dare you," I began, stepping forward, but someone pushed his way through the crowd then, the brown-haired man I'd seen earlier with the girl.

"What's the brat done now?" he growled.

Erinel cringed back against the wall. "Papa," she cried. "They're saying I did something to the buns, but I never—I brought them like you said—"

"What's she whingeing about?" he said to Loris.

"Erinel brought poisoned food to our guests, Madden," said Loris.

Madden didn't even look at his daughter. "Can anyone be

surprised? You know what she is."

Erinel let out a wail.

"Yes," said Loris softly, "we know what she is. Which is why we all know that Erinel does not have the wits for this."

The people outside the cell exchanged uncertain looks.

Madden went completely still, and then his lips broke into a sneer. "The Learned One speaks," he said. "Did you work that out for yourself, or have your new masters been whispering in your ear?"

Loris blinked, but did not otherwise react to the insult. "Did you send your daughter to poison the councilors, Madden?" he asked in a low voice.

"Yes, I sent her. Thought she might as well do one useful thing in her worthless life." Madden was a head taller than Loris, but thinner. He shouldn't have been intimidating, with his wispy hair and plain gray tunic, but the snarl that twisted his face made him look like some feral creature. He hurled his next words at the Melarim crowded at the bars. "He sits talking to them, after they dragged us from our homes. We're not slaves, they say, so why are we penned up like slaves? Your brother died on that ship, Rorie. Sana, they killed your husband. They murdered my wife and children. And he"—Madden flung out an arm to point at Loris—"is helping them." He turned his lethal gaze on me. "When we should be taking every chance to end them."

In the space of a breath, Valdis had dropped the bun and twisted both Madden's arms up behind his back. A wave of agitated murmurs arose among the Melarim. Erinel let out a hiccuping sob.

Jonis stepped forward. "You are not slaves here," he said loudly. "We're doing everything we can to get you home."

"And how long will that take?" shouted a woman's voice from the back of the crowd.

Jonis glanced at me. "Eight days," he said. This set off another wave of muttering.

"You see?" shouted Madden. "They lie. They want to keep us quiet and locked up here, and he's helping them—"

Valdis cuffed the man on the side of the head. "Shut your mouth," he growled.

"Valdis," I said evenly. He glanced at me and subsided. I ignored the claustrophobic glares of the Melarim and the suppressed fear blooming into a headache behind my eyes, and said, "Garvin, arrest this man and—"

"No," said Jonis. "The Melarim are under Loris's leadership. He decides, not us."

Even as I opened my mouth to argue, I understood that he was right. We would never convince the Melarim that we were serious about treating them as equals if we didn't respect the authority of their leader.

Knowing that did not lessen my irritation at being contradicted so publicly. Maybe that was what sharpened my tone when I turned to Loris and said, "Very well. This man has committed attempted murder and endangered his own child's life to do it. What will you do about it?"

Loris looked startled and slightly sick. "You must understand," he said, "this man does not speak for all of us. We are a peaceful people."

There was a discontented murmur from the crowd of Melarim, and Tira shot Loris a worried look. "However," said Loris loudly, "we have all suffered at Qilarite hands, and that must be taken into account."

My hands clenched into fists. Jonis would probably agree with whatever light punishment Loris was about to give this man, and would probably lecture me later about how the treatment this man had received justified his behavior.

All was quiet now, except for the rise and fall of Erinel's sobs. Loris studied Madden, absently pushing his curls out of his face. The gesture was uncertain, almost endearing, and I couldn't help thinking, *He's too young for this. We all are.*

Finally, Loris spoke. Though his face was pale and he looked as if he might vomit at any moment, his voice was low and sure. "Sotia's laws are clear. One can expect no more from others than one is willing to give oneself."

There was a collective intake of breath; the Melarim had understood something from Loris's words that I had not. I glanced at Jonis, but he looked just as puzzled as I was.

Loris, meanwhile, faced his people. "Is this punishment out of step with anything in the Book of Years?" He turned his head, taking the time to meet each pair of eyes, his voice firm. "Do our laws change depending on what is done to us?"

A few people shook their heads. Loris gave a decisive nod, then stooped and gingerly retrieved the poisoned bun from the floor. "Eat it," he said quietly, holding it out to Madden.

I gasped. Madden, still held by Valdis, looked from the bun in Loris's hand to the people on the other side of the bars. He opened his mouth as if to shout, but then closed it uncertainly.

"It will only mean death if death is what you planned for her," Loris said, almost gently. "This is the sentence of the Learned Ones . . . One. It is as Sotia wills it. You may choose to eat it yourself or have it fed to you."

Valdis smiled grimly under his mustache, looking like he wouldn't mind doing the force-feeding.

"Give it to me," said Madden, and Valdis let him pull his hand free to grab the bun, which he stuffed into his mouth defiantly.

Madden's mouth flapped as Valdis's had, and a series of loud gulps, like some comical imitation of a frog, came from his throat.

Erinel let out a piercing wail. Despite everyone's insistence that she was witless, the girl seemed to understand exactly what was happening. Garvin tried to shush her. Tira, ashen-faced, stepped around him, took Erinel's hand, and led her out of the cell.

Madden swayed on his feet, and Valdis stepped aside and let him crash to the floor. The man's hands began to shake and his eyes blinked rapidly, and the only sounds were his wretched gulping and his daughter's muffled sobs fading down the hallway.

Many of the Melarim had moved away, but some remained, clutching the bars with white fingers as they watched Madden's legs twitch, his arms flail as he slowly lost control of his body and eventually, limb by limb, went still.

That would have happened to me, I thought, my breathing shallow. I flexed my fingers almost convulsively, to assure myself that I could still move them.

Loris, too, was watching Madden on the floor, and his pale

skin had a greenish cast. Abruptly he called out to two of the Melarim and ordered them to take Madden to a cell down the hall. As soon as they had done so, people dispersed into small, murmuring groups.

Loris beckoned us out into the hallway. "Please accept our apologies."

"You have nothing to apologize for," said Jonis shakily.

I pursed my lips and hoped that I was hiding my own pounding heart better than either of them. I didn't agree that there was nothing to apologize for, but it wasn't an argument I wanted to have surrounded by the Melarim. I did my best not to run back up the corridor.

Jonis and I were both on edge when we got back to the carriage. "And you want to give them weapons," I said.

He stiffened and laced his fingers together in front of him. "It makes sense to arm them if we can't protect them."

"I would be dead right now if—"

"If you didn't have a taster. But you do. You have protection. They don't."

"You're ashamed." The words spilled out before I could consider them. "You think that man was justified, trying to kill me."

"You know that's not true," said Jonis angrily. "That was one man, and Loris made it very clear he doesn't represent them all." He shook his head. "This country has enslaved countless people, has destroyed their homeland again and again. Aren't you ashamed of that?"

I frowned. "I didn't do it, though. Why should I be ashamed? We're just trying to pick up the pieces!"

He shook his head. "Your people did this to them."

"Mati did this, because he was driven to it."

"By your people."

"And by yours," I shot back. "The Scholars Council was terrified of the Arnath Resistance. Every time you struck, it made them more determined to get revenge. That's why they pushed Mati to send the raiders."

Jonis shook his head and exhaled loudly. "Raisa should be here. She should be the one to talk to them."

"Maybe." But I wasn't sure whether Raisa's presence would have made things better, or worse. She had come to Qilara by the same kind of raider ship, had been sold from the platform at the slave market. Would she have been better able to communicate with the Melarim? Or would she have crumbled from the reminders of her past? Would men like Madden want to kill her too, see her as a traitor to her people for trying to make peace?

Mati would have been useless, I was sure, mired in his own guilt about sending the raiders in the first place, no matter that he had only done it to save Raisa's life.

"You miss her too," said Jonis. "You could admit that." When I didn't respond, he added, in a different tone, "She is, after all, one of the few people who can stand you."

I tossed my hair and turned away, determined not to let him see how much that hurt.

ELEVEN

OUR COUNCIL MEETING that night was contentious. Jonis only wanted to discuss the Melarim, while I had spent the hours since leaving them going over ration plans and writing letters, anything to push the image of Madden's flapping mouth and twitching fingers out of my mind. I didn't say that to Jonis; to him I only pointed out that Qilara was not going to come to a halt until the Melarim left. We still had to set repair crew orders, review petitions, and listen to an update brought by a messenger from Commander Gage of the South Company. Mati and Raisa had met with Gage in Lilano, and their letters had described him as largely supportive of our Ruling Council's reforms. Gage's men were famously loyal to him, so if he supported us, then most of the South Company would too. The messenger delivered Gage's request for more supplies as a memorized speech, as not even Gage had embraced writing yet.

I smiled and gave my standard answer about considering everyone's needs and making just decisions, while clenching my fists under the table. Did no one else in this country understand what a mess our finances were?

As soon as the messenger had left, Jonis pushed back his chair and stood. "Are we done here?"

"There are still the repair crew orders. We don't have enough money to do both the aqueduct and the garrison bathhouse, so we'll have to prioritize. And with the ship expense, we can't—"

Jonis raised one eyebrow. "Why isn't there enough? What did you do with it?"

"Do you have any idea how much it costs," I spluttered, "to hire a ship on short notice, and feed two hundred people, and pay guards for extra shifts? And now we can't count on the southern vizier to loan us anything until his ship returns. Where are you going?"

Jonis was halfway to the door. "In case you haven't noticed, a lot of Arnathim are pretty upset right now. I've got my hands full convincing them that they're not going to be made into slaves again, and dealing with all the ones who want to take their long-lost relatives home with them instead of leaving them in the slave pens."

I frowned. "We can't reimburse them for expenses if they do that."

Jonis scoffed. "We can't *protect* them if they do that. But I'm a bastard for telling them so." His face was stony, as it had been at the docks when people in the crowd had called him a traitor. "By all means, stay here and keep going over your papers."

He left, slamming the door behind him, before I could come up with a response.

I spent the evening working in my study, trying to ignore the sick feeling in my stomach that had been there ever since Valdis had detected the poison in the bun. It was one thing to be a proud member of the Gamo family, knowing that our power had made us targets ever since my great-great-great-great-grandfather first maneuvered his way into the post of Trade Minister, the first in an unbroken line of Gamos holding influential government positions. It was quite another to look into the eyes of a man who wanted me dead simply for what he thought I represented.

Alshara came to see me and gave a detailed account of everything that had gone on in the Library of the People that day. I'd let her in because I'd hoped that her chatter would be a distraction, but in the lamplight, her features looked more like her lost twin's than usual, and the reminder of Aliana's death made the hollow in my stomach even worse.

Alshara, however, went blithely on. She didn't know about the poisoned bun, of course, but she didn't seem to care much about the arrival of the slave ship or to understand that I had far more important things to consider than how many scrolls she had been asked to copy.

Let her be clueless, I thought. It was how she should be, how Aliana should have been too—carefree, untouched by the evils of this world. I hadn't been able to protect Aliana, but maybe I could keep Alshara safe from them.

I finally sent her off to her bed, but didn't go to my own. Instead, I sat back down at my desk and stared at the ring on my thumb.

I'd been right to insist that Gelti teach me how to defend myself. I was half tempted to summon him for another lesson, despite the late hour, despite how desperate that would make me look.

I settled for throwing myself into my work, scribbling different scenarios for making up the quill tax shortfall. That tax, levied on Scholars for writing the language of the gods and those of the lower classes who employed scribes, had once made up a huge portion of Qilara's income. But now that writing was available to everyone, we'd had to do away with it. I believed in the value of education as much as my fellow councilors did, but revolutionaries, I thought sourly, didn't consider the paperwork involved when they were plotting their reforms; they just left it to people like me to sort out the details.

Even though the budget was impossible, it was soothing to submit to the pull of the numbers on the page; budgets were so much less complicated than people. The income and expenses columns badly wanted to be balanced. I wanted to prove that I could balance them.

I worked until I could barely keep my head up, then dragged myself to my bed, hoping for a deep, dreamless sleep.

The nightmare came anyway. I'd expected to dream about Madden; after all, his feral look as he admitted to planning my death had been repeating itself behind my eyelids every time I closed my eyes.

I hadn't expected to dream about his daughter, Erinel. I hadn't expected to be there in the dream beside her, watching her father fall, twitching, to the ground, her sobs echoing in my ears as if they might have been my own.

I woke with my sheets tangled around my legs, my hair matted and sweaty, the lamp flickering in the early-morning light. I rubbed my eyes, ignoring my mother's voice in my head warning me that doing so would cause premature wrinkles.

The memory of my wedding day, so often carefully suppressed, swept over me with the force of Sotia's tidal wave.

"You will never have to suffer his touch again after this day, my dear."

I'd stared at my father, but he'd only smiled and helped me up onto the litter that would bear me through the garden to the bower where Mati and I would make our marriage vows. Symbols of my substantial dowry surrounded me: small trunks of gold and jewels, and ten slaves tied to the litter with golden ropes.

I settled myself in the center and straightened my purple skirts. The guests had taken their seats, but Mati was nowhere to be seen. I pondered my father's cryptic words.

And then the sky ripped open, with thunder so loud that it continued booming long after I had covered my ears. The litter lurched as the slave in front fell to his knees. I screamed, clutching the sides. Trunks slid to the ground and burst open, scattering gleaming treasure across the grass.

The palace bells tolled once, again, then on without stopping. Scholars ran in every direction, men among them with swords, flailing their weapons without seeming to care what they hit.

My litter crashed to the ground so hard that my teeth jarred. I kicked my legs out over the side, my satin slippers sliding in the dirt. *They aren't supposed to touch the earth*, I thought in dim panic. Mati was supposed to carry me to my bridal tent and remove them along with the rest of my garments, and my mother and sisters would put sturdier shoes on me when they came to dress me after the consummation. That was what was supposed to happen.

Hands were thrust into my face. "The ropes, please help!" It was one of the slaves tied to my litter.

A slave in the back had managed to free himself and was untying the man next to him. The others were frantically pulling at their bonds, but none looked as terrified as the man before me.

Pushing myself to my feet, I debated which way to run.

The slave clawed at my skirts. "Please," he begged.

My father's voice rang out behind me. "Don't touch her!"

The slave fell, blood spraying over the gold and jewels. In seconds Father had dealt with the others too. They sprawled against the litter, most still tied to it.

I stared in horror at the bodies. The first slave's hand still reached out toward me.

A cry rose over the babble in the garden. Father and I both whipped our heads toward the sound. It took me a moment to locate Alshara, cowering behind the priests' canopy. I followed her horrified gaze and saw a Qilarite servant dragging Aliana away through the crowd, a knife at her throat. The man's eyes were on my father. He obviously wanted him to see this.

One of Father's enemies, taking advantage of the chaos, I thought numbly.

Father roared and leaped forward, mowing down a slave woman in his way. I ran to Alshara, and, huddled together, we watched Father battle two men, one with fair hair, the other dark. Father held them off easily, his attention not entirely on them, but on the one dragging his youngest daughter away. I could see that his opponents were but gnats to him, obstacles keeping him from getting at the man holding Aliana. Even I could tell that they hardly knew how to fight; all they were doing was delaying him.

And then.

And then another man, burly, bald, and fair, sprang into the open space behind Father and plunged a sword into his back.

Father swung around. Bile rose in my throat at the sight of steel protruding from his chest, but Father didn't even seem to notice; he hacked at the bald Arnath, driving him to his knees, removing his arm, slicing the scalp from his shiny head. The two other men stabbed at Father from the back, but he paid them no mind. He was elegant and unstoppable, a god of death. A Gamo in every way.

Until one of the men behind him grabbed the handle of the blade protruding from Father's back and jerked it out. Father convulsed and blood gushed out of his mouth, over his fine vest of blue satin, staining his white tunic.

"No!" I screamed as he fell facedown to the dirt and went still. This was not the way for a Gamo to die!

The two men had spat upon my father's body, I remembered now, my fingers clenching my sheets. They'd hated him, just as Madden hated me. Just as any number of Arnathim in the city hated me, for what I was or what they thought I was.

I hauled myself out of bed so quickly that it made my ankle twinge. I needed another self-defense lesson as soon as possible.

Gelti reported on his investigation as we made our way into the garden maze in the golden light of sunrise. The talk in the alehouses had gotten more violent, and there was much complaining about how food rations were sure to be cut to feed the Melarim.

I rubbed my eyes. "Will your volunteers still man the food distribution points?" I asked. "That will help keep order."

"Yes," he said. "But I doubt it will stop the talk. And I've been hearing more about these 'Swords of Qilara' the assassin mentioned. No one would say much before, but now some of the men in Portside are using that name, talking about defending the sailors. So far it's all talk, so if that boy was with them, maybe he was a radical. But it doesn't sit right, you keeping Coe and his men locked up."

"It's for their own protection. But surely no one will dare start anything, not with the financial incentives in place."

"Hope you're right. But holding Coe in the dungeon seems a bit harsh."

One of Coe's spies had killed a guard, which was plenty of justification for holding him. But to Qilarites in the city, it looked like we were keeping the sailors captive simply for following orders. "Would it be viewed differently if we held him elsewhere in the palace?"

"Definitely."

I bit my lip. Gelti had worried about me being around the Melarim, and then one of them had tried to kill me. He'd been right about that, so I had to consider that he was also right about moving Coe.

"What is it?" he asked.

I hesitated, knowing how he would take the news of what Madden had done, but in the end I told him what had happened, keeping to the barest details.

He listened, stone-faced, a muscle twitching in his jaw. "Poison is a coward's weapon," he said.

"And yet it kills just as effectively as a blade," I responded, striving for a light tone.

He shook his head. "You don't have to pretend. You must have been terrified." He reached one hand out as we arrived at the center of the maze, but stopped short of touching mine.

I looked at his hand, then up at his face. "I just want to be able to defend myself."

"Qilarites won't stand for this happening to you. Once word gets out—"

"It won't," I said firmly. "It can't. I'm only telling you because you can't investigate attacks on the council without having all the facts. We just need to hold things together until the Melarim leave."

He stared at me. "Why are you defending them?"

"I'm not," I said icily. "But more violence won't help anything. And I don't need anyone starting riots on my behalf. The best way to get through this is to learn to take care of myself."

He reluctantly agreed, and soon we were deep into the lesson. He had me practice using found weapons again, and this time I'd thought to wear a hair comb that, to my surprise, drew a few drops of blood when I jammed it into his arm. Then he showed me how to strike toward an opponent's eyes while angling my feet so that I could dart away immediately afterward. He had me practice this for what seemed like an hour, until my thighs were burning and my arms felt like wood and my ankle, which had been fine in the beginning, started to twinge. He said my muscles needed to know what to do without my brain having to tell them, or these skills would be useless in a panic situation.

"One more time," he said, and I shifted my weight onto my right foot as I struck, using my momentum to carry me past him. His hand shot out, though, and he grabbed my waist, whirling me back around.

Without thinking, I struck toward his eyes and stepped out of his reach again.

"Good!" he shouted, even as he rubbed the bridge of his nose, where I had jabbed him rather hard. "Good. That's exactly what you have to do. Adapt."

Adrenaline pumped through my body, nearly nauseating me, but I couldn't help beaming at his praise. Gelti grinned at me, then picked up something from the ground—my hair comb—and tucked it back into my hair. His eyes lingered over my face, and my skin buzzed with his attention, but I wasn't about to let him humiliate me again.

I neatly stepped away and said, "Tomorrow, same time?"

But it turned out I had reason to see Gelti much sooner than that. Later that afternoon, a man was murdered outside the doors of the slave pen building.

Jonis got there before I did, and I arrived to find him kneeling beside a body that had been propped up against the wall. A short sword had been thrust through the man's chest, pinning a large piece of yellowed paper to him—a map of Qilara.

"We should have realized he'd be a target," said Jonis hollowly. Adin, standing behind him, reached out and squeezed Jonis's shoulder.

I didn't understand what he meant at first, until I tore my eyes away from the sword in the man's chest and looked at his bloody, battered face. It was Hodder, the Arnath guard who had killed Coe's spy in front of the crowd at the docks. It hadn't occurred to me that anyone would hold him personally accountable for that sailor's death. Like the sailors, he'd only been following orders.

I looked around at the guards—a handful of Arnath guards was grouped around Jonis, and four Qilarite guards stood at the edge of the building, blocking the way toward the market. Those four kept looking back over their shoulders uncomfortably. Garvin and Vance, my guards, hovered behind me.

I was about to ask where Kirol was when he came around the corner from the market with Gelti. From the panicked look on Kirol's face, he must have gone to fetch his cousin immediately. Gelti's eyes swept over the scene, and he leaned close to Kirol and said something in a low voice.

Kirol flushed and ordered several of the Arnath guards down to other corner of the building, so that both entrances would be secure.

In the bustle of their movements, Gelti stepped close to me. "You shouldn't be here," he said softly.

"Nonsense," I said. "I'm a councilor. This is my responsibility."

He frowned but didn't object further, only said to Jonis, "May I?"

Jonis and Adin exchanged a look, but Jonis stood and retreated a few paces to let Gelti examine the body.

"His name is Hodder," I said. "He is—was—a guard. He was the one who killed Coe's spy at the docks."

Gelti nodded as he held up the dead man's hand, which was bruised and swollen. "That makes sense. They broke his fingers."

Behind him, Jonis looked like he might vomit. Breaking or cutting off the fingers, or cutting off the hands entirely—those had once been common punishments for slaves who dared to even look at the language of the gods.

Gelti prodded Hodder's legs, then lifted his eyelids and felt along the man's scalp, under his matted auburn curls. "He's got lumps on his head. They must have beaten him badly, so he was probably already dead when they stabbed him."

"They," I repeated. "The Swords of Qilara. The sword and the map are not exactly subtle. This is a message."

"A threat, more like." Gelti unfurled the edges of the map, revealing two symbols in brown ink—or was it blood?—scrawled in the northwest corner, over the City of Kings. His whole body went rigid, the automatic response of a man who had lived his whole life in a place where writing meant death.

Reading the message, I had gone rigid too, but for a different reason.

"What does this say?" Gelti asked, an edge in his voice.

Jonis's fingers were laced in front of him again, so tightly that his knuckles were white. "It says, 'Tialiks go home.'"

Tialik. It was an ugly word, an ugly symbol even written in the language of the gods. An ugly idea—a thing to be burned like unwanted scrolls. I'd heard the slur used against Arnathim all my life. And now the Swords of Qilara were using it to threaten the Melarim, to threaten all of us if the Melarim didn't leave. Anger rolled through me in waves, and I didn't understand the reasons for all of it. That word didn't refer to me—was I even allowed to feel the sick horror clenching my hands into fists?

"They used what they learned at our Library for this," I finally managed to get out. "We changed the laws of this country so they could learn to write, and this is what we get for it."

Gelti glanced uncertainly at me.

"Ungrateful swine," I spat. "Learning to write was supposed to make them less ignorant. It was supposed to stop things like this from happening." Somewhere behind my fury, I knew that I was reacting to the wrong thing. But I was raised a Scholar, and writing . . . writing was not supposed to be used this way.

Jonis stared at me, apparently just as surprised by this outburst as I was.

Gelti stood and wiped his hands on his tunic. "We still don't have any solid evidence that the Swords of Qilara were behind the assassination attempt, but they're obviously happy to take advantage of the dissatisfaction in the city. They want attention, and they'll do whatever they have to in order to get it."

Jonis scrubbed his face with his hand. "We should move the Melarim."

"We can't," I said sharply. "There's nowhere else for them to go, and the ship will be ready in seven days. We'll have to double their guards though." I stepped closer to Gelti. "We need to know who's leading the Swords of Qilara, and we need them arrested."

Gelti nodded. "I'll question all the guards here first, and go from there." He turned to Jonis. "Did you see anything unusual here . . . Councilor?"

From the way Jonis's eyes narrowed, he'd noticed Gelti's pause before saying his title. But Gelti listened patiently to Jonis's answers, then asked a few more questions that drew far more information out of Jonis than I had expected. Then he questioned the two Arnath guards who had found the body.

It quickly became clear why Gelti had become such a leader among the people in the Web. He listened more than he spoke, and managed to project an air that was at once friendly and professional. One of the guards even volunteered the names of three other men Gelti might want to talk to about unusual activities in the market area.

Kirol and two other men finally came to take the body away, and Gelti reminded his cousin not to dispose of the sword and map, as he would need to examine them more thoroughly. A mutinous expression passed over Kirol's face at this reminder, and I had to turn away to hide the rolling of my eyes. Sometimes it felt like Kirol's incompetence was so exaggerated that it had to be deliberate.

"You should go back to the palace," Gelti said to me. "Once word about this gets out, the situation on the streets will be tense."

And word would get out. Kirol had practically guaranteed that by letting the body sit outside long enough that it could be seen by all the guards and anyone who happened to wander down this way from the marketplace. If he wasn't working for these Swords of Qilara, he certainly wasn't working against them. The question was whether it was purposeful or not.

I frowned, resolving to bring this up when Gelti reported to me tomorrow morning. "Find out whatever you can," I told him. "We need to make some arrests as soon as possible."

Gelti nodded, then glanced around and lowered his voice. "I'll come early tomorrow. You need those lessons more than ever."

"Certainly," I said at regular volume, as Jonis looked over at us. "I look forward to your report."

TWELVE

BY THE NEXT morning, Gelti had very little to add; the people who had been complaining were only complaining more loudly, but it was difficult to determine who had gone from talk to action. And half of the ridiculous stories going around the alehouses were alcohol-soaked conspiracy theories about how the Melarim had killed Hodder and left the sword and map to divert suspicion.

The stupidity of the public could be truly astounding sometimes.

Delicately I brought up my concerns about Kirol, but Gelti assured me that his cousin would never work against the Ruling Council. When I pressed him to explain why, he laughed.

"Do you know how many times Kirol showed up at my door to try to convince me to meet with you? Seventeen." He shook his head. "Kirol doesn't have a deceptive bone in his body. That'll probably get him killed one day."

"And do you regret that he convinced you to come for that meeting?" I asked. I hadn't forgotten that he was only working for us because I had threatened to blackmail him.

Gelti looked at me for such a long time that I grew restless, worrying that my question had been too revealing. "No," he said at last. "I don't regret it."

The situation in the city was still tense the next day. Gelti spent ten minutes of our early-morning fighting lesson trying to convince me to cancel the public audience scheduled to begin at midmorning bells. But these audiences were always held on the fourth day of each Shining and each Veiling, and canceling one would be an admission that our Ruling Council couldn't handle its responsibilities.

A few hours into it, though, I was wishing I had taken his advice. Not because it felt especially dangerous—two guards stood at the door, and petitioners had passed through two guard stations and been relieved of any weapons. But the room was stuffy, and the fact that I wore a long-sleeved dress didn't help. I'd chosen the long sleeves to hide the bruises on my arms, as my last two days of fighting lessons had focused on using my elbows to strike an opponent.

I'd been prepared for the dangerous parts of holding power, but no one had mentioned the tedium. I'd already seen more than thirty petitioners, and the scribe beside me had filled two scrolls with notes. Interspersed with fearful or angry questions about the Melarim, Coe and his men, and Hodder's murder—all of which I answered with a smile and a noncommittal statement that the council was handling it—the requests were the same kind we had been fielding all along: more food, a place to live, help locating missing relatives.

But then a hefty Qilarite man walked in, his manner confident. His black hair was curiously cut—thick in the middle, sparse on the sides—and his smile was polite even though the broken teeth it showed made me recoil. He looked familiar, but I couldn't place him.

"I am here," he announced, "representing the Captains Alliance. We formally protest the increased docking fees."

"The only alternative would be to close the port entirely," I said firmly. "It is only fair that those who use the docks pay for their upkeep."

"But the increase unfairly targets Qilarite businessmen, my lady. It is nothing short of prejudice," he returned.

I'd heard similar claims from others this morning, mostly merchants. Many of the Scholars and peasants had fled the capital after the monarchy fell, but the merchant class were so tied to their shops and their homes that they couldn't imagine leaving, even if they had to struggle to get by, and suffer the indignity of paying their former slaves. Many of them ascribed any ruling they didn't like to prejudice.

I knew how to respond. I'd been repeating it all morning. "The Ruling Council has many competing demands to weigh. This is a difficult time, so everyone will suffer somewhat. We strive to make decisions that will limit that suffering for everyone."

The man grimaced and placed a bundle on the table. I tensed and looked at the nearest guard, who nodded to indicate that it had already been searched.

"A gift," the captain said. "A reminder of the trade that the Captains Alliance brings to this city." He pulled back the red cloth—the finest Emtirian silk, I noted—and revealed three golden saltcellars, each a miniature of the stubby, round Temple of Poro in Emtiria's capital city.

"These are lovely, but—" *But they hardly support your case about the captains not being able to afford their docking fees.* That was what I would have said, if he hadn't cut me off in an entirely infuriating manner.

"Please, examine them. They are of the finest make, and stamped with the maker's seal."

The seal on the bottom showed me what I should have understood as soon as I'd seen the Emtirian silk. The design was small, the curling horns of the ram just visible. It was the seal of Lord Romit, erstwhile ambassador to Qilara from Emtiria.

Which meant that the man sitting across from me wasn't just any captain, but the one I'd sent to Lord Romit with my invitation to buy the salt mine: Horel Stit. No wonder he looked familiar. I'd seen him when he had been escorted out of the palace after being questioned about the attempt on Raisa's life.

I'd made it clear, when I had sent Valdis to him with the message, that communication about the sale was to be handled *discreetly.* Obviously Romit was reminding me how easily he could make this sale public knowledge and play on the history of the Gamo family as traitors to Qilara. He was counting on that to make me cautious enough to accept his insulting offer.

My message had said that I would sell the salt mine for five hundred thousand Emtirian dinas. Three saltcellars sat on the cloth before me, representing his counteroffer: three hundred thousand.

And Stit's earlier words hadn't been a protest at all, but part of the message.

"What exactly does the . . . Captains Alliance wish to see, in regard to the docking fees?" I asked carefully. The scribe's quill paused beside me, but I ignored him.

Stit's face broke into that mangled smile again. He knew now that I understood who he was and what was going on here. "Free access to all ports would be ideal."

I laughed along with him, hoping mine didn't sound forced. So that was the condition Lord Romit wanted: tax-free access to Qilara's ports in exchange for his silence. Surely he expected a counteroffer; the trio of saltcellars begged for a fourth to complete the set, and I could casually ask for it as a code for more money. But the stipulation about the ports would be harder to get around. Romit would know that I could make it happen; one of the advantages to being the only financially competent person in this government was that everyone had to trust my figures.

But if I let Romit have free rein at the ports, I'd be giving him exactly what the Ruling Council had been trying to keep away from Emperor Adelrik. The others would see that as me breaking my vow not to treat with Emtiria. Selling the salt mine was one thing; I could and would defend my right to dispose of my property as I saw fit. But tampering with official records to record false payments was quite another.

Still . . . with all the needs in the city, with the loss of financial support from the southern vizier now that we were using his ship to transport the Melarim home, could I afford to let the chance slip away? Could I afford to let my family's legacy decline? My father's ring suddenly seemed heavier on my thumb.

I rewrapped the saltcellars and pushed the bundle across the table. "We cannot accept this gift. It's lovely, but not a complete set. There are four councilors, after all." I paused, making sure he got the message. His mouth tightened, so I thought he had. "As for your concerns about the docking fees, they have been noted, but I'm afraid that reducing them is impossible at this time. Thank you for coming, Captain . . ." For the scribe's benefit, I trailed off as if I didn't know his name.

"Stit," he said with a grim smile. He seemed amused at watching me play this game.

The scribe went still and looked up at Stit, then dipped his quill and started writing furiously. I pretended not to notice, but cursed inwardly. There was no chance that word of Stit's appearance wouldn't get back to Jonis; Stit's visit would be recorded right there in the audience notes, along with his request for waived port taxes, which Jonis would surely find odd. He might even drag Stit in for questioning again, and if he went poking into Stit's business he might learn about the negotiations with Romit.

"The trade brought in by the Captains Alliance keeps the city going," said Stit. "You wouldn't want to lose its support, I'm sure."

I wrapped my fingers around a quill to keep them from twitching. "It certainly does," I said smoothly. "And the goodwill of the council allows the Captains Alliance to keep doing business."

All at once, a warning hand seemed to press down on my shoulder. I looked up, wondering how the guard had gotten close to me so quickly, but he still stood at the door. On my other side, the scribe's quill hadn't stopped moving. No one stood behind me. I touched my shoulder, frowning.

I haven't done anything wrong, I reminded myself. I hadn't accepted Romit's terms regarding port access, and I wouldn't. If he agreed to my counteroffer, then this would be a clean business deal, albeit one I would rather not advertise lest people misunderstand my loyalties.

But I couldn't take the chance of Jonis looking too closely at Stit's visit. And the only way to do that was to be proactive, to show Jonis that I was just as concerned about Stit as he was.

Even as Stit was being escorted out, I was making plans to send Gelti to question him.

I explained what I needed to Gelti in my study a few hours later, letting my lip quiver a bit as I described Stit's appearance at the audience and how it had supposedly unnerved me.

Gelti's eyes softened. "Don't worry. We'll bring him in and—"

"No," I said quickly. "Go to Stit's house and question him there. We can't bring him in because Jonis can't be trusted to be unbiased about this. And you'd better take Valdis with you."

"Do you think I can't handle Stit alone?" he asked. I couldn't tell if he was amused or offended, or both.

"We can't afford for anything to happen to you right now," I said, but I made sure my tone implied that *I* couldn't afford for anything to happen to him. I was only letting him hear my concern because I wanted him to agree to taking Valdis, but that didn't mean what I was saying was untrue. "It would make me feel better if you didn't go alone."

Gelti smiled. "All right, then."

"And remember," I couldn't help adding, "Stit is likely to claim all kinds of ridiculous things about . . . about the council. Who knows what lies he'll try to tell you?"

"Don't worry," he said with a nod. "I'll figure out how things are."

Gelti and Valdis went to find Stit right away. That night, in the deserted dining room before the council meeting, Valdis reported to me on what had happened. Gelti had questioned Stit about his whereabouts during the attack on Hodder, and Stit had an alibi, as he had been at sea and just returned last night. Valdis, as I had instructed him to, had stepped in before Gelti could ask too many questions about Stit's business dealings, and had asked Stit what he knew about the Swords of Qilara.

"He insisted he didn't know anything about them," Valdis said as the door opened behind him and Jonis entered the room. I expected Valdis to stop talking, but he took one look at Jonis and went on. "He said he thought they were right about one thing, though. Apparently most of the men using that name are talking about how you should be queen."

Jonis stopped three steps into the room and looked from Valdis to me. "What's going on?"

My cheeks went warm. I had the feeling that Valdis had wanted Jonis to hear that last bit. Maybe Valdis thought that would please me, that people wanted me to be queen, or that it was putting Jonis in his place. It was hardly helpful, though, when the point of sending him to question Stit had been to forestall Jonis's suspicions, not stoke them.

"Horel Stit showed up at the public audience this morning," I told Jonis. "He made demands on behalf of the Captains Alliance about port fees. I knew you would find it as suspicious as I did, so I sent Gelti and Valdis to question him."

Jonis frowned. "Why didn't you have him brought in?"

"And make it public that we're questioning him? No one would believe it wasn't just you trying to get revenge on Stit." I shook my head. "They didn't find anything, though."

Jonis shot a suspicious look at Valdis. "Except that the Swords of Qilara want to make you a queen, apparently. Bet you'd like that."

Once, I might have. But those men didn't want a queen; they wanted a return to the past, and I was the most conveniently located Qilarite noble. "Don't be ridiculous," I snapped. "That's just foolish talk from a pack of murderers."

"But it won't be seen that way by Arnathim in the city. They already think that we aren't doing enough to protect the Melarim."

I held in a sigh. I'd only wanted to keep Jonis from looking too closely at Stit's business, and it seemed I had succeeded—only now he was suspicious of me. "We've already doubled the guards at the market. What else are we supposed to do?"

He folded his arms. "It doesn't help that you avoid the Melarim, you know."

I'd intended to be appeasing, but this was too much. "Pardon me if I have no desire to spend time around people who tried to kill me!"

"*One* of them tried to kill you, and Loris punished him for it."

"Fine," I said. "I'll . . . go see them." I waved to the pile of scrolls on the table in front of me. "Now, shall we start on the repair orders?"

THIRTEEN

I WAS KNEELING in a dark, airless place, rough stone scraping my legs. When I lifted my hands, chains clanked, trailing from the manacles around my wrists. Laughter echoed beyond the walls.

My mouth was so dry that I couldn't swallow, and my breath came in little frightened pants. They were going to come for me soon. My family name wouldn't save me. It would only make them more determined to hurt me.

The stone door scraped open, and I skittered back against the wall as light flooded the tomb, stabbing into my brain. I tried to shield my eyes as a figure stepped inside.

But then my vision adjusted, and I wasn't in a tomb at all, but at the slave pens, inside a locked cell. Jonis glared down at me from the other side of the bars, backlit by torchlight. Behind him stood rows of silent Melarim, glaring at me.

"What are you hiding?" he snarled.

"What are you talking about?" I tried to say, but only a whimper came out. Manacles still bit into my wrists, and, as I moved my hands, someone behind me cried out. I turned and saw Alshara behind me, huddled on the floor, her cheeks tear-stained, her wrists bound by manacles too, the chains attached to mine. And next to her, a sight that made my throat close up: Aliana, lying lifeless on the stone floor, staring glassily at the ceiling, her throat slashed open.

"Once a Gamo, always a Gamo," said Jonis. "This is where you should have been all along."

I woke with a start, blinking in the gray morning light. *Just a dream*, I told myself, shaking my hands to release the sensation of metal cuffs around the wrists.

I'd been having disturbing dreams ever since Madden had tried to poison me. There was no reason this one should unnerve me any more than the others. I was safe here in the palace, and I was learning to defend myself against attackers.

I knew, though, there would be no going back to sleep. I kicked off my sheets and got dressed. It was early enough that the shared dining hall was empty, so I didn't have to talk to anyone as I fetched an orange and bowl of porridge to take up to my study. But I was muzzy with lack of sleep and had forgotten what day it was, and Deshti had to send Alshara at midmorning bells to remind me that I was scheduled to teach in the Library of the People. My sister fell into the other chair as if she'd come leagues, not just up one flight of steps, and gasped out her message.

"She treats me like a servant. Delivering messages? Honestly!" said Alshara hotly.

"Sometimes spying isn't very glamorous," I reminded her as I locked up my papers. "But I'm counting on you to keep an eye on her."

This led to a fresh torrent of complaints, but I did my best to muster a patient tone as we left the room. "Thank you for coming to get me," I said. From the way Alshara rolled her eyes, I gathered that it had come off as condescending. I frowned; I never could seem to find the line between the two. I tried again. "I lost track of time while I was working."

"Deshti said it didn't matter that you weren't there, since no one ever asks for you. But then someone *did*," Alshara said.

I frowned, fear spiking through my chest. I wasn't a popular teacher; while I agreed with the other councilors in principle that a better-educated populace was key to an improved economy, I had little patience for guiding the uneducated through the symbols of the language of the gods. I paused by the guard at the door, scanning the people in the Library warily.

My eyes were drawn to the figure that looked most out of place: Gelti Dimmin, seated at a table near the doors that opened to the outside, shoulders tense as if surrounded by enemy combatants instead of wall slots full of scrolls.

I blew out a breath as my racing heart returned to normal.

"Is that who I think it is?" hissed Alshara, but I ignored her as I pushed chairs aside and slid between students.

I sat down across from Gelti. "Not exactly the most secure location for a report, is it?" I said in a low voice.

He glanced around uneasily. About thirty heads bent over scrolls, but two empty tables stood between us and the nearest people. The low buzz of chatter made nearby conversations indecipherable. "It'll do," he said.

"Valdis already told me what happened with Stit," I said softly. "No leads there?"

He shook his head. "That man loves to hear himself talk. I checked out his alibi, though, and it's solid. He wasn't in the city when the Arnath guard was killed, and he wasn't here when the first attack happened either." He grimaced. "He's got all sorts of opinions about what's going on, though. But then, his wife was attacked by . . . by Arnathim. After the earthquakes and all. He was away, and they stormed the house and . . . well. She died after." He paused. "That's her, the figurehead of his ship. With the flowers."

I frowned, a knot of discomfort in my stomach. I did not want to feel sympathy for Horel Stit. I just needed him to quietly deliver my messages, far from Jonis's notice.

Gelti lowered his voice even more. "The talk in the pubs now is that the Swords of Qilara say you should be queen."

"Valdis told me." I grimaced. "In front of Jonis."

Gelti let out a low whistle. "I imagine he didn't like that much."

"No. He doesn't trust me any more than I trust him, and that didn't help." I rubbed my eyes. "But I thought the merchants hated me. *'You're telling people they'd better behave or they won't get their grain.'* Isn't that what you said?"

He flinched. "Maybe that was too harsh."

I frowned, considering him. "You could have told me all this in the garden. Why did you really come to the Library?"

Gelti placed his hands flat on the table in front of him and looked down at them for a moment. "You were right," he said at last. "It was cowardly of me not to come before. I couldn't even understand that threat written on the map. I can't help you if I can't read and write. I want you to teach me."

I nodded, as affected as any woman would be by having a handsome man tell her she was right. "How did you know I was supposed to be here?"

"Wouldn't be much of an investigator if I couldn't find that out. I asked her." He jerked his head toward the other end of the Library, where Deshti, formerly of the Arnath Resistance and currently the head librarian, was watching us more closely than I liked. For all that she enjoyed bossing my sister around, she was only a few years older than Alshara. And, as Deshti was utterly devoted to Jonis, I knew he would hear about this scene in great detail.

Let him. He ought to be pleased that I had convinced Gelti to learn to write.

I showed Gelti the first tenset, and he was slow and clumsy at first, but I found it easier to keep my patience with him than I had with others I'd taught. It had nothing to do with the fact that each time he ruined a symbol I had to put my hand over his to help him correct it. No, nothing at all.

"That's it!" I said when he finally managed to approximate the symbol *man* on the eighteenth try. "Now a few more times to make it stick." I smiled; that was something Mati and Raisa always said when they were teaching.

Gelti wrote the symbol again. "This is lower order writing?

That the Scholar class used?"

"Yes. Now that you've got the taste for it, you want to learn the higher order too, do you?" I indicated the scrolls in their slots along the walls. Those had been written by the kings of Qilara; for centuries only the monarchs and their oracle-chosen Tutors had been allowed to know the higher order writing, the sole purpose of which was to communicate with the gods. Back when this room had been known as the Library of the Gods, it would have been death for a nonroyal to even touch one of those scrolls.

"Maybe," he said slowly. "Might be interesting to read some of those."

I considered telling him about the Arnath writing. It was also taught in the Library, and the higher order writing would be too, once Mati and Raisa returned; they were the only ones who knew it. We used Arnath writing among the Ruling Council, though, because the fact that fewer people could read it made our communications more secure, especially when combined with our ciphers. The sound-based Arnath script was far easier to use than the complicated pictographs of the Qilarite writing I had grown up with, but I doubted that Gelti would be interested in anything from the Nath Tarin. So I just said, "The lower order Qilarite symbols will take some time to teach you. There are over four thousand."

"I don't mind how long it takes, if I have a good teacher."

I smiled and wrote another symbol on the paper. I pushed it across to him and rubbed my right wrist, which still ached from where I had twisted it out of his grip during yesterday's early-morning fighting lesson. I'd been too distracted by his nearness to feel it at the time, but after a morning of writing I was wishing for some of the physician's sharma sludge to dull the pain.

He frowned. "Still hurts?"

I nodded, and he put down his quill. "Let me see." His tone was so commanding that it didn't occur to me not to hold out my hand to him, even though we were in the middle of the Library.

He examined my wrist, his touch clinical but still warm enough to set my heart thumping. "It's not bruised," he said. Then he turned my hand over and ran his fingers from the backs of my knuckles to my wrist, separating the bones. His thumb brushed my signet ring. "Better?"

I nodded, though I couldn't feel my hand at all. Too many other sensations crowded my brain.

He squeezed my hand and let go. It went directly to my lap, where my other hand clutched it like a Scholar girl begging for gossip after a ball.

"How," I began, then forced my voice into a less squeaky tone before I went on, "how did you know to do that?"

"My mother was a seamstress. Her hands bothered her a lot."

I studied him. "That's why you joined the guards, to take care of her."

"And Kirol. He came to live with us when he was nine, after his parents died. But you already knew that, I wager." There was no bitterness in his tone, just acknowledgment, and somehow, that warmed me as much as his touch had. "This afternoon, I'll teach you how to break an attacker's grip without hurting yourself."

I nodded. An idea was blossoming in my mind, born of

Gelti's willingness to come and learn in the Library. "I think it's time your work for the council was made public. We need the merchants to—"

A basket thumped onto the edge of the table, making us both sit up sharply; we'd leaned so close together that our foreheads were almost touching.

"Fresh quills?" said Alshara, flashing Gelti a wide, dimpled smile.

I shoved the basket away, but Gelti sorted through the feathers as though choosing a weapon for a duel, and finally selected two gray quills identical to the ones already inked on the table.

"I sharpened them myself," Alshara cooed, as if she hadn't spent the past twelve days complaining that this was "slave work."

Gelti examined the tips and pronounced them well done. Alshara hovered so long that I had to introduce them, and she fell all over herself exclaiming that *of course*, she should have recognized him, and what a fine job he had done as guard captain, how *safe* she had always felt in the palace when he was in command. Gelti was so gracious that I found myself irritated with him too, until he flashed me a long-suffering smile that said he was only putting up with Alshara for my sake.

"Alshara!" called Deshti from the other end of the room. "Please finish tagging that basket. It really ought to be done by now."

Alshara glared at her, but trudged away. I shot Deshti a grateful smile that she ignored.

Gelti's eyes lingered on Deshti's straight, jet-black hair, which would have made her look Qilarite if not for the Arnath paleness of her skin. Deshti made no secret of her dislike for me, and it had taken me a while to figure out that it had nothing to do with my family connections, or my wealth, or being a Qilarite. For her, it had everything to do with where I spent my evenings—in council meetings with Jonis—and where Deshti wished she spent hers.

Gelti's jaw tightened, and I braced myself for a comment about Deshti's insolent behavior. But then he glanced at me, and I saw him decide not to say whatever he'd been thinking. I'd had the same experience so many times since joining the council that I couldn't help a rush of affection for him.

It also made me certain that what I was about to suggest was the right course. "I know you don't think we're doing enough for the merchant class, but we really do want to do what's best for everyone in Qilara. It would help if people in the Web knew you support us."

Gelti tapped the table thoughtfully. "What about the investigation?"

"That can still stay quiet. We'll say you're . . . an adviser. Which is true, in a way."

His mouth pressed into a thin line. "People come to me because they don't think your council is listening. You want to use that to your advantage."

"I want to use that to *listen* to people. Why is that so hard to understand?"

He crossed his arms over his chest.

"Did you know," I said, pitching my voice low enough that he had to lean in to hear me, "that Raisa was the one who suggested hiring you?" Other than a twitch of his jaw, he didn't react. "It's not a trick. We really are trying to change things for the better. But we can't do it alone."

I watched his face, my fingers clenched in my lap. Had I pushed him too far, too fast? But every instinct told me he was on my side; he'd agreed to teach me to fight, and he'd questioned Stit for me, and he'd overcome his doubts about learning to write. And I definitely hadn't imagined the attraction between us.

"All right," he said at last. "I'll help you."

I smiled. "Perhaps we can arrange a reception here at the palace—"

He shook his head. "You're thinking like a Scholar. You have to come to the Web." He paused, then said, "I'll take you around to meet people. Nothing formal. And after, you can come to dinner at my house." Then he added, almost defensively, "It won't be fancy. Not what you're used to."

I swallowed. "That's all right. I'd like to see . . . your home. And meet your mother." The thought put an odd, bubbly feeling in my stomach. "But . . . I'll have to take guards."

"Of course," he said. "But you'll be safe with me."

"According to my investigator, I'm supposed to have two guards within arm's reach at all times when I'm outside the palace."

He smiled. "Then we'll invite Kirol too. And why not your sister as well? Maybe the two of them will hit it off."

"Kirol?" I asked. Gelti's frown told me that I had not hidden my instinctive dismay at the idea of a lowborn guard with my sister. "I mean," I fumbled, "she's only sixteen. She's too young for him."

"He's not that much older than she is."

I wondered if we were really talking about Alshara and Kirol. "Well . . . all right. She's been missing going out. Thank you for the invitation." I realized too late that my voice had come out all Scholar manners, but this seemed to amuse him.

My fingers shook with excitement as I showed him the next symbol. He flubbed it so badly that I had to guide his quill again, which didn't help with the shaking either.

And that was how Kirol found us when he escorted Loris into the Library.

FOURTEEN

THOUGH I HAD rather forgotten that there was anything in the world but the Library table where we sat, Gelti's head rose as soon as Kirol and Loris entered.

I stood so fast that I had to grab the table to steady myself. What on earth was Kirol thinking, bringing Loris here? We had all agreed that the Melarim would stay at the marketplace. The last time I had seen Loris had been four days ago, when he had sentenced Madden to eat the poisoned bun.

Today Loris wore a faded blue tunic belted with a length of linen; though the clothes were hardly formal, he seemed to have made an effort to dress for this visit. He followed Kirol through the Library, but his steps slowed as he took in the rows of scroll slots and the cabinets we had brought in to house new scrolls. The other students and teachers must have left for luncheon while I had been so focused on teaching Gelti. Only Deshti remained, watching from her desk in the corner.

"Welcome," I said when they reached us. "But why are you here? Has something happened?"

Loris finally took his eyes off the scrolls and faced me. "I wanted to speak with you," he said.

He glanced uncertainly at Gelti, who had stood up behind me, and I abruptly remembered my manners and introduced him. "Gelti is . . . here learning to write," I explained. "Just started today, but is making progress."

Loris's eyebrows went up, and Gelti's mouth was an unpleasant line as I turned to him and said, "This is Loris ko Puli, of the Nath Tarin."

"Of Longa," Loris corrected quietly. "We don't say 'Nath Tarin.' I am from the island of Longa."

Gelti took in Loris, from his copper curls to his scuffed boots, and I sensed that he was insulted on my behalf. I didn't have time to examine the little burst of satisfaction in my chest.

"Pleased to meet you," Gelti said, not sounding pleased at all.

We stood in awkward silence until I finally turned to Gelti and said, "I'll see you this afternoon. Kirol, please see Gelti out."

Gelti's eyes darted to the guard at the door, and then did another assessing sweep over Loris before he finally clapped Kirol on the shoulder and said, "I need to talk to you anyway. About a dinner invitation." He shot me a little sideways grin. I couldn't hide my answering smile.

Loris waited until Gelti and Kirol had left before he said softly, "I came to tell you that Madden is dead. It happened early this morning."

I nodded stonily. What was I supposed to do? Thank him? If

Madden had succeeded, it would have been me lingering in pain and paralysis for four days.

Loris gripped the back of a chair. "His was the act of one man, driven by hate. We are a peaceful people. Please do not judge all of us by what he did."

"And how many of your 'peaceful people' are saying that he was right?" I said. "I saw how they looked at me."

Loris flinched. "None say it out loud. Madden's punishment did that much, at least."

I tapped my fingers on the table, considering him. I'd assumed that the sentence he had pronounced had simply been about forcing Madden to accept the consequences of his actions for himself. But now I understood that it had also been carefully calibrated to assert Loris's leadership to the other Melarim. Loris may have seemed impossibly mild, but that didn't mean he didn't know what he was doing.

I frowned. "How did you know that he poisoned the food, not his daughter?"

"Erinel is karas." He lowered his gaze as if he had said something foul. "She does nothing but what her father tells her to. She cannot read or write. We don't know why the gods afflict some people this way, but she is incapable of learning."

I remembered the vicious words of Erinel's father—*"She might as well do one useful thing in her worthless life"*—and how he'd spoken of his wife and children dying, as if Erinel didn't exist. Her father had used her without a second thought.

I squeezed my signet ring. "Is that why everyone was avoiding her?"

"Those who cannot read and write the language of the gods are unable to receive the grace of Sotia," Loris said, a bit defensively. "They can't participate in our rituals. How could a man marry, for example, if he couldn't write the sacred symbols on his bride's arms in the yearlong ink?"

"Up until recently, most of the people here couldn't read or write," I returned, a bit defensive myself. "Many still can't. But at least we don't punish children for having problems learning." This wasn't strictly true; here in Qilara, Scholar families with children who could not read had often claimed that their offspring had been switched for a peasant soon after birth, and sent them to the local village. It hadn't occurred to me that the islander expectations about writing might be as cruel, in their own way, as Qilara's laws had once been.

Loris made a considering noise and looked around. "You lied to me before."

My head snapped up. "I most certainly did not," I responded automatically, though I had no idea what he was talking about.

He smiled. "You said you had no temples left, but what is this place if not a temple to Sotia, celebrating her gift of writing?"

He'd obviously just been trying to change the subject, but he had a point. The Library of the People was open and full of light and scrolls, though, according to Mati and Raisa, the Library was nowhere near as splendid as it had once been; I myself had never seen it before the day of its destruction. Once, the high walls had been lined with friezes telling the stories of the gods, but Raisa had insisted on removing those—too many Arnath children, she said, had died falling from cleaning platforms. We'd sold the friezes to collectors all over the peninsula, and kept only the portion that told the story of Sotia, goddess of wisdom, and her punishment by the other gods for giving the tablet of language to humans—but that had been moved closer to the floor.

I cleared my throat. "Would you like to meet our head librarian?"

He accepted eagerly, so I took him over to Deshti's desk, and she made a great show of looking up from the scroll she was rolling, as if she hadn't been trying to eavesdrop since Loris had arrived.

She told him animatedly of her work on salvaging scrolls from the former Library of the Gods, and he had many questions for her on the staffing of teachers and how she planned to obtain new writings.

"We would love to have some scrolls from the islands in our collection," she said.

"Deshti!" I hissed. Things with the Melarim were touchy enough without us asking favors before we even got them home.

Loris, however, beamed. "Certainly! An exchange. I hope to expand our people's library too. So many of our records have been burned in the raids."

It was hard not to feel defensive at that, but Loris seemed to have meant it simply enough.

Deshti rooted through a basket of scrolls and pulled one out. "You might be interested in this—an account of the last days of the old kingdom, in the Arnath script."

"Raisa's account?" I asked as Loris accepted the scroll eagerly.

Deshti's nose wrinkled as she nodded. She might dislike me,

but she hated Raisa beyond all reason. Jonis's crush on Raisa had ensured that.

I frowned. That scroll was a brutally detailed retelling of all that had led up to the destruction of the palace, including my father's role in the coup. Raisa's depiction of me had done nothing to dispel my reputation as an ambitious, spoiled brat. I didn't care for the idea of Loris reading that.

I cleared my throat. "I'm not sure that there will be time today to read all—"

"It's a gift," said Deshti. "The original is the only scroll we have so far in the Arnath script, so the advanced students use it as a model for practice. We have plenty of copies."

Chagrined, I let the matter drop and offered to show Loris the courtyard before Deshti could stir up any more trouble.

He followed me outside, where I showed him what had once been a cloistered study space for the heirs to the throne and their Tutors, but now had become a place for students to take a break and enjoy the ocean breezes. To me, it still had a mysterious, forbidden quality, but Loris didn't seem impressed.

"You didn't like that she gave me this scroll," he said. "Why?"

My face flushed. "It's . . . I just don't understand why everyone is so obsessed with the past. We're trying to rebuild and it's not . . . helpful."

Loris went still, the scroll resting across his palms like some kind of offering. "Do you really believe that anyone can just let go of the past so quickly?"

"I know that it won't happen if people don't try," I said acidly.

"You mean us."

"I—no, I just meant . . . in general."

He cocked his head. "For hundreds of years, your people have hunted mine. How are we to put aside what has been done to us? You came from the sea, again and again, without warning. Everyone on Longa lost someone to the raiders. Some killed, some taken." He paused. "Do you know what the raiders did to the Learned Ones?"

I didn't want to answer, but I also didn't want to be the coward who refused. "I imagine they . . . cut off their hands and executed them," I said, with only a slight tremor. That was what had been done to the royal Tutor before Raisa, Tyasha ke Demit, after she had been caught teaching the Arnath Resistance to write. Removing the hands was symbolic, but the rest had been slow and gruesome and staged on a public viewing platform, to keep Scholars and future Tutors from getting any ideas about breaking the writing laws. The Scholars Council would have executed Raisa in the same fashion, if Mati hadn't agreed to send the raiders.

"Yes," Loris said, so quietly that the word seemed to meld with the ocean breeze.

I didn't have to ask whether he had witnessed this; the set of his shoulders told me he had. "That was why the others didn't want you to say who you were, on the ship."

"I told them I'm only an apprentice, but . . . they're right. It is unlikely that Calantha lives, and I am her successor." He took a deep breath. "I was never supposed to be her apprentice. The Learned Ones train their own children to replace them. Father to daughter and mother to son, that is how it is supposed to go. But Calantha's husband and children were killed by raiders, and she refused to remarry. That was . . . unthinkable, for a Learned One. But Calantha never worried about what people thought of her."

I could understand why Calantha hadn't wanted to remarry; from what I'd seen, few women benefited from marriage, and I doubted things were different on the islands. "How did you come to be her apprentice, if you weren't her son?" I asked.

He gave a pained laugh. "When I was fourteen, Calantha hired me to cook and clean and chop firewood, and every day she posed questions to me about conflicts between people or groups, and I had to work out a just response. I thought it was a test. I didn't realize until I was eighteen that it was my training."

"She sounds like a great mind," I said politely.

Loris snorted. "She was a terror, and she reveled in it. But she knew her business. People respected her, even if they didn't like her."

I felt an odd rush of affection for this woman I had never met. It was much harder to make people respect you than like you when you were a woman.

"When the raiders came," Loris went on, "Calantha sent everyone to the caves. She is—was—a fair shot with a bow and arrow. She killed at least ten raiders before they took her down." He stared into the Library, but didn't seem to see it at all. "They chopped off her hands before they—"

He broke off, but I didn't need him to tell me the rest. They were men, she was a woman, and they would have wanted to prove their superiority in every way. Bile rose in my throat.

"I tried to stop them," Loris said in a choked voice. "But there were too many."

I reached out in an instinctive, useless gesture of comfort, but Loris was too far away to touch. "Why didn't they kill you too?"

Smiling wanly, he showed me his callused palms. "I didn't fit their picture of a Learned One. I heard them saying I'd fetch a good price. I never thought I would thank Calantha for years of making me chop and carry."

I nodded. With his broad shoulders and quiet demeanor, he was exactly the kind of slave my father would have purchased for his mines. "Did she do that on purpose? To protect you?"

"No telling with her. Maybe."

"May the gods smile on her spirit," I said. When Loris looked at me in surprise, I amended, "Goddess, I mean."

He cocked his head. "You don't believe that Sotia destroyed the other gods?"

"I don't presume to know what the gods—"

"But surely you feel how this place is full of the goddess. How she watches over us."

I hesitated. There was a spirit of something that hummed through the Library, more than just the thrill of people accessing what had once been forbidden.

And hadn't I felt a warning hand on my shoulder just yesterday?

Something rustled behind me, and I turned to see an asoti perched on the wall, regarding me expectantly with one round black eye. My stomach swooped.

"What difference does it make? With all that's happened—what can any of us do to change things, against all that?" I asked, unsure if I was addressing Loris or the bird.

The bird remained silent, but Loris repeated my earlier words back to me. "I know it won't happen if people don't try." He smiled. "This Library is a start. I wish the others could see it."

"They would be welcome here, but it's too dangerous."

Loris shook his head. "They wouldn't come anyway. Most of them are too afraid to even go out into the market."

I thought for a long moment. We needed their cooperation, and I needed to prove to myself that I wasn't frightened of them. "What if . . . we bring the Library to them? The spirit of it, anyway. Suppose I come for a lesson with the children."

Loris nodded, looking impressed that I would think of such a thing. "That would be a powerful symbol."

"Yes." I straightened my shoulders. "And I want to Erinel to be there."

He frowned. "I don't think that is a good idea."

"Let me work with her," I insisted. "She must think I hate her. Let me show her that I don't."

Loris pursed his lips and looked down at the scroll in his hand. "Every symbol written is a prayer, but she cannot do it. It is cruel to remind her of that."

"Well, we all need prayers right now, including her." I waited, and finally Loris gave a shrug of acquiescence. "Raisa says that too," I told him, "that all writing is a prayer. But really. I wrote a letter about the city latrines yesterday—would Sotia find that sacred?"

I half expected Loris to be offended. But he only smiled and said, "Latrines are just as important as temples. Perhaps more so. The fact that some people can't see that doesn't make it less true."

I was fairly certain that there had been a compliment in there somewhere.

When my carriage pulled into the market the next day, I blinked. Everywhere I looked, it seemed, I saw armed Arnathim. We'd assigned more guards to the market area after Hodder's murder, of course, but most of these men weren't wearing uniforms. I hadn't been around this many armed Arnathim since the battle on my wedding day, and the sight brought on a sudden panic that made me curl my fingers into my skirts.

"What's going on?" I demanded of Kirol, who'd ridden down with me.

"They've been showing up over the last few days," he said grimly. "Arnathim from all over the city. They say they're here to protect the Melarim."

"From the Swords of Qilara?" I asked. "But there haven't been any more attacks." I'd gotten a full briefing from Gelti that morning when he had come for a report and a fighting lesson. Though he'd had the guards arrest three men in Portside who had been drunkenly singing a song about the Swords of Qilara, no one spreading the rumors seemed to be able to identify the men using that name. Gelti was obviously frustrated, but at least the increased guard presence had been effective in preventing any more incidents.

"It's not just the Swords of Qilara they say they are protecting the Melarim from," said Kirol carefully. "It's the guards too. They don't trust that the Ruling Council really will send the Melarim home. They're here to make sure you do."

I knew we'd had more Arnathim joining the guards, but this was different. "Where did they get the weapons?" I asked. I would have bet my family's fortune that Jonis had been involved in that, but of course he hadn't said a word about it.

Kirol grimaced. "They showed up armed. The sailors in Portside have done the same thing around the Bleeding Oyster."

Gelti had warned me that Qilarites in the city were angry about the sailors being locked up, so I wasn't surprised that they too had decided to defend their own. But at least we could do something to reassure people about that. "Move Captain Coe to a guarded room," I said. "And make an official announcement that he's been released from the dungeon. That might help ease tensions there. We just need to keep the situation contained for three more days."

The last time I had come to the slave pen building, I'd often held the wall for support. But today I made it out of the carriage and down the hallway almost as quickly as Kirol. It helped that the doctor had reapplied the hard wax around my bandages the night before, so they again held my ankle like a vise. I longed to get rid of them entirely and have a proper soak at the bathhouse, but Nelnar insisted that they stay on for another Shining and Veiling at least. Broken bones, he said, did not heal that quickly.

"Perhaps they do in those of superior will," I'd responded, only half joking, but he'd ignored me and slathered on more wax.

Loris was waiting for me in the crowded front room with more than a dozen children. He insisted that they had been looking forward to meeting me. Their wary expressions said otherwise, but they sat down obediently when Loris asked them to—except one little boy who squeaked and scuttled away, straight into the arms of a squat woman who sat on a bench with a few others, watching me warily.

Loris introduced me and had the children tell me their names, which I had no hope of remembering, even if I could have understood them all.

Erinel sat alone on a bench in the corner, curled in on herself like she was trying to melt into the shadows. I went to sit beside her, acutely aware of the eyes of the adults on me.

"Would you like to come sit with the others?" I asked, trying to keep my voice low, but it echoed in the silence.

Mutely she shook her head. Her hair was still in braids, but wisps had come loose and the ends looked crunchy, like she had been sucking on them.

"All right," I said. "We'll sit here then."

Loris was passing out the wooden tablets he had described, which he called ervadesha, and I motioned for him to give one to me and one to Erinel. He frowned, but he did not refuse. I examined the device, a wooden slab coated with wax, with a flat-edged writing stick tied to one corner. His face softened when I asked him to send one to Deshti so we could have more made for the Library.

Loris began the lesson by holding up his own ervadesha, which already had several lines of script pressed into the wax, and chanting, "Light of wisdom, bold, brave, bright, bless us all and what we write. The lesson begins, with thanks to the Great Goddess."

"Light of wisdom, bold, brave, bright, bless us all and what we write," repeated the children.

Loris nodded and smoothed the wax with the flat side of the writing stick. Then he wrote one symbol, large enough to fill the whole board, and held it up.

"*Sa*," he said. "With me." I expected the children to copy the symbol onto their ervadesha, but they raised their fingers and traced the symbol in the air with him. Then he had them stand and use their whole arms to create the shape, and once he was satisfied that they had done it with enough care, they were allowed to sit and try it in the wax.

Erinel sat next to me with her head bowed, the ervadesha untouched on her lap.

"Can you write the symbol with your finger like that?" I asked her with false cheerfulness. "That isn't how I learned to write. I'm not sure I can do it that way. Can you help me?" I raised my finger and traced the symbol in the air, and a few of the older girls in the circle around Loris let out giggles.

Erinel's hands were clutching the bench below her, but I saw her eyes following my finger.

Encouraged, I took her hand. "Here, you try."

But she pulled her hand back as if I had burned her, and shook her head. I picked up the ervadesha and wrote the symbol *sa* on it, then offered the writing stick to Erinel.

Her eyes flicked to the other children. "Don't worry about them," I said in a low voice.

For once, I must have managed to make my tone sufficiently encouraging, because Erinel actually picked up the writing stick and attempted the symbol. She bit down hard on her lower lip while she wrote, and Loris had taken the others through three more symbols by the time she was done. Hesitantly she turned her tablet to me, and I inspected the symbol—or rather, ragged attempt at one—she had written.

When she saw my face, she quickly smoothed the wax with the flat edge of the stick, her shoulders hunching.

I cleared my throat. "When I was little, it sometimes took me hours to get a symbol right," I said. "Sometimes my tutor would make me skip meals to practice."

Erinel's eyes flashed up to mine, and then away. "Sometimes Papa would beat me when I couldn't write something," she said, her voice barely above a breath. "He said it was better if I didn't try, so he wouldn't have to get angry about it."

I stared at her openmouthed for a long moment. "Well," I said firmly, "that won't happen here. Just try your best. Let's do *sa* again."

Erinel hesitated, but tried the symbol again. It was just as awful the second time.

"See this line here?" I said, pointing to the symbol on my tablet. "Can you make it straight like that?" I had her practice the line by itself a few times.

"Good!" I said, though it wasn't. The corners of her mouth lifted slightly. "Now do the top crossline." Biting her lip, she put the line in the wrong place. "No," I said, reaching for patience, "see how the line goes at the top? You've got it in the middle. Try again."

Her chin trembled, but she tried it—and still put it too low.

"Here," I said, pointing to the sample symbol again. "This line, not the lower one."

Her hand shaking, Erinel smoothed the wax and tried again. The women on the bench across from me started to murmur, but I ignored them.

Erinel looked up timidly. I sighed. The contents of her tablet looked less like the language of the gods than a series of scratches made by some wild animal.

I put my hand over hers. "Here, let me—"

But Erinel leaped up, letting the ervadesha clatter to the floor. "I can't do it," she choked out. The other children scrambled out of her way as she charged out of the room.

I stood to follow, but Loris put a hand on my arm. "Let her go. Forcing her won't help."

"Yes," said a woman on the bench, "it is better not to tempt her with things she can never have." She shot me a pitying smile. "But you did try, and that's something."

Loris studied me with those cream-tea eyes. "Come, help me check the other children's writing," he said.

Reluctantly, I agreed. To my surprise, the children seemed more comfortable with me now. One girl flinched when I corrected her grip on the writing stick, but none of them scooted away. And one little boy of about four demanded that I help him write his name, while a girl I guessed to be his older sister watched beadily. Between his mumbling and his accent, I had to ask him to repeat his name three times. Impatiently he took my face between his hands to make sure I was paying attention, and said, "Awon."

"Aron," said Loris softly.

Aron nodded as if to say, "Yes, that's exactly what I said." I scraped my ervadesha smooth and showed him the symbols that made up his name.

He plopped himself down in my lap and happily copied the symbols over and over. His yellowish hair tickled my chin and his warm weight was oddly comforting.

When Loris announced that the writing lesson was over, Aron hugged me before his sister snatched him away. Some of the children thanked me for coming, without even being prompted by Loris, before they left.

Loris offered his hand. I hesitated a moment, but took it and let him pull me up from the floor. "It was kind of you to try to work with Erinel," he said.

Well. No one, as far as I knew, had ever accused a Gamo of being kind. "I thought you said it was a bad idea."

Loris shrugged. "It was. Completely pointless. But still kind."

I pursed my lips. I couldn't help feeling sympathy for Erinel; I had been used by my father too. I'd been thinking about that conversation with Loris in the Library yesterday, and how the illiteracy that made Erinel's own people shun her was still fairly normal in Qilara. But I had to tread carefully. "Maybe if she had a more patient teacher. There's a woman who teaches in the Library, Marisa—she's taught some of the former guards and they say she can teach anyone."

Loris shook his head. "Erinel has had many teachers. Some children just cannot do it."

“Do what?” said Jonis, walking in, followed by Adin and Kirol.

“Write,” I said shortly. I wasn’t about to explain myself to him any more than that. “When were you planning to tell me about those men outside?”

“We can use the help. I’m sure they want their extra grain as much as the sailors over at the Bleeding Oyster. None of them want a fight.” Jonis folded his arms. “When were *you* planning to tell me about your dinner invitation?”

“How did you—” Kirol’s guilty face behind him gave me the answer. I drew myself up. “We need to make connections with the merchant class. I told Gelti that, and he offered,” I said, my voice unnaturally high-pitched. We’d talked more about the details during this morning’s fighting lesson, and I’d gotten the sense that Gelti was excited to show me where he’d grown up. And if that pleased me, well . . . that was none of Jonis’s business.

“As Dimmin’s so concerned about the success of the council,” said Jonis with a nasty smile, “I’m sure he won’t mind if I come too.”

FIFTEEN

THE NEXT EVENING, I rode into the Web with Raisa's maschari plant balanced in my lap. I hoped Raisa wouldn't be offended that I was giving the plant to Gelti's mother; I hadn't been able to find anything else, and showing up without some token for the hostess was an unforgiveable slight. Skinny shoots had pushed out of the dirt a few days after Raisa left; now she had been gone for twenty days and the plant stood six inches tall with shiny green leaves, but had not yet flowered. I'd gotten a letter from her that morning, confirming that Vizier Tren wouldn't loan the council a thing until his ship had been returned to him in excellent condition. Her tone had been distant and formal; I imagined that the news of the Melarim's arrival had hit her hard, and possibly even driven a wedge between her and Mati. Once, that would have pleased me, but now, the idea was unsettling. The council needed them to return safely.

And I missed them both, even Raisa's irritating openness and

Mati's insufferable righteousness. I could admit that, if only to myself.

Or maybe I was just missing them because I was facing an evening with Jonis. At least I didn't have to listen to my sister's nattering in the carriage, as she had proclaimed the goodwill-visit portion of the evening "boring" and would be coming down with Valdis for dinner later.

Jonis, however, had spent most of the ride complaining about me moving Captain Coe out of the dungeon.

"Keeping him in the dungeon was unnecessarily provocative," I said coolly.

"And keeping the Melarim in the slave pens isn't?"

"You know there was no other choice when they refused to split up." I took a deep breath. "They leave the day after tomorrow. We just need to keep things under control until then." Those words were starting to feel like some kind of incantation; I'd said them so often.

Part of the reason Jonis and I were sniping at each other was nerves over the evening ahead. Jonis seemed less sure of himself now that we were on our way. Adin, next to him in an ill-fitting guard tunic, obviously thought the whole business was stupid. Kirol kept drumming his fingers on the window frame.

I ran my hand nervously over my hair; I'd spent half an hour combing orange blossom oil through it, so it hung straight and soft down my back. I'd chosen the yellow dress today, the one that always felt like freedom to me because I'd worn it the day that my betrothal to Mati had been dissolved and Raisa had asked me to join the Ruling Council. But now it seemed too bright and gaudy.

A familiar figure on the street outside caught my attention. "Is that Deshti?" I asked.

Jonis, who had been muttering with Adin, whipped his head around and leaned out the window. "Deshti!" He banged on the side of the carriage and called to the driver to stop, and Deshti came over, her expression guarded.

"You should have told me you were headed down here. We'd have given you a ride," said Jonis.

Deshti licked her lips. "I don't mind the walk. I'm just visiting . . . a friend."

Jonis frowned. "You shouldn't go out alone."

"I'll be *fine*," she responded, with much more vehemence than his words had warranted, and then she smiled sweetly. "Enjoy your dinner." As she walked away, I wondered how she knew about that, but then, Alshara probably hadn't shut up about it since I'd told her of the invitation. Deshti was probably burning with jealousy that Alshara and I were attending a dinner with Jonis, and she wasn't.

But Jonis's distraction as the carriage continued down the street was something new. However oblivious he was to Deshti's feelings for him, he clearly didn't like the idea of her visiting someone else.

"What?" demanded Jonis, catching my grin.

"I wonder who Deshti's visiting. A friend in the Web, someone she goes off to see alone? Hmmm."

"It's Tana," said Jonis flatly. "Her, uh—"

"The woman who used to own her," supplied Adin in a gruff voice.

Jonis nodded. "She goes to help with her candlemaking shop."

"Oh," I said. "But that woman, Tana, was kind to her, wasn't she? I mean, it wasn't like . . ." I trailed off, gesturing at Jonis. He hadn't said anything else about Horel Stit's appearance at that public audience, so I wasn't about to bring it up.

"Do you really think that *kindness* makes a difference?" Jonis snapped.

"It should," I said, staring him down.

Jonis shook his head. The run-in with Deshti had gotten under his skin in a way I had seen little else do. "How could it, when that woman had all the power? Her kindness wasn't real."

I frowned. "But it's Deshti's choice now. Just because you don't like what she's choosing, that doesn't mean you get to tell her what to do."

Jonis looked away and pulled at his tunic—an old blue one of Mati's that hung loose and high on Jonis's thinner frame.

I had meant to pay attention as we drove along the winding streets that gave the Web its name, but before I knew it, the carriage stopped in front of a squat two-story mud-brick house identical to the others stretching off in both directions. It hadn't taken us more than a quarter of an hour to get here, though it felt like another world. A low wall surrounded the house, with a wooden gate that kept the goats, geese, and chickens wandering the front courtyard from escaping.

It reminded me of the outbuildings of my father's estate in Pira, only this whole house would have fit into our stable with plenty of room to spare.

Kirol helped me down from the carriage as Gelti emerged

from the house, wearing a white tunic that reminded me of his old guard uniform.

I extended my hand, and Gelti took it without hesitation. "Councilor," he said. "Welcome."

Then he faced Jonis and extended his hand sideways, merchant-fashion. "Many Shinings to you," he said. The handshake went on too long—I had the impression that Jonis was refusing to let go. When they broke apart, Jonis smirked like he had won a contest.

Gelti squared his shoulders. "I've arranged visits for you, all on the surrounding streets. Will you be able to walk?" he asked me.

"Adin could carry you," Jonis put in innocently.

"I'll be fine," I said, ignoring Jonis. "Lead the way."

Gelti walked beside me, describing the Qilarite residents of each house we passed: a weaver's assistant who'd recently taken in his sister's family from the Valley of Qora, an elderly couple whose four sons had been killed in the battle at the palace. A trio of unmarried sisters who'd done laundry for most of the street for years, but were struggling now that no one could afford to hire out the washing. Every house had a story, and he knew them all. He mentioned them casually, but I heard what he didn't say: that our council wasn't serving these people.

I was feeling defensive when we arrived at our first destination, a tiny bakery with two narrow floors wedged on top for the family's residence. Gelti introduced the baker as Shovan Ots, maker of the best buns in the Web for forty years. His grown son, Parker, took up most of the space behind the counter, looking slightly ridiculous with his muscled bulk constricted by an apron. I wasn't at all surprised when Gelti told us that Parker and his brother had once served in the palace guard.

The baker looked askance when Valdis stepped forward to taste the buns, so I made a point of praising them. His chest puffed up with pride, but he waved it off. "They'd be better if I could get finer flour, but everything is hard to find these days."

"We're working on that," I assured him.

His eyes cut to Jonis. "And when will I see my other son again, can you tell me that?"

"Shovan's younger son is one of the sailors at the Bleeding Oyster," Gelti explained.

"One of the raiders?" I asked. I saw Jonis stiffen in my peripheral vision and prayed he would keep his mouth shut.

Shovan nodded. "He shouldn't have been in jail in the first place. They said he stole from the other guards, but my boy never stole anything in his life. The king let him out of jail, said he'd come home a free man if he did his duty to Qilara. So why's he locked up again?"

"Your son will be free, and soon," I told him. "The sailors are being well taken care of. It's for their own safety as much as the peace of the city."

Shovan sniffed. "And why do the tialiks get to walk the streets?"

"Shovan," said Gelti in a warning tone.

I forced my lips into a pleasant smile and mouthed the same old things I said at public audiences, about how the Ruling Council had to weigh many choices. By the time we left, the old man seemed satisfied that he had gotten to air his grievances. On the way out, Gelti said something quietly to Parker, who nodded.

"What did you say to Shovan's son?" I asked as we continued down the street.

He looked sideways at me. "Parker's been going to the Library for writing lessons. Wants to join the guards again, but his father doesn't know. I told him I'd talk to his father for him if he wants me to." At my amused expression, he added, "Parker Ots is a good guard. You could use more like him. And he's losing his mind being stuck in that bakery listening to his father complain."

The next stop was the home of a former overseer who'd been beaten so badly by a group of newly freed Arnathim that he couldn't walk, could hardly speak, and his face was lumpy and misshapen. Though Gelti warned him to stay outside for that visit, Jonis insisted on coming in anyway. He stood stonily in the corner while the man's sister glowered at him.

I forced myself to sit by the man's bed, and did my best not to flinch whenever he tried to speak and sprayed me with spittle, and promised to send Nelnar down to see if there was anything he could do for him.

"Raisa tried to visit him after it happened," said Jonis in my ear as we left. "To pray with him. Tried to take the doctor down too. The sister refused to let her in."

I glanced at him. "People need time," I began, but he just scoffed and turned away.

After that there was a dyer who wanted to know how he was supposed to make a profit when he was stuck with vats of kirit dye that no one wanted, now that Arnathim were not required to wear green. Then a widow with five children who gushed about how much help Gelti had been—he was even giving the family his house once he and his mother moved to the new one in the Watch—and clutched his arm with a familiarity that made me uncomfortable. It obviously made Gelti uncomfortable too, because he pulled away from her quickly and said his mother was waiting on us for dinner.

At each stop, Kirol and his guards had examined the inside and outside before Jonis and I entered, and Gelti's house was no exception. Gelti seemed pleased—proud, even—that his cousin was taking such precautions.

Alshara's carriage pulled up while we were waiting for the guards to finish. She took Valdis's hand and stepped down, her blue silk dress comically fine in the dusty animal yard. Her face fell when she saw the house, and I limped over to her quickly.

"We are guests here," I hissed at her. "You will not embarrass me." She opened her mouth, no doubt to say something snotty, but then she saw Gelti and batted her eyelashes.

Gelti shoved aside the goat sniffing at my slipper and smiled at Alshara. "Welcome, to this beautiful young lady."

Alshara lit up as he bowed over her hand. Valdis stepped closer to her, reminding me of my father.

"I never knew merchant homes could be so clean," she cooed. I winced at her rudeness, glancing at the mud already staining her hemline. If she thought this was clean, what had she pictured?

Then again, like me, she'd probably never really thought about where the lower classes lived at all. She'd never had reason to.

Kirol seemed flustered when he came out to tell us that the

house was cleared for our entry. We followed him inside, and I noticed that he and his aunt didn't look at each other.

Nasha Dimmin was a squat woman, a fact emphasized by the gray scarf draped across her vast bosom. Though she was a head shorter than Gelti, she seemed to take up more space than he did. She greeted us soberly, turning her piercing eyes and beaky nose on each member of our party as Gelti introduced us, but she did not extend her hand to anyone.

"Gelti, see to the pig," Nasha said, nodding toward the back door.

"Yes, Mother." Gelti hurried out to what was apparently an outdoor kitchen.

Even after our earlier visits around the Web, it hadn't occurred to me that they wouldn't have servants. I flushed, mortified for Gelti's mother that she'd had to cook this meal herself, but she seemed to think nothing of it.

I hurried to present Nasha with the plant, warning her to keep it away from the animals once it bloomed, as the flowers, though beautiful, were poisonous. Nasha beamed and placed the pot right in the front window.

Gelti returned with a platter of pork. Nasha took the seat at the head of the table, and Gelti led me to the chair on her right. Kirol seated Alshara across from me and sat beside her.

In Scholar circles, the seat to the left of the host would have gone to the next-highest-ranked guest, after the seat to the right. Jonis should have been sitting there. But I didn't know if merchants followed the same customs, and Jonis didn't seem offended as he pulled out the chair next to mine and sat down.

Gelti sat at the foot of the table, facing his mother. The guards had taken up various positions around the room. Adin, of course, stayed close to Jonis.

Valdis came forward and started tasting the food. "No offense is meant to your hospitality," I assured Nasha. "But in the current climate we cannot be too careful."

When Valdis had pronounced everything safe to eat, Nasha, Gelti, Kirol, and Jonis reached for the platters and started ladling food onto their plates. I stirred, belatedly realizing that no one was going to serve me, and I kicked Alshara under the table. She looked briefly appalled, but then she reached for the platter of pork. The meat slid sideways when she lifted it, and Kirol managed to grab it before it went all over the tablecloth. He helped her get some of everything onto her plate, and I prayed that she would keep her mouth shut about the food.

None of it was bad, but it was quite different from what we had been raised to expect. Besides the pork, there was thick, starchy bread with honey; a dish of spiced cucumbers, garlic, and onions; and a sweet, soupy beer.

"You have a lovely home," I said to Nasha. This wasn't true, but I had fallen back onto Scholar manners, where truth had little to do with anything. The house was much like the others we'd seen tonight. A sparsely furnished room ran the length of the first floor, with a low wall separating a storage area full of barrels from the dining room. The table was the only large furniture, though shelves lined the walls. Most of these were empty, but a large plate decorated with gaudy blue stars stood upright on the top shelf, in apparent pride of place. Next to it, a silver cup gleamed.

"Thank you, my lady," said Nasha. I lifted my coarse linen napkin to my mouth, hoping she would take the hint and wipe away the bit of onion dangling from her chin.

I felt Jonis's eyes on me, and I realized what Nasha had said. "Please, call me Soraya."

"And you can call me Councilor," said Jonis loudly.

Nasha gave him a blank nod, but her response was directed at me. "That is very kind of you." She took a bite of pork; the vigor of her chewing, mercifully, knocked the onion on her chin back onto her plate. "We have been great admirers of your family for some time. My late husband, Kassel, served under your uncle in the border war. He would have followed that man anywhere."

I frowned, ticking through the list of my aunts' husbands and failing to find any man who could inspire such loyalty. "Which uncle was this?"

"Why, Captain Jac Gamo. Your father's brother."

Valdis had raised his head and was watching Nasha closely. Even Alshara was paying attention; our father had rarely spoken of his older brother, who had died in battle before I was born. Jac Gamo's wife and children still lived in Lilano, where he had been an adviser to the southern vizier. I'd sent his widow a letter of introduction for Mati and Raisa, and Mati had written that he had visited her, but he'd had little success convincing her to support the council. I wasn't surprised. Ema Gamo was a hard, unforgiving woman who resented that Father had become the heir to the Gamo fortune after his older brother's death.

"We never knew our uncle," I said, "but I'm pleased to hear that he had such devoted admirers."

"Kassel used to say that Jac Gamo could have talked the gods into coming down from their mountain, he was that charming. But then, Kassel had a bit of a silver tongue himself, else I might have married better."

I winced. Not that such things weren't endlessly considered in Scholar circles, but it wasn't polite to speak so frankly of them.

"As soon as they announced that Master Jac had died," Nasha went on, "I knew Kassel was gone too. Before they even brought the cup." She jerked her head at the silver cup on the shelf, which I now recognized as an award for military valor. She shoveled pork into her mouth and said, shaking her head, "He would have fought to the death and all that. Never would have forgiven himself if he'd survived and his captain hadn't. He wasn't a practical man. Kassel always said that was what he married me for."

I cleared my throat. "Well, you must be proud of your son for following in his father's footsteps. And your nephew."

Kirol ducked his head as though he wished I had kept him out of it.

Nasha smiled. "My Gelti really made something of himself. Youngest guard captain in Qilara's history, you know."

We all knew. If Nasha understood that Gelti had only risen so quickly through the ranks because of my father's patronage, I doubted it would bother her.

"Mother, please," said Gelti.

"Why shouldn't a mother be proud?" Nasha gestured with her fork. "It's good to see that someone appreciates a man of quality," she went on, nodding at me.

She only means that I hired him, I told myself, but it was hard not to read deeper meaning into her words. Especially when Jonis let out a loud cough that I suspected covered a snicker.

"Mother," Gelti tried again.

"Gelti wanted to take me to Pira when the floods came," Nasha continued, oblivious to her son's distress. "As if he could have traveled so far, with the knife wound one of those—"

"Mother!"

Nasha sniffed. "I've told you a hundred times, son. You have nothing to be ashamed of. All you ever did was follow orders."

The silence in the room seemed to take on a physical form. Kirol stared into his beer. Jonis gripped the table with both hands. Alshara, who'd left most of her food untouched, paused in the act of pushing pork around her plate. Gelti glanced at Kirol, his color deepening, then shot an oppressive look at his mother.

It was impossible not to think of the day when Gelti had followed orders and Kirol quite definitely hadn't—Gelti had whipped Raisa, and Kirol had run off to get Mati and make it stop. My father and the High Priest of Aqil had given Gelti his orders and maneuvered Kirol into defying his, so that Mati would reveal his feelings for Raisa and weaken his hold on the throne.

"They were only following orders," I had said to Jonis about the men on the raider ship. But if those men weren't responsible for their actions, who was? Captain Coe? Mati? Father and the High Priest of Aqil? Or did we, as the new Ruling Council, take on responsibility for every injustice accrued in Qilara? Who was to blame, anyway?

And then, a thought that drifted into my mind like a feather falling from a passing asoti: *Does it even matter?*

"The council is lucky to have both Gelti's and Kirol's talents," I said at last, raising my voice the way Father used to when overruling arguments between me and my sisters.

"And yours." Nasha eyed me shrewdly. "Many people wanted you as queen."

I felt Jonis tense beside me.

"Many people," I said quickly, "didn't know a thing about me except my last name, and still don't."

"People only see what you do," said Gelti. "But most of them want to follow. Most people are sheep." His smile suggested that his words had been in jest, but I had heard the bitter undercurrent to his tone.

"No, most people want to be safe." Kirol spoke without looking up from his plate.

Gelti and his mother made identical sounds of disdain, as though the people Kirol was talking about didn't deserve consideration. Kirol didn't react; I had the feeling he had a lot of practice in the art of not reacting to them.

"People also want to be free," said Jonis. "No matter who they are."

Nasha chewed noisily, not deigning to respond.

But Gelti nodded. "Now that, Councilor, is very true."

For the first time, it seemed like a good idea that Jonis had wormed his way into this dinner. True, it was just one Arnath and one Qilarite having a moment where they seemed to understand one another. But it felt like progress. Maybe the only thing that would get Qilara past all that had happened was many small interactions like this.

I downed a mouthful of beer. Gods, what was happening to me? I was turning into Raisa.

It was no surprise when, after the table had been cleared, Nasha set up five candles and said the old invocations to Gyotia, Aqil, Lila, Lanea, Suna, and Qora, which ignored Sotia entirely. As she finished, Jonis muttered something quick and rhythmic—a few lines of a prayer to Sotia. I said it with him in my mind, hoping the goddess would understand. Not that she was known for being especially understanding.

SIXTEEN

AFTER DINNER, NASHA sent us up to the roof while she and Gelti prepared a tray of wine and cakes. This was no rooftop garden as we had in Pira, but a bare expanse of brick, edged with wooden benches. Pots of herbs lined one end, and a rope hammock swung under a reed canopy at the other. I'd read that city dwellers often slept on their rooftops when it was too hot indoors, but I could not imagine Nasha Dimmin heaving her bulk onto that hammock. A little thrill ran through me to see the place where Gelti slept.

"So many merchants," Jonis said, studying the streets below. "If they decide to fight us—"

"Why would they fight us?" I said. "Merchants, of all people, are going to be sensible and go where their money does."

"There are things more important than money, you know."

"Maybe to some people. I haven't met those people." Even as the flippant words left my mouth, I rethought them. Jonis and his Resistance hadn't cared about money. Weapons, certainly, but only so they could fight for their cause. On that first, horrible morning in the tombs, I had tried to bribe Jonis to let me go. I'd promised him more gold than he had ever seen in his life, but he had just walked out without a word.

"Kirol! Come get the drinks!" called Nasha from below.

I didn't mean to offend him with my curious glance, but Kirol muttered defensively, "She can't come up the stairs. Her legs bother her," as he passed me to go down.

A few minutes later we were sitting on the benches sipping apricot wine out of cracked mugs. Kirol acted as host in the absence of his aunt and cousin, but he was so awkward that I wished Gelti would come up to the roof and relieve him of that duty.

All right, so that wasn't the only reason I wished Gelti would come up. After we'd endured Kirol's awkward comments on the view for fifteen minutes, I went to the stairs and told Nasha that I'd come down to help. She looked scandalized at the idea and said, "Nonsense, my la—my dear. You just relax and Gelti will be up soon with the cakes."

Alshara was now flirting with a Qilarite guard at the other end of the roof, ignoring Valdis's brooding presence behind her, and Kirol stood with Garvin and an Arnath guard, talking while they scanned the streets below. So much for Gelti's idea about Alshara and Kirol falling in love.

I wandered over to the hammock and skimmed my fingers across the ropes, allowing myself to imagine Gelti lying there, perhaps bare-chested on a steamy night—

"He definitely wants you, in case you were wondering," said Jonis, appearing beside me so abruptly that I almost dropped my wine. "I was wondering what was behind his sudden desire to help the council connect to the merchant class, but after watching you two and your smoldering looks all night—"

I flushed. Had my behavior tonight been that obvious? "I'm not . . . I don't know what you're talking about."

"If you say so." He flopped onto the hammock, tainting my earlier visions of Gelti in it, and swung back and forth a few times. He snorted. "Conspiracy, I thought. But no, this whole evening was just an excuse for him to impress you." He shook his head.

"I thought you didn't trust him," I said witheringly, though I was dying to say, *"Do you really think he feels that way? Tell me exactly why."*

"Oh, I don't." Jonis leaned back and closed his eyes. "But I don't trust you either, so." He smirked. "Who knows? Maybe you'd be a little more pleasant after a few—"

"Dessert!" came Gelti's voice behind me, and I could not have said whether or not it was an accident that my mug clipped Jonis's head as I spun around.

Gelti stood at the top of the stairs with a tray of cakes, the dark hair at his temples damp with exertion. When Gelti saw me near Jonis, who was muttering and rubbing his forehead, he went briefly still, but then he smiled, placed the tray on a bench, and made a circuit of the roof, lighting candles.

Realizing I hadn't seen any lamps inside either, I frowned. Though lamp oil wasn't cheap these days, Gelti's salary ought to have been enough for it, even with other expenses. What was he spending his money on instead? Was it all going to help people like that overfriendly widow and her children?

Gelti passed the cakes around, but they were so dry that no one ate more than a few bites, and Gelti tossed the remains down to the chickens. He tried to laugh it off, but he was obviously embarrassed, so I made a fuss over the dinner and the wine and the view.

As night fell, the houses and streets below were reduced to elegant silhouettes. Gyotia's Lamp was fully veiled, leaving only the stars to puncture the black sky. Here and there, lamps and candles twinkled back from windows below. The occasional braying of a donkey or laughing voices passing on the street were comforting, familiar noises. Despite the darkness, my breathing remained easy—between the starlight and the candles and the open sky above, I felt safe, and free.

Of course, that might have had something to do with the person who settled next to me on the bench. I took the wine that Gelti handed me and smiled.

Jonis had taken his mug down to the hammock, where he had become a slowly swinging shadow. Gelti suggested that Kirol show Alshara the view of the harbor from the far end of the roof, and the two of them refilled their mugs and moved off.

There were still six other people on the roof, all within ten feet of us, but the dark made it feel as if Gelti and I were alone.

"I'm sorry about Alshara's behavior earlier," I said softly. "She doesn't mean to offend." *Most of the time, anyway.*

He shrugged. "She takes it for granted, the things she has.

She's lost more than most people will ever have, and she still has more than they do."

I knew we weren't just talking about Alshara. "What is she supposed to do? Give away everything she has, every gown and trinket and quill? Would that satisfy you?"

He gave me a long look, and I found myself wanting to be deemed capable of handling whatever thought was gathering behind his eyes. At last he said, "She needs to understand that people listen to her more carefully than they listen to others, even when she thinks she's saying nothing."

"She didn't ask for that."

"No," he agreed. "Doesn't change it, though." His mouth twisted. "You saw those people tonight. They're afraid. Suppose the Arnathim grow to outnumber us? Who will look out for Qilarite interests if Scholars don't speak up for the lower classes?"

"How do we assure them that we already are?"

Gelti refilled his mug. "In the old days, it would have been done with a marriage alliance," he said in an offhand way.

My cheeks flamed. Was he implying what I thought he was? I drained my mug, then said lightly, "Oh, I couldn't marry Kirol. We would argue too much."

Gelti laughed. His fingers brushed mine as he took my mug and refilled it.

I tried to regain the thread of the conversation. "Once we get the Melarim on their way home, we can deal with everything else."

"How can you still defend them?" His voice was low, but I

heard the anger vibrating in it. "They tried to kill you."

"One of them did, and he was executed for it. He doesn't represent all of them." I frowned as I heard Jonis and Loris's words coming out of my own mouth. "Sending the Melarim home is the priority. There will be no sensible debate about anything until they're gone."

He studied me for a long moment, and my cheeks warmed under the intensity of his gaze. "You are extraordinary," he said softly. "I've never met a woman like you. It's not fair, all they expect from you. Someone ought to be taking care of you."

My breathing sped up, but I managed to clear my throat and say, "I want to be able to take care of myself."

Gelti smiled. "If you can spare an hour tomorrow afternoon, I'll come for a lesson."

He thought I just meant being able to defend myself. But I was still formulating a picture of the independence I wanted. Once, it had meant sitting on the Scholars Council in the queen's place, but now I understood how hollow that would have been; no one would have taken me seriously, and it would have come at the cost of marrying a man who could barely look at me. Now I was on the Ruling Council and controlled my family's money, but I didn't feel free of my father's machinations or my mother's manipulations or the constraints of growing up a Scholar.

I wanted, I realized with a clarity that brought tears to my eyes, to feel that I had earned my place in the world. To be respected for who I was, not for being Del Gamo's daughter or Mati Villari's former betrothed or the Scholar that Raisa ke Comun had taken pity on. It was, perhaps, a foolishly small desire compared with the things the other people in this city wanted right now—food, safety, freedom—but that didn't make me want it any less.

Fortunately, Alshara interrupted us then, because my feelings were far too close to the surface. She squeezed onto the bench on Gelti's other side and he scooted closer to me to accommodate her. He braced me with one hand at the small of my back.

"It's so pretty up here at night," Alshara said, laying one hand on Gelti's bicep.

Gelti must have felt me tense—the whole of my sensation seemed to have reduced to the set of nerve endings under his warm palm on my back—because he gave me a little smile and said, "One day I'll take you to see the silver linfish jumping in the Aqorin River. When Gyotia's Lamp is shining, they like to put on a show." His hand pressed against my back, as if to say that by 'you,' he really meant me, not Alshara.

Alshara draped herself against him in an alarmingly familiar fashion, and I recalled that she'd eaten very little at dinner and had had at least three mugs of wine. "My sister will want to come," she said petulantly. "She's in love with you."

I sprang up so fast that I almost knocked over the jug of wine. "She's had too much to drink. We need to leave—"

Gelti gave me that slow-burning grin that never did anything good for my willpower. "It's all right," he murmured. "I'll take her down to the carriage." He scooped Alshara into his arms. "Kirol, you ass," he called. "You've let your charge get drunk. She might have fallen off the roof."

Or mortally embarrassed her sister, I thought.

Down in the courtyard, Gelti handed Alshara to Kirol, who

didn't manage her with the same easy grace, but was able to get her into the carriage with Valdis's help. Gelti pulled me aside as the others decided who would ride where.

"I'm sorry about that . . . and about, well, Mother. But"—he dipped his head closer to my ear—"I'm glad you came tonight."

"Me too," I said softly. There were polite things a guest should say when taking leave of her host, but all of them abandoned me in the dark courtyard with him inches away.

He squeezed my fingers. "I'll come at midday bells tomorrow."

"That would be . . . that would be fine." My throat wasn't working properly.

Gelti glanced over at the others—making sure, I was certain, that they weren't watching, because every part of me knew he was about to kiss me, and every part of me wanted him to, no matter that we were in a dark courtyard with chickens cackling a few feet away.

A flash of movement on the street caught my attention. Gelti followed my gaze, and then his hand ripped out of mine, and I blinked in confusion at the place where he had stood.

From somewhere in the darkness, Jonis yelled. More sounds came from the street—fists on flesh, punctuated by grunts.

There was a short scream; I realized belatedly that it was mine. By the time I had limped forward, pushing past the Arnath guard who was babbling that I needed to stay back, the grunting had turned into the slap of running feet against the road, and low, brusque orders being issued.

"Light," a voice growled, and it took a moment for me to

recognize it as Gelti's. Someone pushed past me and went into the house, and soon emerged carrying two lit candles, followed by second figure. Kirol and Adin. Both of their faces were drawn, and I understood why when I saw what the candles illuminated.

Gelti braced himself against the gate, panting. A gash along his collarbone dripped blood all over his tunic, but otherwise he seemed unhurt. Jonis sat on the ground, rubbing the back of his head, with Garvin kneeling beside him. Valdis stood in the door of the carriage, guarding Alshara, who was draped across the seat behind him.

"What happened?" I asked shakily.

"Someone attacked me," said Jonis. "They were outside the gate—"

"Where were your men?" Gelti barked at Kirol. "Did you even have them check the carriages and the road?" The patient older cousin was gone, and Kirol shrank back as if he were still Gelti's second lieutenant.

"I, uh, didn't—"

Gelti waved a disgusted hand toward the carriages. "Get your councilors home."

"You're injured!" I touched his arm. He was so tense that the muscle practically vibrated under my fingers.

"It's shallow. Get out of here before they come back."

He was furious. Because he had trained his cousin, and he thought Kirol ought to have known better? Or because someone in the Web had attacked a guest in his home, and he felt it as a betrayal?

Garvin helped Jonis to his feet. I finally understood what had happened—Gelti had gotten to the attacker before the attacker got to Jonis. I squeezed Gelti's hand in gratitude, but he hardly looked at me now; he pulled Kirol aside and spoke to him in a low, angry voice, the picture of command.

Kirol and Adin climbed into the second carriage with Jonis and me, while Garvin took the driver's seat. That left one guard to drive Valdis and Alshara, as Gelti had sent the other two after the attacker.

I didn't understand why Adin hadn't seen the attacker—he'd been Jonis's shadow as long as I'd known him. But Jonis was still dazed from knocking his head against the wall when Gelti had shoved him aside, and Adin was stubbornly silent on the matter. My mind lingered on the image of Adin emerging from the house behind Kirol—even though he hadn't gone inside with him a few minutes before. Adin hadn't been with us in the courtyard, and probably, I now realized, hadn't been with us up on the roof.

"Did you find anything?" I asked Adin.

"What do you mean?" Even in the dim light his eyes had a cornered look.

"While you were searching the Dimmins' house. That's why you weren't there to protect him, isn't it?" I jerked my head toward Jonis, who looked at me blearily, but didn't say a word.

Adin glanced at Jonis and didn't respond.

I shook my head at Jonis. "After being invited into their home! Gelti has done nothing but help this council, and he just saved your life."

Jonis didn't argue, but I couldn't tell if this was because he thought I had a point, or because his head was bothering him so much. Everything had happened so fast that no one had seen how hard Jonis had hit the wall, but when we got back to the palace I insisted that the doctor tend him, and I sent Valdis to watch over him as well. Then, because I knew that Nelnar and Valdis would leave if Jonis ordered them to, I sent a message to Deshti. She wouldn't let him bully her away, even if she was still angry with him. Maybe *especially* if she was still angry with him.

I left Kirol with orders to wake me when the two guards who'd gone after the attacker returned, no matter what time it was, and locked my door and fell into bed.

When the insistent knocking came, I jolted awake with the feeling that I had hardly slept. But that was only because I'd left the lamp burning, as I did every night; the sky outside the window was the smoky gray of very early morning.

When I finally got my too-big dressing gown tied around me and made it to the door, Kirol waited there. My heart leaped to my throat at the expression on his face.

"Is it Jonis?" I asked. "Or did the guards come back?"

Kirol's face was vaguely greenish in the lamplight. He probably hadn't slept in some time; I probably should order him to bed. "Jonis is fine."

"The guards then?"

"Haven't returned. It's . . . the prisoner, Coe. He's dead."

I grabbed the doorframe to keep from swaying on my feet. "Show me," I demanded.

"Are you sure? It's not very—"

"I am the only councilor available to deal with this situation. Show me."

I didn't realize until we were out in the corridor that I was still in Father's badly embroidered dressing gown. I tamped down my instinctive appalled embarrassment—I didn't have time for that.

Captain Coe had been moved to a small chamber that had once been a guardroom, and now held nothing but a narrow bed, a side table with a low-burning lamp, and a wooden chair.

And of course, a dead body sprawled on the floor, an angry red gash across its throat and a puddle of blood spreading beneath it.

I pushed away thoughts of Aliana. Kirol might have warned me that Coe's throat had been cut.

Two more bodies lay facedown just inside the door—the men who had been guarding Coe. Presumably their throats had been cut too, since they hadn't raised the alarm, but I wasn't about to turn them over to check.

"No one noticed the missing guards?" I asked.

"I found them, Councilor," said one of the men just outside the doorway. "At the shift change just now. Whoever did this killed them and then propped them up against the wall." He gave a mirthless laugh. "I didn't realize myself until I went to clap Nave here on the shoulder and he fell right over."

Kirol frowned at this—as well he should. It was hard to imagine Gelti tolerating his men talking about a dead comrade so lightly. But Kirol didn't reprimand him, only knelt and turned over the nearest body. I looked away. Yes, this man's throat had been cut too.

"How did the killer get in?" I asked.

Kirol shook his head. "The gate guards didn't see anything."

"There are other entrances to this building, you know. Not to mention plenty of people already inside."

"I *know*," said Kirol, with the first flash of temper I had ever seen from him. "I've put more men on every entrance and we'll question everyone inside."

I looked around the room. "Was there anything sharp in here? Is it possible that Coe did this himself?" Coe's death would martyr him in the eyes of Qilarites who thought that holding him was unjust; maybe the man fancied going out like that.

"Nothing."

I hardly heard him; the idea of Coe as a martyr had triggered others involving riots and angry mobs. "We have to keep this quiet as long as we can," I told Kirol urgently. "At least until the Melarim leave tomorrow. If the sailors at the Bleeding Oyster find out, we'll have another mutiny on our hands."

Kirol's eyes widened, as if he hadn't put those pieces together. I wondered again if his ineptitude was an act. It would have been something of a relief to have a guard captain who was devious instead of just dim-witted. "We only have thirty men on shift right now—" he began.

"Then wake the rest of them," I snapped. "We have to be ready to keep the city under control, do you understand? And get Gelti in here to examine the scene." Though it was unlikely that the bodies were decomposing yet, the stench of death filled my nostrils and I had to get out of the room. I stepped over the body closest to the door and made for the fresh air of the hallway. "I told you what to do. Act like a proper captain and do it."

By sunrise bells, word of Coe's murder had somehow gotten out, and roving bands of sailors were shouting Coe's name like a war chant. Kirol set off for Portside with half the palace guards, and I went to order one of the gate guards to rouse any men still in the garrison.

"Has Gelti Dimmin arrived yet?" I asked another, not caring what it looked like. We needed Gelti's expertise, now.

"I'm here," said a voice behind me, and I turned to find Gelti just outside the guardhouse window. He wore a gray tunic that blended with the dim morning streets behind him, but white fabric poked out above it where the gash on his collarbone had been bandaged.

I suppressed a wave of relief and motioned him in, waiting impatiently while he handed over his weapons to the guards. I knew, from our fighting lessons, that he probably still had a dagger in his boot that he didn't tell them about, but I let it go.

"The garden is closest," I said, nodding in the direction of the lightening path and hobbling as quickly as I could away from the listening ears of the guards.

"I found the guards who went after the attacker last night," Gelti reported soberly as he came level with me. "Both dead. Found them in an alley in the Web."

I sighed. "You'll need to tell Kirol, and show him exactly where—"

"I will. But I wanted to check on you first."

"Why?" I asked. "What's happening out there?"

"Fighting here and there, gangs of kids, mostly, getting into it with the guards. They're saying things—I thought you should know . . ." He stopped and touched my arm.

But I had to keep moving. "About Captain Coe? I know."

Gelti hadn't moved. "About Coe, yes. Strangled in his cell in the dungeon, they're saying."

"Throat cut in his room. We moved him out of the dungeon, remember?" I shook my head. I'd had good reason to move Coe, but he would have been harder to get to in the dungeon. "Go on, tell me how terrible our security is. After three assassination attempts and a murderer getting into the palace, I won't argue with you."

"You've got a bigger problem than that," he said. "Word on the streets is that Coe found out the king gave the raiders false maps, so they would drown in the northern wastes. And that the Ruling Council killed Coe to keep him quiet about it."

SEVENTEEN

I STARED AT Gelti. *That the Ruling Council killed Coe . . .* My mind replayed Jonis's reaction when he'd found out the raider ship had fulfilled its mission, how I'd had to step between him and Coe. Could Jonis have been behind this? But what sense would there be in killing Coe? Besides, Coe and the guards had been killed sometime before the shift change, and Jonis had been dazed after his injury. Before that, he'd been right there with us all night.

But Adin wasn't, whispered a voice in my mind. *When he was allegedly searching the Dimmins' house.* And it wouldn't take long for a determined man to get to the palace and back from the Web. . . .

But why would Jonis want to work against the Ruling Council? It didn't make sense . . . unless it was a way to make the council look suspect, so he could justify trying to overthrow it. Then the success of the Arnath Resistance would be complete, wouldn't it?

I shook my head as I continued down the path. "Obviously, whoever killed Coe is trying to stir up the public against us."

Gelti caught up to me. "Isn't it more likely that the Arnathim targeted Coe in revenge? Maybe for that Arnath guard's death?"

My brain seemed to work better with my feet moving. "But why would they take the chance of retribution against the Melarim?" All the Arnathim I knew were habitually vigilant about how their actions might be taken by others, especially Qilarites. I recalled the way that Jonis's little sister had frozen in fear when she'd dropped a cup a few days ago. In her old life, her master would have beaten or whipped her for such a minor thing.

No, killing Coe and the sailors and provoking Qilarite rage was not an Arnath strategy. Even when Jonis had led the Arnath Resistance, dramatic murders and instilling terror hadn't been his style. He'd crafted a long-term plan, putting his people in place at the palace long before my wedding day, so that the Resistance would be poised to attack during the ceremony.

"Whoever did this," I said, "has turned Coe into a martyr, like Tyasha ke Demit was for the Resistance." I stopped and stared at Gelti. "That's what this is, isn't it? Some kind of . . . Qilarite resistance movement. It's probably the Swords of Qilara."

Gelti frowned. "But they took credit, loudly, for the Arnath guard's death. If it was the Swords of Qilara, they'd announce—"

I shook my head, my brain working so fast that I spoke right over him. "They've tried to kill us, but that hasn't worked. You stopped them from killing Jonis. That probably made them angry, so they went for Coe. And they want people to think that we're incompetent or evil. They're trying to discredit us, any way they can." I nodded at my own observation. "Because if we go, then so do the First Laws—the Arnath emancipation, the inheritance laws, all of it. I need you to confirm it's the Swords of Qilara, and we need to make some arrests. We have to show that we are taking steps to secure the city."

On the day the Melarim had arrived, I'd thought I could buy the mob's cooperation, but I hadn't counted on the power of hate. The image of an Arnath guard shooting a poor Qilarite sailor had likely become fixed in the minds of the people who had done this, along with a thousand other slights, real or perceived, that convinced them that striking out against the Ruling Council was the only way to get what they wanted. It was why they had killed Hodder. It might be why someone had killed Coe too.

"If this is the Swords of Qilara," said Gelti, "then they're using much cleverer tactics than they have in the past. It doesn't fit their pattern."

I wrinkled my nose. "It's not that clever. Using fear to start wars is hardly new." My own father had done it, hadn't he?

Gelti still didn't look convinced, but he nodded. "And how will you handle the rumors about the false maps?"

"Charts," I corrected absently. "How did that get out anyway? Maybe one of the scribes who created them—"

"You think Scholars are doing this?" said Gelti, seeming to resent the idea that the lower classes weren't capable of fomenting their own rebellion.

I sighed. "I don't know. We need more information. I have to talk to Jonis."

Gelti opened his mouth and closed it again.

"What is it?"

"Be careful. He's . . . got something to prove, that one. Don't let him do it at your expense."

My hands went cold. The reflexively mistrustful things I had been thinking about Jonis earlier were one thing; it was quite another to have Gelti's professional intuition back them up. "What do you mean?"

"He was clever when he led the Resistance. I can admit that. He bested us, more than once. He stole weapons, stayed hidden in the tombs until you showed up with information about where he was."

I pursed my lips. "Only because he let me go, knowing I would lead you there."

Gelti raised his eyebrows. "Exactly. He likes complicated plans. I wouldn't put it past him to provoke Qilarites and give his own people a reason to fight them."

"I can deal with Jonis," I said.

"I know you can. I just . . ." He rubbed his neck. "Last night, when I saw that attacker, all I could think was that he'd go after you next. I couldn't let that happen." Gelti slid his hand down to wrap around mine. "Just remember . . . people do strange things when they feel strongly about something. They don't always follow sense."

I looked up into his dark eyes, only inches away. My heart thumped painfully, but I said, "Is that why you helped the High Priest of Aqil and my father with their coup? Because you felt strongly about their cause?"

I knew why I'd said it; this was too much like the first time

I'd thought he was going to kiss me and had seen him decide not to. So I'd reached instinctively for the weapon I knew would wound him most: the truth.

Pride flashed in his eyes, as if he had taught me that move himself and was watching me perfect it. "No," he said, "I've always been a man of sense. Until now, at least."

And then he kissed me.

It wasn't gentle. I had expected that; Gelti was not a gentle man. But it was warm, and forceful, and Gelti seemed to be everywhere at once, though his lips didn't leave mine and his hands only gripped my waist. When he nudged my lips open with his, I let him.

For that short time in the garden, I didn't care about assassins or ships or devastating rumors. None of that existed. There was only the perfect bliss of Gelti's hot lips against mine, his lean muscles under my hands, his hair tickling my forehead. For once I had found something effortless; I didn't have to try, to plan, to scheme, to wonder how to make this work. It just worked, all on its own.

I expected—wanted—Gelti's lips to wander down my neck, even arched my back a little, yearning for his hands to move somewhere other than my waist, but he just kept kissing me, deep and slow, until I was so limp that if his hands had moved, I might have collapsed. When at last he lifted his head, it was a slow withdrawal. I was breathing heavily—not panting, I assured myself, as ladies did not pant—and even though my lips were uncomfortably swollen, they also felt bereft, missing something they had never known they wanted.

I half hated the way my face tilted up toward his, inviting him to kiss me again. I also couldn't seem to help it.

He traced one finger slowly over my lips. "I did support them. Your father, at least. But the king was weak, or so I thought."

"That was treason," I said evenly.

He sighed. "I was young and stupid when it began, and I thought a captain's post was the best thing I could hope for in this world. I didn't know that the price of it was becoming the High Priest's dog. By the time I understood that, it was too late to get out."

I ran my hands down the back of his tunic. When I moved them back up, the edge caught and my finger grazed the hot skin of his lower back. My breath hitched and I let the fabric drop.

I cleared my throat, trying not to fixate on that brief touch. "You did what you had to in order to survive."

He shook his head sadly. "I wish you didn't know about the things I've done, so you might think better of me."

"I'm glad I know," I said. "I . . . understand you better that way."

Gelti stroked my cheek. "Whatever happens out there," he said, "I won't let anyone hurt you. I promise you that."

Gripping the front of his tunic, I pressed my lips to his. It was more urgent this time, and Gelti let out a grunt when my hand knocked against his bandaged collarbone. But when I tried to pull away to ask if he was all right, he didn't let me, just wrapped his arms around me and pulled me closer.

Any minute now, I told myself, I would push him away and get back to work.

After Gelti left, I took myself off to Jonis's room for a confrontation.

Jonis and his family had taken over the former royal Tutors' suite, a pair of connecting bedrooms with a sitting room. I thought he was mad, personally; I'd made sure to put my sister in a room as far away from mine as possible. But I suspected that he had a sentimental attachment to these rooms, since they had once been Raisa's, and he couldn't justify taking the whole suite without putting his mother and sister in the second bedroom.

Or maybe he'd just wanted to keep them close by.

I rapped on the sitting room door, and, when no one answered, let myself in. The bedroom door was ajar, and I could see the closed door of the second bedroom beyond, along with the chunk ripped out of the wall where Jonis had removed the second door's lock bar. The restful silence made me move quietly even though I had come to awaken and disrupt.

I had to squint to see them; the shutters were still closed. Jonis slept on his side, sandy curls covering his eyes, his mouth hanging open. He looked incredibly young, which took me aback. Jonis was only a year older than I was, but I usually had to remind myself of that. The fact that my introduction to him had been as his hostage had made him older in my mind.

Deshti was sitting up in the chair by his pillow, her head lolling against the headrest. Jonis would see her first thing if he opened his eyes. I doubted this was accidental.

Deshti jerked awake the moment I stepped into the room. "Don't disturb him," she said at once.

"I need to talk to him." I reached for the shutters, but Deshti hissed at me.

"The light will bother him."

"And the lack of light will bother me," I said testily. But I only pulled the shutter halfway open, allowing a weak beam of sunlight to glance across the floor away from the bed.

Deshti huffed out a sigh. "I'll wake him." She rubbed Jonis's bare back, murmuring into his ear with a tenderness that made me look away; it seemed more intimate than taking off her clothes and climbing on top of him would have been.

I studied the peeling edges of the shutter, calculating how long it would be before we could afford to have it repainted, to drown out the murmurs and rustling coming from the bed. I didn't look back until Jonis said, "Soraya?"

He was propped up, squinting at me, pushing his mop of sandy curls out of his eyes. Deshti fussed with his pillows.

"Something's happened," I said. I looked away. "Put a shirt on, please."

"What?" Jonis sounded confused, as though he hadn't realized he wasn't wearing one, but Deshti snickered as she fetched a tunic for him. *It's a shame you hate Raisa so much,* I thought sourly at her. *The two of you could bond over laughing at what a prude I am.*

Then I ran one finger over my no-longer-unkissed lips, suppressing a smile. What did they know?

I caught a glimpse of the mass of scars on Jonis's back as Deshti helped him slip the tunic over his head. "Is this more acceptable?" he said as he fell back onto the pillows again.

"Yes," I said. "Overnight there was—"

"I'm feeling much better, thanks for asking."

I frowned. "I assumed so, otherwise you wouldn't be able to crack jokes. I need to talk to you." I cut my eyes at Deshti. "Council business."

Jonis looked at Deshti. "Why don't you go get some breakfast, Desh?"

Deshti didn't move. "What if you need something?"

Jonis shook his head, then winced, which made Deshti narrow her eyes. "I'll be fine. Go eat."

Deshti's mouth tightened, but she left the room, throwing me a suspicious look as she pulled the door shut.

As soon as she was gone, I told Jonis about Coe's murder and the rumors flying around the city about the false navigational charts, and asked point-blank if he was responsible.

His brow creased in confusion, but that might have been an act. "I could ask you the same question," he said.

"Why on earth would I have Coe killed?"

"Coe's a martyr now, those sailors too. If someone wants to stir up Qilarites, this is a good way to do it."

I stared at him, astonished at how quickly he'd come up with the idea that had taken me much longer to get to. But then, he'd had experience with rebellion, hadn't he?

And maybe he *wanted* me to think that Qilarites were behind it.

He rubbed his forehead. "It's exactly the kind of thing a small group of people with no real power might do, to inspire fear."

I nudged the shutter open a little more, needing more light to dispel the tightness in my chest. "That's what the Scholars

Council used to say about the Arnath Resistance."

"This is completely different," said Jonis sharply.

"Keep your voice down."

He waved wearily at the second bedroom. "No one's here. Mother and Jera got up hours ago."

"Yes, but Deshti's in the sitting room."

He looked at me like I was the one with a head injury. "She went down to breakfast, remember?"

I tutted. "You really are an idiot, aren't you?"

"What?"

"Never mind." I wasn't at all certain that he was telling the truth, but I decided to let him think I believed him. For now, at least. "It's not exactly like their tactics so far, but it might be the Swords of Qilara. We need to make some arrests to show we're handling it. I sent Gelti out to do more investigating."

Jonis's eyebrow raised the way it usually did right before he made some cutting remark, but then he seemed to recall that Gelti had saved his life the night before, and stayed silent. Reluctantly I placed a mark in the "Jonis didn't do it" column in my mind.

I sighed dramatically. "We need to decide how to handle the rumors about the false charts." I'd already decided what to do, in fact, but his response would tell me where he stood. If Jonis were behind the murders, then he would try to incite the Arnathim to fight. He would want people to know about those charts, because no one would ever trust the council if we admitted to hiding the truth about them.

Jonis closed his eyes for so long that I wondered if he'd gone back to sleep. But then he said, "If we admit it's true, that's practically announcing that we murdered Coe."

"But if we deny it, people will assume we murdered him anyway and are trying to cover it up."

He eyed me warily, probably remembering that I'd suggested keeping the charts secret in the first place. "What do you think we should do?" he said, and I could feel him measuring my response too.

"Ignore the rumors altogether. Just say we're appalled by the murder, and that whoever did it will be apprehended and punished. But we'll have to make a spectacle of the execution once we catch them. To deter others."

Jonis crossed his arms. "Did the Scholars Council say that about Tyasha's execution? That making a spectacle would deter the Resistance?"

"I wasn't there then." But he had a point. Executing an Arnath Tutor had turned her into a martyr who inspired the Resistance further, and whoever was behind this plot already had plenty of martyrs to work with. "Fine," I said. "When we find out who did it, we take them out quietly." I hesitated, then added, "Gelti could do that."

Jonis narrowed his eyes. "And Adin."

"Yes. And maybe Valdis. But we can't do anything until we have more evidence."

Jonis groaned and pulled back the blanket, swinging his legs off the bed.

"Get back in bed," I told him. "I can handle this. Shall I call Deshti and your mother to restrain you?"

Jonis looked alarmed. "Listen, I told my mother it was an

accident last night. Don't tell her about the attack, all right?"

"She serves your meals to make sure you won't get poisoned. Do you really think she doesn't know what's going on?"

"My mother had to be strong for a long time. She doesn't need anything more to worry about." His eyes went to the damaged wall, and it only now occurred to me to wonder about the vehemence with which he had torn out the lock bar.

"All right," I said slowly. "I won't say anything to her."

"Thanks. It's bad enough Deshti found out. I guess Adin told her."

"Hmmm," I said. "I'll check on the ship and make sure everything is set for the day after tomorrow. The sooner we get the Melarim on their way, the better."

"And I'll write to Raisa and Mati. If anything else happens, let me know right away." The way he settled back against his pillows without arguing further was a bit alarming; he must have been feeling awful. I slipped the shutter closed and dived for the exit.

As I had predicted, Deshti waited in the sitting room. She sprang up from the sagging couch as I closed the door to Jonis's room behind me.

"What's going on?" she asked.

Her belligerent tone made me want to refuse to tell her anything, but it had just occurred to me that Deshti might be a useful source. Had Jonis even thought to ask her for information, or had he been too resentful of her visiting her former mistress?

So I told her bluntly about what had happened. She absorbed it all silently.

"Did you see anything unusual last night?" I asked.

She shook her head. "Everything was quiet."

"Jonis said you were visiting your, er—"

"Friend," supplied Deshti pointedly, narrowing her dark eyes.

"Yes. Will you send her a note and ask if she's seen anything that might help us figure out who did this?"

Deshti crossed her arms. "Tana can't read that well."

"Ah. You've been teaching her. That's why you visit her."

"Sometimes." Deshti rubbed at an ink stain on her thumb. "She's still suspicious about learning to write. A lot of the merchants are. I sneak lessons in while I'm helping her make candles. I convinced her that if she sells candles with symbols worked into them, it'll set her business apart."

"Clever," I said. If those candles had been available in the old days, Scholars would have thronged to buy them. "Does Jonis know about that?"

"It's none of his business."

"True." I rubbed my signet ring thoughtfully. I had a question I wanted to ask Deshti, but couldn't quite figure out how to phrase it. "How can you consider her a friend?" I said at last, wincing at how plaintive the words sounded.

Deshti's face closed off entirely.

I sighed. "I'm trying to understand. I see how you are with me, and I never owned you. Why don't you hate her?"

Deshti frowned. "You're a Scholar."

"So?"

"Tana's a merchant. It's different. She never had a chance to do more than get by, with the Scholars Council setting limits on the prices she could charge and raising taxes every year and her having to hire a scribe to keep her records. She understands what it's like to work to survive."

Her passionate words probably should have angered me, but instead they made me sad. No one had ever spoken so forcefully in my defense, not even my own father, when my fiancé had humiliated me. "She's lucky to have you," I said.

Deshti shrugged. "We've always taken care of each other."

"Did she know?" I asked. "About you being in the Resistance? Was she—"

"No. Tana was never involved. I thought she must have suspected, but she was furious when she found out."

"Naturally. If you'd been caught, she could have been implicated."

Deshti shot me a look of disgust. "She was furious that I was putting myself in danger. And that I kept it from her."

"I see. Well, if there's anything she can tell us . . ."

"I'll go see her." Deshti stood. "Jonis's mother is coming up soon."

I nodded. "It makes sense for the Library to close today."

"No," said Deshti vehemently. "The Library has to stay open, no matter what happens. What's the point of any of this if it doesn't? Besides, Alshara can handle things there."

"What?" The thought of my little sister having the wherewithal to handle anything was amusing.

"It's just scheduling, really, matching teachers with students. She's done it before."

"But not well," I said before I could stop myself.

"Then she'll get to practice," said Deshti. "Why are you so hard on her? You want people to give you a chance, but you never give her one."

The accusation stunned me into silence.

"Marisa has a student who wants to take the guard writing test today though. Parker Ots." Deshti frowned. "Guess he'll have to wait."

It took me a moment to place the name, but then the baker's son, looking miserably squeezed in a flour-dusted apron, popped into my mind. "He was in the palace guard before, wasn't he?" I asked.

She nodded.

A guard who was already trained and ready to go—we'd be foolish to say no to that, in our current state. "I'll test him myself," I said. And if he didn't quite pass everything, well, maybe that wouldn't matter. We needed more men on the streets before nightfall.

Before I reached the door, Deshti spoke again. "Thanks for sending for me last night. He never would have. He probably wouldn't have told me what happened at all."

"Well, he's blinder than a cave cricket, isn't he?"

Deshti smiled wanly. "He tries to protect me. You'd think he would have learned by now that nobody likes to be told what to do."

"Blinder and stupider than a cave cricket," I amended.

Deshti laughed softy and gave me a tentative wave as she disappeared into Jonis's room.

EIGHTEEN

BY MIDDAY, THE Web had quieted down, with most people electing to stay inside. We'd closed the market early on, so the only people there were the Arnathim who had shown up to guard the Melarim. There were over fifty volunteer defenders now, so Kirol sent most of the guards over to help in Portside, where the sailors had constructed a barricade. A handful of homes and shops had been looted there, but now it was mainly sailors yelling about taking back the City of Kings and keeping the Arnathim out of "their neighborhood." I ordered Kirol to get some spies into that crowd.

It seemed ridiculous to hold a regular council meeting that evening, but we had business to discuss. Jonis wanted to go down to see the Melarim, but conceded that in the current environment, it was best to stay in the palace.

"We have to go to the docks to see them off tomorrow morning, though," said Jonis, "no matter what anyone says."

"Yes," I replied. "And it should be the biggest send-off we can make it."

Jonis nodded. "To honor them, yes. That will send a message."

I'd been thinking that it would announce to the Qilarites that the divisive Melarim were gone and things could go back to normal, but if the Arnathim wanted to take it as honoring the Melarim, well, then, even better.

"As soon as they're gone, we'll hold a memorial for Coe," I mused.

Jonis's fork paused halfway to his mouth. "What?"

"If we don't, Qilarites will take it as a slight."

"You want to honor that—"

I abandoned all pretense of eating and stared him down. "If we don't do something to honor him, it will only feed the idea that we killed him."

"Or it will make us look like enormous hypocrites."

That was true, but I didn't see any way around that. Half the city would probably believe that we were audaciously memorializing a man we ourselves had murdered. But then, people admired audacity in their leaders. That was why Father had been so successful.

"Just one more day," I said. "Things will settle down once the Melarim are gone." The Melarim were a disruption, a reminder of all the things we were trying to move away from, and their arrival had ripped off the thin scab that had just begun to form over the wound of Qilara's past. It couldn't start to heal until they were gone.

It was obvious before we got halfway to the docks the next morning that something was wrong. Smoke painted the sky, and the driver shouted that we should turn back. Adin agreed, but Jonis and I both demanded to go on. There was hardly any traffic on the road, so when we reached the docks—what was left of them—we had an unimpeded view of the flaming piers, the charred pilings, and two ships burning at their moorings. One of them was *Gyotia's Wrath*, the raider ship that had brought the Melarim. The other was the southern vizier's ship, the *Shorebird*.

Through the window, I could see the driver fighting to control the spooked horses. This was the slowest it would get before he gained control and made them race off.

Jonis must have realized that too, because he sprang up, pushed the door open, and jumped out of the carriage. Adin, who'd probably seen what Jonis was going to do before Jonis had even thought of it, was right behind him, and I was right behind Adin. The carriage door clipped my shoulder as the horses shot forward.

By that time Jonis was already shouting at the nearest guard in the bucket line, demanding to know where Kirol was.

"Jonis! Adin! Come on," I shouted, leading the way to where a man was hauling on a rope, bringing up buckets of water from the harbor, and a small boy was running the buckets over to the end of the line of men passing them.

"What are you doing?" Jonis shouted. "We need to find out who's behind this!"

I pushed my hair out of my face. "The docks are burning!

Right now, this is the most important thing."

Someone thrust a bucket into my hands, almost knocking me off-balance. I slopped half the water on myself as I passed it to the next man, and then someone was there handing me another bucket, and so on and so on. I shifted and let my right foot take more weight.

The buckets kept coming; soon my gown and the waxed bandages around my ankle were soaked, my fingers sore, my shoulders aching. It was numbing, mindless work, but there was also something exciting about being a link in a chain of people working toward a common purpose. All I had to do was pass the bucket, follow directions, and hope for the best.

That shook me right out of my trance, and I let the next bucket slop to the stones. It might be easier to follow, but that wasn't my role. Jonis was right; we didn't have that luxury.

I marched up to the guard at the front of the line. Jonis was still shouting at him as he passed bucket after bucket, but I shouted louder. "Focus on the piers," I ordered. "Let the ships go."

Jonis turned on me, his eyes almost deranged with anger. "What are you doing?"

"The ships are lost! If we waste time trying to save them, we'll lose the pier and the warehouses. We've got to cut the lines and let them drift away from the dock."

"The current will take them out," objected a tall sailor who had stepped out of the line. "But they'll come back in with the tide and slam into the dock, still burning." He looked down his nose at me, clearly offended by the notion of a woman having ideas.

"No, they won't," I said coldly. "Because as soon as they get far enough out, we're going to raise the harbor walls. Cut the ropes," I ordered. "We need to find the harbormaster and get someone up to the floodwall towers."

Jonis grabbed my arm. His soaked brown curls were tighter than usual above his pale face. "What about the Melarim?"

My dread mirrored what I saw in his eyes, but I couldn't allow myself to feel it yet. "We'll deal with that later. Perhaps we could make sure our city is not on fire first."

"We'll deal with it now." Jonis pointed behind me, and I pivoted to see a line of carriages coming up the main road. The lead carriage was close enough to see Loris and Tira at the window, the hope on their faces bleeding away as they took in what was happening at the docks.

It was only later I learned that the ships weren't all we had lost in the fire; while the guards were distracted fighting the blaze, the Swords of Qilara liberated all of Coe's men from the Bleeding Oyster, leaving behind another map pinned to the front door of the inn with a sword. They hadn't left a written message this time, though. Apparently they felt that the deserted inn was enough. By the time Jonis and I learned of the escape from a bedraggled, wary-looking Kirol, the sailors had disappeared and none of the people in Portside would admit to seeing them.

This was right after the harbormaster told us—too obsequiously, barely hiding a grin—that most of the large ships had left port in the past few days. "Could be Gyotia sent those captains warning dreams, to get their ships out before the fire," he added.

The reference to the destroyed god had only made Jonis's mouth go thinner. "Arrest this man."

Jonis hadn't looked back at the two guards behind him, or he might have seen that both were Qilarite, and that both waited for me to nod agreement before they dragged the harbormaster away. We'd have Gelti question him as soon as possible. The harbormaster had to be working with the Swords of Qilara, and we needed names. The escape of the sailors meant that the Swords of Qilara had just added sixteen angry men to their ranks.

"We should have sneaked the Melarim out of the city in the night," said Jonis, staring out the window of our carriage as it made its way to the market. "Why did I ever let you convince me to—"

"Convince you?" I snapped. "You wanted to make a fuss over their departure!"

"That wouldn't have helped," Loris put in. He sat curled into the corner, but his tone was detached, as if we weren't talking about the fact that his people's chance to go home had gone up in smoke. "Between the captain, the crew, the suppliers, and the guards, many people would have known when we were set to leave."

Jonis snorted. "Next you're going to say that we don't even know for sure that this was directed at the Melarim."

"Well, we don't," said Loris and I together. Jonis laced his fingers together and turned away.

I was used to Jonis's disdain, but Loris was not. His eyebrows furrowed. "We don't know how the fire started," he said, his tone eminently reasonable, but I could have told him that reason wouldn't reach Jonis right now.

"And besides, the Swords of Qilara are only taking credit for freeing the sailors," I added. "The fire could have been an accident, or started by Arnathim who wanted the raider ship burned, and they took advantage of it."

Jonis didn't bother to turn his head. "After clearing out the harbor first?"

"True," I conceded, "but it doesn't make sense. Wouldn't the Swords of Qilara be happy to have the Melarim gone? Isn't that why they killed Hodder?"

"They wouldn't want us gone if they're using us to start a rebellion," said Loris. He stared at a cut on the back of his right hand, which he must have gotten at some point during the morning when some of the Melarim had joined in the bucket brigade to save the warehouses. His thumb kept moving over the cut, which was large enough that the contact probably hurt, but he couldn't seem to stop doing it.

"We should seize a merchant ship," said Jonis savagely. "We have to get them home."

"We can't go seizing ships," I said. "Not unless you want the Swords of Qilara to have more reason to turn every merchant in the city against us and against the Melarim. Besides, there aren't any large ships in the harbor, remember?" And we'd be in enough trouble once the southern vizier found out about the loss of his ship. Vizier Tren would surely demand reparations, and might even accuse us of deliberately targeting his property, as so many ships had apparently been warned to clear off before the blaze started. All of this had been whirling unpleasantly through the back of my mind, but I wouldn't let myself think about it yet—or about how we were going to pay for yet another ship to get the Melarim home.

When we arrived at the market, Jonis and Loris helped carry in the crates of supplies that had been salvaged because they hadn't been loaded on the *Shorebird* before the fire. I limped down the hallway after them. My ankle, though cold and stiff, didn't actually hurt, but all the water that had slopped onto my bandages had disintegrated the wax and made them an annoying, floppy mess. By the time I reached the front room, one of the guards was already tugging the lid off a crate, and Melarim in clothing in various states of soakage were crowding around. The guard pulled items out and tossed them into the crowd. I had just seen a flash of green when Jonis roared, "What is this?"

Jonis pushed through the mass of people and plunged both hands into the crate, pulling out bundles of green cloth.

Kirit green. The color once worn by slaves.

Jonis went still. "It's all green." His jaw worked, then he looked straight at me. "Still going to tell me those fires were an accident?"

NINETEEN

"SOMEONE WANTS THEM to fight," said Kirol.

"Of course they do," I said, holding the torch up higher as I continued down the hallway. Jonis had stormed out after finding the green clothes, practically flattening Kirol, who was on his way in. Needing to move, I'd grabbed Kirol and Loris and dragged them to the back of the building, looking for a secluded place to figure out what was going on.

"Why would green clothes make us fight?" said Loris behind me. "Green means nothing to us."

"Not you," said Kirol. "The Arnathim. It's a symbol of slavery, a slap in the face to them. It'll work, too."

I reached the end of the corridor and turned, thrusting the torch into a holder on the wall. We were far enough away from the others, at the opposite end of the building from where the Melarim had been living. I hadn't realized how homey they had managed to make the main hall until I smelled the dank air emanating from the shadowed cells surrounding us now.

Kirol might have been borderline useless as a guard captain, but he was right about one thing: whoever had sent those clothes wanted the Arnathim to rise up and fight. And it seemed to me that Jonis would have more reason than anyone to want that, if he thought—as he clearly did think—that his people weren't getting enough.

I turned to Kirol. "Do you think Jonis was behind those green clothes?" I asked.

Kirol shook his head. "You saw his reaction. Whoever did this wanted to insult him." It was true that Jonis had seemed furious. But that might have been a trick.

"Don't look at me like that," I snapped. "If I want to insult Jonis, I'm perfectly willing to do so to his face."

Kirol sighed. "Whoever's behind it, we're going to be in trouble if the Arnathim riot. As it is, we don't have enough guards to keep an eye on those volunteer defenders outside."

"So the Arnathim are out of our control," I said.

"They always have been. You think any Qilarite guard is going to wade into that crowd? Or that our Arnath guards would stand up to their own people? If the Arnathim decide to fight, we won't be able to do anything but run."

"We don't want to be symbols or martyrs or whatever it is they're trying to make us into," said Loris wearily. "We were never supposed to be here."

I squeezed my signet ring. "We'll get you home, but it will take some time." Most of the ship captains had obviously had warning of the fires and cleared out, but I could use my family's connections in Pira to find another ship. My heart sank at the thought of how long it would take and how much that would cost, on top of rebuilding the docks and providing food and shelter for all the people who had been displaced by this latest round of disasters. Not to mention that we'd have to compensate the southern vizier for the loss of his ship. There hadn't been enough money before, and there certainly wasn't now. "We don't have the resources to—"

Loris lifted his eyes to my face. The defeated disappointment in them cut off my words.

"I'll find a way," I said.

And I would. I had to. Getting the Melarim home was the priority—the city wouldn't be safe, for them or anyone else, until they were gone. Our Ruling Council would fail. The treasury, depleted by disaster after disaster, would collapse, taking me and my family down with it. And more people would die.

Getting the Melarim home was more important than anything else—even a promise made to the others on the council.

It was time to send another message to Lord Romit.

"I told you not to get this wet," Nelnar chided as he cut away the last of my limp bandages in the infirmary later that day. Cool air rushed over my skin, and I knocked his hand aside to scratch the divot under my ankle bone. It felt glorious.

"You're going to need more pain medicine if you've been walking around like this," he said, frowning so deeply that the edges of his mouth practically touched his chin bone.

"I'm fine," I assured him, quite honestly. "It doesn't even hurt.

Just leave the bandages off."

"You're going to need them for at least . . ." His voice trailed off as he looked down at my ankle. The skin was puckered and clammy from the wet bandages, but it was no longer swollen, and I flexed and pointed my foot, enjoying the freedom of movement.

"See? I'm fine," I told him.

"But that's . . . it hasn't even been thirty days since you broke it." Nelnar pressed his fingers into my ankle, my lower leg, and all over my foot, watching my face as if to catch me wincing. But it didn't hurt, not at all.

Nothing like the awful floppy sensation or the gut-stabbing pain when Jonis had carried me out of the marketplace the night of the first assassination attempt.

Uneasily, I thought of Raisa's fingers tracing symbols over my bandages, calling down Sotia's blessing. I thought about how I'd been able to dispense with the walking stick so quickly, and how I'd stopped calling for Nelnar's sharma tincture only a few days after the injury.

Nelnar frowned again. "Perhaps I was mistaken. Perhaps it was only sprained."

"That must be it," I said in relief, hopping down from the bed.

Free from the bandages, I could finally soak in the bathhouse again, but I had no time to enjoy it. There wasn't enough of anything over the next few days. Not enough men to patrol Portside and the harbor, where Qilarites had erected more barricades, claiming that the "Swords of Qilara" would take the city back. Not enough food to feed the Melarim and the city residents who depended on our regular distributions. Not enough money to appease Marieke Gard, who demanded compensation for the southern vizier's lost property, or the warehouse owners who did the same. Not enough we could say to counter the renewed resentment in the city about the false charts Mati had given the raiders, now that the freed sailors had confirmed the rumors. Not enough information from the questioning of the guards and the servants and the harbormaster, though Gelti offered to use "more extreme interrogation techniques."

I wasn't sure any longer whether Jonis would object, so I didn't tell him about Gelti's offer—not that Jonis had spoken to me since discovering the green clothing anyway. He spent nearly all his time with the Melarim now, and I spent as much time as I could in the Library, looking up nervously whenever someone entered. As the next public audience wasn't scheduled for another eight days, teaching in the Library of the People seemed the best way to make myself available to receive messages. I'd sent a coded message to Horel Stit the evening of the dock fires, offering Lord Romit the salt mine and open port access in exchange for four hundred thousand Emtirian dinas.

I'd already found loopholes in the laws that I could exploit, tiny changes in the ways port policies were enforced that would allow Romit's ships in without too much fuss. If Romit continued to be discreet—and why wouldn't he, with his own profit at stake?—it would be years before anyone noticed that he hadn't paid taxes. If they ever noticed at all. Father had taught me how to create a simple, clear financial report—and also how to make one just complicated enough to keep people from asking questions.

Alshara seemed to think I was only spending time in the Library to check up on her. Though it was fascinating to see the way my sister channeled Deshti's no-nonsense attitude when assigning students, I really didn't have time to watch her. I had explained my newfound eagerness to Deshti as a need to have more guards on the rolls, and by midday two days after the fire, I had tested four men who said they were friends of Ots, the baker's son and experienced guard I had helped through the test a few days before.

Ots himself was one of the guards I took with me when I went down to the market that afternoon. Though no message from Lord Romit had arrived, I had gotten three from Loris asking me to come, and the last had threatened, in a very mild Loris sort of way, to visit the palace himself if I didn't show up soon. I couldn't put it off any longer, though I wouldn't be able to tell him about any solid plans for sending his people home until I got confirmation from Romit that he would buy the salt mine.

When I arrived at the former slave pen building, Loris led me down the hallway and past the open cells that composed the Melarim's main living space. He waited while I ordered Ots and Garvin to stay back so we would have privacy, and then he turned to me. "Did you send those green clothes, as Jonis keeps saying?" he asked without preamble.

I took a step backward, resentment burning in my chest, and ran into the bars of the nearest empty cell. I wanted to tell him that the moment Romit accepted the deal on the salt mine, I would be signing a promissory note for the first ship that could get here from Pira, no matter how much it cost. I wanted to point out that I'd have to bargain away the last of my jewelry to keep people's mouths shut and create an endless trail of false records to hide Romit's involvement.

But I couldn't say any of that.

"No," I spat. "I told you—"

"That's what I thought," said Loris, nodding. "I think Jonis knows it too. But you haven't gone out of your way to convince him of it."

"He's the one who disappeared."

Loris shook his head. "Jonis told me that your council is modeled on the Learned Ones. The thing about the Learned Ones is that, even though they live on different islands, they stay in constant communication. They have to learn to trust each other."

I let out a bitter laugh. If there was one rock-solid fact in this world, it was that Jonis ko Rikar did not trust me, and that I did not trust him.

Anger sparked in Loris's cream-tea eyes. "And how I am supposed to reassure my people that they are safe, when the two of you won't even talk to each other? When the men who murdered their friends and family have escaped from that brothel and—"

That drew me up short. "Brothel?"

"The Bleeding Oyster. The place where you were holding those monsters? One of the guards said it's a brothel."

My cheeks went hot. No wonder Kirol had been so shocked that I had known about the Bleeding Oyster. An *inn*, I had assumed.

Aunt Silya's lessons had definitely not prepared me for all I needed to know.

"You've got to talk to Jonis," Loris went on. "My people can't afford for the two of you to be at odds, and neither can yours. If you're really trying to make this work, tell him so."

For a moment, I let myself consider it. Suppose I explained the whole situation with the salt mine to Jonis, and he understood? What if he agreed that making the deal with Romit was the only way to get the Melarim home?

I tried to imagine what Jonis's support would look like, and found that I couldn't. He'd see me as a traitor, as he always did. He'd never given me credit for any motive except profit.

I'd come to understand far more about Jonis in the last Shining and Veiling than I had when I had been his terrified hostage, and one thing I knew: he was both righteous and ruthless. I couldn't tell him a thing.

All this deliberation must have shown on my face, because Loris cocked his head and said, "What troubles?"

I'd heard him use that curious island phrase before; it seemed to be an invitation to share worries, more than just asking what was wrong. Or maybe I was only reading it that way because of all the concerns weighing on my mind and my heart. I hesitated, then asked, "When you told me about your mentor, you said that people didn't always like her, but they respected her. Did people ever think she wasn't . . . good? Even if she was doing the right thing?"

Loris let out a short laugh. "Often. Every time she ruled against someone." He seemed to sense more lurking under my question, but he only said, "Calantha always said it didn't matter what people thought, that we had to keep our own feelings out of it. She was always telling me, 'It has nothing to do with you, Loris.'"

I smiled at his impression of her voice, creaky and commanding all at once. Part of me wanted to tell Loris about the deal with Romit, though I doubted he would have grasped the intricacies of the politics involved. It simply would have been a relief to confide in someone who might not judge me a traitor for what I had done.

As quickly as it rose, I recognized the impulse for what it was: weakness. If my plan to get the money was going to work, I had to see it through alone, with as few people knowing about it as possible.

Still, Loris's response laid to rest the last bit of doubt that I had done the right thing. The Melarim would go back to their islands, and we would rebuild this city. A bit of vigilance in making sure the port tax records told the story I wanted to tell would be nothing compared to the good that would come of the deal.

"We will send you and your people home," I said to Loris. "And we will keep you safe until that happens. We'll triple the guard if we have to."

Even if I couldn't tell Loris the truth about all I was doing to get the money, I wanted him to know that I was serious about sending them home. I shouldn't have promised more guards though—we didn't have the men for it. That was why I hadn't, ultimately, protested the arming of the Arnath volunteers outside the pens; if they wanted to guard the Melarim for free, then why not let them? Jonis had made no secret of his plans to arm the Melarim themselves, but since none of them except Loris had ever ventured outside the market, I doubted it made much difference.

That was when I realized: in the open cells we had passed

were old women and young, mothers and children, but not a single boy older than little Aron.

My stomach swooped. There hadn't been any boys or men around when I had come for the writing lesson either.

"What troubles?" said Jonis's voice behind me.

I turned to face him. His use of the island phrase made me grit my teeth. "Where are the men, Jonis?" His brown curls were dark with sweat, and he glanced defiantly back the way he had come, through the rear hallway that led to the courtyard that served as an outdoor kitchen. And, apparently, a training yard.

"They need to be able to defend themselves. I've made sure they can do that," said Jonis grimly.

"You knew about this?" I asked Loris.

He frowned at Jonis. "It wasn't a secret."

Jonis looked pointedly at my shoes. "I notice *you* took off your bandages."

"My ankle is better," I said shortly. "I don't need them anymore. What makes you think you can get away with—"

"Broken bones don't heal in a Shining and a Veiling," Jonis snarled. "Let me guess—you faked an injury to get rid of Mati and Raisa so you and your Scholar friends could start causing chaos." He shook his head. "You're quite the actress. I can't believe I really thought you were angry about not going—"

"Of course I wanted to go to Lilano," I shot back. "My family has investments there, and—" I bit back the rest. I couldn't draw his attention to the salt mine, not when the deal with Romit was so close to completion. "Nelnar says it was just a bad sprain. It was never broken."

"A sprain. Sure. And it's just a coincidence that all those ships got warning to clear out before the fire, and the raiders just happen to have escaped while you were putting on your little show with the buckets. Is that why you sent your lapdog to Stit? Getting his help?"

"Stit? What are you talking about?" My throat went dry. "You know why I sent Gelti and Valdis to question him. He acted suspiciously when he came on behalf of the Captain's Alliance about the docking fees."

"There was more to it. You contacted him again, the night of the dock fire."

A shiver went down my back. I couldn't let Jonis find out about the salt mine deal; he'd never understand. *It's business, nothing more*, I told myself. "I was inquiring about the use of his ship to take the Melarim home," I lied. "It turned out to be too small. I didn't tell you because I knew how unreasonable you would be about it."

Jonis laughed nastily. "I'd sooner seal the Melarim in a tomb than let Stit near them."

No matter that Jonis had plenty of reason to hate Stit; I couldn't let him look too closely at the man's doings. I had to get him off this topic. "How do I know that *you* didn't set the fire and send those green clothes, to get the Arnathim worked up against the Qilarites?"

"That's ridiculous," he said in a low, dangerous voice.

"Really. And arming all those Arnathim out there is your way of showing faith in the council, is it?"

Jonis took a threatening step toward me. "Giving people the

means to defend themselves is hardly—"

"Jonis, Soraya, stop," said Loris.

But I spoke over him, lobbing my words at Jonis. "And you've been hiding down here, making your own little army." Between the Melarim and the armed Arnathim out in the market, he could storm the palace if he wanted. Even Kirol had said as much. The Arnath guards would aid them, and then what would happen to me and the other Qilarites?

"That's ridiculous," Jonis said again, but something flashed in his eyes, some acknowledgment that he'd considered it.

Of course he had. He was the leader of the Arnath Resistance, and his own people had called him a traitor for working with Qilarites. Why wouldn't he want to prove himself to them?

"Soraya, don't," Loris tried again, but I shook his hand off my arm.

I laughed sarcastically. "For all you know, he burned the ships to keep your people here, to join his little army."

"ENOUGH," shouted Loris, stepping between us.

"You're taking her side?" Jonis's eyes flicked from Loris to me and back again.

Loris shook his head. "I'm trying to stop you both saying things you'll regret. Get my people out of here. Then tear each other apart if you must, but leave us out of it." He speared Jonis with a look until he nodded, then did the same to me.

As soon as Loris turned away, Jonis glared at me. I knew this wasn't over.

TWENTY

WHEN I RETURNED to the palace, I summoned Valdis and ordered him to keep an eye on Jonis and report to me twice a day about his movements. As I expected, he protested that he was only a taster, but I held up my signet ring and reminded him that he owed his loyalty to the Gamo family and me as its head.

I could have asked Gelti to do it, but asking for his help felt more fraught now. Better to give this task to one of my father's loyal men.

Valdis's report later that night was hardly surprising: Jonis had stayed with the Melarim all day, Adin too. The boys and men spent most of their time in a wire-roofed courtyard near the back of the building, with Jonis and other Arnathim training them. Maybe they were just learning to defend themselves, as Jonis insisted, but the thought still made me uneasy, and I knew the other Qilarites in the city would feel that way too.

I almost cried with relief when Lord Romit's response about

the salt mine finally came, slipped across a Library table to me by the harbormaster's wife, of all people, as she sobbed and begged for her husband's release. It was all I could do to wait until the guards escorted the hysterical woman out before I escaped to my study to read the note.

Romit would pay three hundred and fifty thousand dinas, and was so sure that I would accept that he had already sent the money to my family's estate. My fingers curled around the page in anger, but the overwhelming relief of getting the money made me decide to let this insult pass. Romit would send a Qilarite to oversee the mine, or take on the man already there if he was deemed acceptable; he wasn't insensible to my position. In return, he expected that all ships flying his colors would pass without trouble or tax at any Qilarite port.

It was less than I had hoped to get, but the influx of money would be near miraculous. I grabbed my budget scrolls, the tightness in my chest easing with every number I filled in.

And then I signed a promissory note to an old friend of my father's for the use of his ship, *Lila's Arrow*, and sealed it with my ring. The Melarim could go home as soon as the ship arrived from Pira. *I* had made that possible.

The next day Gelti decided I was ready to try one of the light training swords. I accepted the wooden thing and whipped it through the air, imagining a point that would rip open an attacker's flesh, as I told him of my concerns about the Melarim learning to fight.

Gelti didn't seem surprised that Jonis had set up his own little training yard. "After the ships burned, he'd be a fool not to have a backup plan to protect them," he said.

I sighed. "And whatever else Jonis is, he's not a fool."

"No." Gelti grabbed my wrist as I sliced the wooden sword through the air again. "You should know that there are rumors going around that you've been funneling money from the treasury to your family's investments."

My mouth fell open. "That's preposterous! Most of the money keeping this gods-forsaken city going was borrowed from my family in the first place."

"It's possible that he planted those rumors. If he's planning to fight you, then he'd need to discredit you first."

"No rational person will believe that I—"

Gelti shook his head. "And how many rational people do you think you'll find out there?" He took a step closer, his eyes intense. "But the Qilarites of this city will defend you, if it comes to that."

"I want to defend myself, remember?" I said lightly.

"A sword will help with that," he said with that slow grin.

He made me practice a proper stance for more than twenty minutes; as this involved his hands skimming over my shoulders, arms, hips, and knees while he made adjustments, I didn't mind. But the heated pounding of my blood couldn't distract me from a thought that had been plaguing me since my last conversation with Loris.

I lowered the sword. "When you first started working for me," I started. His mouth tightened, but I pushed on. "You said you began investigating at places like the Bleeding Oyster." My cheeks went hot. "You didn't mention that it was a brothel."

He laughed. "Half the alehouses at the docks are."

I turned away, and my voice came out thick and squeaky. "That would have been relevant information to share, before I sent Coe's men there. It's not in the budget to pay for whores."

He touched my shoulder. "What's wrong?"

Would he really make me say it out loud? "You said," I forced out, "that you started where you were already known."

"Oh," said Gelti. "*Oh.*" His tone made me feel young and stupid, and I regretted wholeheartedly that I had ever let him kiss me. It wasn't worth letting him close when that meant he could make me feel so small and foolish.

He tried to pull me around to face him, but I wouldn't budge, so he came to stand in front of me. "Look at me," he said quietly.

I did, reluctantly, but I kept my face blank.

"I would think," he said, "that you of all people would understand about business transactions."

I thrust the wooden blade point-first into the ground and took a step back. "Business," I repeated.

He smiled in a way that made it hard for me to keep glaring at him. "Why, my lady. I do believe you're jealous."

"Me? Jealous of . . . of—"

"Whores," he said flatly. He put his hands on my waist, and I both wanted to pull away and . . . didn't. "Do you think I don't hate every man who has an excuse to talk to you?" His words set off a triumphant ringing in my ears, though that might have had something to do with his lips brushing my neck. "When I heard you'd gone down to the pens to see that . . . I wanted to—"

"How do you know about that?" I asked.

"Ots told me. He seems to think you're mine." Gelti seemed

to think so, too, from the way he claimed my lips with his.

I had never expected to feel this wanted.

And Gelti was wrong. I was jealous, all right, but it wasn't anger that he'd been with those whores. I was jealous that they had been with him in a way that went far beyond these heated kisses, that he had touched them somewhere other than the maddeningly safe zones of waist, back, shoulders, and neck that he stayed in now.

What did it make me, that I wished he would cross those lines with me? I pressed myself against him until he broke off breathlessly and stroked my hair.

"I want you to know," he said, "that I would never take advantage of you."

I sighed. I knew.

His arms tightened around me. "Don't pretend with me, Soraya. I was there when you came back from the tombs."

He was talking about when the Resistance had kidnapped me. Did he think I had lied about what happened there? "They didn't touch me," I told him. "They could have hurt me, but they didn't."

"You don't have to defend them," he said quietly.

"Why on earth would I defend them?" I demanded. I broke away from him and picked up the training sword. "I told you, nothing happened."

I couldn't tell if he believed me or not, but now that I was thinking more clearly, I didn't like the way his possessive gaze warmed me when it should annoy me. So I directed us back to the lesson, and Gelti showed me sword drills, and a basic block, and said I was doing well even when it was clear to me that an opponent who wasn't thinking about kissing me would have slit my throat easily.

Still, it was gratifying that he was as distracted as I was.

He walked me back inside when we were done, which was a first; neither of us could seem to let go of the time together. A letter from Raisa was waiting in my study. I groaned when I read her news.

"What is it?" he asked, stepping around the desk.

Instinctively I pulled the letter away, though he couldn't read it, let alone decipher Raisa's code. His mouth tightened.

"The idea that the Ruling Council murdered Coe has taken hold in Lilano. People are talking openly about secession. The southern vizier isn't doing anything to stop it, and now he has announced his daughter's engagement to the highest lord in Galasi." I rubbed my forehead. The timing of the engagement couldn't be a coincidence. He wanted us, and the people of Lilano, to know that if Lilano were to secede, it would have Galasi's support. Galasi, our populous southern neighbor, was not a wealthy country, but Lilano claiming it as an ally would keep us from doing so, and bolster the southern vizier's confidence.

Gelti frowned. "What about the South Company?"

"Mati and Raisa are focusing on getting a commitment to the council from Commander Gage. Vizier Tren won't dare try anything if Gage supports us."

Gelti nodded solemnly. "Gage is an honorable type. I doubt he'd fight for Tren if he believes your council is looking out for the people."

Surely if anyone could convince Commander Gage of that, it was Mati and Raisa. I stared at the letter, and couldn't help thinking how reluctant Vizier Tren had been to support the Ruling Council in the first place, and how quickly he'd been able to turn Coe's murder and the destruction of his ship into widespread resentment of the Ruling Council and talk of secession. He was working to discredit us as surely as the Swords of Qilara were.

Or maybe the Swords of Qilara were working under Tren's orders.

"Round up any of the southern vizier's known associates and question them," I told Gelti. "Start with Marieke Gard. Then question the harbormaster again and see if you can establish a connection between Vizier Tren and the Swords of Qilara. If they're working for him, we need to figure out how, and stop them."

Gelti flexed his long fingers. "It could get messy," he warned.

I ignored the knot in my stomach and lifted my chin. "Do whatever you have to."

By the next morning, the palace dungeons were filled with shipping agents, scribes, and messengers who had known connections with the southern vizier. Kirol had brought in Marieke Gard, but she had thrown a crying fit and pleaded to speak to me directly, claiming a delicate feminine terror of our guards, particularly the Arnath ones.

This made me roll my eyes even as I remembered attempting such tactics myself when I was taken by the Resistance. Still, if Marieke wanted to see me, it must be because she had information she thought she could use to bargain for her freedom, so

I had her brought to my study.

She wore the same long, sheer veil she had worn on our previous meeting, and through it I could see that her hands were bound in front of her and that her eyes were blazing with fury. Still, she seemed to realize that haughtiness would not get her far, because she sat in the chair across from me and did not speak until invited to do so.

"You have information for me," I said.

"You're trying to connect the Swords of Qilara to the southern vizier," said Marieke in a flat tone. "That much is obvious. Your guard captain's questions were not subtle."

I folded my arms. "And?"

Marieke shook her head. "You're a fool if you think Vizier Tren would involve me in any of his schemes. If he knew that I was handling his business instead of my husband, he'd probably send his men after me himself."

"Perhaps I should write to him and let him know how ill your husband is," I said innocently.

I could practically hear Marieke's teeth grind together. "I don't know if Tren is behind these Swords of Qilara, but I have been a victim of them too. There is no need to pull me from my home and throw me into a—"

"Victim?" I frowned. "What do you mean?"

Marieke lifted her square chin. "Two evenings ago, a man approached me as I was leaving a business meeting, offering to warn me of future attacks by the Swords of Qilara in exchange for a series of payments. He threatened both my property and my life if I did not agree."

"And did you?" I asked.

Her lips pressed together under the veil. "The man had cornered me in an alley out of sight of my driver, and I had a large sum of money on my person because of the . . . business I had just conducted. I was hardly in a position to refuse him."

Her tone made me jiggle my leg under the desk. I knew exactly what sort of choking terror Marieke would have been feeling in that moment. Of course she had given him the money.

She cleared her throat. "He ran off once I paid him."

I breathed out a sigh of relief. That wasn't how I had expected the story to end. "Let me guess," I said. "You want the council to provide reparations for your stolen money."

"No need," said Marieke with a sudden smile. "I sent two of my servants after the man, posing as common street thieves, and they beat him and took it back. I told you before, if your council does not protect Scholar investments, then Scholars will find a way to do it themselves."

I frowned. "Why didn't you report this when it happened?" *If it actually happened,* I thought, *and isn't just a lie to get you free of the dungeons.* "The man who threatened you could lead us to the Swords of Qilara."

"I prefer to keep my business private," said Marieke, and from that I knew that her business that night was likely less than legal. "But I am sure that I could remember more about the man if it would help me get home sooner." She flashed me a sharp-edged smile.

"Fine," I sighed. "Give me your information, and then the guards will see you home." I inked my quill to take down her description, and nodded at her to go on.

"Qilarite, with a thick mustache and horrible little eyes," she said. "A large man, and he seemed quite offended at the very idea of a woman carrying on business, let alone in his corner of the city. I was just south of Portside. He was wearing a coat with gold trim—I remember thinking that a man who wore clothes like that ought to take better care of his teeth, because he had horrible, broken teeth. Oh, and his hair was strange—all in the middle of his head, hardly any on the sides." She nodded decisively. "Yes, if you find that man, you'll find the Swords of Qilara."

My quill slowed on the page as I stared at the symbols. Marieke was, without a doubt, describing Horel Stit.

TWENTY-ONE

AN HOUR LATER, I was waiting nervously in the front courtyard for Gelti to bring Stit in. I'd briefly considered ignoring Marieke's information; after all, arresting Stit would mean that he might reveal my dealings with Lord Romit. With rumors about me stealing from the treasury already in circulation, no one, least of all Jonis, would ever believe that I wasn't a traitor to Qilara. It might be the only excuse he needed to mobilize his Arnath followers and seize the city.

But we had to stop the Swords of Qilara, whether they were in league with the southern vizier or just terrorizing the city on their own. And if Jonis ever got wind of the fact that I had this lead and ignored it, it would absolutely confirm his belief that I was a traitor.

Gelti had been skeptical about Marieke's information, but he couldn't deny that the man she described had to be Stit. "It won't be pretty when word gets out that Stit's been arrested," he said. "You said it yourself when I questioned Stit before. Qilarites will see this as Jonis ko Rikar's bias against his former master."

"Jonis isn't involved in this," I said firmly. "I haven't even told him about the arrest. And I'm trusting you to handle it quietly."

He'd nodded and touched the back of my hand, then taken three guards with him and gone to arrest Stit.

Now, standing in the courtyard, I thought back to Stit's words at the public audience. *"The trade brought in by the Captains Alliance keeps the city going. You wouldn't want to lose its support, I'm sure."* I'd assumed that he was pressing me on behalf of Lord Romit, but perhaps he'd had his own plans. I'd never taken Jonis's suspicion of Stit seriously—how could I, when he had so many reasons to hate the man?—but it seemed, after all, that he had been right to insist that Stit was working against the council. And I was the fool who had forgotten the most important lesson my father had ever taught me: every man looks out for himself first.

I'd been watching the gate, waiting for Gelti to appear with Stit. My heart leaped when Jonis marched through it instead, trailed by Adin and two Arnath guards. When he saw me, his eyes narrowed and he marched up to me so angrily that I felt Garvin and Ots, my guards, move closer behind me.

"You arrested Marieke Gard," he said. "You're putting the blame on another Scholar to lead everyone off the scent."

I might have expected Jonis to fling accusations at me, but I hadn't thought he would know or care who Marieke Gard was. "What are you talking about? I sent you Raisa's letter. You saw what the southern vizier is—"

"Awfully convenient timing, isn't it?" Jonis interrupted. "Just when everyone is talking about you, wondering where all the money's going, another Scholar name rises up to be accused."

"No one's accusing Marieke Gard of anything," I told him coldly. "She was questioned and gave us information leading to the Swords of Qilara. If you had been here, you would know that. In fact, the man we've arrested is being brought in now." I flung out a hand and pointed to the gate, where Gelti and a guard were hauling Stit into the courtyard.

So much for arresting Stit quietly, without Jonis's knowledge.

Jonis turned, and, at the sight of Stit, he stiffened and took a step backward, treading directly on my foot. I shoved him aside, but he didn't even seem to notice; he was too busy staring.

Horel Stit did not look half so tidy as the last time I'd seen him, when he had come to the public audience. His strange hair, which had been perfectly oiled then, now hung limp over one side of his head. One eye was black and swollen, and he had several cuts and bruises on his jaw, presumably from where Marieke's servants had beaten him. His tunic was ripped, as though the guards had handled him roughly, possibly while tying his hands behind his back. He wore only one boot and limped along as his captors dragged him over the paving stones.

"Found him in his bathhouse," said Gelti when he reached me. "Full of weaponry. If he's not with the Swords of Qilara, he's supplying them."

"There's a compartment under the floor in the front room of his house," said Jonis in an odd, breathy voice. "He's probably hidden more there."

Stit had been staring at the ground until this point, but upon hearing Jonis's voice, his head shot up. His dejected manner evaporated, replaced by an aura of hatred so strong that I nearly stepped backward from the assault on my senses.

I didn't step backward though. I was a Gamo, and I stood my ground.

"It's only luck you're still alive, tialik," Stit spat.

I glanced at Jonis. His hands were clenched at his sides, and all the color had drained from his face.

"Is that a confession, Captain Stit?" I asked coldly.

Gelti glowered down at Stit. "Did you send those men after the councilor on the night he visited my home?"

Stit shot a look at Gelti that was pure venom. "There are plenty of us who know the truth about what these tialiks will do if you give them a little power."

"And did you send an assassin after Raisa ke Comun at the Festival of Lanea?" I asked.

Stit looked me up and down smugly. My heart thumped at what he might say, but I held his cold gaze. "Why'd you save her? The Swords of Qilara have tried to get rid of the tialiks for you, but you've been too stupid to take advantage of it."

Gelti yanked on Stit's arm. "Speak to the lady like that again, and my knife will find its way into your gut."

Stit gave a gurgling laugh. "The rumors are true! You've gone soft on her."

"You set the fire at the docks," said Jonis shakily. I'd never heard his voice so thin, and that made me look over at him in concern. His cheeks were two bright spots of red against the sickly pallor of his face.

"Why would we do that before the tialiks were on board, eh?" sneered Stit. "Burning's all they're good for."

Stit's voice had taken on an almost hypnotic quality. I watched in horror as Jonis seemed to shrink a few inches just hearing it.

"Shut up," growled Gelti.

But Stit only grinned that horrible, broken grin at Jonis. "You think you can protect those island tialiks down at the pens, think you're full of big ideas, but you're nothing. The only thing you were ever good for was cleaning up shit in my stable."

I waited for Jonis to fire back one of his pithy, arrogant retorts, but he was disturbingly silent.

"How dare you speak to him like that," I said to Stit. "He is your councilor." I shot a meaningful look at Jonis, urging him to remember this and pull himself together, but he didn't even seem to see it. It was almost as if Jonis wasn't quite here in the courtyard, but was instead locked in some memory.

Stit's eyes blazed. "Careful," he snarled. "Or I might tell the *councilor* about you selling your mine to Romit."

I swallowed hard, but managed to recover and roll my eyes. Gelti looked from Stit to me, puzzled, and Jonis turned to me dazedly.

"Romit? The Emtirian?" Jonis asked. "What's he talking about?"

I folded my arms impatiently. "He's obviously inventing a story to try to make you—"

"She sold her salt mine to Lord Romit of Emtiria for three hundred and fifty thousand dinas and open access to every port in Qilara. I handled the messages myself, with all the secrecy she wanted," said Stit, his eyes on Jonis.

Jonis's face twisted. "You're lying," he said, his tone fervent, like he needed to convince himself that the words were true.

Stit's face broke into a hideous smile, and I understood: though my speaking up in Jonis's defense had made Stit reveal this, his intent had nothing to do with exposing me as a traitor. He was saying this because he wanted Jonis to suffer, wanted Jonis to understand that he'd been played a fool by a Scholar.

"Of course he's lying," I snapped, as much to allay the sick expression on Jonis's face as anything else. "Gelti, get him out of here."

Stit started laughing, a horrible, cackling laugh.

Jonis pressed his fingers to his temples as if to ward off the sound. He still looked pale and shaky. "Go with them," he said to Adin.

Adin shot a concerned look at Jonis's face, but followed Stit and Gelti and the entourage of guards into the palace.

I motioned to Garvin and Ots to stay back and cautiously approached Jonis. "I'll have Gelti interrogate Stit," I said. "We'll get more names, arrest the other men involved."

"Gelti," said Jonis, raising his head. "Of course. Your little friend." He shook his head. "You always wanted to be a queen. How many times did you shout at me about it in the tombs?" He folded his arms and glared at me. "You've got the Swords of Qilara doing your bidding now. Is that why you sent messages to Stit? Or is it Emtiria you're working with? It's hard to keep track of all your intrigues."

"You think I would work with a worm like Stit?" I said haughtily. Something desperate coiled in my stomach; even if Jonis might have understood why I'd sold the mine to Romit, I doubted he would listen to anything else if I admitted that Stit had been the intermediary. But even if I had made mistakes, his accusation ripped something open inside me. I was sick of people making assumptions about me.

I glared at him. "I sank my family's fortune into rebuilding this city, and for that I get attempts on my life, and accusations? Those people out there—"

"You don't give a damn about the people out there. Quit pretending—"

"—wouldn't have roofs over their heads if it weren't for me. This"—I flung a hand at the palace—"would still be a ruin. Why would I work with the people who are destroying all of that?"

He shook his head. "All along, Dimmin's been reporting whatever you told him to."

"Why would I—"

"You think I don't know that you meet with him every day?" Jonis said with a sneer.

"Of course I do! I'm his contact on the council! You agreed to that from the beginning—"

"You sent him to Stit."

"I told you why! So people wouldn't think it was you being—"

"I'm sure it's all *business* with you two."

I took an involuntary step back from the force of his disgust. "What is this about?"

"There's more going on with Dimmin," he announced. "If

you expect me to believe that it's only about rolling around in the—"

"He's teaching me to fight."

Whatever Jonis had been expecting me to say, it obviously hadn't been that. His mouth fell open in unflattering disbelief.

"Yes. So that if, say, someone were to attack me or try to *kidnap* me again, I can fight back." I drew in a shuddering breath. Maybe if I had known how to fight on my wedding day, I could have saved Aliana.

"Really," said Jonis, his voice dripping doubt. He lifted his chin. "Prove it."

"What?"

"Show me what he's taught you. Spar with me."

I took a step back. "You've got to be joking."

His lips spread into an unpleasant grin. He clearly thought I'd been lying and this was how he'd catch me out. "Don't tell me you've never thought about coming at me with a weapon. Here's your chance."

"Fine," I said shortly. "Follow me." I led the way across the garden and into the maze with as much dignity as I could muster.

Jonis furrowed his brow when I pulled the training swords out from under the branches. I tossed him one of the wooden blades and grabbed another for myself. Indignation had carried me this far, but now I recalled that I'd had precisely one lesson with the sword, and that I'd always known that Gelti wouldn't really hurt me. I had no such assurances with Jonis.

His fingers flexed around the wooden sword, his face like stone. Whatever anger I had in me, Jonis had more—vats more, oceans more. His anger had fueled a revolution, had given him the gall to kidnap a king's bride and invade a palace.

Anger makes you weak, I told myself, *and that is something I will not allow myself to be.*

Jonis came at me. I swung my arm up, using the block that Gelti had taught me. To my astonishment, it worked.

Jonis's eyes narrowed, and he struck again. I blocked him and brought the sword around to crack against his ribs. Gelti hadn't taught me that move, but he had spent enough time harping on the vulnerability of bones close to the surface of the skin that it was easy to extrapolate.

Jonis folded sideways with an "Oooof," then straightened and lunged again. I held him off, barely and far less elegantly than I had before. He wasn't even breathing hard, though I was gasping. I'd reached the end of my sword-fighting knowledge—one could only learn so much in a single distracted lesson. I managed to block Jonis twice more before he struck my forearm hard enough to bruise. I bit back a cry and spun my mind furiously over the other things Gelti had taught me: How to break a man's grip. Which areas were most vulnerable.

How to make anything into a weapon.

And just like that, I was coldly cataloging the items in the maze again. Tree branches, my sash, the stone bench that could crack an assailant's skull.

I might not be able to defeat Jonis, but I would be damned by all the gods before I let him have an easy victory.

"Your little lapdog has definitely taught you a few things," Jonis said, circling me. I held the sword with both hands, watching him warily. "Guess he thought you'd need it for whatever you two are planning."

"It was *my* idea to learn to defend myself. I won't let anyone hurt me or my family again."

Jonis lunged, but I was ready; I swung the sword so hard that it almost knocked his from his hands. He caught it, though, cutting under my arm to jab at my knee. "As if you care about anyone but yourself," he spat.

That hurt more than the pain in my knee, and I finally saw how to turn his own weapon against him. It was his words he was tossing around like double-edged blades, slicing through the tentative cords that had bound us together on this council. We were all full of things long unsaid in the interest of keeping the peace, but apparently Jonis wasn't interested in that peace anymore.

Neither was I, I told myself.

I lifted the blade. "What would Raisa say if she saw you like this?"

His mouth tightened. "She's not here."

"No," I said, gliding sideways, making him track my movements now. "She's in Lilano. With Mati. Her husband." Jonis slashed at me, but I ducked back. "Must be awful knowing that she chose him over you, that she's never once thought of you the way you think of her."

Jonis didn't respond, which told me that I'd struck a nerve. He did, however, swing his wooden sword savagely at my side, a move I barely ducked, so I wasn't celebrating yet.

I backed away. Lest that looked too much like letting him gain ground, I said quickly, "That's a pattern, isn't it? Deshti's more interested in spending time with her former mistress than you, too."

Jonis jabbed at my shoulder, and I blocked it. "Shut up about Deshti," he growled.

"Why should I?" I taunted, dancing away from his next strike.

Physically, I was outmatched. But, I reminded myself, I had the ability to see things that he couldn't.

And the ruthlessness to use them.

I stopped abruptly, just out of his reach, and lowered my sword. "You're astonishingly dense," I told him. "Anyone with eyes can see that Deshti is jealous. That's why she hates Raisa."

Jonis still held his sword up, but he seemed to have forgotten it was there. "Deshti hates that Raisa was chosen as royal Tutor instead of her."

I gave my best condescending laugh. I'd occasionally considered saying the next words out of pity, but now they were a dagger, hurled between his eyes. "No, it's because, for some unfathomable reason, Deshti is in love with you. And you're too stupid to see it."

Jonis blinked, and I swept my sword up and knocked his aside. It skittered across the grass and I advanced on him until he backed up to the edge of the maze and lifted his hands in surrender.

I smiled triumphantly and pointed my sword at his chest. "Still think I was lying about the fighting lessons?"

His mouth twisted. "Does Dimmin know you're leading him on, using him for those lessons?"

"I'm not using anyone."

Jonis shook his head, chuckling humorlessly. "I should have

known. You're not capable of getting close enough to someone for an affair *or* a conspiracy. Soraya Gamo doesn't have partners, only underlings. It's always the wall of ice with you."

The sword shook in my hands. Jonis's opinion didn't matter. He didn't know me, I told myself, not really.

That's right, said a gentle voice in the back of my mind. *No one does, because you don't let anyone in.*

Before I had properly thought through the action, I lifted the sword and struck at his shoulder. In an instant, Jonis had grabbed my wrist and forced me around so I was the one pinned to the hedge.

"Drop it," he said tonelessly.

I tried to break his grip the way Gelti had taught me, but I couldn't get enough power with my hand clenched around the sword. Jonis watched my struggles with a thin smile. I thought of kneeing him between the legs, but he had put himself just far enough away that I would probably lose my balance if I did, and anyway, I was abruptly sick of being at odds with him.

I dropped the sword, aiming for his foot, and rotated my wrist and removed it from his grasp before he could let go. That felt like a victory, at least.

The sword had glanced off his boot, but he didn't reach for it; I wasn't sure whether this was because he didn't want to turn his back on me, or because he was as tired of this sniping as I was. How had we even gotten here?

The mistrust had been there for a good long time, but it had been Marieke Gard's arrest that had set Jonis off, and the run-in with Stit had heightened his suspicions. I stepped sideways along the hedge to get farther away from him, and asked the question

I should have asked much sooner. "Why are you so sure that Marieke Gard is innocent?"

Jonis bent and retrieved the sword. I scooted back a few more steps, but he didn't swing it; he only seemed to need something to hold. "She supported the Resistance," he said at last. "One of our best weapon suppliers."

I stared at him. "You worked with a Qilarite," I said doubtfully.

Jonis's jaw tightened. "We had ways to keep an eye on her. Spies in every household."

That was probably why my father had been so adamant about not keeping household slaves at our estate; it hadn't been just the fact that having so many paid Qilarite servants was a show of wealth, as I'd long assumed.

I frowned. "Marieke hates the Arnathim."

He shrugged. "Or pretends to. She didn't mind our money."

"Then she'd sell you out to the highest bidder. Maybe she's working for someone else now, someone who's giving her more incentive."

A nasty smile flashed across Jonis's lips.

"I see. I thought you were above blackmail." I clucked my tongue. "What would Raisa say?"

He gave a satisfying twitch at that, though he tried to hide it.

"Marieke might be working both sides, you know," I mused. "She's the type."

"Takes one to know one, does it?"

I drew myself up. "I'm sick of your accusations. I've done everything I could to stop the Swords of Qilara. And I'm doing everything I can to get the Melarim home."

You have no idea the risks I've taken to get them home, I wanted to say.

"Then what was all that about selling your salt mine to Romit?"

I put my hands on my hips. "If I were to sell my salt mine, it would be my family's private business."

Jonis frowned. "But now that Romit is on the Emtirian imperial cabinet, I'm sure they would have found a way to use it against us."

I stared at him. "When . . . when did that happen?"

Jonis shrugged. "A few days ago. Don't know what Romit did, but whatever it was, the emperor rewarded him well. Made him Minister of Ships."

"Minister of . . ." My voice trailed off as I sank onto the nearest bench; my legs were suddenly shaking too much to support me.

"What is it?" The suspicion was back in full force in Jonis's tone, and I looked up at him slowly. Whatever he saw in my face made him take a step backward and swear.

My hand seemed to burn where I'd held the quill to sign off on the ship. There was no help for it now; I'd have to tell him what I'd done, but I had to frame it in a way he would understand. "We needed the money," I said hollowly. "Romit was the only one who could deliver enough—"

"The money," Jonis repeated. "You did sell the mine."

"Jonis," I began in my most reasonable tone. "I didn't have a choice—"

"You allied with Emtiria," he accused, staring at me. "For the money. With *Stit* as your intermediary."

"I conducted a *business transaction*. Why would I ally with Emtiria?" I exploded, jumping to my feet. "What would I possibly have to gain?"

"Why wouldn't you?" He shook his head, disgust etched on his features. "You wouldn't help someone else unless they held a knife to your throat and forced you to."

I hadn't even told him the worst part yet. "We needed the money," I said again. "More than ever. And . . . Romit demanded duty-free access to our ports for ships flying his colors."

"When were you planning to tell me about this?"

I ignored his question. "If Romit is the Minister of Ships, that means that he commands the entire Emtirian fleet." Commerce and military alike—for the profit-hungry Emtirians, they were largely the same thing.

"And you gave his ships free rein at our ports," said Jonis coldly. "And a stronghold in the Haran Desert. And somehow I'm supposed to believe that you're not a traitor like your father?"

"It was the only way to get the Melarim home. We're running out of options."

"Call off the deal."

"And give Emtiria a reason to attack? That's what they'll do." I pressed my fingers to my temples. "That's probably what Emperor Adelrik planned from the start. Nothing incites a holy war in Emtiria faster than breaching a trade agreement."

Jonis fixed me with a cold look. "Then I guess everyone is about to find out where Soraya Gamo's loyalties have been all along."

I went straight to my study and laid out all my papers relating to the Emtirian deal, determined to go over every line and find some loophole we could exploit. Jonis posted Adin outside my door to keep an eye on me; with so much to do, I didn't waste time arguing with them. I'd also sent down to the Library for every record we had relating to Emtirian law and past trade agreements. I had to write to Romit and the emperor today, but first I had to come up with a position strong enough to keep them from taking advantage of the ports and the salt mine. There was no hope of getting the mine back, not if we wanted to get the Melarim home, but maybe I could convince the emperor that keeping Qilara as an ally was more advantageous than conquering us.

I tried to stay calm, running a dry quill under every line to keep myself focused, but I kept seeing Jonis's disgusted sneer, hearing his threat to expose me as a traitor. I hadn't forgotten my suspicions; if he wanted to spark Arnath anger into fighting, then announcing that I had sold Qilara out to Emtiria would make excellent kindling. I wouldn't give him the chance.

My throat was dry, my lips bitten raw by the time Deshti came up an hour later, bearing a satchel full of scrolls and a tray of tea and rolls.

"Alshara said you missed breakfast," she said.

I had, she was right, but my stomach had been too tied up in knots to realize it. I ignored the tray and seized the satchel, pulling out scrolls and sorting them by date. Emtirians were notoriously litigious; even if I could find some ancient precedent it would be better than nothing.

"You look terrible. Have some tea." Deshti shoved a cup across the desk.

My fingers were cold, so the cup felt good in my hands, and my dry throat welcomed the hot liquid. "Thanks. Is . . . is Jonis still here?"

Her mouth was a thin line. "He went to talk to Loris."

I closed my eyes briefly. Jonis had probably told Loris exactly what I'd done. I'd been stupid to think Loris might understand; he probably didn't trust me any more than Jonis did.

I had to gulp down another mouthful of tea to keep from crying. This wasn't how I had meant for anything to work out. "Did he ask you to watch me too?" I said, trying to keep my tone flip.

Deshti didn't answer, only looked down at her lap. I flushed, remembering how I had used her feelings for Jonis as a weapon. That hadn't been fair to her. My head swirled with all the mistakes I had made, all the ways I had hurt people. "Deshti," I said, "I'm sorry, but I . . . told Jonis how you feel about him."

Deshti rose. "That's all right." She tugged the teacup out of my hands, and I realized that the fingers holding it had grown numb. *Drugged*, I thought hazily.

Her voice seemed to come from far away when she spoke again. "Jonis already knew that I would do anything for him. A lot of us would. You should have thought about that sooner."

Deshti's face slid in and out of focus as I slumped back into darkness.

TWENTY-TWO

SOMETHING LARGE WAS trying to batter its way out of my skull. Even with my eyes closed, everything spun dizzily. I gulped in a breath, and was relieved when I didn't actually vomit, as the gag over my mouth would have made that especially disgusting.

But then, my stomach felt hollow, my mouth dry. A voice in my mind informed me crisply that I hadn't eaten or drunk anything recently except for a few gulps of tea in my study. I pictured it as an efficient valet appearing at the elbow of a hungover monarch, and then laughed at the image, which made my head pound harder.

Focus. I had to focus. The last thing I remembered was sitting at my desk, drinking the tea Deshti had brought. The tea I had, for once, not called Valdis to taste before drinking. I'd let my guard down. My fingers clenched, making me aware of the ropes binding my wrists.

"I would do anything for him," Deshti had said. *"A lot of us would."*

Jonis had kidnapped me. Again.

Not the time, I told myself coldly. I would deal with Jonis later. Now I had to figure out where I was, and how to get away.

And the first step was opening my eyes.

This took a ridiculously long time; light stabbed my brain whenever I opened them a sliver. Finally, I managed to force my eyes open all the way, only to discover that I lay on the floor of a closed carriage. The dizziness turned out to be only partly in my head; the carriage was also in motion. I hadn't noticed this immediately because, though the floor jolted under me, my head had been cushioned with a pillow. I was alone, which meant that either Jonis hadn't wanted anyone but the carriage driver to know where I was being taken, or that he had counted on the drugged tea keeping me unconscious the whole way. Possibly both.

Step two, the brisk little valet in my mind said, *assess your injuries.* The throbbing head must have been from whatever Deshti had put in the tea to knock me out. I also had a tender spot on my right forearm where Jonis had smacked me with the wooden sword. The inevitable bruise had yet to form, which meant that I couldn't have been unconscious for more than a few hours. My left kneecap protested when I moved it, and my ankle twinged, but only my hands were tied. That was something, at least.

Step three: figure out what to do. I didn't know where this carriage was going, but that didn't matter. I would be exiting it as soon as possible.

I pushed myself up, and had to close my eyes as the plush seats spun around me, and my insides swooped. I desperately wanted to shun the comfort of the pillow, but within seconds I had fallen back against it, curling into a ball on my side, my bound hands pressed against the gag at my mouth.

Jonis was probably moving his people into place even now, getting rid of anyone who would contradict the story he wanted to tell, that Soraya Gamo had betrayed Qilara, just like her father. With a wave of nausea, I thought of Alshara, still in the palace. He would hurt her too, use her to control me.

How had I ever, ever thought he would do anything but this when given the excuse?

"Sotia won't let us fail," Raisa had said, so serenely, before she had gone south. I laughed bitterly, surprised when it came out as a sob. I'd let her belief in the possibility of peace and friendship and all that nonsense affect me.

This would be a good time for praying, wouldn't it? But all I could come up with was, *Thanks for nothing, oh honored Sotia.*

Enough. I had to get out of here. I forced my eyes open again. Since I'd rolled onto my side, I was staring at the bottom of the seat, where a loose wooden slat clacked against the other boards with every bump of the carriage—falling apart like everything else in this administration. The slat was separated from the seat enough that I could see the silhouette of the nail that had come loose.

A nail that might be sharp enough to cut rope.

I scooted forward and maneuvered my bound hands under the seat. It took several minutes to pull the slat free, and I got a finger full of splinters in the process, but soon I was balancing the slat between my knees and rubbing the rope against the nail. It cut agonizingly slowly, strand by strand. The carriage jolted, jabbing the nail into my left palm, but I kept going even as blood trickled over the rope.

Once the outermost rope had been cut, the many loops revealed themselves to be all one piece that slipped off easily. I tore the gag from my mouth and used it to wrap my bleeding hand, then hauled myself up onto the seat to peek out the window.

The carriage was on the main road, heading out of the City of Kings. The Valley of Tombs loomed up to the south, and I knew with sickening certainty that this was where Jonis intended to put me. He'd imprison me in a dark tomb as he had before. I'd been wrong when I'd thought he had no idea how much my kidnapping had affected me; he knew, and would do it again.

My throat constricted. There was no time to plan a clever escape; I had to get out of this carriage, right now, before it got any closer to those tombs. When the driver slowed in the traffic near the Aqorin Bridge, I pushed open the door and slipped out.

Landing wrong on my ankle, I toppled down the weed-choked slope at the side of the road. I rolled under a bush at the bottom, ignoring the thorns scraping my arm, praying that the driver hadn't heard the carriage door slam shut behind me, praying even harder that no one had seen me fall. The biggest danger right now wasn't from the driver; he could be bribed, though this one was probably loyal to Jonis, and that could be a problem. But if other well-meaning citizens rushed to my aid, it would quickly get back to Jonis where I was, and I doubted I would escape a second time. I knew now what he was capable of.

A concerned face peered over the edge of the road, but the man must not have seen me in the branches where I hid, because when someone behind him called to him, he shrugged and disappeared. The carriage continued along the road and the carts behind it followed. I eased away from the thorns and watched the roof of the carriage disappear across the Aqorin Bridge, bypassing the turnoff to the Valley of Tombs.

Jonis must have planned to imprison me somewhere else, then. Or dump my body somewhere. The surge of relief in my chest meant nothing; Jonis had still declared himself my enemy with this act, and Gamos did not allow their enemies to succeed.

I crawled out of the ditch, rubbing my scratched arm and brushing debris from my dress. The sun was beating down, so I ripped a loose thread from my hem and tied my hair into a knot to keep it off my neck. My head throbbed with every step I took, but I couldn't stay here. From my most recent survey of the city fountains, I knew there was a working one nearby. I needed water, and eventually food, though I was still so nauseated that food could wait. I needed to get a message to Valdis and get Alshara out of the palace.

What I needed, more than anything, was a reliable investigator. Fortunately, I knew exactly where to find one.

I waited for the last chime of midnight bells to fade before I approached Gelti's house. I knew exactly which beachfront estate in the Watch had been fixed up for him and his mother, but I'd waited out the day in the shadows of an outbuilding next door, running over plans for which Scholar families could be counted on as allies, and how I might quietly spread the word among the Qilarites of the city about Jonis's treachery.

What I had observed since leaving the carriage was a city going about an ordinary day. If Jonis knew about my escape, he would expect me to go to Gelti, which was why I'd watched the house. But the only people I had seen were Gelti and two other men, one of whom I recognized as Ots from his bulky frame. They had come up the path at twilight and entered the house, and the two men had left half an hour ago. Now the house was still and silent, the only sound the crash of the waves on the shore.

Jonis must not know yet that I was free. I had to take advantage of his ignorance while I could.

Gyotia's Lamp, two days from its full shining, had been bright in the sky earlier, but it crouched behind murky clouds as I crept out onto the beach. The west-facing walls of these ocean-front homes were all on wheels, so they could be opened to the spectacular view. I guessed that Gelti, so long accustomed to the closed-in spaces of the Web, would spend his time there looking out at the sea.

Sure enough, he lounged in a chair just outside the open wall, his legs stretched out and a glass in one hand. My throat caught with relief at the sight of him, a confident silhouette against the dim light of the single lamp burning in the house.

That tiny sound captured his attention. Before I'd even seen him move, he was behind me, my arm twisted back and his blade at my neck, just like in our lessons.

"What do you want?" he growled, and then he froze. "Soraya? What are you doing here?" He let go of me and slipped the dagger back into his boot before taking both my hands in his. "Gods, you're freezing. What's going on? What happened to your hand?"

I desperately wanted to say something pithy, and had considered several possibilities as I'd waited in the shadows throughout the day. But now all that came out was, "I need you to send some messages for me." My throat caught at the end, and the last few words were faint and teary.

His eyes widened, and he pulled me inside. I collapsed onto a padded bench as he wrapped a blanket around my shoulders. The story spilled out of me—the deal with Romit, sparring in the maze, waking up in the carriage, making my way here. At some point, he pressed his glass into my hand, and I drank the contents, not even caring how they burned my throat going down. The bare walls and sparse furniture took on keener edges, and my head finally stopped throbbing.

Gelti shook his head. "I will kill him for doing this to you."

"I don't need you to avenge me. I want you to help me get Alshara out of the palace, and then Jonis needs to be dealt with. *Not* killed. I need him held somewhere away from his followers. He's the hostage to keep the Arnathim from fighting." We were headed toward exactly what the Ruling Council had been trying to avoid: open conflict between Qilarites and Arnathim. And the Melarim would be caught in the middle, just as Loris had feared.

No, more likely, Jonis had already recruited the Melarim to his side. He must have been preparing this for a long time. Whenever he'd been off in the city, he'd probably been bolstering support for his Arnath militia, or checking on caches of weapons from his Resistance days.

"But in case that doesn't work," I added heavily, "I need to get a message to my mother in Pira. She'll send enough men to restore order."

"That'll take days. You don't have to wait that long."

"What are you talking about?"

Gelti's lips brushed my temple. "He's already got his little army, hasn't he? You'll need one of your own. The Qilarites of this city will follow you. All you have to do is say the word."

"How am I supposed to reach them, though?"

Gelti smiled. "If only you knew someone who had connections in the Web. You leave that to me."

Jonis started this, I reminded myself. All I was doing was finishing it. I couldn't let him drag Qilara into chaos again.

"I still need to contact my mother," I said, "but . . . I'll meet with your friends tomorrow morning. I'll invite a few of my father's old friends as well. And I want you to take a message to Valdis. I'll write notes for the Scholars. They need to know that Jonis is a threat."

Gelti stroked my hand thoughtfully. "One thing I don't understand. Why didn't he kill you when he had the chance? That was sloppy."

"Because then he couldn't make it seem legitimate," I said bitterly. "He's probably been waiting for an opportunity to get rid of me. If I betrayed the council, proved myself to be the Gamo traitor everyone expected me to be, then no one could say he hadn't tried, right? Not even Raisa."

I couldn't help looking at the line of plants inartistically arranged against the wall, with the pot I had given Nasha in the center, one perfect blue blossom atop the stem. Raisa had been right—the maschari was a beautiful color. She'd given it to me as a token of her belief in me, but surely she and Mati would side with Jonis once they found out about my deal with Romit and the fact that it had been brokered through Stit. It was always the three of them against me.

I was on my own now.

Gelti took my hand, reminding me that this wasn't entirely true. "You can stay here tonight. I'll find someone to watch the house."

"Gelti . . . if Jonis wants to make me look like a traitor, he'll send Kirol after me."

Gelti smiled grimly. "I can handle Kirol."

"I hate to put you in the middle of this," I said, but Gelti didn't seem bothered at all. He jumped up, rolled the wall shut, and locked it, and when he returned to the bench, his knuckles grazed my cheek. There was no pity or judgement in his eyes, nothing but a steady warmth that told me he was completely on my side. The intensity of it stole my breath. When he looked at me, I felt stripped of artifice.

I felt *seen*.

I turned my head away, shivering.

He pulled the blanket tighter around me. "Still cold?" he asked.

I shook my head, but I *was* cold—cold, and hot, and unsure of anything. I couldn't think properly when he looked at me like that.

Nausea swept through me, reminding me that all I'd eaten

today was the unattended half loaf of bread I'd swiped from a table outside one of the beach houses, and I told him I needed food.

I peeked into the rooms on either side as we went down the central hallway to the pantry. The simple furniture was decidedly out of place in the vast spaces of this former Scholar's home, which was easily five times larger than his tiny house in the Web.

He came up with a tin of biscuits, a hunk of cheese, and some dried meat, all of which transformed my nausea into ravenous hunger, and I embarrassed myself with the ferocity with which I fell upon them. Gelti only chuckled, though, and tugged my left hand into his lap to unwrap my makeshift bandage. While I ate, he cleaned the wound and worked the splinters out. Then he dabbed on some ointment before wrapping a strip of linen around my hand.

He returned the ointment to the pantry shelf and ran his hand over the other pots there. "Do you want something for the pain? It'll help you sleep."

I glanced at the shelf. There was a jar with a picture of a round-topped silphium plant scratched into it, beside another bearing a picture of a plant I recognized as sharma. Many people used silphium for headaches and such, but I had been warned all my life about how it had ruined my mother's ability to bear sons. And sharma might dull the pain, but it would also leave me heavy and sleepy, and I needed to keep my wits about me.

"No," I said. "I'm fine."

I wrote my letters after that. They were just notes, really; the Dimmins did not keep ink or paper on hand, so I had to use a piece of charred wood to write on the greasy cheese wrappings, but they would have to do.

Then Gelti led me down the hall. Snores emanated from one closed door, which must have been his mother's room. He opened the door to another room and stepped inside. The lamplight fell onto the simple bed and table, the chest strewn with men's tunics. I stopped in the doorway. It was, without a doubt, Gelti's bedroom.

"Get some sleep," said Gelti. "I'll have some friends guard the house while I send your letters and make arrangements for a meeting tomorrow morning. You'll be safe here."

I had flashed through several reactions in the past few moments: shock, that Gelti had brought me to his bedroom; anger, that he would try to take advantage of me in my current situation; embarrassment, that I had assumed he would stay; relief, that he was, after all, what I had thought him to be.

"You don't have to give up your room for me," I protested. "I can sleep in one of the others." Gods knew this house had plenty.

Gelti looked away. "We don't have any other beds."

My eyes welled up. I'd done it again, hadn't I? I'd bribed Gelti with this enormous house, never once considering that he wouldn't be able to furnish it.

"What is it?" he asked in alarm.

I shook my head. I couldn't even do the right thing for the people I cared about, like Gelti. How was I going to fix any of this? "I've made a mess of everything."

"Hush, now. You've done a fine job. Qilara needs you." Hesitantly he touched my cheek. "And so do I. I'll be back in a few hours. Try to get some rest."

After he left, I stared at the lamp for a long time, thinking through plans. I couldn't do anything until I got more information about what Jonis was up to, until I knew which Scholars and merchants would support me, but the planning was soothing, like filling in numbers on my budget scrolls. The act of going over them calmed my racing heart until finally, I fell asleep.

TWENTY-THREE

WHEN I WOKE, the windows were still dark. I couldn't have been asleep for more than a few hours. There was no disorientation; my head was clear, if achy, and I knew exactly where I was. I'd fallen asleep with a host of half-formed plans in my mind—Scholars I could bribe or blackmail for their support, family friends I could ask to send men. But now my brain was quiet, and my senses were alive.

A blanket that smelled like Gelti was over me, and a bandage that Gelti had wrapped encircled my sore hand. In the wavering light of the oil lamp, the pattern of ferns on the walls was a night forest, shielding me from enemies, and the minimal furnishings made the room not so much bare as intimate. Nasha Dimmin's snores still rumbled down the hall—maybe that was what had awoken me.

Gelti had done so much for me tonight, even after the way I had manipulated him into working for the council. And we had made Jonis's suspicions true—Gelti *was* conspiring with me now to take back the capital city.

Gelti trusts you, whispered a voice in my mind. But how could I let myself trust him?

I'd gone to him in desperation, but was I brave enough to really let him close, after the humiliations I had suffered with Mati? Should I even be thinking about that, with everything else going on right now?

But somehow, with his blanket over me and his bed under me, it was *all* I could think about.

A shuffling on the other side of the door made me sit straight up. I pushed the blanket off me and stood, so slowly that the ropes under the mattress barely creaked. The sound came from outside again, faint but distinct. I inched toward the door, frantically scanning the room for something to use as a weapon. Heart pounding, I untied my sash and held it ready as I eased the door open a crack.

Gelti lay on a mat across the doorway. "Did I frighten you? I was trying to be quiet—"

"What are you doing?" I asked, relief sharpening my tone. I hid my sash behind my back, feeling silly.

Gelti's lips twitched, which told me he'd seen it. "Guarding you. I've got watchers outside, but no sense taking chances. Valdis is taking your sister to a safe place near the market. The meeting is set for midmorning bells in one of the warehouses in Portside."

"And who will be there?" I asked.

"All three of the Scholars you wrote to, and Ren Tatch and a few others from the Captains Alliance."

I frowned. "Most of the Captains Alliance got their ships out of port before it burned. How do we know they weren't behind the fires? Or working with the Swords of Qilara?"

"We don't," he said somberly. "But you need men, and they'll fight for you if you ask them to."

I blew out a breath. It couldn't hurt to meet with them. Hopefully I wouldn't need them to fight at all; once I held Jonis and my mother sent men from Pira, I could keep the city under control. Gelti's friends would be the fail-safe, in case I had overestimated Jonis's importance to the Arnathim.

I looked up at Gelti, suddenly shy when I thought of all he had done for me tonight. "Thank you," I said. "For everything."

He ducked his head with a little shrug, then pulled himself to his feet and held a scroll out to me. "I was going to save this until you were ready for arrows, but . . . I don't know, now seems a good time to give it to you."

The brush of his fingers as I took the scroll was a jolt. It was the room, I told myself. The room, and the lamplight, and the realization that I was in the company of a man who both frightened me and made me feel safer than I ever had.

With shaking fingers, I unrolled the scroll and walked over to the lamp to read it.

Unbent and wary, she stands tall,

Arrows keen as eyes that see all.

It was a piece of a lay about Lila, goddess of war. I looked up at him questioningly.

"I wanted to write something for you," Gelti said quietly. "Those lines have always reminded me of you, ever since you played Lila in the pantomime."

A pleased flush warmed my face. "That was over two years ago."

"You made an impression."

I'd been trying to make an impression on Mati during that pantomime. But to think that Gelti had noticed, even then, that he had gone to the effort to write this for me despite his trepidation about writing . . .

I cleared my throat. "I haven't taught you all these symbols yet."

Gelti smiled. "Your sister helped."

I let out a short laugh. "I'll never hear the end of her teasing now."

He brushed his palms down my arms. "Do you really mind that?"

"No, it's more a matter of what she'll write to my mother." Too late, I realized how this would sound to him. "I only mean—my mother has a lot of opinions about—but after all this, I'm sure—"

"I understand," he said, stepping back. "She would be horrified to learn that a merchant-born is in love with you."

Heat flooded my whole body. He didn't seem to notice the momentousness of this occasion, so I tried to look as though handsome men routinely declared their love for me in dark bedrooms.

Gelti laughed bitterly. "If your father could see us now, he'd probably kill me where I stand."

I touched his arm. "Did I say that I care what my parents would think?"

That earned me a small smile. "You always had your own plans, didn't you? You never let anyone behind that wall."

His words reminded me uncomfortably of what Jonis had said: *"It's always the wall of ice with you."* But that wall seemed to be melting away, with Gelti's warm gaze on me in the pool of lamplight and the proof of his affection in his words, in his actions, on the paper in my hand.

If there was a wall around me, it was of my own making. And it could be of my own breaking, too. I would not let fear control me. I was sick of being adrift and alone, imprisoned by other people's ideas of who I was and what I could be.

And I was sick of waiting to know more of the world.

In the space of a heartbeat, I ran through the practical considerations. Nasha's snores were comfortingly constant. I knew where the silphium was in the pantry, and as long as I took it within a day, there would be nothing to worry about.

And more than anything, outweighing any other concern, I *wanted* this.

I laid the paper on the table and laced my fingers through Gelti's dark hair, pulling him down to me. His kiss was gentle; mine was not. Having made my decision, I chafed at the way he traced his fingers down my back and feathered his lips over my face. I grasped his shoulders and pressed myself against him, hoping he would get the message.

He pulled away, breathing hard. "I should go."

I grinned. "No, you shouldn't."

"You don't understand." He shook his head. "I don't want to take advantage of you. If I don't leave—"

"And what about what I want?" My heart stuttered. It hadn't occurred to me that he might reject my advances.

Gelti's look of shock was satisfying, only because it was accompanied by one of hope, and the proof, where our bodies pressed against one another, that he wanted this too.

Gelti glanced at the hallway. "My mother is three rooms away."

"And sleeping soundly," I countered. I was fairly certain this was token resistance; Gelti's body seemed quite certain what it wanted, and he had made no effort to put space between us. In fact, his hand hadn't stopped caressing my hip for the past few minutes.

He let go of me, but only to shut the door, and then he was back. The fabric of my gown slid down my shoulder as his lips went exploring. I sank down onto the bed, and he came with me, and soon the clothes slipped off and there was nothing between us at all.

It was not all soft kisses and romantic sighs, gentle caresses and slow murmurs building to shuddering cries of ecstasy. Gelti warned me that it might hurt the first time, and that it would be best to get the pain over quickly. And he was right.

It hurt less after that. He suggested different ways for me to hold my body that would not only minimize the pain, but feel pleasurable. I laughed and said to him, over my shoulder, "You're my teacher again, are you?"

He ran his fingers down my back, moving his hips in a way that turned my laughter into a gasp. "These lessons are *much* less frustrating," he replied.

I didn't have the breath for banter after that; I simply gave myself over to the pleasures of being wrapped up with him, and the even more illicit thrill of falling, exhausted, into Gelti's arms when it was over and letting myself sleep nestled against him.

I woke at sunrise bells to the murky light of morning. The lamp had gone out, but I felt so safe in the arms that encircled me that this didn't bring the usual hitch to my chest.

Gods, what have I done? was my first thought, followed by, *Exactly what I wanted to, for once.*

I marveled at how utterly unchanged I felt. Wasn't this experience supposed to awaken me as a woman, to open up vast new plains of knowledge to me? I felt the same as before, except somewhat itchy and in need of a bath.

Carefully I disentangled my arm from Gelti's body. He stirred and lifted his head. "Good morning," he murmured with a smile. His hair was tousled and his eyes heavy with sleep.

"Good morning." I sat up and raked my fingers through my hair. "We should get up before your mother—"

Gelti pulled me into a kiss that, despite the initially unpleasant tang of morning stickiness, sorely tested my resolve to get up. "Soraya," he murmured. "When I said I was in love with you, I meant it."

I swallowed, my heart pattering. "I know that," I said faintly. Did he expect me to say that I was in love with him too? *Was* I in love with him? Was that what this was, this overpowering want I felt each time he was near?

Despite the choice I had made last night, I balked at the idea of saying those words. That was too much, too far past the wall.

But Gelti, it seemed, was already leagues past that wall, and I hadn't noticed.

"Marry me," he said.

I smiled. "You're joking." He had to be—he couldn't possibly expect me to make such a choice right now, when I had to secure the city against Jonis. His face fell, and I pulled back, his hands sliding off my arms. "I can't—that is, I—"

His jaw clenched. "You can't marry beneath you. Guess you care what your parents think after all." He tossed a resentful look at my ring.

"No," I said sharply. "I don't intend to marry anyone. Not now. Maybe not ever." As I heard myself say this aloud, I recognized that it had been simmering in me ever since my disastrous, aborted wedding day. I had narrowly escaped shackling myself to Mati—why would I risk a similar fate with any man, no matter how rakish his smile or how inviting his caresses?

Abruptly I rose and pulled on my clothes. Gelti watched me, his expression wounded, and the fact that he was still only partially covered by the thin blanket when I sat back down on the bed seemed indecently vulnerable.

I laid my palm on his cheek. "It's nothing to do with you. You've only ever been kind to me." *Kind* was an understatement; he'd unhesitatingly thrown his lot in with mine. But that didn't mean I owed him this.

"Is that why you invited me in last night?" His fingers stroked down from my throat to the neckline of my dress, then slipped under the fabric. "Because I'm so kind?"

My eyes fluttered shut of their own accord, but I wrapped my fingers around his wrist and lifted his hand to my lips. "I can't marry you," I told him as I kissed his fingers. "Please don't be offended."

He pulled away and rolled off the bed, barking a laugh. "I see. I'm fine for a tumble or two—"

Or five, I thought, and struggled not to let my lips quirk.

"—but not enough of an equal to be considered as your husband," he finished, yanking a tunic over his head. "Well, it's nice to finally know where I stand with you, *my lady*."

I sighed. "Gelti, it's not—"

He shrugged violently as he turned away and pulled on the rest of his clothes, and I fell silent, ridiculously embarrassed at the intimacy of watching him dress. Or maybe it was the things he had said, the deeper feelings he had revealed.

And, worse, I understood his anger. I had worried about opening myself up to him, but he had made himself vulnerable to me in a way I had never expected. I didn't know how to make him understand that my refusal had nothing to do with him.

I crossed the room and touched his arm. "Please don't be like this. I . . . I need you on my side."

His shoulders sagged. "I am on your side."

I let tears well in my eyes, let emotion put a catch in my voice. "I don't know what I'd do without you. You've been there for me when I couldn't trust anyone else. But I can't consider marrying anyone right now. Please try to understand."

Was I manipulating him? Maybe. Did it count as manipulation if the things I was saying were entirely true?

But I knew with desperate certainty that I didn't want to lose whatever this was with Gelti, even if I hadn't been relying on him to help me fight Jonis.

I just didn't want to lose control of it either.

Gelti put his arms around me and I laid my head on his shoulder. "I understand," he said, but the words had a resentful undercurrent. I wondered if any man could really understand a woman's desire for independence, the constant struggle between being what the world told you to be and being what you wanted to be.

I kissed his neck. "I'm glad to hear it, because if not, it would make this morning's meeting rather awkward," I teased.

He shot me a look that said he knew what I was doing. He'd probably noticed that my eyes were now dry too. But he played along. "I've got something for you to wear," he said, arms still around me. I looked at him questioningly, and he shrugged. "I know people. Do you want breakfast?"

I hesitated. "What about your mother?"

"Mother won't be awake for hours yet. She sleeps in now that she doesn't have to see to the animals."

I went off to the bathhouse to wash away the evidence of last night's activities in the cold water. When I unwrapped the bundle of clothes Gelti had given me, I found a blue dress that looked so much like the one I had worn to the Festival of Aqil banquet before my wedding that I wondered if Gelti had raided my own closet. But then I saw that the stitching was shoddy, the fabric thin and cheap, and knew that it was one of the reproductions of my gowns that had been popular among the lower classes when I had been the king's betrothed. My former maid had made a small fortune selling information about my gowns to city dressmakers.

I slipped the dress on, along with the matching slippers, and went back inside, where Gelti waited with a breakfast of eggs and hard biscuits. His eyes ran down my body in a way that suggested he was remembering everything under the dress, but all he said was, "It fits."

I nodded. "Will you button up the back?"

He did, and it shouldn't have felt as intimate as it did, considering all we had done last night, but my spine shivered every time his fingers brushed my skin.

When he was done, I ran my fingers through my tangled mess of hair. "I need hairpins. I want to put my hair up, so as not to advertise what I've been doing all night," I said, aiming a coy smile at him.

Oh, he liked that. He grinned and wrapped a tendril of my hair around his finger. "Let me see what Mother has." He tugged on my hair before he let it go and disappeared down the hall.

As soon as he was out of sight, I slipped into the pantry and grabbed the silphium jar. I'd heard that the taste was best dealt with in a tincture, but consuming three of the rotten-tasting dried leaves would be just as effective in preventing unwanted consequences from last night. Though my mother had never let us take silphium, I'd listened when the servants gossiped.

The jar, however, was completely empty.

I was staring, horrified, into its hollow depths when Gelti returned.

"Why didn't you tell me there was no silphium?" I demanded.

He furrowed his brow. "You didn't ask."

I slammed the lid on the pot and shoved it back onto the shelf. "How am I supposed to—"

"I did propose to you," Gelti pointed out, smirking. "Want to change your answer?"

"This isn't something to joke about," I said, though I'd heard the hard edge of his tone; he hadn't gotten over that rejection yet, and would probably smart about it for a good long time.

"Relax. After the meeting, I'll get some. You've got thirty-six hours or something, don't you?"

"Twenty-four," I muttered. One would think that a man of his *experience* would know that.

"Plenty of time," he said. "I got you hairpins."

I took them and went back into the main room to use the spotted mirror. When I was done with my hair, the sides and back looked fine, but the top was a mess of pins. My silver comb would have been perfect to hide them, but it was on my dressing table at the palace.

My eyes fell on the plants along the wall. The blue of Raisa's maschari flower was just a few shades paler than my dress. The stem was thin enough to break easily, so I tucked it into my hair, but my fingers faltered as I remembered what she'd said after giving it to me. *"Don't murder Jonis. Even if you have a really tempting opportunity."*

The flower was poisonous. If it came down to it, I would use whatever weapons I had to against him.

I didn't need my reflection in the cracked mirror to tell me that, in the slapdash hairstyle and knockoff dress, I was nothing more than an imitation of the Soraya Gamo who should have been queen.

Over breakfast, I questioned Gelti about the men from the Captains Alliance he had invited to the meeting. I still didn't like the idea of involving them, but he assured me that few of them had any love for Horel Stit.

"When you questioned Stit, did you find out anything else we can use?" I asked.

"He gave up a whole list of names," said Gelti. "But it seems to me those are exactly the men you want on your side. They want to make you a queen, after all."

Something in his tone made me put down the hard biscuit I'd been gnawing on and frown. When he and Valdis had said this before, I'd dismissed it as ridiculous; our council had been making progress. But now that Jonis had kidnapped me and was arming his people, maybe seizing power as queen was what I had to do. I sighed heavily. "I just want to keep a war from breaking out."

He smiled fondly. "That's because you're a woman. Maybe war is what we need to clean up the mess."

"No," I said firmly. "It's not."

He shook his head. "The Qilarites in the city will be just as glad as I am to see you finally standing up for yourself. Ever since that ship arrived, you've let those island tialiks control everything."

That word made my stomach turn. "Don't say that."

His eyes were soft, but his voice was a tight coil. "They tried to kill you, Soraya. If you're not going to protect yourself, then I will."

I looked at him uncertainly. "This isn't about the Melarim," I said. "This is about Jonis and how he plans to incite the Arnathim to fight."

Gelti smiled. "Oh, we'll give them a fight all right."

I pushed my plate away; suddenly I had lost my appetite. "Why were you gone so long last night?" I asked tightly, hating the awful suspicion rising in my mind.

"I told you, I was delivering your messages and setting up the meeting. Putting everything in place for you." He reached across the table and took my hand. "I told you I wouldn't let those tialiks hurt you, and I meant it."

A weight seemed to land on my lungs. "What have you done?" I whispered.

"We've got Jonis ko Rikar, and we took the slave pens last night. When his people fight it, we'll put them down and restore order." He came around the table and pulled me up into his arms. "It's a simple solution, don't you see?"

The Melarim. He had turned my request for help into an excuse to capture the Melarim.

My heart plummeted as I realized: there was only one group of men he could have called on to do such a hateful thing so quickly.

My mind spun back over the past several days. Gelti had come to the Library, had agreed to take me to meet merchants in the Web. No wonder he had become interested in learning to write and supporting the council; it was the way he had earned my trust, made me think he was ready to accept the changes in Qilara.

I fought to keep my voice even as I said, "How long have you been working with the Swords of Qilara?"

Gelti's answering smile was full of relief and delight and, absurdly, pride that I had figured this out so quickly. "Since you asked me to question Stit. I knew you wanted my help. When he went on about how the Swords of Qilara thought you should be queen, I saw that they were just what we needed." He ran his hands possessively down my arms.

"Coe's murder," I said. "The dock fire. The sailors' escape. The green clothes. All of that happened after you questioned Stit." I looked up at him. "When you said they started using smarter tactics."

He grinned. "My idea, yes. I wanted to tell you, but I knew you wouldn't understand yet. But now you see what a danger they are, don't you? I did what I had to in order to protect you." He nuzzled my neck. "The Swords of Qilara were just the tool we needed."

I looked at him incredulously, but didn't step out of his reach. Not yet. Part of me was still frozen with shock, and another was trying to find the best way to play this. Ignoring the hollow in my chest, the way my body felt tainted by his touch, I focused on the fact that Gelti was still claiming that he had done this because he cared about me. That meant there was something else, besides my pride and my heart and my body, that he thought he could wring out of me. I couldn't formulate a plan until I knew what that was.

"The tool we needed," I repeated faintly. And then I thought I understood. "We?"

"Soraya," he said, as though I were a petulant child. "Every queen needs a king."

My earlier refusal of his marriage proposal echoed in my ears. That was what he would take from me, the thing I had already made clear that I prized most: my independence. He would use my name and my fortune and my body to secure a throne, just as my father had planned to.

To think that I'd believed that he truly cared for me. That I had felt guilty for hurting him when he'd made himself so vulnerable to me.

That I had chosen to spend the night with him.

Gelti watched me warily, his hands gripping my waist. I lowered my head, lest he see the fury and pain that were surely playing over my face. Images from my fighting lessons flashed through my mind—how to knee a man to make him crumple in pain, how to strike at his eyes and get away. But there was nowhere to go, and he was stronger than I was.

It wasn't Gelti's lessons but my mother's that would help me now.

Without a word, I molded my hands to the back of Gelti's head and pulled him into a kiss just as passionate as the ones we had shared last night. I only hoped he wouldn't taste the fear and disgust that now laced it as well. I pressed myself against him for a count of ten and then broke away breathlessly. Smiling demurely, I laid my head against Gelti's shoulder, the picture of a contented bride-to-be. This would be a delicate operation, but I had to play along until I figured out what to do next.

"Soraya," Gelti said tenderly. He touched my cheek and whispered, "That was . . . almost believable."

TWENTY-FOUR

MY HEAD CAME up at once.

"Do you think I can't read you?" he said, his gaze still tender, but his voice cold. "Do you think I don't know that you're already planning some manipulation or other? It won't work, Soraya. The Swords of Qilara are loyal to me. The tialiks would kill you as soon as look at you. Cooperating with me is your only choice."

I tore myself out of Gelti's grasp. "The Swords of Qilara are loyal to you?" I spat. "Are you so sure of that? You arrested Horel Stit, after all." Or had it all been an act for my benefit? Just like every time he had held himself back from insulting the Arnathim or the Melarim, to make me think he was changing?

Gelti's eyes flashed with anger at Stit's name. "I gave them incentive to work with you instead of against you," he snarled. "I did this for you."

"For me?" My voice had gotten higher, and there was a thrumming inside my head. "I don't need your help! And how dare you decide what I need or don't need."

Gelti scoffed. "Of course. You don't *need* a husband." He said the words as if he could not conceive of a more ridiculous thought.

"Gelti?" said a voice behind me. I turned to find Nasha in the doorway in a beige sleeping shift, hair sleep-tousled. "I heard shouting."

"Everything's fine, Mother. Go back to bed," said Gelti.

"Is it happening?" she asked, her tone sharp.

Gelti's eyes shifted to her, and he smiled. "Yes, you'll get to plan a wedding soon."

"Oh, my dear, that's—"

Gelti put up a hand to silence her as a knock sounded at the door. He strode down the hall to open it, revealing Ots and another man.

"Carriage is ready," said Ots.

Gelti motioned the men inside and came to take my hand. "We are going to the meeting now," he said, his voice equal parts reasonableness and threat. "Time to meet the men who will put you on the throne."

I couldn't help it; the situation was so absurd. Did he honestly believe I was just going to let him use me the way my father had? I ripped my hand out of his and said, with a bitter laugh, "Don't you mean put *you* on the throne? Do you really think anyone would follow you?"

Gelti's face was blank, but his jaw clenched. "Obviously I will have to handle the meeting for you, since you can't be rational right now. Ots, take her in the carriage to the pens and lock her in with her sister. I'll find my own way to the warehouse." He touched my cheek. "We'll talk about this later, after you've calmed down."

"How dare you," I began, but Gelti turned away from me dismissively.

"Ots, take her," he said. "And don't let the pretty package fool you. She can be ruthless when she wants to be." He motioned to the other man to follow him, and disappeared out the front door.

Before I'd even had a chance to consider moving, Ots was behind me, my arms in an iron grip.

"You let Gelti handle it, dear," called Nasha as Ots dragged me out the front door. "He knows what he's doing."

In the carriage, I tried to reason with Ots. But no matter what I said, he refused to speak or look at me or loosen his grip on my wrist, so I gave up and focused on being ready when the carriage stopped. Mentally I ran over the moves Gelti had taught me that would distract an attacker long enough to get away.

And then once I got away, I would have time to figure out what to do next.

When the carriage stopped, I tensed, ready to kick out at Ots as soon as my feet touched the ground. But he didn't even give me a chance to climb out of the carriage, just threw me roughly over his shoulder and strode through the door of the slave pen building, grunting a greeting at a man in a dirty tunic stationed there.

I struggled as the door fell shut behind him, cutting off the morning light. Perhaps that was stupid, as even if I got away now, there was no place for me to go. But I couldn't stand the idea of going along with this quietly, allowing Ots to haul me along like a sack of flour over his shoulder. The struggling didn't matter; Ots only held me more tightly.

"Put me down, you oaf," I said. "This instant."

"What's this?" said an oily voice. All I could see was Ots's back and the dim hallway behind us, but I recognized that voice. Horel Stit.

"The girl," said Ots. "Dimmin said to—"

"Bring her here," said Stit sharply.

Ots hesitated a moment before depositing me on the stone floor of the front room.

Stit's beady eyes were black in the torchlight. Six other men stood behind him. All were armed, most with knives, though one had an ax and one a heavy chain. Stit's hair was now carefully oiled, his boots polished, in stark contrast to the mismatched clothes and ragged hair of the men behind him. He'd taken the time to clean himself up, despite the fact that he still had a black eye and bruises on his face. He clearly thought himself a cut above the others. *I can use that*, I thought automatically.

If only I had some idea how.

"She didn't go along as Dimmin expected, eh?" Stit said. "Shame. He was so certain she would turn. But there's still the sister."

"You leave my sister alone," I said through clenched teeth.

"Dimmin thinks you're the key to taking back this country," Stit said, stalking toward me. "Set up this whole plan around it. Make things bad enough, he said, and Soraya Gamo would be forced to turn to the Swords of Qilara for help. And damn if he wasn't right. When he heard how you'd sold away your salt mine and port access to Romit, he said it was the perfect opportunity to sell the whole penful of slaves to the Emtirians too. Then spread the word that Soraya Gamo was behind it, and watch the tialiks riot, watch the Qilarites crush them." Stit dug his fingers into my hair and wrenched my head up, so violently that it knocked the flower out of my twist. He tilted his head, considering me. "Ah well, if she won't cooperate, at least she'll fetch a pretty price from the Emtirians."

A yawning pit of fear opened in my chest, but I forced myself to sniff disdainfully. "Slavery is illegal in Emtiria, just as it is in Qilara. You can't sell the Melarim any more than you can sell me."

Stit laughed and let go of me. "Slavery is illegal. Indenture isn't. And why would we let all this profit burn when we could get some gold out of it and earn the goodwill of the Emtirian emperor too? When he heard about the good work of the Swords of Qilara, he was happy to help put our pick on the throne."

I wanted to say something cutting about how ironic it was that they had given themselves such a grand name when none of them actually carried a sword. But all I could manage to force out was, "Even in Emtiria, there are laws. You'll never convince anyone that all those people sold themselves into service."

"We got a little Scholar upstairs who'll write up any damn record we tell her to, if she doesn't want her pretty throat cut." He grabbed my arm, his fingers pressing into the bruise Jonis had left there yesterday, and ripped my father's signet ring off my thumb. "We'll make it all official with this. Now, we *could* do it more easily with you making the sale. But we don't need you. Think on that."

I curled my fingers into my skirts, waiting for the black spots in my vision to pass.

Stit looked extremely pleased with himself. "You're not for the salt mines, though. I know a brothel in Cation that specializes in fallen ladies of breeding. Oh, I know what you're thinking—" He put on a high, false, simpering voice. "But my daddy's friends in Emtiria will help me." He laughed. "Who do you think that brothel's best clients are, princess?" He bent to retrieve the flower from the floor and tucked it back into my hair. "Keep yourself pretty, and you might stay alive."

He grinned, his foul breath in my face, and I imagined shoving that maschari flower down his throat.

Stit straightened up. "And we'll put out that the tialik found out she sold the islanders, and he killed her. The goats in this city would believe it, of both of them."

The other men laughed, and Stit seemed to swell with the force of their obsequious approval.

"Put her in the pit with the tialik," he said to Ots. Given the venom in his voice, he could only have been referring to Jonis. "Give her time to think about her choices."

I felt Ots shift his weight behind me. "Dimmin said to put her in with her sister."

"Dimmin's not in charge," Stit growled.

There were murmurs of agreement from other men.

"Halder, go with them in case Ots gets lost," said Stit.

Stit obviously hated the idea of the other men deferring to Gelti. I tried to translate that fact into some useful scheme, but soon I had to focus all my attention on keeping my footing as

Halder and Ots dragged me down the torchlit hallway.

The Melarim were silent shapes in the darkness of the cells at the back. In the hold of the ship, they had watched me and Jonis warily, wondering if we had come to free them or hurt them. Now they watched me being paraded past them as a prisoner.

I'd failed so many people that it shouldn't have pained me anymore, but when I saw Erinel huddled in a corner, my throat went dry.

The brutes pulled me down a hallway and to the right, and I could see metal bars glimmering in rows off in the distance. I hadn't appreciated before just how large the building was.

Think of something, I ordered myself. Nothing on my dress was sharp; I didn't even have a sash. I had no jewelry with which to bribe the men. My right hand felt naked without my father's ring.

I hung my head, squinting through the murky light to catalog the men and their weapons. Ots had a knife at his belt; the stiffness of his wrist made me suspect he had a weapon sheathed there too. And there was his massive size to consider. His grip on my right arm was bruising, and I had to force myself to stay limp to avoid provoking him.

Halder had a chain hanging from his belt. He kept leering at me; I might be able to use that, but not unless I got him alone.

And then there was the snarl of hairpins and the poisonous flower still in my hair. Once they put me in that cell with Jonis, my hairpins could be useful. If anyone in this blasted city knew how to pick locks, surely Jonis did.

Assuming I could convince him that I wasn't his enemy.

TWENTY-FIVE

HALDER GRABBED A torch from the wall and led the way down shallow stairs into a vast, dim space reeking of mold and human waste.

Something splattered from the ceiling, and I leaped backward, knocking into Ots, who caught me around the waist with a vicious laugh. I squinted into the shadows and made out a small grate in the ceiling, and couldn't help gagging as I realized that this was where those imprisoned above relieved themselves.

The men's harsh voices echoed so much that I couldn't sort out what they were saying, especially when a loud scraping sound obscured their words.

"How you doing down there?" one of the men shouted.

"He'd better still be alive. Stit wants to kill that one himself. He's going to burn him alive at sunrise," said another.

"Ah, it was only a twenty-foot drop. He's still alive. I can see him twitching. Stit won't mind a few broken bones."

I'd expected a particularly nasty cell, but what I saw when Ots dragged me forward, his arms clamped around my elbows so tightly that I thought I might never bend them again, was just a dark hole in the floor, about six feet across. The stone cover lay to one side, beside a pulley with a rope attached to a rotten-looking bucket dangling above the hole.

"Want to go down the way he did, princess, or will you play nice and ride in the bucket?" said the greasy-haired man near the hole.

I tossed my head, even though my heart was pounding, my half-formed escape plan disintegrating. "Why on earth would I invite broken bones? That would be idiotic."

They guffawed as though it were a carnival trick, a woman spouting common sense.

"I'll make it worth your while if you help me get out of here," I said desperately. "All of you. My family has money, you know, and having a Gamo in your debt is not an insignificant asset."

"You never shut up, do you?" said Ots as he stuffed me into the bucket.

The bandage had come off my hand at some point, but I clutched the rope so tightly that my palms bled—I didn't trust the bucket not to splinter beneath me. I swung wildly, descending deeper into the darkness, holding my elbows close so they wouldn't bang the slimy stone walls.

My feet hit something soft—Jonis's body. I pushed away in shock and smashed into the wall, jarring my spine.

The men above shouted insults, but it took me several seconds to unclench my fingers from the rope. The open air on the rope burns stung, and the wound in my left palm was bleeding freely. The moment I was out of the bucket, the men started cranking it back up. I ducked to avoid being struck in the head.

An inch or so of cold, foul water covered the bottom of the pit, which must have once been a well. My slippers were immediately soaked. In the dim light from the torch twenty feet above, I could see that some of the bricks had barely visible symbols etched on them. Halfheartedly I felt for handholds, but I already knew it was useless; the slick, smooth walls extended upward in a perfect, unclimbable column.

Jonis lay slumped against the wall. I crouched beside him.

"Are you hurt?" I hissed.

He laughed, presumably because my question was ridiculous, and didn't answer.

"Jonis!" I clung to the belief that we would get out of here. I hadn't been broken by the Resistance when they had captured me, and I wouldn't let Horel Stit and Gelti Dimmin break me either.

That resolve lasted until the men pushed the cover of the well back into place, cutting off the distant twinkle of the torch. I shouted; I may even have begged. I hadn't realized how precariously I had been keeping my terror of the dark at bay until that tiny spark of reflected light disappeared, and I found myself huddled on the wet floor, whimpering and fighting for breath.

Nothing but darkness, like a boot heel of the gods grinding me into the cold stone, stealing the air from my lungs. *You deserve this*, it whispered in my bones. *This is what you are. Powerless against the dark.*

I clawed at the shadows creeping over my skin like oil.

Screams and burning flesh. A scarlet slash across Aliana's throat. My father's body, cold and lifeless.

A hand grabbed mine, and a voice cut through the clamor in my head. "Stop it! What are you doing?"

It felt wrong to grip that hand, to reach for that voice like it was a float thrown from a ship, but I couldn't help it; the sea of shadows was swallowing me whole. I pulled in a shuddering breath, willing my lungs to work, forcing my pulse to slow.

It was the thought that somewhere, the gods were laughing at the irony of *Jonis*, of all people, rescuing me from the panic of the shadows, that let me push the fear far enough away to laugh bitterly.

"What's wrong with you?" he said angrily. "What are you doing here? Did your conspirators get sick of you?" He tried to pull his hand out of mine, but I kept a death grip on it.

"Not conspirators," I whimpered. "Don't let go."

"Don't give me that. Dimmin and his friends freed Stit and dragged me here. They've got Kirol up there somewhere too. They killed Adin. He died holding them off so that Deshti and my mother and sister could escape." He was silent for a long moment, and when he spoke again his voice shook with rage. "Stit made sure to tell me all about your plans for the Melarim."

"Why would I be in this pit if they were my plans?" I managed. I forced my eyebrow to arch sardonically, as though he could see me in the blackness. I didn't know another way to steady my voice as I said, "I went to Gelti for help. I didn't know that he was mixed up in all this."

Jonis swore and tugged his hand out of my grasp. I started

hyperventilating and grabbed it again. "What's wrong with you?" he demanded.

A burst of welcome anger kept my voice from shaking. "I've had problems with the dark ever since *someone* locked me up in a pitch-black tomb."

"We only took the torch away because we thought you'd try to kill yourself with it," he snapped. "After that time you set your dress on fire."

I coughed out a laugh. My throat was raw, which made me wonder if I had been screaming earlier. "I was trying to throw the torch at the brutes who were chaining me up." The haughtier my tone, the less the shadows frightened me. It had been that way in the tombs too. Which was why I had shouted at my jailers as often as I had.

"That sounds like you," he said snidely.

"Did you think I would just let you do it again? That's why I went to Gelti. I wasn't going to let you take over the city."

Jonis snorted. "I think you're confusing things. I was getting you out of the way until the Melarim left."

"Oh, really. And where was that carriage heading?"

"The Valley of Qora. Adin was taking you to an estate there to be held until Raisa and Mati got back, and then we would . . . figure out what to do with you. Who let you out? The guards?"

"I got myself out."

"Of course you did."

I remembered waking up in the carriage—it was hard to believe that had been only a day ago—and my mind snagged on one small detail. "There was a pillow."

"What?"

"There was a pillow under my head in the carriage." I didn't want the relief that coursed through me; anger had been helping me keep myself under control. I blew out a breath. "You never really believed I was a traitor, did you?"

Jonis was silent for a long moment, then he said, "I didn't know what to think. But I couldn't take any chances. You worked with Stit and sold us out to Emtiria! The Melarim had to get home."

"Sending them home is exactly what I was trying to do, you idiot." He hadn't seemed to notice that I was still clutching his hand, but I tightened my grip in case insulting him made him let go. "I was trying to fix it. You could have let me."

"And you could have told me about the salt mine in the first place." He shook his head; I could tell because the movement stirred the dank air in the pit. "For all I know this is still part of your plans."

"If I had planned to betray you," I said stiffly, "I'd have pulled it off with far more finesse, and in a much cleaner place. If I'd wanted you dead, you would have been gone ages ago."

Jonis laughed sardonically. "That, I believe."

He did, I could tell, and that loosened something in me. Absurd, perhaps, considering how we had gotten here, but the idea of Jonis understanding what I was capable of—understanding that I *was* capable—was a tiny spark of warmth against the icy fear in my heart.

"So they tricked us both," he said, dousing the spark. He coughed, then groaned.

"You *are* hurt, aren't you?"

I felt his shrug, but his breath went ragged as he did it. "A couple of broken ribs, I think. I've had worse. Think Stit'll send a doctor before he starts disemboweling me?"

"Stop that." I shook our joined hands chidingly. My palm stung where the rope burns pressed against his skin, but I wasn't letting go. I couldn't. "We have to figure out how to get out. They have my sister, and—"

"There's no way out of here until they decide to let us out," said Jonis, chilling certainty in his tone. "We can't do anything until that happens, so we might as well rest up for when it does."

"Have you . . . been in here before?"

"No, but I've heard from enough people who have. This is where they threw the ones who fought the hardest, to break them before the slave auctions."

"They have to let us out, if they want to make a show of us," I said, my voice rising.

"Stit will make a show, that's certain. He wants revenge, as if everything the Resistance did was designed to humiliate him personally." Jonis let out a shaky laugh. "I expected it, every time he came home from sea. Every minute I thought he would see through the act and figure out what I'd been doing while he was gone. It was stupid to stop expecting it. As long as Stit was alive, it was bound to happen."

I knew I should tell him that Gelti was, even now, meeting with Scholars and ship captains in my name to incite a war. I turned it over in my mind, the way that Gelti had insisted that the Swords of Qilara were loyal to him, the way that Stit had overruled Gelti's orders and thrown me into this pit. Dishonest people never trusted others; hadn't Jonis and I proved that? There had to be a way to use that against them.

Or maybe I was wrong. Maybe Stit had only put me here to demonstrate just how helpless I really was. He didn't just want me to do his bidding; he wanted to break my spirit and make me do his bidding with a smile. And he'd wanted me to see Jonis like this, lost and hopeless.

"Nothing is bound to happen," I said, my throat tight. "We have a choice."

Jonis let out a noncommittal sound and slid down onto the floor. "Need to sleep," he mumbled. He pried his hand out of mine, but before my breathing could become too erratic, he reached across me and took my left hand with his right. "I won't let go," he murmured.

"Thanks," I whispered.

He slipped into sleep so quickly that I was certain he'd been lying about his injuries. I let my eyes drift shut—not that it made much difference, as I couldn't see anything either way. Hateful voices swirled in my mind: my mother, my father, my sister. The echoes of Stit's malicious laugh. The whispers of every Scholar who had gossiped about me while I stood by my fiancé's side. Gelti's voice a sensuous buzz along my skin, full of lies more potent than any of the others, because of how much I had longed to believe them.

They all agreed on one thing: I had gotten what I deserved. I'd thought that I was special, because I was a Gamo, because I was a Scholar, because of the way I could manipulate people. I could almost hear the laughter of the gods, mocking the fallen fortunes of the mighty when they were alone and friendless.

But the Qilarite gods were gone now. Sotia, goddess of wisdom, ruled in their place.

"And I'm not alone," I told the darkness, squeezing Jonis's hand, the words somehow both a statement and a prayer.

Jonis didn't answer. I slid down onto the floor next to him and rested my head on his shoulder, letting his slow breathing lull me to sleep.

I woke with my face mashed into Jonis's shoulder, my body stiff from lying on hard, wet stone. I opened my eyes, and then had the sensation that I *hadn't* opened them, that I couldn't open them, and pushed myself up in a blind panic.

I'd let go of Jonis's hand in my terror, and I thrashed in the dark until I found his arm. He shouted and struck me across the face. I fell backward into the wall with a cry, cradling my nose.

"Soraya? Where are you?"

The air was disturbed, presumably from his flailing as he tried to find me, and I was relieved for the excuse to reach out and take his hands.

"What happened?" he said, using his grip on my hands to pull himself up to a sitting position, with many a groan.

"You hit me in the nose." I tried to sound haughty about it, but my heart still hadn't quite recovered from waking in the darkness.

"Are you all right?"

I had to laugh at that. "All right" was the furthest thing from what I was. "I don't feel any blood."

He scooted closer, wrapping one arm around my shoulders.

My mind may have considered pulling away, but my body didn't, not for one second. Jonis and I were both shivering, and I leaned into his warmth. I drew my knees up and gathered my sodden dress around me. I thought of the way Jonis had woken in the dark, lashing out and frightened, and wondered what nightmares from his past he'd been fighting off.

We were quite a pair. I considered how I might say this out loud, a humorous, wry observation, laughing in the face of danger, using the phrase to put us together, make us a duo. But the words stuck in my throat. *It's only the fear,* I thought. *When we get out of here, we'll go back to hating each other. Don't mistake this for something it's not. He doesn't really trust you.*

And I didn't trust him either, I told myself. How would I ever again be able to trust that arms around me meant comfort and not betrayal?

Jonis and I were of a height, so being tucked under his arm felt nothing like being in Gelti's embrace, but the moment I thought of Gelti, I bent over and dry-heaved into the darkness. Nothing came up, but my stomach convulsed as if trying to expel the very memories of last night. The empty silphium jar flashed through my mind, leaving a gleaming pebble of worry, but I shied away from it. I couldn't think about that, not now, not with everything else that was happening.

"Talk about something," I said, unable to be alone in my head any longer. "Anything. Tell me how you met Deshti."

His arm tightened across my shoulders. It had been the wrong thing to say, and I opened my mouth to take it back, but Jonis spoke quietly before I could.

"Her brother Loti was the first friend I ever had. We joined the Resistance at the same time. He was a jokey type, always said I was too serious. Mati reminds me a lot of Loti, actually. Maybe that's why he and I get along."

And why you haven't imploded with jealousy over Raisa, I thought, but didn't say. It wasn't the time to pick at that wound.

Jonis had paused, as if leaving space for the insult he expected, but when I remained silent, he went on. "Loti was . . . idealistic like Mati too. The many matter more than the one, and all that."

"You led the Arnath Resistance, and you don't consider yourself idealistic?"

"Look where idealism has gotten us," he murmured, and I knew exactly what he meant. It struck me as fiercely appropriate that Jonis and I were the ones in this pit. We had both been expecting betrayal and disappointment all along, only we'd each assumed it would come from the other.

"Anyway," he continued. "Loti and I were leading a group of escapees to the border, and he volunteered to draw the guards away. Knew it was suicide, but just grinned and took off." He paused. "His head was on a pike at the market the next day. And I had to go tell his sister. Their parents were dead, so I'd promised to take care of her if anything happened to him. And also"—his voice grew heavier—"to never, ever let her get mixed up with the Resistance. But she guilted me into telling her enough about the Resistance for her to figure out how to approach the leaders herself. When the palace started rounding up orphans for the Tutor Selection, they sent her in to be our spy."

"And you tried to stop her."

"Locked her in the basement of the candle shop." He sighed. "She broke the window and went anyway. But it didn't matter. The oracle chose Raisa." I felt his head tip toward me. "I always thought that was why Deshti couldn't stand Raisa, until you said . . ."

"She is in love with you, you dolt. But I wonder if you even realize that you love her too." A spark of hope kindled in my heart. "You said Deshti got away! She'll send a message to Raisa and Mati and they'll—"

"They can't help anyone right now," said Jonis heavily.

"What do you mean?"

"Last night a message arrived from the southern vizier. Gage and the South Company are supporting him, and he announced that Lilano is officially seceding from Qilara. Mati and Raisa fled the city two days ago. No one knows where they are."

"They're not dead," I said at once, as if by saying it out loud I could will it to be so. I had to believe that they were still alive. Even if Jonis and I failed, they would fix things. That was who they were, Mati and Raisa, the golden hero and heroine. "Raisa says . . . that Sotia won't let us fail, that she works through us." Those words seemed even more hopelessly naive now, especially because my thin, quivering voice held none of the conviction Raisa's had.

"That sounds like her." Jonis's voice was gentle when he spoke of Raisa, but it turned bitter as he went on. "But maybe we're just tools. Just the knife Sotia holds to the throat of her enemies. Maybe that's all the Resistance ever was, all our council ever was."

"And a broken blade gets tossed away," I murmured. Just as Jonis and I had been.

Jonis coughed, then grunted. "How much did Dimmin know about council business?"

My throat burned, and my face did too. I wrinkled my nose to stop the stupid, hot tears that welled in my eyes. "More than he should have," I said at last. "After he helped us . . . after he saved *you*, I thought . . ."

"Why did you really have him teach you to fight?"

"I told you, I don't like feeling helpless. My family's money and my name were all I've ever had. I could never defend myself. I couldn't defend my sister." Suddenly I was so, so tired. I was losing my grip on the idea that we might get out of this, as I thought about all the ways our captors planned to destroy us.

The ways they maybe already had.

Jonis grunted. "I should have known there was more to it. I thought you were just sleeping with him."

The tiniest whimpering gasp escaped my throat.

"Oh," said Jonis softly. I braced myself for his arm to tighten sympathetically around me—I didn't want his pity—but he didn't move at all.

I swallowed the lump in my throat. "He proposed to me afterward," I forced out. "I thought he meant it—isn't that stupid? I even felt bad for turning him down. He said I was only saying no because he was merchant-born, made me out to be a terrible snob."

I paused, but Jonis didn't fill in the obvious, *"Well, aren't you?"*

I sniffed. "It's stupid, to trust anyone like that."

Jonis's arm did tighten around my shoulder then. "No, it's not. Trusting people isn't the mistake. It's not your fault he was untrustworthy."

It's not your fault. His words echoed around the dank pit. Did I believe that, really?

Hadn't the voices in my head told me for ages that it was my fault, everything that had happened? If only I'd been born a boy who could properly become my father's heir. If only I'd been able to make Mati love me. If only I'd been able to see through Gelti's lies, instead of being so desperate for affection that I had fallen into his trap. And now the Melarim would become slaves, Jonis would die, Qilara would fall, and I would be ruined, all because of my failings.

But those voices in the dark lied. I knew that.

Those voices had told me that I didn't trust Jonis, that I *couldn't* trust him. But maybe trust didn't happen all at once. Maybe it was built from a thousand small moments—a hand to hold in the dark, an unvoiced insult, a shameful secret shared. I remembered Raisa, hands clenched at her sides, deciding again and again to believe that people could be good despite all evidence to the contrary.

I'd made mistakes—we all had—but we couldn't change those. All that mattered was what we did now.

It's not your fault.

I believed him, I realized. I trusted him, and I no longer cared whether it was prudent, or clever, or politic to do so.

Like a lamp twinkling at the end of a long, shadowy corridor,

I saw a way out of this. I sat up and patted at my hair, securing the maschari flower.

"Do you trust me?" I asked Jonis abruptly.

"What?"

"Do you trust me?"

"I—I suppose. I mean, we don't exactly have a choice—"

"I'm going to get us out of here. All of us. But you have to follow my lead." I pulled myself up and started shouting, not letting go of Jonis's hand until the cover scraped off the hole above and the dim light of the torch made me pull away to cover my eyes.

"Quit your yelping," yelled one of the men.

"I must speak to Horel Stit at once," I announced crisply.

"What are you doing?" Jonis hissed, tugging at my sodden skirt.

"Hear that, boys?" said another man above. "Lady High and Mighty has a demand."

"If you have a jot of sense in those thick heads of yours, you will listen to me," I said in my haughtiest tones—far more effective with men like these than flattery. "How would Stit reward you if you cost him the secrets of the Gamo fortune?"

Raucous laughter from above. "You think we won't get those secrets out of your little sister?"

I waited for their distasteful comments to cease before I said, "Alshara knows nothing. *I* am the head of the Gamo family." I sniffed. "I've just been learning of Stit's nature from the tedious ramblings of this slave, and I doubt Stit would be forgiving if he knew you had passed up such an offer on his behalf."

The men above conferred in an undertone. I felt Jonis staring at me, but I didn't turn my head, didn't shoot him a look to warn him to be quiet or remind him to trust me. I'd set my course, and a Gamo didn't waver.

After a bit, I gathered that the men had sent someone with a message to Stit. It didn't surprise me that they wouldn't make a decision on their own; if I'd read the power dynamics right, then the only man here who might do so was Gelti. I used the time to consider how Stit had secured his men's loyalty. Perhaps with money, though even a well-to-do merchant couldn't spread too much around. He'd promised them favors, no doubt, played on their fears of the Arnathim. He had a certain hateful charisma—not like Gelti's, not the light that made you want to be in the path of his smile—but more a shadow that engulfed you with its power and made you despair of ever escaping it.

I would not let that shadow get to me.

A clattering cut the silence, and I moved aside as the bucket descended to the bottom of the well. "Get in," growled a voice from above. "Any funny business and we drop you."

"Do try to hold it steady this time, will you?" I sniffed.

My already burned hands slipped on the rope and the wound from the carriage nail opened again, but the sound of my labored breathing was drowned out when Jonis started shouting obscenities from below. Every vile insult I'd ever heard whispered behind my back came out of his mouth, with a sincere hatred that left no one in doubt. I hadn't expected how painful it would be to have him behaving like my enemy again.

Don't be hurt, I told myself. *Be angry. And then use that anger like Jonis does.*

So I clung tightly to the fire in my blood, and when I got to the top I pried myself out of the bucket with as much dignity as I could muster, and said, "Cover up that hole. No one needs to hear that rat whining."

TWENTY-SIX

MY HEART CONSTRICTED as the cover screeched back over the hole and I pictured Jonis alone in the darkness below.

That was all the sentiment I allowed myself before I said, "Now, I'll need proper clothing and a wash, and then I must see Horel Stit."

The greasy-haired man laughed. "And dinner brought on a silver tray, too?" he mocked. He grabbed my arms and wrapped a leather strap around them several times, then buckled it. He and another man led me up the stairs and along a corridor. I caught a glimpse of a lone figure lying motionless in a cell near the back—Loris. I had no idea why he was being held separately from the other Melarim, but whatever the reason, it couldn't be good.

When we passed the Melarim, the men holding me started talking loudly about how they were escorting me to see Stit so I could finish selling them out—only they used a variety of uncouth words to refer to the people watching from the surrounding cells. I kept my head down and held my tongue.

There were things about the bowels of this place that these men knew that I hadn't—like the presence of the pit below—but I knew more about the upper level. When this building had served as the slave pens, high-ranking Scholars had not stood in the marketplace purchasing slaves from the auction platform, or even had slaves brought to them in the waiting room at the front of the building.

No, Scholars had been escorted up the outside stairs to one of the luxurious rooms on the second floor, which had become a makeshift infirmary for the Melarim. Stit, of course, would have set himself up there after tossing the sick and wounded into cells below.

The first floor of the building had only one entrance, to minimize the possibility of escapes, so the men dragged me all the way to the front door, then around the side of the building and up the stairs I had once climbed with my father. The greasy-haired one kept his foul hand clamped over my mouth the whole time we were outside. My eyes stung in the bright sunlight, even as it allowed me to pull in my first easy breath in hours. The men lounging outside were more sailors, hats pulled low over their faces, disguised to keep the oblivious shoppers in the marketplace from knowing anything was amiss. The Arnath defenders were probably all either dead or imprisoned inside with the Melarim.

I almost sobbed with relief when my soaked, disgusting slippers hit the soft carpet of the upstairs hallway. Maybe I was a snob, but I was a snob who had reached her own territory, and that could only help me now.

They dragged me past a closed door and stopped to knock at a second. Stit himself opened it, and he took his time looking me over, from my bedraggled hair to my filthy slippers. A satisfied smile spread over his face. He stood back and the two men shoved me inside.

In the time it took Stit to order the men out and shut the door, I cataloged the room. No windows, which meant that this room was set inside the long hallway that wrapped around the upper story of the building. A long, wide settee. A scattering of comfortable chairs. A table along the back wall with pitchers, crystal glasses, a jewel-toned array of wines and liquors, and in front of them, several small tincture jars and a pile of bandages. The medical supplies, along with the depressions in the carpet from the beds Stit must have removed, and a faint scent of willow bark in the air, were the only indications of the room's recent use as an infirmary.

A tall mirror hung on the wall, making the room seem larger than it was. I would have bet that it hid a secret door. The fact that the men had brought me up the outside stairs meant they likely had no idea about the hidden passages the slavers had once used to transport slaves from the pens to these upper rooms and to spy on their customers.

"Well," said Stit, "what do you have to say?"

I lifted my chin. "I require a wash and change of clothes before I tell you anything."

Stit barked out a laugh. "No. I like seeing you this way. Highborn lady looking like she rolled in the harbor. Plenty of men in that brothel will want to see it too." He scratched his neck, displaying my father's ring on the first finger of his right hand, and I gritted my teeth.

He wanted me obsequious and begging, but I knew I couldn't pull that off convincingly. I went with my strengths instead. "That would be wasteful, and you know it. You'll never have a hint of legitimacy if you take my family's money through Alshara, signet ring or not. But if I were on your side, everything would be so much easier for you. I'm the one you need to work with, not Dimmin." I peered up from under my lashes at Stit, hoping that this move still had some effect even when I was soaked and covered in grime. "He's weak, can't you see that? He's a fool to think he could control me."

"And you think no one can control you." Stit was starting to look bored with the conversation, and my skin grew clammy. If he threw me back into the pit, I didn't have a backup plan.

The next words left my mouth with a strong taste of bile, but I knew they would appeal to Stit. "My father always said women are like horses," I said lightly. "The best ones require the firmest hand." I lowered my joined wrists to allow a better view of my cleavage.

His eyes flicked to my bodice, but without any real interest, and he didn't answer.

Doubt flared in my chest, but I pressed on; I had to say something. "I heard what happened to your wife. I imagine you must be . . . lonely for feminine companionship."

Stit strode across the space between us and grabbed my chin, spitting into my face as he spoke. "You heard, did you? Heard how

I came home and found my house full of squatters and my wife upstairs?"

I nodded, remembering the houses Jonis and I had passed near the docks, the ones that had been taken over by Arnathim. "How horrible," I whispered.

Stit gripped my chin harder. I was sure there would be finger-nail marks in my skin if he ever let go. "You're not understanding, *my lady*," he spat. "They didn't kill her. I did. She was a good woman. She begged me to do it—they'd raped her, see, and she didn't want a tialik inside her." He flashed a smile that was little more than a baring of his misshapen teeth. "I gutted my own wife, so what do you think I'll do to you?"

I forced myself to hold his oily gaze. "You do have a firm enough hand, then," I said, as though we were discussing a shipping agreement and not my own demise. "You could sell me away, but you could accomplish much more with me at your side."

He pushed me away so hard that I stumbled backward. "By my side, ready to knife me in the back," he said.

"I thought you were a man who could handle risk. And I think you underestimate the lengths to which a Gamo would go to save her own neck."

Stit tilted his head. "Dimmin said you were a ruthless one."

"My favorite compliment," I lied. "You keep me here, and take my money, and it will be you on that throne, not him."

He laughed raucously, and I understood that I had misstepped again. "Don't want a throne. I'll take your money, though, and you can be a puppet queen and do any damn thing I tell you to."

It's hardly worse than what my father was ready to do, I thought, but I plastered on a smile.

"Hmmm," said Stit. "Dimmin on the throne, beside the great Soraya Gamo. Think how the merchant class will lap that up." His lips spread in a slow smile. "Think how they'll explode when he's killed on his wedding night and we announce the tialiks are behind it. Are you ruthless enough to stab him in the marriage bed, girl?"

I swallowed hard. "That would be immensely satisfying," I answered coolly.

He laughed. "You sign every gods-damned document there is giving me full rights to your money."

"Only if my sister goes free." Whatever happened to me, I had to get Alshara away from Stit as soon as possible. She would never be free if Stit could threaten her to keep me under control. She was probably being held in one of these upstairs rooms, with no idea that she was even a prisoner. Gelti had probably charmed her across Library tables too.

Stit nodded thoughtfully, but I could tell that he still wasn't convinced.

I let my hands fall down again—it couldn't hurt to give him an unobstructed view of my heaving chest as I said tearily, "Dimmin took advantage of me. Do you have any idea how it feels to be humiliated like that? After suffering the indignities of pretending to work beside those wretched Arnathim for so long?" I peeked up at Stit from under my eyelashes. "And then the one in the pit wouldn't stop talking about the things you'd done. I realized that you were like me—ruthless." I spoke the word like a caress.

"And so you thought to make yourself worth the trouble of keeping you."

"Oh, I promise to be worth it," I purred.

Stit backhanded me so hard that I was on the floor before I even registered the pain of my father's ring against my cheekbone. "Maybe you will be," he growled into my face. "But the first thing you'll learn is to keep your mouth shut except when I tell you to open it."

I blinked away the stars in my vision, imagining sweeping my bound hands into his legs to knock him off-balance. But there was no follow-up to that move that wouldn't result in more pain for me, so I didn't struggle when Stit hauled me to my feet and threw me into an armchair. He took a chain that was attached to the wall and pulled it through my bound arms, refastening it to itself and then turning a key in the lock with a click.

I watched the ring of keys disappear into his pocket as he said, "Don't go anywhere, now. Got a few things to take care of, but I'll think on your generous offer. It's getting on to sunset, and I have the tialik's execution to plan for the morning."

"Will you let me watch it?" I forced out, as eagerly as I could. "Please?"

Stit laughed, but I couldn't tell if it was delight or mockery.

As soon as the door shut behind him, I let my head fall forward and took several shuddering breaths. I was only marginally better off than I had been down in the pit, but at least there were lamps lit here. I nudged off my slippers and dug my feet into the thick carpet; it wasn't warm, but it was a reprieve from the cold, wet discomfort of the shoes.

I had a clear view of myself in the large mirror. My skirts had begun to dry, stains blooming over the fabric like vulgar designs. Dirt streaked my arms and face, and even from across the room I could see the mark on my cheek where Stit had hit me. The coils of my hair hung halfway down my head in a stringy mass, but the battered blue flower poked out of the top like a flag planted in an ash heap.

I'd teased Raisa about giving me a prickly seed pod that grew into a poisonous plant, but it had been an appropriate gift, hadn't it? I poisoned everything I touched, and her greatest mistake had been trusting me. The things my father and his father and his father and on and on, back through the years, had set in motion were larger than any of us—how could we possibly fight them?

I didn't know how to believe in Raisa's vision anymore. There was only one thing I knew how to do well: lie.

So I would be the poisonous flower, if that was what it took to get out of here alive. I'd get Alshara and the Melarim and even Jonis out of here too, if I could.

And if I can't? How far would I go to save them, if it meant not saving myself?

In the mirror, I saw the way my face crumpled into an ugly mass, saw how my shoulders heaved with sobs, and considered how I could re-create this exact crying jag later, when I needed to manipulate Stit. Even while I was falling apart, I was searching for ways to use it to my advantage. My parents had taught me well.

I didn't notice the mirror moving until it swung all the way out from the wall and a figure emerged from behind it.

Gelti.

He glanced at the door and then shut the mirror behind him. Without a word, he strode over to me and examined my cheek.

"I will kill Stit," he growled.

So he'd been watching. Stit and the others must not have known about the passages, but of course Gelti did. He'd been captain of the king's guard, after all. He'd probably used similar passages in the palace on the night he had killed Captain Coe.

I wiped my eyes on my bare arm and considered how to use this. How much had Gelti heard?

I should have played innocent, at least until I found out how much he knew. But I couldn't tolerate his closeness, his familiar scent that made my stomach heave. I cringed away from him, and then, because I saw in the mirror how weak that made me look, I forced myself to sit up straight and say, "What are you doing here?"

"Ots told me they'd put you in the pit, so I went to get you out. But you were already here."

I laughed. "They don't seem to follow your orders very well. Some king you'll make. You do whatever Stit says, just like you did with my father." I darted a glance at the mirror to check my sneering expression. It was perfect. But then, it was absolutely sincere.

He grabbed my wrists, and I recoiled automatically. But he only unbuckled the strap and tossed it aside, then lifted the chain over my head. "I would be more polite if I were you. I am the only thing between you and execution."

I slapped him across the face. It was a stupid thing to do, but my hands had been itching to do it ever since he'd walked in. He didn't even flinch.

I tossed my head, trying to find my Scholar pride and my councilor bravery. "Haven't you heard?" I said coldly. "Stit plans to sell me to an Emtirian brothel."

Gelti's face went ashen. I wasn't surprised that he didn't know about Stit's plans; I *was* surprised that he actually seemed to care what happened to me. That realization tugged at my heart.

But he only minded the idea of other men having his plaything. That didn't mean he loved me.

I could almost feel the few tender pieces left of my heart desiccating as I said, "No wonder he didn't tell you. He seems determined to make sure that you die. I would think that by now you would have learned how to pick your conspirators more wisely." I pushed myself to my feet. "But I've made my own deal with Stit, as I am sure you overheard while you were skulking in the passage."

He shook his head. "You were lying to him. It won't work, Soraya. You can't trust a man like Stit."

"I can't trust any man," I said, though this wasn't true. There was one man in this place I trusted, and it wasn't the one I ever would have expected it to be.

Gelti took my hand, as naturally as if it was his right to do so. "You're overreacting. You think you know what you want, but you don't."

That made me want to slap him again, but I held back. The most dangerous thing I had done was reject Gelti, because he would use that as an excuse for anything he did to me afterward. In his twisted mind, it would be a valid one.

"You deserve better than having to pretend these island vermin don't disgust you," he went on. "You played their game well, because you had to. But I've seen who you are underneath. I know you, Soraya." He closed the last few inches between us, and then his fingers gripped my waist and his mouth was on mine and for an instant—the tiniest instant—I couldn't help falling into his kiss. It was hot and needy and made me feel wanted, and reminded me why I had let him fool me in the first place.

But I wouldn't let anyone deceive me like that ever again. I planted my hands on his shoulders and pushed as hard as I could, twisting out of his grip in a move that he himself had taught me.

"Don't. Touch. Me," I said.

Gelti shook his head, looking for all the world like my father had when I had complained about Aunt Silya—disappointed in my shortsightedness. "I've only ever tried to help you. You should be a queen, not beholden to tialiks. Everything I've done has been with that goal."

"Liar. You've been looking out for yourself."

He shrugged. "I can do both." He spoke as if I should have known that he would have been working for himself all along. As if I should have recognized it, because I was like that too.

And he was right. When had I stopped assuming that everyone in this world was out for themselves?

I snorted. "And this bunch of petty thugs is your grand army."

"They *were* petty thugs until I got my hands on them and made them something more. Stit is a blunt instrument, maybe, but an effective one. One I can control."

"You're doing a wonderful job so far."

Gelti's eyes narrowed. "One I can get rid of when I need to. You let me worry about Stit."

He'd been so certain I would follow along with his schemes. I wondered what would have happened if I had accepted his proposal this morning. Apparently, he'd planned for every eventuality but that of me having my own mind.

If he saw Stit as a tool, then it was obvious that Stit saw him the same way. I remembered the venom with which he had spoken to Stit in the palace courtyard. Gelti had been genuinely furious at Stit about the attack on Jonis at his house.

I laughed out loud at the realization. "That was why you were so angry when Jonis was attacked. Because Stit did that without consulting you."

His jaw tightened, and that was answer enough. "Stit won't honor any agreement you make with him. I'm your only chance."

"Are you," I said flatly.

He took my hand and let his lips play over my palm as he spoke. I got a deep sense of satisfaction in remembering how much muck I had touched in the past several hours, but that didn't seem to bother Gelti. "We belong together, don't you see? You're like me. You put yourself where the opportunities are, and then take what you can."

I yanked my hand out of his. "I'm nothing like you."

His face grew stormy. "Don't be stupid. I *will* marry you. I'll get you out of this and I'll take care of Stit. But I can't have you thinking you're in charge. That was your mistake earlier. I was just teaching you a lesson." His fingers roved over my face and hair possessively. "I'll be your husband and your king, and you can be a queen, a real queen, beside me."

I kept my face blank. He honestly didn't seem to hear the contradiction in what he was saying.

He put his lips close to mine. "Let me take care of you."

I considered how to answer. Would being ruled by Gelti be any better than being ruled by Horel Stit?

The door opened. I tried to pull away, but Gelti held me in place, his fingers woven into my hair.

"What's this?" said Horel Stit.

Gelti didn't take his eyes off me. "I'm giving the lady another chance."

I held his gaze. Neither option before me was pleasant, but Gelti at least seemed to be under the delusion that he cared about me. Gelti might think twice before hurting me or Alshara. And a man motivated by his own interests could be reasoned with. I doubted reason would ever reach Horel Stit. I gave Gelti the smallest of nods, so tiny that Stit probably didn't even see it, but Gelti's hands were still cradling my head, and I knew from the triumphant flash of his eyes that he had felt it.

My neck was stiff when Gelti finally let go of me and we both turned to face Stit.

Stit didn't look surprised, or dismayed, or anything at all as he said, "The sister's the extra, then."

My hands went cold. He would sell Alshara to the brothel in Cation instead of me. His eyes shifted to me, his deadly smile making his face a house with broken windows, and I could practically hear his voice hissing in my ear, *"You will do everything you promised, if you don't want me to destroy your sister."*

"Yes," I said to Stit, and I knew he was taking it as I meant it, an answer to his unspoken message.

Stit waved his hand dismissively. "Ah, well, one rich bitch is as good as another."

Gelti's jaw clenched—he had the nerve to take offense on my behalf. I marveled at the sincerity with which this lived beside the things he had said and done to me. He forced a laugh and said, "We should discuss the timeline."

"Certainly," answered Stit. "Have your girl pour some wine."

Gelti indicated the bottles on the table. It was a test, obviously, of whether I would obey him, though he didn't seem to see that Stit was doing the same thing. I nodded as the two of them sat down across from each other in the armchairs. It soon became clear that Gelti had no intention of revealing that he had learned of Stit's plan to sell me to the brothel. That made me breathe a little easier as I pushed the medical supplies aside and wiped dust out of two wine glasses. I could feel both men's eyes on my back as they spoke, each trying to gauge the other without revealing his own plans.

Neither of the options Stit and Gelti presented were even options at all. Which meant that I would have to create my own.

I let the cloth slip out of my hands, and as I knelt to retrieve it, I tilted my head to the side and snatched a few of the drying maschari petals from my rapidly disintegrating hairstyle. I kneaded them into shreds with my left hand while I worked the wax seal off a wine jug with my right. The cloying scent of the wine hit me like a blow, but I pressed my lips together and forced myself not to vomit.

Gelti and Stit were discussing their alliance with Emtiria and their plans to take over the capital, and from there, the rest of Qilara; I should have been listening for information I could use, weaknesses they might reveal, but the blood pounding in my ears made it impossible to follow the barbs of their conversation.

I started to pour the wine, keeping one hand clamped around the shredded petals, ready to slip it into one of the glasses, but Stit's voice stopped me. "Pour that over here, where we can see it."

I turned to him, and he gave me a caustic smile. Gelti seemed chagrined that he hadn't thought of this. "If you wish," I said evenly.

Fine. Both of them, then.

I lifted the cloth with my left hand and pulled it over the wine as I had seen servants do, and as my hand passed over the lip of the jug I uncurled my fingers and let the scraps of maschari petals fall into the burgundy liquid, where they were immediately obscured. I only hoped it would be enough.

A few petal shreds had gotten lodged in the wound on my palm, so I surreptitiously wiped them away on my filthy skirt. Maschari was only supposed to be poisonous if consumed, but my left hand had gone numb, and the muscles in my left wrist had to work extra hard to balance the tray containing the wine jug and glasses. And it was *heavy*. I thought of all the times the servant girls back in Pira had carried platters as if they were nothing.

As I placed the tray on the low table between them, Stit looked openly pleased to see me reduced to being his serving wench. Gelti hid his contentment better, but I saw it in the set of his shoulders. Each of them thought he had me neatly netted, and the other too.

I wrapped both hands around the jug and poured two glasses. The flower shreds were invisible in the dark liquid, but I prayed that they were spinning their poison into every bit of the wine. I managed to replace the jug on the tray without spilling it, and stood back, my heart thumping painfully.

"My wife always insisted on tasting the wine first," said Stit. "Just the kind of woman she was." He smirked. "It's a procedure I'd recommend for any married man."

Gelti's shoulders stiffened, and he threw a protective glance at me. For the barest moment, I wished that I had been able to poison Stit's glass only.

"Mark my words," Stit said, giving me a sly look. "She's the type that'll stab you in your sleep."

"Hasn't so far," Gelti returned in a tone full of implications, and Stit hacked out a laugh.

Gelti's lips spread into a smug smile, and I stared at the carpet, fighting down the heat crawling up my neck. *Drink the wine*, I thought at them both.

"Luckily, I've recently acquired a taster," Stit said. He turned toward the door and barked an order to someone on the other side.

When the door opened, my heart sank. I'd been wrong earlier, when I'd thought there was only one man in this place that I trusted. There had been two.

Valdis stopped short at the sight of me, though I was surprised that he even recognized me in my grimy state. Had he been part of this too, spying on me and delivering my sister into Stit's clutches? Or was he also a prisoner here?

He didn't say anything, only turned his attention to Stit, who was watching me with amusement. I dug my fingernails into the cuts on my hands, to ground myself in physical pain and distract myself from the idea that Valdis, too, might have betrayed me.

Stit handed Valdis his own glass. He was so uncouth he didn't even know that the taster was supposed to observe the wine being poured.

Valdis raised the glass and sniffed it.

Stop him, cried a voice in the back of my mind. But if I stopped him, it would be as good as admitting that I had tried to poison Stit and Gelti, and I would condemn myself and my sister and remove all chance of saving the Melarim and Jonis. It was a simple matter of numbers; it shouldn't even have been a question.

But my mouth opened anyway as Valdis drank. Any words that might have come out were strangled by the immediate knowledge in his eyes. He'd tasted the maschari. He knew.

I held my breath as he placed the glass on the table and said, "It's a fine vintage."

When he'd tasted the pinkbane-poisoned bun that Erinel had brought me, he'd reached for his remedy pouch right away, had scarcely been able to speak. Maschari was supposed to be even more potent, so much so that it worked almost immediately. But Valdis showed no signs of distress as Stit dismissed him.

Had I been wrong? Had he not tasted the maschari—perhaps because I hadn't put in enough to do any damage? Valdis swept one undecipherable look over me as he left. I turned away. I'd had good reason to stay silent, and anyway it seemed as if my brilliant plan had come to naught.

But if Valdis suspected anything, he hadn't told Stit. That meant that I might get a second chance at this; I had several more petals in my hair. Perhaps I could slip more into their glasses while they were distracted.

Gelti took his glass from the table, swirling the contents. "The wedding will take place at midday bells."

"The tialik *might* be dead by then if we start the execution at sunrise." Stit lifted his glass to clink it against Gelti's. "If not, we'll cut out his tongue before the wedding starts so he can't make a fuss."

I edged away from their chairs; I'd just spotted the leather strap that had been binding my hands earlier, in the corner where Gelti had tossed it. As a weapon it wasn't much, but if I could get one of the men alone and get it around his throat in a moment of surprise . . .

"At the temple platform, you thinking?" asked Gelti.

"Could," said Stit. "What do you think, girl?"

Both men turned to me, and I stopped. They didn't care about my opinion; this was another test, to see whether they had broken me. I foresaw an endless procession of these tests, regardless of which of them won this battle of wills.

I tilted my head and puffed out my lips in imitation of Alshara trying to decide which gown to wear. "It's up to you, of course . . . but I think that, if you don't mind the suggestion, the docks might be a good place. It would make everything more visible, wouldn't it?" And there were plenty of spots nearby where archers could conceal themselves, if I was able to figure out how to get a message to my mother, but they didn't need to know that. I despised the mewling, weak way I'd had to couch the words, but that was what it would take for them to even hear a suggestion from a woman.

It worked. Stit nodded. "Symbolism. Oh, she's a canny one," he said, delivering the compliment to Gelti as if he were responsible for my intelligence. "It's not the gods that rule this city any longer, but the masters of trade." He lifted his wineglass in a triumphant gesture. "And we march the slaves through the streets in chains to the ship, and launch it right after the wedding, after we announce how she sold them to Emtiria. The tialiks riot, we burn them, and there you are—we've quashed a dangerous rebellion and taken our city back."

"No," said Gelti. "Too risky. We'll put the slaves on the ship in the night, and bring out the leaders to witness the execution and the wedding. Then we have the leaders announce how she sold them away, and we execute them too. You want a riot, that'll do it. The woman is related to Raisa ke Margara and the man's half-dead anyway."

Raisa ke Comun, I wanted to say. That was her proper name. It was an absurd detail to want to correct, when there was so much wrong with the words that had just come from Gelti's mouth. I thought of the glimpse I'd had of Loris, lying motionless in the cell below. What had they done to him? I gripped the back of an empty armchair for support.

"How can you be sure they'll say she sold them?" asked Stit.

Gelti gave a thin-lipped smile. "I can make them say whatever we want them to say."

"I'm sure you can at that." Stit laughed.

Gelti grinned smugly and drained his glass. Even though I knew the wine wasn't properly poisoned, I couldn't help a little gasp. Stit heard me and stopped his own glass at his lips. His eyes slanted to my face, and I tried to hunch my shoulders in a downtrodden way.

Slowly, Stit lowered his untouched glass to the table. Gelti set his own glass down and wiped his mouth with the back of his hand like a sailor—how did he think he would ever make an acceptable king?

My mind worked frantically. Stit suspected me of trying to poison them, even though Valdis had already tasted the wine. I had but an instant to take advantage of his indecision, before he saw that Gelti was unharmed. I seized the leather strap from the corner and flung it around Stit's neck. I only had to incapacitate him for a few seconds, until Gelti saw what I was doing. Surely he would spring to my aid, and together we could kill Stit.

And I would deal with Gelti later.

TWENTY-SEVEN

I TWISTED THE ends of the leather strap behind Stit's neck, and he clawed at the front of it, ghastly strangled sounds coming out of him.

No, not out of him. Across the table, Gelti doubled over, clutching his chest, white froth spewing from his mouth. I struggled to keep my grasp on the strap as Gelti slid to the floor. "Soraya!" he choked out.

I'd thought my heart was hardened. I'd thought nothing he did could touch me, now that I knew what he was. But the ruined, begging sound that should have disgusted me made something in me burst open, and I let out a sob. My weakened left hand slipped on the strap, and Stit reached up and punched one meaty fist into my throat so hard that I slammed against the wall, gasping for breath.

Stit reared up, face contorted in rage. He shoved the armchair aside, but Gelti pushed the low table over into the backs of his legs, sending the wine jug and glasses onto the floor, and Stit stumbled.

I skittered sideways, still fighting for breath. Gelti grunted. I saw in his eyes that he knew I had poisoned him. I didn't have time to feel guilt or satisfaction or horror, because Stit was righting himself and reaching for his knife, wheezing about how he would flay me alive and make my sister watch before he sold her away.

But I did have time to take in what Gelti's hand was doing—pointing emphatically at his right boot.

I launched myself at Gelti, rolling down his body as Stit barely missed me with his knife. Plunging my hand into Gelti's boot, I found the dagger and forced myself to wait until Stit came closer. He snarled at me and grabbed my hair, forcing my face up.

"Should cut your throat for that, girl. But I'll enjoy carving you apart more. I'll start with that arrogant smile." Stit's knife traced my lips, and then dug into my cheek.

In one motion, I drew the dagger from Gelti's boot and slipped it between Stit's ribs. Gelti had shown me how to find the soft spot between the bones—had shown me quite intimately, in our lessons last night—but still I was surprised at how easily the blade slipped through skin and tissue and organs, like shears through silk.

Stit made a gasping, gurgling sound as I stabbed again. I pulled the blade out and swung my interlocked hands into his legs, taking him down the way I had longed to earlier. He fell amid the smashed table and bits of glass and clutched at his side as if to keep the blood in.

Gelti made a strangled noise—he was trying to say my name.

He'd helped me, in the end. Didn't that mean that I should feel something as I looked down at the foam at his mouth, the knowledge of death in his eyes?

"Tell . . . Kirol," he forced out.

"Tell him what?" *That you're a traitor? A murderer? Or that you helped me?*

But I couldn't get any of that out, and Gelti was in no state to answer. He touched my cheek, in that tender way that had disarmed me so often, and the fact that I held still and let him was the only concession I would make to the fact that he was dying.

I felt the moment the life went out of him, before I saw it in his face, before his body went still and his hand dropped from my cheek.

The numbness had spread up my left arm now, and it took every bit of determination I had to get myself up on my feet and approach Stit where he lay wheezing and gasping on the floor, eyes closed.

I held my blade to his throat and said, "Tell me where my sister is."

I was ready to spring back, away from the grip of those meaty hands, but his arms had fallen slack and a line of drool hung from his mouth, and I couldn't remember when I had seen anything so weak and repulsive. I had only seen death a handful of times, but I knew that the way I had inserted the blade had probably punctured Stit's lung. I'd read about such things, but I hadn't imagined the gasping noises, the agonized wheezing with every breath Stit took. It would have been a kindness to kill him and end it quickly.

Which was why I didn't.

Cautiously I worked my ring off his finger and placed it back on my thumb. Then I reached into his pocket and found the hard edge of the ring of keys. He had fallen with the keys half under him, and I didn't have the strength in my left hand to pull them out, so I cut the pocket away, then I grabbed them with both hands and pulled. The force of it rolled him onto his back and made him groan, and I leaped away, flailing the knife. But his eyes didn't open, so I pocketed the keys and went to the door, my mind oddly clear and light.

I had to find Alshara.

I listened at the door; at least one of Stit's men had been right outside earlier when he had called for him. But then why hadn't he burst in at all the commotion in the past few minutes?

I found the answer as soon as I eased the door open and saw the dead man outside. He lay on his back, staring unseeing at the ceiling above. From the angle of his head, it looked as if his neck had been broken.

An odd gurgling sound came from farther away, and I cautiously poked my head out and saw Valdis slumped against the wall. I ran to him and stopped a few feet away, hissing his name.

I stepped backward when I saw that he too held a blade, but his was longer and duller than mine. And then I took another step backward at the odd, unfocused look in his eyes.

Of course. Because the wine had been poisoned after all. And he'd known it, but he'd hidden it until he was out of the room. *He's built up immunity to so many poisons,* I told myself. *He'll be all right.*

He didn't look all right. It was wrong, more wrong than anything that had happened in the past hour, to see the strong and sure Valdis on the floor with that hazy expression. It was as wrong as seeing my father fall facedown in the palace garden.

"Hurry," Valdis croaked, holding the blade out to me.

"I have one." I showed him Gelti's dagger. Stit's blood still smeared the blade. "Where is Alshara?"

His eyes moved to the door a little farther down the hall, as though he couldn't control his head enough to turn it. Another dead man lay in front of it, his throat cut.

Valdis grabbed my hand. "Did it . . . work?"

I nodded. "Dimmin is dead. Stit's dying." I paused. "Are you . . ."

He let out a low, shuddering breath. "Take her . . . go out the side. Go home. Leave . . . them." *Them.* He meant the Melarim and Jonis. Valdis would have me do exactly what my father would have wanted, what I'd done on the day of my wedding: grab my sister and escape, leaving everyone else to their fates.

"I'll find her." I squeezed his hand.

"He was a good man," he said, so loudly that I shushed him; who knew how many more of Stit's men were lurking up here? "Your father. He only did what he had to. Don't let them . . . say . . . different."

"What?" I said, but Valdis's gaze was completely unfocused now. He obviously had no idea what he was saying. "I'll find her," I told him again, and I pulled my hand out of his and started down the hallway.

"Soraya!" he called, so abruptly that I whirled around. "He

would be proud," he rasped, and this was so far from the truth that the poison must have been in his brain. I had to look away from his tears, had to force my bare feet to count off the steps to the door that hid my sister.

I stepped over the body and tried the door; locked, of course. I knocked forcefully, like Stit or Gelti would, and then sprang back, in case Alshara wasn't alone.

My sister opened the door. I shoved her aside and darted into the room, but it was empty. She screamed, then saw the dead man in the doorway and screamed again. I grabbed her and covered her mouth.

"Shut up!" I growled.

The room was furnished in the same style as the other, right down to the large framed mirror on the inside wall. The only difference was the curtained window to my left, and the stack of folded cots by the far wall.

It was easy enough for Alshara to pull my left hand off her mouth; it felt like a lump of dough at the end of my arm. "You have blood all over you!" she cried. "Where's Gelti?"

"Dead."

"No!" Alshara's hands flew up to cover her mouth.

"He was a liar," I told her. "He never cared about either of us."

She stared at me uncomprehendingly. "You look like you've been dragged through a sewer." She wrinkled her nose. "And you smell like it too. Oh! Is this part of the plan? Gelti told me that—"

A distant noise made me hold up a hand to silence her. When all was quiet, I crept to the door and peered out; the hall was empty, save for Valdis still slouched by the wall, and the two dead men. I could hear the rattle of Valdis's breath.

"Help me get Valdis in here," I said to Alshara.

"No." She crossed her arms. "I'm not doing anything until you tell me what's going on."

I turned on her. "Gelti Dimmin tricked us both. Stit planned to sell us to a brothel. I killed Gelti and Stit, and Valdis has been poisoned, and possibly so have I, and Jonis and the Melarim are all going to die unless I can figure out a way to get Stit's men under control."

Alshara rolled her eyes. "Fine, don't tell me."

I dragged her out into the hallway. Together we managed to heave Valdis into the room and onto the settee.

Alshara looked in alarm at his unseeing eyes and then at me. "He *has* been poisoned."

I shoved a chair beneath the doorknob and locked the door. Then I went to the window. The sun was low, and the crowds in the marketplace were thinning. Stit's men, in their Arnath disguises, still patrolled outside.

I picked up Gelti's dagger and ran my fingers over the polished wooden handle while I considered what to do next. Finally I pried the knife out of Valdis's hand and gave it to Alshara. "After I leave, move the chest in front of the mirror," I told her. "Don't let anyone else in. If I'm not back by midnight bells, go out the outside door and down the stairs. Don't let anyone see you. Find the candlemaker's shop in the Web and ask for Tana. Tell her you're Deshti's friend and you need help. She'll keep you safe." I prayed that this was true.

Alshara's eyes were huge. "What are you going to do?"

"My best," I said. "Before you leave, rub some dirt on your gown and your face. You'll stand out otherwise."

Her shocked expression induced an unexpected fondness in me; I darted forward and kissed her forehead before I snatched a lamp from a side table.

The mirror swung easily, if squeakily, away from the wall; these passage hinges had not been oiled as recently as the downstairs cells had. I pulled the mirrored door shut behind me, letting my eyes adjust to the dimmer light. The shadows played so much that it might have been easier to move along in full dark, but I wouldn't willingly blow out the lamp. I found another door farther along, with a few spy holes alongside it. Peering through one, I saw the room where I had confronted Stit and Gelti. Gelti's body lay on the floor, facing away from me. Beyond that was the wreckage of the table and the smashed wine jug, and an overturned chair.

Horel Stit was nowhere to be seen.

TWENTY-EIGHT

MY WHOLE BODY went cold. Stit had been dying; I was sure of it. How could he have left the room? But the trail of blood on the carpet led to the door.

And I had heard something in the hallway earlier.

Maybe I'd been wrong; maybe I hadn't punctured any of Stit's organs at all. Maybe he'd only been pretending to be dying, had let me take the keys so that he could set a trap and capture me when he was surrounded by his men.

Maybe he really was a monster, one we couldn't win against.

No, I told myself firmly. That was ridiculous. Stit wasn't a creature from a children's tale; he was a man, and I'd stabbed him already, and I wouldn't make the mistake of leaving him alive a second time.

This only meant that I had to move faster, but still I went back and peeked through the spy hole to Alshara's room to make sure that she was all right. The chair was still under the doorknob, and she had pushed the chest in front of the mirror as I'd told her to. She stood looking out the window.

It's the best I can do for her, I told myself. *Time to go.* I couldn't abandon Jonis or the Melarim. Especially not now that I knew Stit was, impossibly, still alive.

The clink of the keys in my pocket echoed when I walked, so I paused and ripped a length of fabric from my dress to wrap around them. This took longer than it should have; my left hand was losing dexterity fast. I shoved the padded bundle of keys in my pocket and took up the lamp again, but my fingers wouldn't curl around the handle, so I laid it flat in my left palm. It should have burned, but I felt nothing.

The dagger comfortingly solid in my right hand, I advanced down the corridor. I would follow this passage down to the cells and find a corner from which to watch while I figured out what to do next. I wanted to free Jonis first; maybe he would have some brilliant idea about how to save the Melarim, and even if he didn't, at least I wouldn't be alone. I knew this was impractical—Jonis was in the pit, guarded by at least four men, and Horel Stit was intent on his death. If Stit guessed that I hadn't fled, then he would surely assume that I would try to rescue Jonis. It would only make sense for him to double the guards on Jonis, or—more likely—pull his men back and set a trap for me.

Even Jonis would say that freeing the Melarim was more important. It was a question of numbers again; it simply made sense.

I groped for the comforting lump of the keys in my pocket, hoping that they opened the cells below. Stit was absolutely the kind of man to insist on carrying the keys that opened every lock in this place.

I'd been shuffling along, squinting into the shadows ahead, but I paused as something pressed against my chest. I lifted the lamp, my skin suddenly slick with sweat—that had felt like a hand, stopping me from going forward. I panicked when I saw what the light revealed: the floor seemed to have fallen away.

I focused on the flame to calm my breathing, and then forced myself to look more carefully. There was no broken floor, only steep stairs that disappeared into the blackness below. If I had taken another step, I'd have tumbled straight down them.

Clutching the dagger, I pressed my fist against my hammering heart. "Hand of wisdom, lead us true, lend your might to all we do," I murmured, a line from Raisa's invocation to Sotia. If I was going to be subject to strange presences in the dark, I might as well pretend they were welcome.

A door stood at the bottom of the stairs, practically against the lowest step, so that there was no room to brace myself to push it open. I really didn't have time to pause, dreading the thought of extinguishing the lamp. But if Stit's men were waiting on the other side, I couldn't afford to be blinded by the lamplight either. I might only have a few seconds to surprise them.

My breathing went so shallow that it took me several tries to blow out the lamp, and I had to stuff my forearm into my mouth to stifle my whimper once the flame had gone out. I squeezed my eyes shut, as though pretending the darkness was under my control would make it better, and realized only when I pried my teeth off it that I had been biting my own arm in fright. My entire left arm was now numb.

Grim as that was, it improved my outlook. If I couldn't feel pain, then why should I feel fear?

I forced my eyes open; it wasn't quite as black as the pit had been, as I could see variations in the shadows around me, though that was hardly comforting. Bracing myself against the second step, I pushed the door. It scraped open with a racket that must have echoed all around the lower levels, and as soon as the gap was wide enough, I slipped out, crouched and ready to strike. A torch twinkled far away to the left, past the ominous outlines of iron bars. I held still, listening, but the darkness around me was silent.

I crept forward, trying to get my bearings. There were so many empty cells around me that I guessed I was in the back corridor, which I had glimpsed when Stit's men had taken me down to the pit. They'd have been wiser to spread the Melarim out among these cells. The fact that they hadn't probably meant that their numbers were not large enough to keep watch on so many cells at once.

Or perhaps it only meant that the Melarim had gone peacefully into the cells, once they had seen what Stit's men would do to them if they didn't. I could picture that easily; it would have taken only one or two examples for the rest of them to fall into line, and they would have wanted to stay together, as they had the entire time they had been here.

Either way, it made my task harder. If Stit's men were concentrated around the occupied cells, there was no chance of freeing the Melarim quietly, even if I could somehow convince them to fight. Why would any of them listen to me?

I came to a turn in the corridor where a torch was missing. That made me examine the door next to it more carefully, and sure enough, it was the door Stit's men had taken me through earlier, down to the pit.

That meant the cells holding the Melarim were down the corridor to my left. Stit's men were there too; I could hear their coarse laughter, but their voices echoed too much for me to make out their number. I wondered if Gelti would have been able to tell, if this was a skill he could have taught me eventually if he weren't—

No, I told myself sternly. *Don't think about that.*

There was no help for it; I had to get closer. If I could see what the men were doing, maybe I could formulate a plan. As if by reflex to soothe the Gamo voice inside of me, I thought, *That will also put me closer to the exit if I decide to run for it.*

I grimaced as I crept down the corridor. Maybe I could still convince others that I didn't care what happened to Jonis or the Melarim—and I would do my best to do so, if Stit and his men caught me again—but I couldn't convince myself any longer. If I had been planning to run, I would have done so already. If that made me a fool, so be it.

A rustling to my right made me freeze. It had been a tiny sound compared to the voices up ahead, but I knew I hadn't imagined it.

I crept closer to the bars. The shadowy figure lay on the floor, clutching its right hand to its chest, rocking back and forth, though there was no sniffling, no crying to go with the movement.

"Loris!" I hissed.

No answer.

"Loris, it's me, Soraya," I tried again.

This got a soft moan.

"I have the keys. I think I can get you out." The distant glimmer of a plan was forming in my mind, though it depended on a number of things going right, and I no longer believed that things did that.

Pressing close to the bars to stay out of the torchlight, I pulled the keys from my pocket. I had to put the dagger down to do so; my left hand simply didn't have the strength to hold anything. Steadying the keys between my knees, I worked the fabric off them, and then it was a matter of standing, holding on to the bars to wait out the rush of blood to my head, and fumbling through the keys to try one in the lock.

It didn't work. I pushed that key to the right on the ring and lifted the next one, forcing myself to go through them methodically.

The sixth key stuck, but didn't turn the lock. I cursed quietly and jiggled it, trying to pull it out, and became aware of footsteps approaching from the left. My heart leaped into my throat—one of the men must have heard me and was coming to investigate. I mouthed prayers to every god I'd ever heard of as I struggled to work the key out. Just as I was telling myself I would have to give up and dive into the shadows, the key came free. I swept up the dagger and retreated to a corner.

I recognized the bulky silhouette coming down the hallway at once—Ots. I pressed the keys silent against my thigh with my left hand, and my blade was firmly in my right.

Ots banged on the bars of Loris's cell and said something foul, then spat. The spittle didn't touch Loris, but Ots laughed as if it had, as if he were superior simply by virtue of being outside the bars.

I forced myself to take silent, shallow breaths.

Loris moaned. This entertained Ots enough that he hung around for a few minutes more, hurling insults, and then, with another bang and more spit, he turned and took a torch out of its bracket.

I tensed, terrified that he would see me when the light flashed over my hiding place, but he was already heading down to the lower level.

I stayed still for long minutes after his footsteps retreated, trying to slow my heartbeat. When I accepted that this was impossible, I crept forward and tried the keys again—I had no idea which I'd already tried, so I had to start over, pausing to wipe my sweaty palms between each attempt. Sweat poured down my face, too, even though I was cold, and I had to work to hold my hands steady.

The lock popped open so smoothly and quietly that I didn't notice until the door swung into my toe. I stifled a curse as I slipped inside and pulled the door shut.

The floor beside Loris was filthy; I gagged away from it when I realized that it was one of the waste grates. He reeked of vomit, and his forehead was hot to the touch. I crept around to his other side, shaking his shoulder. "Loris, wake up."

I thought he was turning toward me, but it was only the rocking movement I had seen earlier. He clutched his right arm, ceaselessly rubbing it with his left hand, like a mother comforting a frightened child.

And then I saw, in the dim light, that there wasn't anything at the end of his right arm, that what he was clutching was a bloody stump.

This must have been what Stit's men did to get the Melarim into the cells quietly. I'd thought before, ever so clinically, that it would only take one or two examples.

I had just found their example.

"Oh, Loris," I breathed.

I'd promised him that I would get him home, and now everything had gone wrong. I couldn't do anything right, the voices in the darkness seemed to whisper all around me, so I might as well give up.

Why not? said a voice in my head that sounded like my mother's. I could sneak back to the upstairs room and get Alshara and flee to Pira. No one could fault me for wanting to survive.

No, I told the voice. That might have been who I was once, but it wasn't anymore.

"Loris," I said, patting his cheek. "It's me, Soraya."

His eyelashes fluttered. I leaned closer, then reared back in surprise; he was looking straight at me, his eyes far more lucid than I had expected.

They were also filled with despair.

I clutched his shoulder. "I have the keys. We can get everyone out, but I need your help."

He let out a sound that was so foreign, coming from him, that I stared for a moment before recognizing it as a sarcastic laugh. "I can't help anyone. Leave me alone. Sotia has abandoned us."

"But I haven't," I hissed. "Get up. Your people need you."

He shoved me away, with more strength than I had expected. I righted myself and crawled back over to him. "Calantha died for you," I spat. "She spent years preparing you to survive, preparing you to lead, and now you're curled up in a feeble little ball. You're pathetic!" It may have been my own hateful internal voices that came shrilling out of me in a cut-glass whisper, but it had gotten his attention far more effectively than sympathy had. He sat up, his left arm wrapped across his right, his eyes afire.

"Don't be mad at me," I said. "Be mad at them." I pushed the keys into his left hand, alarmed at how easily they slipped out of my weak grasp. "I'm going to create a distraction. Open the cells as quietly as you can and get the others out. When you see a chance to run for the doors, take it." I wished I could give him more, suggest a place to go once they got out, perhaps even send him to Pira—but if this plan worked, there was a strong likelihood that I would not survive, and my mother would never help them.

"Soraya!" he hissed, but I waved at him to be quiet and forced myself to my feet. I was starting to push the door open when shouting erupted from the direction of the main hallway. I crouched low as several men ran up from the lower level and past the cell.

When it was clear, I worked the cell door open and slipped outside. "Get them out," I told Loris. "It's up to you."

I didn't wait for him to respond, only ran toward the shouts and scuffling coming from the open area ahead. I pressed myself against the bars of the nearest cell, waiting for the moving shapes to resolve into something that made sense.

Something touched my arm, making me jump. It was an old woman in the cell; the others had crowded near the back wall, but she hissed in my ear, "Go back before they see you."

She looked just as somber as the last time I'd seen her, when she had written symbols in the air to ward me off.

I shook my head. "I need them to see me," I muttered. If Stit's men were focused on me, it might give Loris the chance he needed to free the Melarim. "Be ready to move when Loris comes. He has the key. Tell the others."

I crept forward. The shouting had stopped, and a loud voice was talking. Under that, there was a panting sound. It wasn't until I got almost to the torches that I understood what I was seeing. Stit's men surrounded three figures on the floor: Jonis and two Qilarites, both dressed in the ragged clothes and head scarves of sailors. The two sailors knelt, held by two men apiece, but Jonis lay on his stomach, Ots pressing one foot into his back. Jonis's face twisted in agony from his broken ribs. That was why he wasn't fighting Ots; he was barely surviving the pain.

A voice, wheezing but loud, rose over the laughter of the other men, and I couldn't help cringing against the bars. It spoke as if from the realms of the dead, mocking me with my failures.

If Sotia watched over us, then what darker god aided Horel Stit?

"Thought you'd mount a heroic rescue, did you?" Stit said to one of the kneeling sailors. When he plucked the head scarf off the man's head and dragged his face up to the light, I had to stifle a gasp. It was Kirol. I looked more carefully at the second kneeling sailor and recognized Garvin.

"See, lads? Dimmin betrayed us all. Set his cousin free and tried to kill me too." Stit paused for a good loud wheeze and then added, "But I got him in the end."

You did not! I wanted to shout. *That was me. I killed Gelti, and I almost got you, too, you toad.* Hot fury and indignation swelled in me so that I had to press my lips shut to keep the words in.

Gelti probably *had* let his cousin go, had probably threatened him with something dire if he came back. But that wouldn't have stopped Kirol—he and Garvin must have tried to rescue Jonis.

That didn't mean that Gelti had been on my side, or the side of the Melarim. He'd only ever been on his own side, and he hadn't understood Kirol any better than he had understood me.

Think, I ordered myself. The key to any negotiation was knowing what the other side wanted. How many times had my father drilled that into me? That was what I had been trying to do, using my money as a lure for Stit.

But there was something else Stit wanted—or rather, something he desperately wanted to avoid. He'd practically announced it just now, when he had insisted that Gelti was the one who attacked him.

There were things I could do because of who I was, things that Jonis and Loris couldn't. That had always been true. But now I could use who I was—or who Stit thought I was—to help the Melarim. And I would.

I stuffed Gelti's dagger into my pocket, rubbed my face to get some of the dirt off, and glided into the light.

TWENTY-NINE

PROJECTING THE DELIGHTED laugh I had once used at Mati's stupid jokes, I took Stit's arm. "Dimmin was a fool, and so are these," I said haughtily. "With the Gamo fortune behind us, we will take back this nation."

Stit didn't flinch, but I saw the surprise behind his eyes; clearly, he'd expected me to take my sister and flee. The surprise was quickly replaced by amusement.

Let him be amused. I was gambling on his pride being slightly more powerful than his hatred. I could tell his men what really happened, and though they might not believe me, it would stir doubts and rumors. I watched Stit play out the scenario in his mind, and decide that now, at least, was not the time to kill me.

"I see you've found my ring, my lady," he said, holding out his hand. "Wondered where I'd dropped that."

I hesitated, then clumsily slipped my father's ring off my thumb and handed it to him. It didn't matter, I told myself. Even he knew the ring would do him little good without me behind it, but he wanted me to know he was in charge.

I tossed a glance at Jonis writhing under Ots's foot. "If you want him to survive until morning, you'd better have that oaf back off," I told Stit in a bored tone.

"Ots," said Stit, admiring the ring on his finger.

Out of the corner of my eye I saw Ots remove his foot from Jonis's back. Jonis heaved himself to his hands and knees, grunting with pain, and I turned away, letting disgust curl my lip—but I took care to turn in Stit's direction, so he would see my reaction.

I stood so close to Stit that spittle sprayed my cheeks with every wheezing breath he took, close enough to see the marks on his neck from the leather strap I had tried to strangle him with. It would be a wet day in the desert before Stit truly believed I was his ally, but I just had to keep him and his men distracted long enough for Loris to get the cells open.

Stit tightened his arm around mine, but I forced myself not to flinch. "And how should the execution proceed, for maximum suffering?" he said. "Surely a bloodthirsty wench like you has some ideas. Since you were the one behind selling all these tialiks to the mines."

The men around him guffawed. I realized that I had misjudged Stit yet again. He had mountains of pride, and would have slit his own throat before admitting that a woman had nearly killed him, that was true—but his hatred was stronger. And not just his hatred of Arnathim, but his hatred of Jonis specifically—the Arnath whom he blamed for everything that had happened in this city, and everything that had happened to his wife.

And I was only still alive because he saw me as a tool to make Jonis suffer.

Well, then, I thought coldly, *use that.*

I didn't dare look at Jonis. I didn't have to, as I could practically feel his eyes boring into me, full of loathing. Either he was acting, just as I was, or he thought I had truly joined with Stit. It was probably too much to hope that he would trust me after all this.

That didn't change what I had to do. I'd made my decision to trust him, and I would see this through. I needed to find a way of letting him know that we had to stall Stit and his men.

I brushed my hand along the right side of my dress, confirming that Gelti's blade was still in the pocket. "There's burning," I said, keeping my bored tone.

"Too quick," said Stit.

"Oh, not mere flames," I assured him, my heartbeat accelerating. "He should be branded, as Tyasha ke Demit was. I'm sure you all enjoyed the royal Tutor's execution, yes? Think how satisfying this one will be. We will brand him with the symbols he wanted so badly, the thing that made him tear Qilara apart."

I heard a few mutters of agreement around me, and I tamped down my automatic disgust at the ignorance of these men. Were they so afraid of writing that they saw it only as a tool of execution?

"The brands are still there in the palace dungeon," I lied; the brands had been destroyed as soon as we had found them. I went to stand in front of Jonis. Blood dripped down his face from a cut near his temple, and he seemed to be keeping himself upright only by force of will. I half expected him to grab me when I came near, but Ots looming behind him was apparently enough of a deterrent.

"They start with the face," I said, reaching out to trace a symbol on Jonis's cheek. "*Traitor*, the symbol that Aqil branded onto Sotia in the old stories." My finger came away covered in his blood. "Then the right palm: *death*." I wrote in his hand, upside down, so the symbols written in the ink of his own blood faced him. "And the left: *destruction*." I finished the second palm and moved around behind him. "And then the back of the neck: *nothing*." I pushed his head forward and traced the symbol on Jonis's neck.

His head was bowed, staring at the bloody symbols on his palms, which, despite what I'd said, were not Qilarite at all, but Arnath: *Be Sotia's knife.* I could tell from the way he went utterly still that he was puzzling them out, and I prayed that his head was clear enough to understand the meaning. Would he even remember our conversation in the pit?

"Maybe we're just tools," he'd said. *"Just the knife Sotia holds to the throat of her enemies."*

I let my finger rest on the nape of his neck after I had finished writing the symbol, keeping his head down, and then I bent and spoke in his ear, but loud enough for the surrounding men to hear. "Do you understand what will happen to you?"

Jonis's hands fell to his sides. "Yes."

I couldn't tell whether he was feigning the fire in his voice or not, until I felt his hand move up behind his back and take the dagger I had slipped out of my pocket and held there.

I swirled around in front of him in a flounce of skirts that hid Jonis slipping the weapon into his own belt, and gripped his shoulder. "You should have known," I told him, "that it was only a matter of *time*." I dug my fingers into his shoulder on this final word so hard that he winced.

He bowed his head again, so I couldn't tell if he understood that he had to wait for my signal. But he didn't jump up to attack, so he must have.

"It goes on," I told Stit. "You get the idea. You can cover him with symbols if you like. Would that be sufficiently slow and agonizing for you?"

I worried that I had let too much sarcasm seep into my tone, but Stit didn't seem to hear it. "It'll do for a start," he said.

"What about these two?" asked the older man behind Stit, gesturing at Kirol and Garvin.

I shrugged. "Burn them all, if you like. It can't hurt to give the public many examples of what happens to tialik lovers." The words coated my tongue like oil, but I managed to get them out.

I smiled at Stit and let my eyes rove over his men, but I wasn't really looking at them. I was searching the shadows behind them. And I saw movement, a cell door swinging soundlessly open, dark figures gliding out. If I hadn't known that Loris had the key, I might have thought it some grotesque hallucination.

"How do you know that your own men are so trustworthy?" I said baldly to Stit. "Have you tested their loyalties?"

I was just trying to keep Stit's attention on me so that none of the men would look behind them, but tension sizzled in the air at my words. Some of the men must have been loyal to Gelti, not Stit.

"Those that haven't been will be," wheezed Stit.

I tossed my head, using the movement to eye the hallway; another cell had opened. I saw a man turn, saw hands come out of the shadows and pull him backward, covering his mouth, before he could alert his mates. I laughed loudly to cover the sound of whatever the Melarim were doing to the sailor.

Stit's mouth twisted, and he took a step toward me. But before he could say anything, Jonis had sprung up behind me, one arm a bar around my waist, the other holding Gelti's dagger to my throat.

"No!" I cried. What was he doing?

"Let them go," he growled at Stit. "Or I'll kill her."

He's acting, I told myself. *He understood about the plan, and he's acting to buy time for the Melarim to escape the cells.*

But Jonis's venomous voice was right next to my ear, and utterly believable.

I trust him. He held my hand in the dark and he believes in the council and he didn't hurt me even when he could have. But pressure was building in my head, a scream that wanted to get out, a cringing child that wanted to pull away from his body pressed against mine.

"Go on," said Stit. "Do it."

I swallowed hard; the blade undulated against my neck. "You need my money!" I protested shrilly. "You'll never get a thing from the Gamos if you let me die."

Stit shrugged. "Money I can get anywhere. Where else will I get entertainment like this?" His lips spread into a grimace. "What do you think of all your puffed-up ideas about cooperation and equality now, tialik?" He sputtered out a cackle. "In fact, I'll tell you what. You kill her and admit that your council and everything it stands for is rot, and I'll let every damned tialik in this place go."

THIRTY

JONIS'S HEARTBEAT RACED against my back, and I was hyperaware of every hair on my head. It was only a matter of numbers, I thought dimly. *You should take his offer, Jonis.*

Jonis readjusted his grip on the dagger. I couldn't help a terrified squeak as the blade scraped my skin. I could feel Jonis considering Stit's offer, weighing the fate of the Melarim.

And then he let go of me so abruptly that I almost collapsed. He stepped up beside me, one hand holding his ribs, the other pointing the knife at Stit. "No," he said firmly. "You don't get to tell me what to do ever again."

Stit cackled out a laugh. "Enough of this. Ots, take them both—"

But a shout from the hallway cut him off, and the last row of Stit's men melted away. I didn't understand what I was seeing, but I only saw it for a second before Jonis shoved me aside and leaped at Stit. I slammed into the bars of the nearest cell and gulped air into my strained lungs as the hallway erupted into fighting.

Someone inside the cell grabbed my arm, and I jumped back. The Melarim inside pressed forward, begging me to let them out. "I don't have the key," I told them.

"Watch out!" shouted the boy who'd grabbed my arm, and I whirled in time to see a sailor coming at me. I leaped aside, and the sailor cursed and stabbed at the boy through the bars, opening a gash in his arm before he and the others rushed to the rear of the cell.

The sailor turned his attention on me. I scuttled backward into a wall, my head banging painfully against a torch bracket. *"Anything can be a weapon,"* chanted Gelti's voice in my mind, and I swung my right arm up and grabbed the torch, flailing it in front of me to keep the man and his knife at bay. He jumped back, snarling, but my ears weren't working right; they were filled with shouts and bangs and the thuds of fists on flesh all around me. Whatever had held me together while I was talking to Stit was dissolving in a wash of fear and numbness and maschari.

Another man joined the first, and I slid sideways along the wall. But the newcomer slammed the sailor against the bars and put an elbow into his neck in a way that made him slump sideways.

Only when the second man held the sailor's knife out to me did I realize that it was Kirol. He shouted something at me, but the rushing in my ears was too loud. I blinked and forced myself to focus on what he was saying.

"—let the rest of the Melarim out. Who has the keys?"

I shook my head numbly. I couldn't see anything in the mass

of people, except for flashes in the dim light—a flailing limb here, a bloody head scarf there. Then I made out Tira, moving along the row of bars, looking terrified, hunched over something. Behind her, Erinel hovered with a sword, her eyes sweeping the fighting a few feet away; she had clearly appointed herself Tira's guard.

I pointed her out to Kirol with an inarticulate cry. He whirled, bashing aside a sailor, and ran to meet her. I moved after him, swiping the torch to and fro, catching the back of one of Stit's men and making him roll on the ground to put out the flames. My head pounded, and the stench of burning flesh took me back to the battle at the palace, and Aliana's lifeless face, and my legs almost gave out. But I pushed on, clearing a place around Tira with the torch as she unlocked the last cell and the Melarim inside came rushing out. Tira was shouting, and they were shouting, and Kirol was telling them to drive Stit's men into the cells.

"Go out the front! Take the children!" I told Erinel.

She shook her head. "Loris took them down the back."

"There's no way out down there!" I shouted. There was the passage to the upstairs, but Loris wouldn't know about that. And Loris was in no shape to defend them from Stit's men.

I thrust the torch at Tira and pushed toward the back hallway. The fight was on in earnest now, the Melarim fighting with cooking pots, torches, writing tablets, and weapons taken from the men they had overwhelmed. I even saw the old woman stabbing at a sailor with the pointed ends of writing sticks.

All I could make out at the end of the corridor was a hulking shadow. My quickened breathing understood what it was before I did: Ots.

I caught a glimpse of Loris's reddish hair and pale face in the torchlight. Ots had him pinned against the wall and was doing something to the stump of his right hand that made Loris's mouth open in a scream.

I didn't stop to consider that Ots was three times my size, or that what I knew about fighting would hardly fill a teacup, or that my left arm was heavy and pointless. I slammed into Ots's side, hardly moving him but surprising him enough that he let go of Loris.

Before he got a chance to grab me, I plunged my knife into his back. Ots growled and swung at me with a nasty, serrated blade. It sliced my left arm, and blood spurted up, but I didn't feel it at all thanks to the maschari.

The maschari. I almost dropped the knife as I reached up and ripped out the flower that was—possibly only by Sotia's grace—still in my hair. A chunk of hair came with it, but I hardly felt it. It seemed like someone else who swiped the knife down Ots's chest, opening a trench of blood, and then ground the flower into the wound.

Ots roared and came at me, and I tripped over something as I scrambled backward, my fingers and toes numb as they met cold stone.

It was Loris's leg I had stumbled over, and he kicked it out, grunting, to keep Ots off me. Ots said something my ringing ears couldn't hear, and as he came at me again, Loris spat in his face.

It wasn't much—a gesture of defiance, that was all—but the extra time it took for Ots to wipe his face and roar at Loris must have been all the maschari needed. Ots's eyes went wide, and he clutched at his throat, and foam bubbled from his lips. Loris shielded me with his good arm as Ots took a swaying step, then crashed onto the stones.

I didn't know if the wetness on my cheeks was tears or blood, but I didn't have time to find out. "There's a passage up to the second floor," I told Loris, panting. "We can get the children out."

But Loris was staring behind me, back at the open space between the cells. Most of the torches had gone out—or been used for weapons, judging by the smoke and the stench of burning flesh—and a figure strode toward us. All at once, my ears registered the lack of clanging and punching. The only sounds now were sobbing and cries of pain.

The figure was a menacing shadow as it approached. I told myself that I had known going into this what Stit would do to me, that I was prepared for it, but I couldn't help cringing against Loris's side as the reality approached me.

Then the figure passed the closest torch and resolved into the familiar, exhausted, limping form of Jonis ko Rikar.

"Soraya! Loris!" he cried, hurrying toward us. He was favoring his left side and cradling his right elbow with his left hand, and his face was a mass of blood and cuts.

"Is it . . . over?" I panted.

"Stit's men are all dead or in cells, but we still have to deal with the ones outside. At least five of the Melarim are dead too." He gasped at the sight of Loris's arm.

I ripped off another length of my skirt—it was nearly up to my knees now—and wrapped it around the bloody stump. "Nelnar needs to see him as soon as possible. He's lost a lot of blood."

"The children," Loris gasped, trying to pull away from me. I held him firm, despite the fact that my hands were shaking. My ability to hold him probably had more to do with his weakness than my strength.

"They're down there," I told Jonis, nodding toward the dim hallway.

Jonis started after them, but a shout from Kirol stopped him. "Jonis! Soraya! We've got Stit."

Kirol jogged down the corridor toward us. My heart constricted at how much he resembled Gelti in the dim light. He wiped his forehead with the back of the hand holding a knife, leaving a smear of red. "We put him in a separate cell, but I wasn't sure what you would want us to do with him."

Jonis and I exchanged a look.

"We'll deal with him," Jonis said, something grim and dreading in his voice that I had never heard there before. "Go get the children—they're down here—and get Loris to the doctor."

"Are you sure you don't want me to come with—"

"We'll deal with him," Jonis repeated.

Kirol took one look at his face and nodded.

I squeezed Loris's shoulder and stood, so clumsily that Jonis had to grab my arm to steady me.

"Can you handle this?" he asked.

"Can you?" I responded automatically, but there was none of the sarcasm that once would have laced the words.

Jonis didn't answer, only pressed his lips together.

The numbness seemed to have spread to my whole body now. I limped as much as Jonis did on the way back up the corridor.

"This is yours," Jonis said abruptly, handing me Gelti's dagger.

I hesitated, but took it and gripped the smooth cherrywood handle; it was comforting, especially because the open area was dimly lit now. The Melarim were dragging bodies into one of the empty cells, and everyone spoke in hushed tones. Or maybe my ears still weren't working properly.

I wiped the bloody blade of Gelti's dagger on my skirt. "I thought . . . you were really going to kill me."

"For a moment, I thought so too," Jonis said in a low voice.

The brutal honesty of this quiet admission meant far more to me than a denial would have. "But you didn't," I said thickly. Obvious and stupid, but it needed to be said.

"Neither did you."

We looked at each other. Jonis nodded, and I nodded back, and with no more said, there was a contract between us: we would not doubt each other again.

My head must have been absolutely whirling with the maschari by that point, because I looked down at Gelti's dagger and thought that I would rather have this—this respect and trust—than a thousand heated nights in the dark.

Still, I couldn't help remembering Gelti's eyes at the end, how he had tried to protect me from Stit even after I had poisoned him. I would have to explain it all to Jonis eventually. But I had no idea how to begin.

We had other things to deal with now, most pressingly, the man who waited in the cell that Tira led us toward.

"The punishment for a murderer and traitor is execution," I said, because it felt good to quote solid fact, with the world sliding in and out of focus around me.

Jonis nodded silently.

"But he's supposed to have a trial before the entire council."

Jonis grunted. "We might be all that's left of it."

"We don't know that." The idea of Mati and Raisa dead on the road somewhere was impossible to process. My mind refused to even hold on to the notion.

Tira unlocked Stit's cell and hurried away down the hall. Jonis stood with his hand on the door, and we both peered inside. Stit lay near the wall, eyes closed, blood seeping from a fresh wound in his gut and another on his right thigh. Someone had rolled up a blanket to cushion his head on the stone floor. This unexpected mercy both angered me, that anyone would give this to such a man, and shamed me, that I didn't have those instincts. I hadn't killed Stit when it was the merciful thing to do, and look how that had turned out.

"With those wounds," I said, "he won't live long enough for a trial."

Jonis's throat bobbed as he swallowed. "Mati and Raisa wouldn't like it."

"They're not here."

"But it shouldn't be like this! He should be fighting back. There's no honor in this."

"Nothing is like it should be. But that doesn't change

anything." I faltered, remembering my terror when I had seen that Stit's body was missing. "I'll . . . I'll do it, if you want, but I thought you would—"

Jonis swung the cell door open. "No. It should be me. It has to be me."

He strode forward, taking a notched and stained knife from his belt. I slid into the cell behind him.

He kicked Stit in the side. "Wake up." When Stit didn't move, Jonis bent and slapped his face. Stit opened his eyes, but his gaze was bleary and unfocused. His breath rattled in his throat.

"Do you know who I am?" said Jonis.

I shivered. I had never heard quite that ugly a tone in his voice, and I'd had ugliness aplenty directed my way from him. Whatever hatred Stit had for Jonis, Jonis had it in quantities ten times larger for Stit.

"You . . . I know you, but . . . ," wheezed Stit, his mouth slack. Jonis took a step back, his face twisting violently. Stit's confusion would rob Jonis of even the satisfaction of his death.

"Jonis, wait," I said, putting a hand on his arm.

He rounded on me. "Don't tell me not to do it," he spat. "He's earned it more than any of them. We've tried forgiveness and mercy, and it hasn't worked. There will always be men like him, and the only way to deal with them is at the end of a blade."

I quailed under his fierce gaze. "No, I didn't mean . . . just, use this knife." I held out Gelti's dagger. "It's sharper." It seemed very important that Stit die by Gelti's weapon. Gelti's last act had been to protect me from Stit, after all.

Jonis took the blade and turned back to Stit. I gripped the

bars to steady myself and watched as he knelt beside the man who had tormented him for years. I half hoped that Stit would beg for his life—Jonis deserved at least that much, didn't he? But Stit only gurgled pathetically. Jonis bent over him and said something too softly for me to hear, and then the blade flashed and Stit's ragged breath stopped.

Jonis let the dagger clatter to the floor. He'd done it much more quickly and cleanly than I'd expected. I understood something about Jonis then, and how he was different from the dead man on the floor. He would fight when he had to; he would kill when he had to. But he would never enjoy it, not even now, not even when it meant ridding the world of a man like Stit.

Not so long ago, I would have called that weakness.

Jonis let out a long, shuddering sigh, as if he had exorcised some demon that had been weighing on him for years. He looked up at me. "This is yours," he said, holding out my father's ring.

I stared at it, part of me longing to toss it into the shadows and never wear it again. But that wouldn't change anything. I took the ring, but didn't put it on, only clutched the cold metal in my fist.

"Come on," said Jonis. "Let's go home."

THIRTY-ONE

I WOKE UP alone in the palace infirmary. Well, not exactly alone—there were people in the other beds and the doctor's assistants scurrying around, but I was a small bird bobbing on the waves of their constant movements, ignored and unseen.

My last memory was of leaving Stit's cell with Jonis and walking up the corridor toward the doors. I couldn't remember reaching them; I must have fainted from the maschari in my system.

I put a hand to my head, which was pounding, and discovered that my palms and left arm were wrapped in bandages. Someone had put the signet ring back on my thumb. I wondered how long I had been unconscious, and whether there had been any new attacks, and how I had been brought back to the palace, and whether they had used the palace carriages to do it or had hired outside help, and if they had hired carriages how that would further ruin the budget. And hovering behind all that were several unpleasant memories that wanted to drown me, but I took a deep breath, my lungs gurgling strangely, and pushed them away.

The blanket stirred in the bed to my left, and then Loris's face peered over at me. The sight of the cleanly bandaged stump at the end of his right arm made my chest hitch, and suddenly I couldn't breathe. Vaguely I heard Loris calling for the doctor, and then calm, professional hands eased me back onto the pillow as someone pressed a warm compress onto my chest. Darkness surrounded me—I was in the tombs, in the pit . . .

"Breathe, Soraya," said a voice. Loris. He had pushed between the assistants and taken my hand. I focused on his face and made my breathing slow.

Finally Nelnar sent his assistants off and nudged Loris back to his bed. He lifted one of my eyelids and then the other, and I would have slapped his hand away if I'd had the strength.

"Where's my sister? Where are Jonis and Kirol?" I demanded wheezily.

"Your sister is collecting cloths for bandages. I would guess that Kirol is overseeing the cleanup at the market. And Jonis should be right there"—he nodded at the empty bed to my right—"but he insisted on leaving as soon as we bandaged him up. Said he had too much to do to lie around."

"So do I." I swung my legs off the bed. At some point while I was unconscious, someone had removed my filthy dress—I hoped they'd burned it—and wrapped me in my father's old dressing gown.

Nelnar grabbed my shoulder. The effort of fighting him sapped all my energy and I collapsed against the pillows, coughing wetly. "You're not going anywhere," he said. "Your injuries wouldn't have caused the blackout or the coughing. What else happened to you?"

"Maschari," I said weakly. I held up my bandaged left hand. "I crumbled it in this hand after the cuts."

"Valdis too? Is that why he's been unresponsive?"

I nodded. "He drank it. I only touched it."

Nelnar's eyes were so unbearably sad that I couldn't breathe for a moment. He didn't have to tell me what Valdis's prognosis was. Then he became businesslike again, unwrapped my left hand and examined the wounds. "My assistant cleaned this well, so you'll just have to work out what's already in your blood. If you've managed to stay alive this long, it's unlikely to kill you now." He prodded at my palm, and I flinched. "That's a good sign. You probably haven't been able to feel anything for some time."

I jerked my hand back. "How long, exactly, have I been here?"

"A few hours. It's almost sunrise bells now."

It had been nearly a day since I had left Gelti's house, longer since . . .

I forced myself up, wincing at the pressure on my hands. "I need silphium," I said softly. "Immediately."

Nelnar frowned. "I can give you something else for pain. Silphium and maschari are a bad mix."

"How, exactly?"

"The mixture can cause infertility. It's hardly worth risking that when there are other pain remedies—"

"And suppose," I said, dropping my voice even lower, so that Nelnar had to lean forward to hear me, "a woman meant to take silphium sooner, but missed her . . . opportunity to do so?" I was acutely aware of Loris in the next bed, though he had turned his face away and my voice was so low that I didn't think he could have heard me.

Nelnar's eyebrows rose to his hairline. "For that . . . only a larger dose of silphium would help. But the amount I'd have to give you, combined with the maschari in your system, would almost certainly cause a . . . permanent effect. In addition to, ahem, taking care of the immediate need. Are you willing to trade one for the other?"

My right hand went to my stomach as I recalled the previous night in Gelti's room. It hadn't been real, any of it, no matter what his face at the end had said. He might even have believed that he loved me, but his way of showing it was broken, hideous. I didn't want any part of him in me, not even the memories of him.

And it was easy, too easy, for a woman to be reduced to one role in this world. Wife. Mother. A vessel for the unformed frustrations of whatever man believed he could own her. I thought of my mother, risking death again and again attempting to give my father a son, because that was the only way she knew to prove her worth.

I wouldn't be that. I wouldn't ever let myself be that. If that required sacrifice, then so be it.

"Give me the silphium," I said.

I'd told Nelnar that I would leave the infirmary as soon as I had taken the silphium, and was surprised that he didn't argue with me. I choked down the tumblerful of brown liquid and accepted the glass of water he handed me, glad to have something to chase away the foul taste.

But as soon as I handed back the empty glass and tried to push the blanket off me, I realized that it hadn't been water at all. My limbs went heavy, but I managed to get out a few curses at him before I passed out.

When I woke again, the sounds in the infirmary were muted, giving me the sense that it was late at night.

Then I became aware of low voices to my left—that must have been what woke me. My mutinous eyelids wanted to flutter open, but I kept them firmly closed, instinctively taking the opportunity to listen in.

"—the day after tomorrow," Jonis was saying. "Both ships will be stocked by then. It won't be fancy, but . . ."

"It will be better than the way we came," returned Loris. "We're finally heading home."

"Yes," said Jonis. He paused. "I should wait until I talk to Soraya to say this, but . . . I'd like to send an ambassador back with you."

"All right. We should have an ambassador here as well. Tira will probably want to stay to see her niece anyway."

It took me a moment to untangle the implications of those words, and my eyes flew open when I did. "Raisa and Mati are alive?" I said, cutting across whatever Jonis was saying.

They both swung toward me, Loris propped against his pillows and Jonis sitting on the end of Loris's bed with one leg tucked beneath him.

Jonis grinned. "You can never assume that a Gamo is really sleeping."

"How are you feeling?" asked Loris.

"Fine," I said. This was not, strictly speaking, true—my head felt heavy and my palms and arm burned and my ankle ached and there was an odd pinching in my abdomen—but none of that was important right now. "They're alive?" I asked again.

"As far as we know," Jonis said. "Lilano did secede, and they had to run. But they sent one of the guards ahead with a message. The last time he saw them they were heading for a village on the western coast. Their plan was to get to Pira by boat and then ask your mother for help returning here. In the meantime, we've commandeered Stit's ship to take the Melarim back home. It'll be ready in two days."

"With an ambassador, I hear," I said tartly. Jonis nodded sheepishly, and started to say something, but I interrupted him. "Wait, you said 'both ships' before."

Jonis looked chagrined. "Exactly how long were you listening?"

I shrugged. "Never assume a Gamo is really sleeping."

"When it got out what had happened, some of the merchants started up a collection for food and clothes for the Melarim. Tana Meer led it, and she—"

"Tana? Deshti's friend?"

Jonis nodded. "She and Deshti were there when we came out of the pens. Your sister had sneaked out and gotten them, and Tana rallied some of the other merchants. By the time we made it outside they had already taken care of the rest of Stit's men. Turns out that she and a lot of other Qilarites were pretty appalled when they saw what Stit had done. I guess they wanted to ease their guilt for not doing something before—"

I winced at a pain in my stomach. "Don't do that," I said. "It might be true, but . . . don't discount that they did something good. Even if they should have done it sooner." I couldn't even begin to process what it meant that Alshara had been the one to set that in motion.

Jonis rubbed his elbow, then nodded. "Anyway, they took up a collection for supplies. And Marieke Gard got wind of it, and came to me this afternoon and offered a second ship. Once the southern vizier found out she was doing business for her husband, he refused to pay her. So she seized one of his ships. Said she's done serving as the southern vizier's agent, and is running her own business now."

"She only offered us the use of the ship so we would defend her against retaliation from the southern vizier," I said flatly.

"Obviously," said Jonis. "But I didn't see how we could say no. Stit's ship wasn't big enough, so we needed another."

Jonis sat stiffly, due to the broken ribs, I supposed, and he kept rubbing at his elbow. He'd cleaned up, but still bore the bruises and cuts of the day before. And there was a tight sadness around his eyes. He seemed smaller, somehow, than I remembered.

Oh, I thought. That was probably because he used to have a very large shadow.

"Jonis," I said abruptly. "I'm sorry about Adin."

Jonis's face contorted so sharply that I regretting bringing it up, at least until he said softly, "Thanks."

I cleared my throat into the uncomfortable silence. "I'll need to start working up a new budget. Anything else I should know?"

Jonis seemed relieved at the change of subject. He moved from Loris's bed to mine, and described the cleanup at the pen building and how the remaining Melarim had come to camp out in the Library until the ships were ready. To my astonishment, that had been Alshara's idea, and Loris chimed in to say that none of them minded sleeping on the hard floor when they were surrounded by scrolls.

Losing Lilano and the South Company meant that fortifying the defenses around the Valley of Qora was our new top priority. The rainy season was fast approaching, which would give us some time, as neither Emtiria nor Lilano would bother to mount a campaign until the weather turned fairer, but we had to be ready when it did, or risk losing our main food supply. I had several letters to write in the morning; I was sure that Lord Romit's political enemies would be very interested in the way he had used his cabinet position to back the Swords of Qilara and drag Emtiria into a failed coup.

In the meantime, fifteen of Stit's men in the dungeon awaited trials, and we had to decide whether the demands of justice and the demands of public opinion were the same. I tried to explain that we had to deal with them as harshly as we had Stit, but Jonis resisted the idea of making a spectacle of their execution. Even if the spectacle might keep us in power.

By this time, Loris was pretending to sleep—I could tell by the unevenness of his breathing that he was listening in, but didn't want to be drawn into our argument.

"We can decide in the morning," said Jonis, pushing himself off the bed. "You need rest."

I narrowed my eyes at his unusual solicitousness. "What has Nelnar told you?"

"That you and Valdis were both poisoned with maschari, that he's dying of it but you had less and will recover, but will probably be even more impossible than usual to deal with until you do." He eyed me. "And Kirol found his cousin dead and foaming at the mouth. I imagine there's quite a story there."

"I imagine you're right," I said faintly. "I should tell you about . . ." My eyes were leaking stupid, nonsensical tears, and I swiped them away.

Jonis shook his head. "You don't have to, not now. Write it down. Deshti will want all this chronicled for the Library anyway."

I sniffed. "Will you tell Kirol I need to talk to him?"

Jonis nodded. "Alshara too. Loris said she's been in at least five times today checking on you." He hovered by my bed—I had the ridiculous notion that he was about to kiss my forehead as Raisa had done when she left for Lilano. But he only gripped my shoulder in a brotherly sort of way and said, "Whatever happened, I'm glad you're the one who made it out alive."

And then he left. My body was heavy and achy, but my mind whirred too much for sleep. All the lamps were out except the one between my bed and Loris's, and the one glowing from the room where Nelnar dozed in a chair at his desk. I suspected that Jonis was behind this, and that made my eyes water again.

Loris lay motionless in the next bed, his bandaged stump resting on his chest.

"Mati learned to write with his left hand, after his right was burned," I said softly.

He didn't bother to pretend I had woken him, just turned his head and looked at me. "Jonis told me."

"How can you be so calm?" I demanded. "They took . . . part of you. How do you go on from that?" Whatever it was that kept him from cursing and crying, I wanted it for myself, to quell the churning doubts, the sense that I had lost something vital, even though my limbs were all intact.

Loris studied the shadows above. "Calantha always said only fools see the world through clouded eyes. You have to accept what is before you can see what could be."

"And what about what was?" I asked softly.

The corner of Loris's mouth lifted. "That, you have to let go." He laughed softly. "You remind me of her. In that cell, the way you yelled at me . . . she never let me wallow either."

I settled onto my side facing him. "You're stronger than you give yourself credit for."

He regarded me, his hair wine-dark in the lamplight. "And you're kinder than you give yourself credit for."

I laughed. "Kind?"

He nodded somberly. "It's the best part of you. You don't have to hide it."

I cleared my throat. "You can blow out the lamp if it bothers you," I said, hoping that the light at the other end of the room would be enough to prevent nightmares.

"It's all right," he said softly. "After the past few days, I am not fond of the dark either."

I must have fallen asleep eventually, because I was awakened the next morning when something dropped onto the foot of my bed.

"I've brought your breakfast, sleepy," said a familiar voice.

I opened my eyes to find Alshara holding a tray. The smell of meat made me wrinkle my nose—it reminded me too much of the taste of the silphium tincture. I hadn't eaten anything since breakfast at Gelti's house, and judging by the light, it was mid-morning, over a day since I had arrived in the infirmary and two since going to the slave pen building.

I quickly realized why Nelnar hadn't offered me food before: my stomach seemed to be trying to exit my body. I pressed my hand over my mouth and nose. The gurgling in my lungs was gone, but it seemed to have moved down into my gut. "Take it away," I managed to croak.

Alshara's weight left the bed, and the overpowering smell of meat mercifully dissipated. But then she was poking at my shoulder. "At least drink some tea. Nelnar says you've got to have something."

I pushed myself up, and, to my surprise, Alshara helped position my pillows.

The taste of the tea was mild enough not to nauseate me, and the warm liquid felt good slipping down my throat. "Thank you," I said.

I glanced over at Loris's bed to see what he thought of all this, and found it empty and stripped of blankets.

"The doctor let him leave this morning," Alshara said, clearly pleased to have information I didn't. "He moved to the Library with the others."

I nodded and concentrated on my tea. But I'd only drunk half of it when my body revolted. I slapped the cup onto the table, and Alshara shoved a bucket into my lap. All the tea came back up, along with a thick, greenish sludge that burned my throat. I retched until nothing was left, and then wiped my mouth with my bandaged hand.

Alshara handed the bucket off to one of the assistants and patted my arm. "That's a good sign," she said cheerfully. "I've been reading about maschari poisoning. Once you get to the vomiting, you're almost through it."

"Excellent," I said weakly.

Alshara sat on the edge of the bed. "Will you tell me the plan this time, or do I have to guess?" she whispered.

I stared at her. "What are you talking about?"

"The plan! You're back to pretending to be on the council, right? Though I'm not sure how you convinced—"

I shook my head, my stomach threatening to rebel again. "I'm not pretending, Alshara. I *am* on the council." I closed my eyes wearily. "If you need to go write to Mother about that, do it. Everything is different now. We need to be different too."

Alshara cocked her head. "So . . . you really want me to be Deshti's assistant?"

I nodded, and was amazed to see her shoulders sag in relief.

"Gelti said you were planning things with him," she said, the words tumbling out in a low rush, "and that if I didn't do what he said, that those men would—"

I put my hand on her arm. "Jonis told me that you went for help. You were supposed to run away."

"But you were still there," she said defiantly.

I looked at her for a long moment. Her hair was still perfectly beaded, and the dress she wore was just a little too fine for the infirmary, but those things no longer blinded me to the stubborn set of her chin and the uncertainty in her eyes.

"You did an amazing job," I told her. "Thank you."

She smiled, but then her face fell. "I'm not like you," she whispered.

"What do you mean?" I asked.

"I really like working in the Library . . . with Deshti. I'm not good at . . . the planning, the politics." But I had a strong feeling that she had been about to say something else. I opened my mouth to ask what, but she hurriedly spoke over me. "You were always Father's favorite, the most like him."

"You don't have to be like me, or like Father. You just have to be yourself. I'm proud of you." I hesitated, then hugged her. She sat stiffly at first, before she relaxed and put her arms around me too.

"Soraya?"

"Hmm?"

"You smell disgusting."

There was the old Alshara. I laughed. "I'd love to go to the baths. Will you help me?"

Her face registered surprise, but she nodded eagerly. "I'll get my rose-scented soap!"

I smiled, swallowing the wave of nausea brought on by the idea of that overwhelming scent. It was her favorite, and I wasn't about to quash this unexpected generosity from her.

Alshara stood, chattering about gathering supplies for a bath and how I'd been paying less attention to my appearance of late than was appropriate.

"Do you know where Valdis is?" I asked her.

She immediately shut up and looked forlornly down the rows of beds.

"I want to see him." I pulled the blankets back and swung my legs off the bed, holding out my hand to her, but she only stood frozen.

"He won't know you," she said in a small voice.

I forced a smile. "But I'll know him."

I was panting and sore by the time we reached the bed at the end, but I could see why they had put Valdis here; the ceiling was so low that most patients would have complained. But Valdis only lay motionless on his back, eyes open but seeing nothing. Like he was already gone.

Alshara pulled a chair next to the bed for me, then said something about getting the soap and hurried out. She must have spoken to Nelnar on the way, however, because he soon appeared at my elbow and offered a dose of silphium for the pain.

"It won't matter how much you take now," he said in a low voice. "The damage has already been done."

I swallowed the tincture, and the glass of what he swore by Sotia was water he handed me afterward. "Is there nothing you can do for Valdis?" I asked.

Nelnar sighed. "It's only because of his astonishing tolerance for poisons that he's even still alive. It's possible that, with time, he will be able to sit up, maybe even walk. But he'll never be what he was."

I nodded sadly.

Nelnar's eyes lit on someone behind me, and I turned, expecting to see Alshara. But it was Kirol who stood there, hands in his pockets. Nelnar abruptly excused himself.

I put both hands over my abdomen, grunting as a wave of nausea or pain or both rolled through me. *"I'm sorry about your cousin"* was what I would have said, once upon a time when that was just a banality to smooth an interaction. But the words stuck in my throat, because I wasn't sure what I should be sorry for. Sorry that his cousin had betrayed both my trust and Kirol's? Sorry that I hadn't warned Gelti with a look that the wine had been poisoned? Sorry that he hadn't been properly evil enough at the end, so that I would be free of regrets?

Sorry wasn't the right word, I decided. Only a fool would be sorry for doing what she had to do to stay alive.

It seemed a shortcoming of the language of the gods that there wasn't a word to describe this sick, heavy feeling, all twisted up with despair and sorrow and helplessness and guilt over things I couldn't prevent. I couldn't express it, so I decided not to try.

"Gelti is dead," I said. His name burned on my tongue.

Kirol nodded. "Stit killed him."

"No. I did." Kirol knew what his cousin was, but still I couldn't look at him as I told him about the maschari and how Gelti had fought for me at the end.

Kirol was silent for a long moment, and when he started talking his words tumbled out in a low stream. I'd been right about Gelti freeing his cousin, and also about the threats he had employed to get Kirol to leave. The words they had traded hadn't been kind, and Kirol couldn't look at me as he told it either.

"He knew you wouldn't listen," I said. "He knew you'd get help and come back." I wasn't at all certain this was true; if I had learned anything in the past few days, it was that I hadn't known Gelti Dimmin at all. But the way Kirol's shoulders lifted made me glad I had said it.

"I went to see Aunt Nasha," Kirol said. "I didn't tell her the details, but . . ." His lip curled. "She wanted to know if the Ruling Council would provide survivor's pay."

"I hardly think that—"

"Let her keep the house. Take it out of my wages if you have to."

"Kirol. You don't have to do that."

"Yes, I do. If only to prove I'm not like them. You of all people should understand that."

I nodded slowly.

He looked down at his hands, which were balled into fists. "I heard you're planning to send an ambassador back with the Melarim."

I nodded, relieved for the change of subject. "Yes, we'll have to find someone with diplomatic—"

"Send me."

I blinked. Ah. Not a change of subject after all. "You don't have any experience as an ambassador."

He snorted. "Do you have a pool of qualified candidates you're hiding somewhere?" His tone sounded so much like Gelti that I winced.

"We need you here."

Kirol shook his head. "I'm rubbish as guard captain and you know it. I only got the job because you all were desperate and I was willing. I'm tired of being in my cousin's shadow. I only ever joined the guard because that was what he was." He looked away, blinking rapidly. "I'm tired of pretending to be something I'm not. Maybe there, on the islands, I can do something good that doesn't turn to dust."

I was suddenly pierced with that very same longing, to get out from under my family legacy, to start over somewhere new. In my mind, the beaches of the Nath Tarin spread out, white sand and black rock and asotis wheeling over the trees. The waves lapped against the shore, murmuring of new beginnings.

A nice dream, maybe, but there were things to do, goals to reach here. That was Kirol's dream, not mine.

I nodded. "You'll make a fine ambassador."

His answering smile was so much like his cousin's that it pierced my heart.

THIRTY-TWO

THE NEXT MORNING dawned fair and clear, as if the goddess herself wanted to give the Melarim a proper send-off. Alshara helped me down from the carriage at the docks. Two guards fell into step behind us. Perhaps there should have been more, but two was all we could spare, and I had Gelti's dagger hidden under the scarf at my waist, and frankly, I was tired of being afraid. I'd finally been able to eat something this morning without immediately vomiting it back up. My bleeding had begun during the night, ten days early, and I couldn't tell if I imagined it being heavier and more painful than usual.

What's done is done, I reminded myself.

We'd planned for the ships to leave soon after sunrise, early enough, we hoped, that not too many people would be on the streets. There had been an aura of guilt-fed goodwill hanging over the city ever since the incident at the slave pen building—similar to, if less intense than, the we-are-one-people sentiment that had flourished after the floods. I expected it to burn out soon, at least until the next dreadful incident forced everyone together again. Perhaps this was all our council's reign would be—a series of crises punctuated by periods of naive optimism.

But word had gotten out about the departure, and while the crowd milling around between the burned-out warehouses and the terminal building was nothing compared with what it had been on the day that the raider ship returned, it was large enough to make me nervous. Until, that is, we got close enough to hear the exhausted benevolence that laced the buzz of the crowd. It was hard, at first glance, to tell who was Arnath and who was Qilarite.

At least until I saw the group that had gathered near the warehouses. These were clearly sailors, and clearly disgruntled. But they were small in number, and the crowds nearby were ignoring them.

I squinted and saw that most people in that area were gathered around a stall run by a portly Qilarite woman. "Peace Candles" read the sign above it.

"There's Deshti!" said Alshara, pointing to the second figure behind the stall. She waved maniacally and Deshti waved back, holding up a candle emblazoned with symbols. Judging by the steady business they were doing, Deshti's idea had caught on.

Another idea had caught on too—over near the terminal building, a line of people sat on the ground, leaning against packs. These were the city residents who hoped to take the places on the ships made by the handful of Melarim who had elected to stay in Qilara, and they had been lining up since the day before. Jonis and Loris and I had agreed that those places would be opened to anyone who wanted to go to the islands, on a first-come, first-served basis. Loris had warned that most of them would probably want to return as soon as they saw how confining life on the islands was, but Jonis had been sure that many Arnathim would want to track down long-lost family or simply make a new life away from the place where they had been enslaved.

Jonis stood near the front of the line, talking seriously with a white-haired man. I pointed him out to Alshara and we made our way through the crowd to him.

"Thinking of joining them?" I said as he turned away from the man.

Jonis smiled. "No, someone has to keep you out of trouble until Mati and Raisa get back."

"As I recall, I was the one getting you out of trouble."

"Fair enough," he said mildly. "Have you seen Kirol?"

I shook my head. "We just got here. The Melarim were right behind us. Loris was still packing scrolls when I left the palace."

Jonis indicated the path toward the ships, where Kirol had stayed last night with ten of his men, to make sure that no one tried to sabotage them. The city's mood for the past few days had been gentler, and we'd made sure to bolster it by planting stories about Mati and Raisa's imminent return, but we weren't taking any chances this time.

Kirol came down the gangplank to meet us. He'd already traded his white guard uniform for a tailored tunic of maroon.

"No trouble last night. Everything's ready," he said.

"As are you, obviously," I observed. He practically bounced with excitement. It saddened me to see how much he longed to get away.

He smiled and pointed behind me. I turned to find the Melarim streaming from the line of carriages that had parked along the road. A new sound arose from the crowds on either side of them. Someone threw something, making me tense, but then I realized that it was . . . flowers. The front rows of people were tossing flowers at the Melarim, cheering and shouting wishes for a pleasant journey. There were jeers too, from the back, but the flower throwers had pushed in front of those people and were making a concerted effort to drown them out. I saw Erinel passing out flowers with Marisa, the Qilarite teacher who had taken her on, and the girl actually smiled when Marisa spoke to her.

Alshara laughed. "The flowers were Deshti's idea! Isn't she brilliant?"

Next to me, Jonis's mouth was opening and closing in surprise, and he shot a look across the crowd at Deshti that made me grin.

Alshara giggled proudly. "Deshti got Tana to gather people and—"

The rest of her explanation was drowned out as the Melarim neared us, and their own cheers were added to the throng.

Loris and Tira were at the front of the group, Loris wearing a dark-blue tunic with long, slashed sleeves in the Emtirian style. I had dug it, along with the maroon that Kirol was wearing, out of the trunk of decent clothes salvaged from Mati's and my father's wardrobes. Loris had looked dubiously at the embroidery down the front—it couldn't have been less his style—but I could tell that he liked the way the sleeves hid his bandaged stump. He stood tall and straight, looking like a leader.

By now, most of the city had heard what had gone on in the slave pen building. The flower throwers cheered Loris by name, and to my surprise, I heard Jonis's name and my own in there too.

Loris hesitated as he approached us; in our long discussion last night, we hadn't talked about how we would all interact in front of crowds. I stepped forward and held out my right hand to Loris, palm up. It was the greeting a male Scholar would have used with another Scholar to show respect, though it would normally have been done with two hands, and I wasn't about to draw attention to Loris's right hand. This gesture never would have been used by a woman in the past, but we would just have to adjust.

Everyone would just have to adjust.

"Take my hand," I whispered with a smile. He did, looking bemused, and repeated the greeting with Jonis. "They're going to expect a speech. Just say a few words about hope and cooperation, and then get on the ship."

We went to the top of the gangplank, and it was clear Loris didn't know how to start, so I stepped up and mouthed some platitudes about a new dawn for the people of Qilara and the people of the islands. That left little for Loris to do but introduce Kirol and Tira as ambassadors. Jonis, in a perfect finale, spoke up and offered an invocation to Sotia for fair winds and a calm sea for the journey.

Then the Melarim were boarding the ships, and the guards were counting off the additional passengers, and Tira was going around hugging the Melarim. Loris and Jonis and I stepped over to the rail. To my amusement, Loris was sweating.

"That went better than I expected," he said.

"They were already in a good mood, so they just wanted that reinforced," I said. "It's only hard when you have to tell them something they don't want to hear."

He grimaced. "As I recall, you're good at that too."

Jonis barked out a knowing laugh.

Loris brushed his copper curls out of his face. "Come visit Longa sometime. Both of you. Although," he added, looking at me, "you'd be in my territory then. Could you handle that?"

"I think so," I said, meeting his eyes. I was surprised at how appealing I found the idea of visiting the islands; for so long I had focused on getting rid of the Melarim, but now the thought of never seeing Loris again did something strange to my throat. And I understood, in a way I could not have even a Shining ago, how much trust he was offering in that invitation. I would not take it lightly.

Everything was a bustle of goodbyes after that. Soon I found myself with Tira and Jonis—and Alshara, who had reclaimed her place at my elbow—standing on the dock, waving as the ships pulled away. This was the first time in hundreds of years that ships had set sail toward the northern islands without the intention of raiding and killing. How pathetic, that this was major progress.

A quartet of asotis circled over Loris's ship, their cries piercing the babble of the crowd, and for some reason, tears pricked my eyes.

"Why, Councilor Gamo, are you getting sentimental?" said Jonis next to me.

"Of course not," I snapped. "I was just thinking of all the

work I'm going to have to do to figure out a new budget."

Jonis huffed out a fond laugh and squeezed my shoulder.

Mati and Raisa arrived a few days later. I was in the Library; I had taken to working there instead of the second-floor study, which I now found stifling. Alshara had been delighted to set me up in a corner, though Deshti had been frosty at first, declaring that she had no intention of apologizing for drugging my tea, and would do it again if necessary.

"I don't doubt it for an instant," I replied honestly.

Deshti narrowed her eyes, but then seemed to decide that I wasn't mocking her. After that, we got along just fine.

One reason I liked working in the Library was seeing how competent and helpful my sister could be when she wanted. Knowing that she was allowed to enjoy this, that she wouldn't be expected to lie or cheat or be something else in service to her family, seemed to have freed her. I understood the feeling. She'd even begun training Erinel to help with some of the basic Library tasks like sharpening quills.

To my surprise, I also relished the bustle of the Library during the day—and more people than ever had come to study here since the Melarim had left. Jonis and I had done as much teaching as we could squeeze in, but with the entire budget to redo, I'd come back tonight after dinner to work alone.

Gyotia's Lamp was a bright half coin in the clear, starry sky, and I had opened the outside doors to evening breeze. The budget was coming together more easily than expected—shedding the massive expense of feeding and housing the South Company, which was now Lilano's problem, had freed up resources for the north, even if it also meant that I would have to put more of my family's money into the defenses for the Valley of Qora. But if we could convince the farmers there to contribute—

"I told you she'd be in here," said a voice, and I looked up to see Jonis at the door, with Mati and Raisa behind him.

I pushed back my chair, unable to hide my smile. Raisa seized me and hugged me, and Jonis and Mati were laughing, and we were all talking over each other, and no one could understand what anyone else was saying but it didn't matter because we were all just so relieved to be together again.

We sent for food and adjourned to the outer courtyard when it arrived. Jonis brought out lamps and dropped into the seat next to mine. Mati and Raisa, despite their protests that they weren't hungry, had already tucked into the stew.

"Surprised you didn't make us wake Valdis first," said Mati between bites.

I stiffened, and Jonis shot me a sympathetic look. "We have a lot to tell you," he said.

Mati nodded soberly. "We do too. Only so much you can put into letters, and I don't even know if you got all of them."

"We'll talk first. You eat." I looked at Jonis. "Do you want to tell it, or should I?"

Jonis indicated that I should go ahead, and I turned to Mati and Raisa to find them sharing an amused grin. But their faces quickly fell when I described the unrest in the city, which they'd known about from our letters, and the events of the past several days, which they hadn't. When I got to the confrontation in the upstairs room, my throat closed up, and Jonis jumped in, telling how Kirol had gotten him out of the pit with a combination of flattery, bribery, and sharma-laced liquor.

Mati and Raisa pushed their bowls away and told us about Lilano, and I could see that Jonis and I weren't the only ones who had changed. Raisa's face was freckled, her skin tan from her time on the road. Mati needed a shave and haircut, and his eyes had a tired, cautious look that made him seem older than he was. They sat differently too; I remembered vividly the way they had pressed against each other during our council meetings, because it had given me unwanted pangs. Although they had the same warmth in their eyes when they looked at each other, Mati no longer hovered close to Raisa. It seemed he had finally accepted that he didn't have to protect her every single second.

This realization made me like him more than I had at any previous point, including during our betrothal.

Even though they'd been run out of Lilano, Raisa was optimistic about the progress they'd made there. I was about to comment on this when Jonis asked, "What changed? You said Commander Gage was supporting us. How did the southern vizier get to him?"

Mati gripped the edge of the table. Raisa glanced at him and said, "When Gage got the news about Coe's murder, he believed that the council was behind it and—"

"That was Gelti," I said. Raisa's eyes darted to my face. She must have heard something in my tone, even though I had avoided mentioning anything about my relationship with Gelti, and Jonis had, mercifully, let the omission stand. No doubt I was going to be subjected to girl talk very soon.

"It wasn't just about Coe," said Mati. "Gage found out about the false maps I gave those raiders. He was ready to give us a chance until then. I'm the reason we lost Lilano."

Raisa touched his shoulder, but didn't say anything; I had the feeling that she'd already used up any comforting words on the subject.

Mati shook his head. "If I hadn't—"

"But you did," I said. "It happened, and the consequences happened, and there will probably be other consequences that we don't see yet." The level of sympathy in my voice was on par with that I had shown to Loris in the cell, with that I had shown to myself when I thought about recent events. But Mati had surely been beating himself up about it ever since he'd heard of the Melarim's arrival, and he was no use to anyone like this. "Lilano wouldn't even have been at risk if the southern vizier wasn't such a worm. Not everything is a direct result of *your* actions, you know." All three of them stared at me. I took a deep breath. "Let it go already."

Mati nodded, and the way Raisa's mouth quirked made me wonder if she had wanted to say those harsh things to him, and what had possessed me to do so. I guess I'd finally stopped worrying about his opinion of me.

There were decisions to make after that, and we stayed up well past the muted tones of final bells discussing them. We all agreed that a peace treaty with Lilano would be ideal, as we didn't have the resources to fight its secession. Once the failure of the Swords of Qilara had been made public—as I had made sure it would, by sending messengers to Lord Romit's political enemies—the Emtirian emperor had disavowed all knowledge of the plot, arrested Lord Romit, and confiscated his property. He apparently only wanted to be associated with *successful* coups. Under Emtirian law, Romit's arrest nullified any contracts relating to the incident, and I had sent Romit's money to the emperor at once, in case he got any ideas about access to our ports. I'd resigned myself to regaining a useless salt mine; maybe if we managed to negotiate a peace with Lilano I could find a buyer there.

The others finally agreed to open cautious—"*very* cautious," Mati insisted—trade discussions with Emtiria. I then shocked them all with my suggestion that we add seats to the Ruling Council, but they agreed it made sense to ensure Qilarite merchant and peasant representation. Gelti had planted this idea in my mind—no doubt trying to lay the groundwork for him being on the throne. But just because the seeds of it came from a despicable place, that didn't make it a bad idea. I could admit that now.

We were so caught up in our discussion that none of us realized how long we'd been at it until the lamp in the middle of the table sputtered out.

"Oh!" said Raisa. "We should go to bed. I'll take these to the kitchen." She stacked the stew bowls and stood.

"Soraya and I will get the lamps," Mati said. He kissed Raisa's forehead and she smiled.

Jonis shot him a curious look as he reached for the goblets, but I could tell, as he followed Raisa out of the Library, that he didn't mind having a few minutes alone with her. Jonis might be coming to terms with the fact that he loved Deshti, though I had no idea whether he would ever do anything about it. I suspected that part of him would always idealize Raisa.

I went to get the lamps on the ledge, but Mati's words stopped me. "Soraya," he said softly. "I . . . never thanked you."

I turned, puzzled. Mati hovered by the table, his hands clasped loosely in front of him. The puckered skin of his scarred right hand was visible beneath his sleeve, and I thought, with a flare of anger, of Loris's missing hand.

"Thanked me for what?" I asked.

He looked at me like I was insane. "For saving Raisa's life."

That had been so long ago that it felt like a different person who had tackled the boy with the dagger.

"I—I didn't do it for *you*." My voice was more strident than I meant it to be.

He smiled. "I know that. But I thank you all the same." He looked down. "And . . . I'm sorry, for the way I treated you. None of what our fathers did was your fault. You didn't deserve to be, well . . ."

"Humiliated," I supplied. A nicer person probably would have tried to make this easier for him, but Mati had never made anything easier for me, and I had never claimed to be nice. Mati bowed his head, accepting the accusation without protest. Part of me wanted to put to rest any notions he might have had about me pining after him, and tell him that I had been humiliated by someone far better at it than he was. But I'd found a way to trust Jonis, of all people; learning to trust Mati again shouldn't be so hard.

So when he opened his mouth to offer more self-flagellation, I lifted my hand and said, "Stop. What's past is past."

"There's . . . something else I need to tell you. Sit down."

I did, his grave expression making my heart stutter.

Mati dragged a hand through his hair and dropped into the seat across from me. "In Lilano, I met with your aunt Ema. She was cagey about supporting us, wanted me to promise a high post for her son." I shrugged; he should have expected that going in. I would have. "I . . . found something out, about her husband, your uncle Jac, and I, well, I tried to blackmail her with it."

I watched him shift in his seat. "What did you find out?"

"I haven't told anyone. You deserved to know first." He blew out a breath. "Your uncle Jac was Tyasha ke Demit's father. He had an affair with Laiyonea while he was representing the southern vizier on the Scholars Council."

Now that *was* a scandal: a Scholar noble impregnating an Arnath Tutor. I could only imagine how my prim and proper aunt Ema would react to that tidbit. Mati looked fairly stricken about it himself; Laiyonea had been his own beloved Tutor, and had died defending him and Raisa from the High Priest of Aqil during the battle at the palace.

"You said you *tried* to blackmail my aunt," I said. "What happened?"

He dropped his eyes to the table and told me how Ema Gamo had countered with a story of her own: Mati's father had found out about the affair, and he had enlisted the aid of another officer to have Jac Gamo ambushed and killed. That other officer had been Jac's younger brother—my father—who would go on to inherit the Gamo fortune and build a legacy he never could have attained with his older brother in the way.

I listened, stunned, staring at my father's ring on my thumb.

Once I would have laughed in Mati's face and protested that it was all lies told by Father's enemies. I knew better now. This was what my father had been; that was what had made me. Cunning, and lies, and naked ambition.

It felt like mourning him all over again, only I knew that this sick feeling was just a shadow. I was mourning the loss of my illusions, nothing more. And hadn't they been slipping away for some time now?

For so long I had worried about whether Father would have been proud of me. Now I knew for sure that he wouldn't, and that it was probably better that way.

I cleared my throat. "I guess this means that we're both huge disappointments to our fathers."

Mati gave a little shrug, as if it was an idea he was used to, if not especially pleased about. "If we offer her son the commander post of the North Company, your aunt will keep quiet."

I stared at him. "What are you talking about?"

"Your aunt will tell everyone about this if we don't—"

"Let her," I said. "Better yet, let's put it out there ourselves, so she can't hurt us with it."

"But . . . fratricide is . . . I thought you would want to—"

"Hide it? What's the point? Our fathers' crimes are not our fault, Mati. If we try to hide it we only give our enemies ammunition." This was a lesson I had learned the hard way, at the end of a wooden blade in the garden.

He looked at me, really looked at me, maybe for the first time. "You've changed."

"So have you," I returned. He smiled, and, as if it were a vision provided by Sotia, I glimpsed the future we might have had as king and queen if things had worked out differently. There wouldn't have been passion, but there might have been respect.

"Are you two still here?" said Raisa from the door. Mati and I started out of our seats and gathered up the rest of the lamps, blowing out all but two, which we carried over to the door where Raisa and Jonis waited. Raisa's eyes darted between me and Mati uncertainly, but whatever she read in our faces seemed to please her, and she took the lamp from me and looped her arm through mine as we all made our way upstairs.

"Tira will be thrilled to see you tomorrow," I said.

Raisa nodded pensively. "I haven't seen her since I was very small. That life seems so far away now. I want to visit the islands, as soon as things settle down here." She sighed. "If such a thing is imaginable."

"I'd like to go with you," I said. "If we can convince Mati to unglue himself from your side and allow someone else to go, that is."

Raisa looked at me searchingly, then smiled. "I think there's a lot you're not telling me."

"Hmm," I said. "Jonis says I should write a chronicle of everything that happened, like you did."

Raisa frowned. "Nothing has turned out quite like we expected, has it?" She glanced over her shoulder at Mati, as if to make sure that he hadn't seen her lack of faith. "I was wrong about Dimmin. If I hadn't pushed that so hard—"

"It's not wrong to give people a chance," I said. "And it doesn't matter if we fail. It only matters that we keep trying." I thought of that phantom hand on my shoulder during the public audience, and the one that had kept me from tumbling down the stairs in the tombs. Now that I'd had my own otherworldly encounters, did I believe that Sotia fought for peace through us, as Raisa insisted? I couldn't say. I only knew that I couldn't regret the choices I had made, and that whether I was an agent of the goddess, or just her bloody knife, I wasn't giving up anytime soon.

"Keep trying, and forgive ourselves for our failures," said Raisa thoughtfully.

"That's the best any of us can do, isn't it?"

We stopped in the hallway between our rooms, and she handed me the lamp. "Definitely."

I said good night to her and pushed open my door. The exchange with Raisa echoed in my mind as I shed my gown.

I lay down and stared at the golden glow of the lamp. For so long I had let other people define who I was and what I did. Even joining the Ruling Council had only happened because Raisa had asked me to. For so long I had stewed in the guilt and shame of my father's misdeeds, the effects of the things my people had done, the decisions I myself had made.

Forgive ourselves for our failures.

I would make my own choices now. And I would take whatever came as a result.

I took off my signet ring and set it on the table. Taking a deep breath, I blew out the lamp, and for the first time in ages, didn't fear the shadows.

ACKNOWLEDGMENTS

MY DEEPEST GRATITUDE to everyone who had a hand in bringing this book to publication, especially Alexandra Cooper, Alyssa Miele, Heather Daugherty, Colin Anderson, Megan Gendell, Jon Howard, and the whole team at HarperTeen, and Steven Malk and Hannah Mann at Writers House.

This book would not have been possible without my team of early readers, especially Manuela Bernardi, who read every single draft and always managed to turn my frustration into inspiration. Thank you to the many others who read various drafts and gave feedback: Stephen Devilbiss, Megan Morrison, Mary Fan, Melanie Conklin, Tobie Easton, Alyssa Susanna, Erin Harrison, Helen Harrison, Merrick Harrison, Kelly Emerson, Erin Krug, and Olivia Yancey.

Thank you to those who have supported my work, especially: Erin Matthews of Books with a Past; Lori Conforti of Howard County Library; my critique group, Lisa McShane,

Kate Bradley-Ferrall, Deborah Schaumberg, and Meg Eden; my fellow authors in the Sweet Sixteens (hope you enjoy your cameos, admins!); the members of SCBWI's MD/DE/WV region; and my family and friends who haven't shied away from asking, "How's the revision going?"—even when the length of the answer makes their eyes glaze over.

And thanks to *you*, Dear Reader. Whether you read *Sword and Verse* or met Soraya for the first time in these pages, thanks for going on this journey with me.